T.W.S.C.

A Shrouded Autobiography

TENACITY

PAPERBACK: 978-1-948962-42-1
EBOOK: 978-1-948962-43-8

Ordering Information:

For orders and inquiries, please contact:
1-888-375-9818
www.toplinkpublishing.com
bookorder@toplinkpublishing.com

Printed in the United States of America

CONTENTS

For my Father Tom who never got to see his son grow up…

INTRODUCTION

I wrote this for my family and anyone interested in life. I made mistakes but never stopped living. I recommend reading straight through and letting yourself live vicariously through my eyes. This book encompasses my first twenty-five years of life, including childhood highs and lows, my education, puppy love, incarcerations, drug experimentation, and service in Vietnam. I traveled in many circles and had many adventures.

I wrote in college and school, but those were usually about things I wanted to know or imagine. I wrote this because I lived it and felt it, as I hope you might just a little. I had to use a pen name and change names to protect the guilty, but it's okay. I'm not out to ruin anyone or aggrandize myself. Learn from my travails, avoid the bad, and find what you need.

I learned not to be too judgmental of people and their situations. Remember even a broken analog clock is right twice a day.

For a good takeaway from my book, I'll give you my favorite quote: "Life is short. Eat your dessert first."

CHAPTER 1

Early Years

At 12:31 a.m. on August 29, 1947, my body exited the womb. I don't know why in describing the yin and yang the male is described as being light, dry, and warm while the female is cold, dark, and damp. Light and dry may fit, but the womb is not cold, and I have always attributed women with warmth.

My first true memory was at thirty-two months old in the suburbs of Chicago under a neighbor's porch. Jan, who lived next to us, was playing by me. I was pushing a truck in the dirt, and the cute girl with blonde ringlets came up from behind and hit me in the back of the head with a hammer. I must have been stunned, because I didn't cry and walked home. The shock came from the pain and all the blood staining everything, including my socks. (The experience could have been a warning on how women can treat you.) My mother got me stitched up, and I was fine, but my first vivid memory was rather traumatic. I did get to pay her back couple of years later by accidentally sticking a fork in her eye at her fourth birthday party). I guess the early fifties had their violent moments.

When I was four (and my sister was two), we moved to Subby's Corner. My father had decided to go into business for himself and run a soda fountain and magazine store. It was a wondrous place with penny candy, a huge comic book rack (before plastic wrap, so I could read them all at nap time), and draft root beer in mugs that frosted over when you took one out of cooler and poured the dark liquid from the large wooden barrel's faucet. There's nothing like getting up before everyone and pouring a frosty draft root beer and indulging in an Uncle Scrooge comic book. I also had my only childhood disease here: the chicken pox. My mother always tried to get me infected with mumps, measles, etc., because she heard that if you didn't get sick young, you could be seriously hurt by catching them in your later years. I was often placed with diseased children or made to get shots that would infect me, but my immune system was apparently uncooperative. I was never infected with any other childhood diseases. Mom would have been a total failure as Typhoid Mary.

I remember playing with fire out back (unfortunately, a recurring theme in my youth), and one of the neighborhood kids caught his coat on fire and was wildly running around and screaming. I instinctively tackled him and rolled him on the ground to extinguish the flames. Looking back, I think I did it more out of fear (being discovered by adults playing with fire) than by any heroic notion. He was okay, but like all kids, he couldn't take the pressure and cracked under parental questioning and ratted me out at the first opportunity. I was the neighborhood bad influence overnight, banned from interaction with decent children and grounded for life (more than a week). The local bullies started to pick on me, as my reputation with adults was sullied and my tattling could be construed as prevarication. I hated being tortured by older kids and vowed to end the reign of terror. I found a left-handed number four iron golf club in some bushes. I saw the main bully coming on his bike toward me (he was twice my age), so I whipped the club at him and caught him in the forehead. Down he went with his bike. That was the last time I was harassed.

One day I found a very small purse. It turned out to be a man's change purse with the crossed metal beads on top you had to pinch to get the metal frame to open. The side and bottom reminded me of a thin carpet. I wasn't strong enough to open it and retrieve my found fortune. I went into the store to have my father help me. Unfortunately, either my father knew the owner or he'd come by and asked about his purse. The man came to the store, and I sourly returned it to him. It had many dollar bills in it and lots of change. The man gave me a dime for my honesty and left. I couldn't believe I had let all that loot get away. My father was happy, so I let it go and quickly squandered the dime on five of those huge strips of paper with the candy buttons all over them. My father apparently wasn't a businessman, and we quickly lost the store. (Maybe he should have kept the purse.)

Puzzles and games were my passion, and I learned how to move all the chess pieces by kindergarten. I didn't go to nursery school, but Mom began to work as my father became incapacitated. We moved to the home of my father's mother's (Grandma Gene) in rural Illinois. It was on an acre of land and in the country, with lots of soy, corn, and a neighbor (Mrs. Anthony) who raised stinky chickens. She had a parakeet that she would "let" me hold to my objection. It would peck me unmercifully, and I disliked the bird with a passion.

Grandma Gene was a rare person. She collected rainwater for rinsing her hair and grew her own spices. Gene campaigned for Adlai Stevenson when everyone "Liked Ike" (Dwight D. Eisenhower). She loved her jokes about bums and cow pies and had a pump on the sink and a wringer washer. We had Mom's dog Sandy (purebred cocker spaniel) that was knocked up as soon as she got rid of a litter. She had more than a hundred puppies in her life. The neighbors on the other side had a half terrier mongrel with a gimp leg that would knock Sandy up—and anything else in the area that moved.

Grandpa Sam (Gene's husband) had worked for the IC railroad since he was fifteen. He liked pretending he was agrarian and had a huge garden and lots of fruit trees. We had peaches, apples, blackberries, strawberries, corn, cherries, rhubarb, raspberries, plums, tomatoes, beans, radishes, carrots, Concord grapes, peas, watermelons, peppers, rutabagas, turnips, and pumpkins, as well as an herb garden. We even grew our own mint for mint tea. Grandma Gene thought I was her personal experiment. She bought one of the early blenders and would take all the veggies and mix them together with a whole egg (shell included) and grind it up. Then, I would hear the fateful call of my name and I would have to drink from her cauldron. It was horrible tasting, despite the "goodness" of contents. I would convulse and almost regurgitate when the chunks slid down my throat. She did have some good philosophy, though. Grandma Gene never believed in coloring books. She felt plain paper and a pencil was much more creative instead of staying in the lines. (This is probably where I got most of my rebelliousness.) She also felt a toy was a waste of time and that pots and pans were better for little kids to bang and play with. She made me a horse with a broomstick, a paper bag face, and string reins; I rode it everywhere.

We got chicks one Easter as a present (no doubt from Mrs. Anthony next door), and as they grew, aggression set in. They loved to attack my sister's bare legs. (All girls wore dresses in those days.) She would run, and they would peck the heck out of her. I never ran, and they didn't bother me. Finally, even though they were technically pets, Grandma Gene wrung their necks and cooked them for dinner. I was told not to reiterate the incident to my sister. Well, how could I resist? I sat down at dinner and patiently waited until Lauren had taken several bites of the meal before bringing up the missing pets. I asked her if she'd seen her chicken, and she said no. I then spilled the beans that it was in front of her and she was consuming her "beloved" chicken. Well, true to form, she ran to the bathroom and began to throw up dinner, and I was summarily chastised for my despicable behavior.

I apparently didn't learn my lesson, because a short time later my grandfather on my mother's side (whom we called Poppy) killed some rabbits hunting. Grandma Gene cooked them as a hasenpfeffer stew and served it over toast. I, once again, patiently waited until she tasted the stew and then told her she was eating a bunny. And, once again, she ran to the bathroom to relinquish her supper. This time I was berated and confined to quarters. I doubt if the punishment convinced me not to get her to upchuck in the future, but I was never again afforded the opportunity to exercise the choice.

I went to morning kindergarten in one town, and then Mom picked me up at noon and took me to an elementary school for afternoon kindergarten. I do remember liking rest period; if I positioned my rug right, I could look up the girls' skirts to see what color underpants they had on. Girls were fascinating; some even made a fashion statement by wearing light terrycloth panties.

After that, I went to first and part of second grade at Flossmoor's Western Avenue Grade School. I remember one kid (Ronny) who put a tack on everyone's chair in first grade. I felt it in my rump, but it had caught the side of my Davy Crockett wallet and I didn't get the full penetration Ron had intended. Unfortunately for Ron, he had placed one on everyone's chair but his own, including the teacher's. He was quickly captured and paid the price by being shunned by fellow students and admonished by the teaching staff and parents. I always wondered what happened to him and how that one act ultimately affected his entire life.

Grandma Gene had an old-fashioned icebox and a pump at the sink (instead of a faucet). The water was awful and both tasted and smelled like sulfur. I remember being in the kitchen with shorts on in the summer, and the heavy icebox door came off and fell perfectly flat on the cat. (His milk saucer was under the icebox.) The impact splattered warm cat blood all over my exposed shins, and the cat never made a sound. The kitchen was a mess with blood strewn a few inches off the ground for an eight-foot circle. Grandma and I cleaned it up before Lauren saw it. We got a new, real refrigerator that made its own ice out of the accident.

In second grade, we moved away from Grandma Gene's home to our own home. I went to Willow School, and we were located on the border between walking and getting to ride the school bus.

My father was dying of melanoma in the lymph nodes, and in 1954, most doctors were pretty ignorant on what caused cancer. Dad would lie on our aqua couch in his white boxers and have a sun lamp glowing down on him. I remember him as energetic and the charismatic center of attention. Even people who knew him at the University of Illinois said he was the BMOC (big man on campus) in plays and at parties.

We went to the creek together and had a rope we could swing out on and take a cool summer dip. One time we were jumping fences and ended up in a field with one cow that turned out to be a bull. The bull had an attitude about his pasture and wanted to impress us with his ability to enforce it. My father sent me to the nearest fence and distracted the bull not unlike the clowns at a rodeo. The bull missed goring him by less than an arm's length. He was unfazed and we continued to the creek for another swim.

I remember him yelling "bullshit" at Mom behind the bedroom door. They would never fight in front of Lauren and me.

I got to go often on the Peter Wheat truck, which delivered fresh bread to homes daily. I didn't care about the bread, but Peter Wheat had a company comic book and that was a priority in my life. I was disappointed when he moved on from that profession.

My father also took me door to door selling candy. He would make up bags of penny candy and hawk them in neighborhoods. He never held a job longer that six months, but he was a brilliant artist. He could sketch hands and feet. My favorite piece he did was an oil painting of Plains Indians attacking buffalo with spears.

My father died at the age of thirty-one in December 1954 of cancer of the lymph system and other parts unknown. Mom didn't want to spoil Christmas, so she foolishly didn't tell my sister (age five) and me (seven) he had died. I developed a fantasy that he was a G-man (government man equivalent to CIA today) and on a secret mission. I didn't grieve, and I didn't accept. Actual closure was brought about two years later with my grandfather.

My mom's father (Grandpa Poppy) took over somewhat in the interim. We saw him more than usual, but the father figure was gone. Mom gave me the classic line that strikes fear in to the hearts of psychotherapists everywhere: "You're the man of the house now." My father hadn't bothered with life insurance, so we were destitute and just as poor as Tiny Tim was.

I went into the Flossmoor Pharmacy and stole a pack of baseball cards with the bubble gum inside. When Mom saw me, she asked where I had gotten them, because she knew I didn't have any money. I confessed, and she was severely disappointed. She gave me a nickel and made me go to the manager, tell my mistake, and pay for the cards.

I was humiliated, but it was a lesson that served me well for my own daughter thirty-seven years later.

We had a girl across the street a year older than me named Christine. It was a large Catholic family with five or six kids. Christine (like me) was the oldest. We had a shed out back and would play many games, but she liked the one where she was the queen and we had to do what she said if she captured us. Back then, boys thought of girls as yucky, but I wasn't quite sure. She caught me mostly because I was curious and then took me into the shed where we sat down. I had to sit with her as she "punished me" with a long kiss that made my socks roll down. I was hounded by my peers and jeered about being kissed, but after that day, I never succumbed to any peer pressure.

My next kiss was from Barbara who pretended to be a horse at recess and had a ponytail. She would chase and kick me, but if I could chase and catch her, then I got a kiss. Boy was I sorry when she moved away.

My sister, Lauren, became a problem for my freedom. We fought like any kids, and we cared about each other and had a common bond in our poverty and loss. I remember her pulling on a pair of my corduroy pants, and my loose eyetooth got caught during the ensuing tug-of-war. She ripped my tooth right out of my mouth.

When she started school, she became a horrible tattletale about everything. I learned from a Sgt. Rock comic book that she had the same birthday as Adolf Hitler. It turned out she was a little Gestapo agent for Mom.

One day I was going to take a bath but had left my submarine in the sandbox outside. The sub was one of those I got off a cereal box, and it worked by putting baking soda in it to make it rise and fall. I ran outside naked, procured the submarine, raced naked back inside, and got in the tub. She immediately ratted on me to Mom. I knew I had to take corrective action and straighten out my sister for both of us. If we fought, Lauren only had her legs for strength, so she would run to her room, jump on her bed, get her legs up, and begin kicking while on her back. Once I got through her legs, she was finished.

Mom's standard punishment for hitting my sister was banishment to my room for an unspecified period of time, which varied depending on the severity of the bashing, my sister's length of sustained crying, and Mom's mood when disturbed. I put milk and cookies under my bed, hooked my AM crystal radio to the gutter, and stashed my cherished collection of comic books. I then told my sister I was going to hit her in the stomach for tattling on me, and if she told on me, I would get her again later. She ran to her room and flopped on the bed and began kicking. I quickly followed, swept her legs to the side, and punched her in the gut. She doubled over and began crying. Once she got a good volume of tears and sound up, she raced to Mom with the terrifying tale. I was sent to my room, and I stayed for several hours listening, eating, drinking, and reading. I then went to Mom and apologized to her and Lauren in front of each other and went to the back of the house.

The next time I saw my sister alone I told her she was toast and promised I would get her for tattling on me for punishing her. She immediately ran to Mom and told on me. I, of course, denied any complicity of the terrorizing of her stoolie (my sister). I did that several more times, and my sister would tell but again had no evidence. Mom was losing interest in tales being tattled. Then I reset my room with goodies and comic books. I told her she was toast and had to pay the piper, and if she told, I promised I would get her worse the next time. She ran to her room; I swept her legs and punched her twice in the stomach. She doubled up and took even more time for a stellar grief performance for Mom and ran off. I was again sequestered to my quarters where I consumed my libation and foraged via comic relief.

When I saw her alone (after the customary apology), I reiterated that she was up to three shots and pretty soon wouldn't be able to eat if she continued in her evil tattling ways. I set the stage again with the comics and food under the bed and went to strike her. This time she took her shots and rolled over to cry in the pillow. I felt sorry for her and finally respected her. She didn't tattle again unless it was something morally abhorrent to her (which I was often capable of executing), so I never again used the anti-Gestapo terror technique. (Of course, being a brother, I developed other techniques.)

My Aunt Kay (Mom's sister) lived in a co-op in Park Forest. It was the type of community where residents made an initial investment to get into a rental apartment but then paid really low monthly payments after that. If you made improvements, they were added to your "selling" price when you left for the next "owner" and then they got the lower monthly price. She had a Siamese cat named Sooty who had not been declawed yet. It was summertime, and we were running through sprinklers and cooking eggs on the sewer covers because it was so hot. I ran in Aunt Kay's house, and the cat jumped on my bare back and rode me to the ground like a lion on an antelope. When I hit the floor, she took off, but I was cut up pretty bad. We always got along, and Sooty lived many years after that. But for that one day, I knew what prey felt like.

I wisely invested several allowances in a yellow Flash Gordon squirt gun. I had an evil idea to fill it with my own urine, and the color would be masked by the gun's own color. I filled the gun at my next opportunity, and it was curiously warm. I waited for my chance and talked my innocent sister into opening her mouth and allowing me to fire the demonic contents of my weapons on her pallet. After she complied, my cousin Lee couldn't wait to relate her mistake and my indiscretion. Lauren began to gag and ran upstairs to tell Mom, Aunt Kay, President Eisenhower, and anyone else who had potential disciplinary capability. I was summarily court- martialed, stripped of freedom, had my weapon destroyed, and forced to watch a clock for several hours. I stood my time, but the loss of ability to continue mischief with the gun hurt the worst. After all, it was a genuine Flash Gordon weapon.

When I was nine, I was in my bed one night when Mom had a call late. Lauren and I had a bedroom in an old garage. A wall was built between us, and a separate doorway was built through a half wall perpendicular to the splitting wall. The half wall had one-inch wood dowel rods going to the ceiling to mock a finished wall. One of the dowel rods would turn, and an attached cord would pull on a light. We could hear everything and really had no privacy. I heard Mom talking to Aunt Kay; Poppy had died of a heart attack. This finished me, and I sobbed in my pillow for hours so no one would hear. My pillow was soaked with tears and saliva. I cried for my father, my grandfather, and myself that night.

I was still so upset several months later that I climbed the local water tower in the middle of a rainstorm, hung out over the railing, and cursed God. I wanted to know why he was ruining my life and why he was taking my loved ones away. I gave him an easy opportunity to take me as I cussed him in the lightning and rain. He only growled. Eventually, I realized I was wet and nothing would be resolved. I decided that I should go home. I always figured God was closer in a thunderstorm, and I could hear and feel him more then. I never felt him much in church except much later in life in California. Maybe the other people were soaking him up. I never bothered God much after that. I figured prayer was a waste of time when I listened to what others were asking and expecting. God had to be a busy man, and I vowed to only pray in extreme conditions. I knew (hoped) that he'd listen. (My belief was that if I didn't waste his time, God might lend an ear more readily.) I had my closure with my father's death through Poppy's passing. Even today, when I'm at a funeral, I cry for the little boy on the water tower in the storm. I was growing up too fast, running it myself, and attitudes against authority were beginning to form.

The neighborhood boys played sandlot baseball. I could play with the older boys hitting, but I wasn't very confident about my fielding. They would always stick me in right field, which was where they put the losers when I was growing up. I wanted to play Little League ball when I was eight, but after my father died, we didn't have the money for a bike, glove, shirt, and hat, which were required to be in the league. Few parents drove their kids in those days, and we all rode our bikes to whatever practice field we could find. Mom made about sixty dollars a week and saved enough to get me a used bike for twenty dollars. I tried out for the team using Cousin Lee's glove, and I made it on the Baltimore Orioles. I would go to the sites of new homes being built and collect all the pop bottles in a red wagon I pulled behind me. With the money I earned from the bottles and Mom's help, we managed to buy a fielder's glove and have enough left over for a hat and Orioles T-shirt. I was so proud.

I went to the practices and hit the ball okay, but I had to learn how to judge pop flies better so I focused on that at practice. We got to game day, and I felt all the pressure of my first at bat in front of the crowd at Isaac Walton Park. It was a big deal, with lots of parents and older kids there watching us compete. I didn't start, but I came in for the fourth inning and was fortunate to walk my first time up. I never even got the bat off my shoulder, and I felt silly taking a walk down to first base. To me, it was like getting a bye in a sporting event (winning and advancing because there is no competition). When it was our turn to take the field, I was given left field, which was an honor in my eyes. Some other poor sap had the sentence of right field.

I was all keyed up for my big moment in life. I yelled all the correct chatter to humiliate the other team's batter (like we were taught) and sounded confident as I could in my new role. All of a sudden, the kid at the plate belted one out to left field. There was no one I could hide behind—the ball was coming to me. I finally realized it was going to be short of me, so I started to run in to catch it. I realized I was way too late, so I figured if I tripped, no one could blame me for missing the ball and losing the game. It would just be an unfortunate accident, and I would still be able to keep left field and not be relegated to right field. I acted the stumble as best I could and lurched forward before the ball hit the ground and anyone could see how badly I had misplayed it. I heard a roar from the crowd as I tumbled face down in the turf. When I looked up to see what transpired, everyone was cheering. To my complete surprise, the ball was in the web of my mitt. I had made the greatest play of my life and missed the whole thing. I quickly got up and threw the ball in like an old pro. I figured everyone watching surely thought I did this every day. I was now a hero and found I had to play better just to be equal with my new reputation. I worked a lot harder in practice and got quite good at fielding. I never played right field again. To this day, I still say, "It's better to be lucky than good."

Organized sports can be a great or horrible experience, depending on who's running them and how much they want to win.

Snowballs are always fun. My cousin Lee and I were snowball "experts" and constantly honing our skills. After all, a good snowball thrower is a good baseball player. Unfortunately, as we grew more proficient, it became boring unless we were being chased. The chase was terror, but the rush of just barely getting away was quite addictive. We were thrill-seeker junkies, and when people stopped chasing, we made the mistake of escalating the danger. We loaded the snowballs with pebbles. Lee struck first, but his just grazed the vehicle he was aiming for, and it didn't even slow down. Not to be outdone, I increase the size of my projectile and hit the next car in the driver's side door, causing a small dent and much chipped paint. Lee and I managed to escape the foot race, but one of the other kids (a nonparticipant but active observer) was apprehended in the ensuing rundown. He immediately told the driver where we lived, who our parents were, and what we'd had for breakfast. When we got home, relatively soaked from the adventure, Lee and I got the hard news of the other child's treachery and had to face the dreaded clock.

I think the clock punishment gave me my desire for independence. This punishment entailed looking at the face of a clock for several hours and just watching the hands go around while not doing anything. It doesn't sound bad, but neither does Chinese water torture where just a drop of water is released every minute on the same spot on a person's head. As time goes by, the drop becomes so loud. In the same way, as time goes, by the clock almost stops. For a kid with a million ideas, it's forever!

In the spring, the trouble didn't stop just because the snow melted; it just took on a new look. Lee and I would go to the top of the hill to Bob K's house, which was a huge three-story gray house. Strategically, it offered many escape routes to prairies or back alleys and many levels from which we could launch mischief. On a particularly warm spring day, just after a storm, Lee and I felt it would be a good time to ambush cars. We had collected cattails in the fall, and they were dried out in the basement. We tied them up in bundles of three and went up by the road. We hid behind a hedgerow and waited till we heard a car ascending the hill. Lee and I leapt up and tossed handfuls of bundled cattails at the hapless vehicle, only it turned out to be a Homewood Police car. I hit the front grill, and Lee hit the windshield. The cattails exploded with a myriad of seeds and fluff that literally coated the car. We should have gotten away easily, but I started laughing. In those days, we called the police "fuzz," and it was now definitely a fuzz-mobile. When I told Lee, we were both laughing so hard that the chubby cop almost caught us. It was only adrenaline that saved capture and parental humiliation.

Later, we did the box trick. This is a trap for the unwary or destructive motorist. We would build a pile of bricks on the road on the double yellow line and cover it with a cardboard box. It did not impede traffic, but many people like striking orange construction cones or boxes. Sure enough, when we came back, someone had struck it. There was glass, coolant, and broken bricks everywhere. We were bad kids pushing the envelope.

I met my first best friend, Peter S, at Willow Elementary. Everyone needs a crazy family to make him feel normal. Peter's mom was the secretary for our church's pastor. She was also divorced with four kids. Stanley was the oldest at seventeen and a juvenile delinquent, Donna was fifteen going on thirty and totally boy crazy, and Eddie was psychotic at 10 and a year older than Pete and me. Pete's dad lived in Matteson about ten miles away. It took a long time to ride there on balloon-tired bicycles.

Eddie was very jealous of the friendship Pete and I had and was forever our nemesis. If we built forts, he would attack and wreck them. If we rode bikes, he would follow. If we made a tent, he would cover it with kerosene and light it on fire with us in it. If we played in the driveway, he would throw something heavy from an upper floor. In those days, milk came in gallon bottles. Eddie threw almost an entire gallon at me from the second floor that just missed my head. Had it hit, I would have been dead. Pete and I could not deal with this and play Monopoly. We put our heads together and decided to sabotage

Ed's bike. We loosened all the fork screws that held the wheels on his bike and left the house in a hurry, because we knew he'd follow. To our surprise, after three blocks, he was still coming after us. I decided to take action and told Pete to follow me. We proceeded to jump curbs and ruts. Sure enough, Eddie followed, and his bike was quickly dispatched to our instant delight. He lost both wheels and went down hard over the handlebars. Pete and I were delighted with a "free" day. Unfortunately, the day ended, and Pete had to go home and face the music. As the youngest, he faced all three siblings, none of whom was on his side. Sometimes he couldn't leave home for a three-week stretch.

Behind our house were all prairies, then Western Avenue and up a hill to the railroad tracks. To the north was a prairie that had been cut down for a baseball field and then Mrs. T's house. Fortunately, she cut back the prairie enough to save her from my later prairie fires. Mrs. T was a stocky, gray-haired woman with a braid around the top of her head like a halo and the hair in the back all pinned up. She had those cat's-eye glasses with a jeweled chain to hold them on her neck. She was often our babysitter, and we just kept away from her. Her son was Richard, the local garbage collector; he was quiet, but if he turned out to be a mass murderer, we wouldn't have been surprised. While Pete was incarcerated, I had to let my mind exercise.

Rocketry was popular in the fifties. I wanted to be an enthusiast, but Illinois didn't allow fireworks sales. I had a water pressure rocket that I could pump pressure in. When it was released, it would go eighty feet up, but I would get wet. We had many new homes being built on the prairies of Homewood. I would go there to collect pop bottles with my wagon to collect money, and I discovered conduit. This is the pipe the workers put electrical wires through in new construction. I would collect scrap pieces that were maybe eight to twelve inches long and some gutter pieces. Selling the pop bottles for two cents each and the larger ones for a nickel gave me the ability to purchase matches in sizeable quantity. I used the gutter and some two-by-fours to build a launch pad. This was pre-Sputnik, so I was part of the space race.

I took a piece of electrical conduit and a three-foot gutter. I cut the pipe to about a foot long, hammered one end to a point, and hammered the other end to another point leaving enough space in the middle to allow one match head to fit through. I bought a big box of matches and began breaking off the heads. I ran out of wooden matches and had to use cardboard ones after a while. When my rocket was completely packed, I set up the gutter at about a forty-five-degree angle across the baseball field from our yard. I placed my rocket in and ignited it. It sat for a moment, building pressure from the internal match heads igniting, and then took off in a miraculous flash. I was so pleased and proud until it crossed my yard, the baseball infield, right field, and Mrs. T's yard before flying right smack into Mrs. T's bedroom window. I bet a rocket scientist never ran so fast away from a success. I stayed in the other part of town at a park for the rest of the day, skipping lunch and returning at dusk for my supper. I managed to get away with that one, but I couldn't ever look Mrs. T in the eye after that. Of course, back then, she was so scary that I never looked in her eyes anyway.

Marion was another babysitter I had issues with. She was in late high school and had short brown hair, glasses, and a blue bike just like the one the witch rode in The Wizard of Oz. She was always trying to emasculate me by forcing my sister and me to play with dolls and not letting us go outside. Lauren was okay with it, but not me. I wandered off and retrieved my toy rifle. It was a replica of the 1903 Springfield (like drill teams use), but in those days, toy manufacturers made them of wood, not plastic. It had most of the heft of a real gun. Marion liked to crack us with a slap in the face if we were mouthy. She really demanded respect all the time and found out I was the wrong kid to push. I was sassing her back one day, and when she came after me, I hit her in the knee with the rifle. It amazed me that I had made someone so much older and larger cry. I was delighted beyond all reason that she quit and never returned. Poor Mom had to find another sitter. I felt like Dorothy in The Wizard of Oz when she threw the water at the Wicked Witch of the West.

I took my "matches" skill to a new level with my spool gun. I took a wooden spool for large thread and hammered a headless nail in one end and bent it to just come over the hole. I used a large rubber band around it from top to bottom (not the direction the thread was wound) and poked a light-anywhere wooden match in the spool hole. I pulled the rubber band with the match end on it back, and when I released it, the nail was struck with the light- anywhere wooden match, which smoked as it flew through the air and ignited to a brilliant flame. I was on our shed roof at the time, and it wasn't until I fired the third match that I realized my grievous error. Unfortunately, the prairie had caught on fire on a windy day and was raging by the time I got down and acquired water. Over the next few years, I would burn the prairie down three more times.

When the police or fire department arrived on the scene, the first question was: "Where is the S kid?" And rightfully so. One time I went into a caboose and got the track explosive that warned the engineer to stop. It had two wires coming out of a slice of dynamite with a compression detonator. They were also effective on the end of a broomstick (like an exploding spear on impact). I also found some flares, and once again, the prairie started on fire. I ran home and put water in the tub. I retrieved my blanket and soaked it, but by the time I was back at the fire, it was raging. I was in the middle of it trying to contain the flames when the fire department arrived with the police to really put it out. Once again, I was the scandal of Homewood.

It is strange to be so poor and in debt at such a tender age. Money is money, so I went and got a job with the local Tribune carrier; my boss was Bill Hamilton. Interestingly, this man married my future best friend's mom after her second divorce. I got a route with eighty Tribunes, which required three baskets on my bike. Thursday and Sunday were extremely tough with all the advertisements. I worked seven days a week, before school on weekdays, delivering the papers. I picked up my papers in the dark and started rolling them and then took off when dawn was barely breaking. It took more than six weeks to pay for the first customer's window that I broke. I was getting pretty good at tossing the paper, and after about three weeks, I bounced a Thursday paper and took out the glass in another customer's storm door. Another three weeks of work down the drain. Paperboy work was hardly glamorous or profitable. Snow on the ground was tough to negotiate, but I was a quick learner. One day before school it had sleeted on top of seven inches of snow, forming a two-inch crust. I could only ride where the trucks were or in tire tracks. If I tried to go on the sidewalks, the crust gave out, leaving me stuck and having to pull the bike by hand with all the papers. A woman finally drove me to finish my route at nine and take me to school, but I was two hours late and got detention. To this day, I don't understand why it wasn't a snow day at school.

My mom's mother, Clara, decided we all needed a vacation to Ft. Lauderdale, Florida. Aunt Kay; my cousins, Lee and Mike; and my sister, Lauren, were all invited to a place by the beach. Grandma Clara loved to breaststroke in the ocean, and we were very excited to get in the Atlantic for the first time. The sisters (Aunt Kay and my mom) made us stand in a line before we would take the four-block walk to the beach. Lee and Mike were fighting as usual when Mike tried to scratch Lee and missed. He struck my arm and took out a huge hunk of flesh with his nail; the wound was about one and a quarter inches by a quarter inch. It was a bloody mess, but I said nothing because we wouldn't have been able to swim. I paid the price and learned about the saying "don't rub salt in the wound" when I began to swim. My arm screamed in pain from the seawater and it mucous overflowed the wound.

A couple of days later I had an even worse experience when swimming. First, I stepped on a manta ray so big that when it took off, it swept my feet out from under me. This was fortunate, because the stinger tail missed my legs. Then the Portuguese Man of War flotilla hit the beach like a fleet of purple balloons. Once again, I was attacked, but this time I was stung in the crotch. The lifeguard was cute, but I was embarrassed so I just borrowed the medicine to spray on my newest wounds.

Fourth grade was a good, intellectually stimulating experience. I was in love with my teacher, Mrs. Erickson, who was very curvy and blonde. I stayed after class to clean the chalkboards and help her move stuff. In those days, the teacher kissed everyone good- bye, and I got to the line first and stayed to be the last too. She was a good math teacher, and I learned my times tables quickly. I also liked to read comic books, including the ads. The Hallmark card/stationary ad on the back was the most persuasive. If you could sell one hundred boxes, you could get your very own BB gun. I worked very hard, and Mom was impressed with my diligence. After I sold to everyone at school and in walking distance from my house, I had sold ninety-five. Mom bought the last five, and I was able to get my precious weapon of choice. I got the Daisy pump BB gun, and while it held only fifty BBs, they were force-fed. You could keep your gun on target while you pumped like a police shotgun. The other ones held four hundred to five hundred BBs, but you had to hold the barrel end up while you cocked the lever, or it wouldn't grab a new BB.

In those days, all kids had raincoats with galoshes (rubber boots that went over your shoes) and funny black buckles to close them. When you had a BB gun, you could play with the local boys. You wore your raincoat, galoshes, rain hat, and goggles. I hated the goggles because of the vision impairment they caused. I also lost the galoshes, because the buckles would get entangled in the prairie weeds. I wore the rain hat and coat for a while, as most of the boys were older and had no problem shooting kids in the back. My gun was superior in a close-up fight of thirty feet or less. I could fire faster, and the feet per second velocity on my BBs were 150 faster than theirs. My plan was to get in close early and outshoot the others. Once someone broke to run, he was finished. In battle lulls, I quickly unscrewed my tube and reloaded as much as possible. If the other guys were well covered with ski masks, goggles, and gloves, I would shoot at the ski mask (which still hurt) and then at the soft inner legs or any other exposed area. I got quite good and always attacked the biggest bullies first and then took aim at their minions when the bully ran. My status in the neighborhood rose quickly.

Unfortunately, we had the battles only once a week, and the rest of the time I had target practice. Birds were my primary targets and then glass. Glass was tough to break, especially on streetlights and stoplights. I learned it took four hits to take them out. This was frowned upon by our local police, and within a month, the alert had spread to capture the culprit. When they found out that "prairie fire boy" was the bad guy, my gun was quickly incarcerated and donated to a policeman's son who was more responsible. I was devastated at the loss, so I tried a normal life and rejoined Little League baseball.

I took a long time collecting pop bottles to be able to afford my second-year entry fee for the uniform, etc. In the minor league, we only needed a glove, T-shirt, and a hat. I had none but decided to try my luck. An older kid went on to the majors (where you had a full uniform) and was getting a new glove, so I got him to give me his old beater glove. It was like a half catcher's mitt with fat padded fingers and a terrible web. I raised the five dollars necessary for the team hat, registration, and T-shirt. We had practice for a couple of weeks trying to catch grounders and fly balls. I sucked at first but quickly learned to block grounders with my body and right leg, knee down to protect between your legs, because the ball that went through your legs got recrimination from everyone. My batting was mostly strikeouts and foul balls. I took an old bat home and began to hit golf balls and then rocks till the wood bat was hamburger.

When tryouts arrived, the individual team managers picked their own kids and drafted the rest in order till the roster was full. The event was held at Isaac Walton League Park in Homewood near the Washington Park race track. Maybe 10 to 15 percent of the boys would not be admitted. I did not want to be one of them. In fielding, I missed a fly ball that bounced off my old glove's fat fingers, but I did stop all grounders and threw out the runners. When I went up to bat, the pressure was immense. I was lucky and got a walk on a 3/2 pitch. The next time I was pumped and missed them all swinging. During my final at bat, I tried to bunt but did it incorrectly; it looked like a check swing, but I watched the ball hit the bat and go over the first baseman's head. I had a hit. I probably should have gone to second base, but I stayed on first, very proud. I was drafted by the Homewood Red Sox and got my hat and T-shirt.

The local kids had games in my prairie. (There were no weeds due to late summer fires caused by yours truly.) I learned a lot about base running and placing an easy hit. At the Red Sox practice, I learned proper hitting and fielding. This was cut short by tree climbing. I climbed a tree maybe twenty feet up and was enjoying the view on a large, dead limb. I heard it crack a little, so I tried to shimmy back to the trunk. The bark came loose, and I began to fall headfirst to the earth. I instinctively put my hands out to break the fall; my body flopped over my head, while my right hand stayed as a fulcrum. My right wrist was trashed, and I had to wear a cast for seven weeks. I was still in school but would miss the first half of the season's Little League games.

Another boy had also broken his arm, so we had Robin Hood and Little John fights banging each other's casts. His was wood and eventually fell prey to my plastered arm. He had to return to the doctor for a new one. It was warmer, so I went in the creek only to have my plastered arm disintegrate in the water. I too had to return to the doctor for a new cast. When he sawed the cast off with a new little power saw, blood came up from the crack. He had cut too deep, and I lost confidence in doctors. My arm looked so skinny when the cast came off, but by week's end, I was throwing well again and returned to team practice.

The rule was you got to play three innings if you made the roster. Newbies and general sucks got to be right field. Good players were infield or left field. Center field was for in between. The manager's son got to play wherever he wanted. For my first game, I was in right field, and I struck out at bat. We had the best pitcher in the league; he was named Ralph. He was a religious kid who crossed himself a lot, but he was effective. He had twelve strikeouts that game, so I didn't see any action. The next game some other kid had my spot, so I just warmed the bench, as they say. The next game I played I didn't have any real fielding except a missed line drive that I stopped on the ground and threw to second base. I did get a double on an errant throw to first.

The next game was awesome because they put me in left field for some reason at the beginning of the game. I was so pumped. It was a weekend game, so the stands were full. I felt like I was in the majors on television and was very alive and important. My first up was a walk, and I scored on someone else's hit. I had no action the first two innings, and then the other team's pitcher got up to bat. He was two years older and hit a pop fly to left. I ran forward and caught his ball then kept going to tag out the base runner for the unassisted double play. When we got the third out, everyone was patting me on the back as we came in to the dugout.

The trains at the top of the hill were always an opportunity for flares or explosive track caps. Now Peter & I would jump the freight cars and ride from 185th Street to 147th Street to roller skate at Art's Roller Rink. We had to sneak in if we didn't have enough money and then just pay for the skate rental. Speed skating was fun, but I couldn't get the hang of the turn. I would crash into the rail and then realign myself and take off fast. There was a much older girl skating clumsily around, and as I was speed skating, she moved in front of me and I crashed into her. I found out that she had just had an arm cast removed, and when she fell, my impact caused her arm to break again in the same place. Pete and I got out of there and jumped a freight train back to Homewood. To jump a train, you need to run as fast as it is going and then pull yourself up on the ladder or door opening.

Later, we had a kid try our stunt catching the train, but he just grabbed the ladder bar. It jerked him so his foot went under and the train and severed his foot at the ankle. We tried to stop him, but he was crazy with shock and ran to his home on the cinder stones. He lost the leg up to his knee because of infection.

I was so good at math that the school promoted me to the fifth grade super accelerated class. At the time (1957–58), math and science were treated special because of the space race with Russia. I was in all the accelerated math classes through my freshman year at college. Math made sense to me and was a building process. I received maximum scores and accolades and really enjoyed finishing way before the others with a perfect score. My new teacher, Ms. Crawford, worked extra hard with me, and I was transferred to Standard School in downtown Homewood to be with her math class when she was promoted. She taught sixth grade math, and Ms. Foster taught the rest of my classes. Standard was an old-style school—three stories high and no gymnasium. We had to go over to Ridge or Central schools for PE class. It was a ten- minute formation walk, so gym class was only forty minutes of actual time. I was doing high school algebra by this time, and it was a breeze for me. Social studies became more important, and I loved the history stories. Math class was mostly boys then, but this class had girls, and some were wearing bras already. New Interests were forming.

I joined Cub Scouts, but I was older, so the Bobcat and Wolf ranks were practically given to me so I could be a Bear with my age group. Troop 242 was our local, and I liked the shirt and the pocketknife. I seemed to know more than the group and was the only one to start a fire without matches. My fire experience had really grown by this time, as had my rifle skills. The only thing new I learned besides tying knots was how to wipe snot (phlegm) on my socks so no one would notice. It seemed very political, and the kids were a little sweet and naive. I did enjoy the night campfire and snipe hunt with flashlights and paper bags. They told us the snipe was a weasel-like creature (looked it up later and discovered that it's just a bird) and explained it could only be caught at night (nocturnal mammal). It was attracted to light, so they would place us at the woods' edge at the perimeter of the camp so we could see the campfire. We would hunker down with our paper bags open on the ground with the flashlight above, aiming into the bag. When the snipe jumped in, you were to drop your flashlight into the bag, close the top quickly, and run back to the campfire. Of course, from the adults' perspective, it was hilarious seeing all the little bags lit up around the perimeter. After a half hour, I became skeptical, so I dropped my light in the bag, yelled "got him," and shook the closed bag with the light in it as I ran to the fire. I thought the rest would get it, but I think my "success" only enhanced their resolve to capture the critter. After a couple of hours, the other Scouts were all back at the fire and learned of the snipe hunt ruse.

At the end of the summer, I had a gray cat named Smokie. He disappeared for a month, and I thought he was lost forever. I found him under Mom's car, and he wouldn't come out. He acted very strange and made growling noises I'd never heard before. I got hold of his leg and tried to pull him out, but he savagely ripped up my left hand. There was lots of blood (which probably saved me), and Mom carted me to the doctor for three penicillin shots. The police had found the cat in my prairie and shot him with a pump shotgun. They cut the head off and took it to the vet. Unfortunately, the results came back positive for rabies, and I had to get fourteen more shots. I had to go by bike to the doctor two miles away every day for two weeks. Going there was the longest ride ever, and leaving was the shortest. Twelve shots were in my back, and two were in my stomach. The needle was large and the vaccine thick, so he timed the shot for sixty seconds as he slowly pushed the plunger into the syringe. The process was very painful, and I couldn't move at all. School was now starting, and I was far enough away to ride the yellow bus.

The basement of Standard had a coal furnace with two huge piles of coal at opposite ends. Students would sneak down there at lunch and have coal fights by throwing large pieces at each other. If a chunk hit your bare skin, you would get infected (on the head or arm when it penetrated the skin). I threw well and quickly became a leader.

My cousin Lee (who was my age) also went to the same school, and since he'd been there since the fourth grade, he was well known by the administration. He was not in the super math class, but he was captain of the patrol boys. Nepotism kicked in, and I was a lieutenant instantly. The patrol boys protected the access under the highway to the downtown. We ruled with simple extortion. If you wanted to pass, we had to be paid in candy. Many were eager, so we got lots of trade. We would also accept quarters and whether it cost one or two depended on the person in question. Total idiots were charged a dollar. It was a fruitful year. I was a patrol at Willow School in fifth grade, but it was just work and nowhere to visit. This was a good beginning for business acumen.

Steve B (in Miss Foster's class) was destroyed by me in a coal fight down in the basement. He was outside waiting for me, and when I appeared, he punched me in the balls as hard as he could. I doubled over and took a few minutes to recover from the trauma. I went upstairs to the second floor and waited until I saw him walking toward the corner below. I got a bottle of permanent ink and threw it just before he turned to a blind corner beneath me. The timing was perfect except Miss Foster came around the corner in her blonde hair, white blouse, and yellow pencil skirt. I liked her and was devastated as her outfit and day were ruined by my act of revenge on Steve. A parent- teacher conference was called, and I was sentenced to after-school work for a couple of weeks. Poor Mom had to be called from her job at Cabinet Top Shop. She was a secretary there dating the boss, Bob, who was to become my future dad.

We still said the Pledge of Allegiance in those days, and with my paper route, I had to buy a huge box of green rubber bands. I used the bands to roll the papers, but as any kid would do, I shot them at things. I would build huge card forts with eight or more decks of cards and then see how many shots it would take to destroy the hours of work. I shot insects, spiders, and other kids. At school, I notched my wooden ruler to get maximum stretch from the rubber band and better, more consistent accuracy. One morning, from the back of the class, I shot a rubber band at the little flag over the blackboard and knocked the flag out of the holder. Obviously, during the Pledge, everyone saw it, and another conference ensued. No one appreciated my technical achievement, and we all ceremoniously burned the little flag. I also received detention and had to pay for the flag.

In May 1959, my mom married her boss, Bob. I was eleven going on twelve, and it was weird drinking champagne at my parents' wedding. It was a great party, and they took off to Nassau in the Bahamas for their honeymoon, leaving us with a babysitter. We moved into a beautiful tri-level in a new subdivision in Homewood. The life was a radical change from a poor and rundown part of town by the rail tracks to a new and clean neighborhood. We had drive-in movies and burger stands and big fins on new cars. Times were great.

At the end of the block was a Jewish golf club. The fourteenth hole was near our house, so I jumped the fence to explore. I found the caddy shack by the clubhouse and checked it out. I was still only eleven, and you had to be fourteen to get a work permit and sixteen for a Social Security card. In the mid- seventies, my kids could get Social Security cards when they were born, but in the fifties and sixties, that was the rule. I was big for my age and strong enough to carry a golf bag, so I signed up, not telling the truth so I could be employed. We had moved away from the old newspaper route, so this was a new source for cash.

The caddy master was older with a little gray hair and a very shiny bald head. We called him Chrome Dome. The way caddying worked is I had to get out to be paid. The lower a caddy's number, the sooner he got out. Points received for good ratings by the golfers helped, and caddies could get extra points by ball picking at the practice tee while waiting for a club member. Doubles were the best, because I would make eight to ten dollars and get a hamburger at the halfway house. The only problem is I had to hustle for eighteen holes to get them their clubs and replace their divots. The good thing was I only walked the course once for two pay vouchers, and then I was done for the day.

I worked hard and got my number down and my points high. Unfortunately, the older boys were lazier and, of course, bullies. This one fifteen-year-old was much taller and loved to push everyone around. I was thrown in the urinal trough by him, so I had to get him back. On another day, he had taken the only basketball away and was running around with it playing his own form of keep away. I stood up, picked up a large rock, and aimed at him perfectly. The stone careened off his jaw. He got up bloody and extremely angry, and I was ratted out by other oppressed observers who really feared him. I knew there was no chance of escape (he was fast), so I sat down on the ground hugged my knees and put my face to my legs. He screamed, bled, cursed, kicked, and punched my balled-up body, but I knew I'd gotten him. I took my licks and never squealed to Chrome Dome. My respect went way up (for an underage caddy). The fifteen-year-old was teased by his peers and soon quit. I made a lot of money for my age. My new dad even hired me to put Formica samples together at his business for forty-five cents an hour.

My first real date was with Aleda, who lived behind the prairie at Cousin Lee's house. She had eyes like a doe and a very attractive personality. My allowance was twenty-five cents a week, and that was the same price as the local movie theater. Popcorn was a dime, so I had to collect pop bottles (five at two cents each) to go in the winter. I met her inside the movie on the right side near the back. I shared my popcorn, and she shared her lips. It was grand.

CHAPTER 2

Junior High

I won my first mail-in contest just before school started in junior high. I must have been trying for whatever the first-place prize was, because the second-place prize I was awarded had absolutely no value to me. I won custom drapery rods for the house. Mom had plenty, but Aunt Kay needed them, so I gave her the prize. She was very happy, but I was disappointed with my first ever win.

That summer had a rough ending. We had a hoodlum gang fight at our local theater, and one sixteen-year-old died from knife wounds. A big deal was made about carrying knives, but the bad guys never listen, so it was stupid. We had a new high school opening that school year that combined students from a couple of towns. My class, from 1961–65, was actually the first four-year class to graduate from the school. It started with only juniors and seniors.

One of the students, Calvin, was dumped by his girlfriend. He was a spoiled rich kid and couldn't stand the rejection, so he blew his head off with his dad's shotgun. It put more pressure on the rest of the students from adults doing Band-Aid fixes after the fact. Calvin's parents felt so guilty they created an ongoing scholarship in his honor. He even has a simulated tombstone flat on the ground right outside the administration entrance of the school for everyone to see.

Now that Mom and Dad were happily married, Dad, whom we still called Bob, asked for a family meeting with Mom, Lauren, and me. He asked Lauren and me if he could adopt us and change our last name. He said it wasn't out of disrespect for our father but a way for us to be a closer family. Now, I'd been an S my whole life of twelve years and had to wait at the back of lines for everything. I could see Lauren (ten years old at the time) waiting for my response. I quickly chimed in yes, and then Lauren did too. Bob was now Dad and very happy, as was Mom. I was happy because my new name was toward the beginning of the alphabet. It took junior and senior high to get my acquaintances to recognize my new name.

We had to go downtown to Chicago over Christmas vacation 1959. We went to the official Cook County courthouse, and Judge Otto K was presiding. He seemed nice; he put me on his lap, asked us questions, and signed some papers. A short time later, he ran for governor and was sworn in in 1961. He was a World War II veteran and had received a Bronze Star in Italy with the Ninth Infantry. He retired from the Reserves in 1954 as a major general. Otto was a friend of Mayor Richard J. Daley and remained a judge until 1968. He was then convicted in a racetrack scandal with stock bribes and spent time in prison until they let him out for terminal cancer. He passed in 1976, and at times, I have wondered if my adoption was legal (it is).

Thursday night was dance class in junior high. The boys dressed up in sport coats and ties, and the girls dressed their best. I met a girl there named Joyce. She was very animated and full of energy with a great sense of humor. I enjoyed talking and dancing with her. I decided to buy her a friendship ring, which was the first step before going steady. I saved my money and bought a sterling silver ring with swirly cutouts in it. I thought it was gorgeous and was sure she would say yes. I took it out of the package and went down the hall between classes to offer my admiration and deepen our relationship. The hall was crowded, and just before I got to her, someone bumped me and the ring rolled down the floor. I chased after it, but by the time I caught up to it, someone had already stepped on it. It was flattened like the proverbial pancake. My deep relationship was terminated, and at the next dance class, I asked someone else on free choice.

After Joyce, I fell in love with Sandy. My uncle knew her family, and he would grind me about my interest in "beanpole" Sandy (she was tall and thin). She danced with me at the junior high dance class, and I fantasized about marriage, children, and our life together. Sandy's best friend was a chubby girl named Marsha, so to get Sandy's attention, I danced with her friend (whom nobody would pick as a partner)—what a bad plan. I had my first official date with Marsha where my parents picked her up, and we went to a church Halloween party dressed up. We danced, bobbed for apples, and ate. After that, Sandy wouldn't even dance with me but would invite me to her parties and social clique. I was now Marsha's boyfriend. After I "broke up" with her, I still never got a chance with Sandy but continued to be invited to the clique parties. I would still dance with any girl who would ask but life was changing. Guys are so easily messed up.

My seventh grade accelerated math teacher was also in charge of the chess club. His abilities were pretty good compared to mine then, so I invited him home to play my mom. He won, so I played Mom and could beat her continually. I had to get my game up. Me and my chess club friends began to play speed chess and could get in four or five games during lunch. To better prepare ourselves, we then would play without a chessboard and write the moves down (in case there was a dispute). This really got the concentration up, and I began to beat everyone, even the math teacher. It was boring after a while, because everyone lost to me. My interest level was only older people with good chess backgrounds.

We had a neighbor who invited me to play chess. He had played European masters and had spent lots of time playing good chess players. The first game, he slaughtered me, so I played with him sans rooks and queen. As I improved and began to beat him, he would start with one rook (castle) and then two. Finally, I could play him with the whole board and occasionally win. When he moved away, I lost my best adversary. My skills, however, had been elevated considerably. I didn't play regularly again until my sophomore year in high school.

The cheerleaders looked good, so I turned to sports. I was fairly tall, so I chose basketball. My cousin Lee was on the team, so I tried out and made the lightweights. They made me a center (jersey number twenty-five), but it was fun. I learned my position and got to go with the team on away games. The cheerleaders knew me from dancing and now basketball, so life was good. I never got as good as my cousin, but they needed the height, so I played both years.

School brings the vandals together to compare notes and test their skills. We had fountain pens for penmanship back then, which was another area where I did not excel. I did have an Ester brook pen that I could shoot ink out of pretty good. They were quickly outlawed by the school as cartridge pens came in vogue. I would take a refill cartridge and put it under the leg on a chair. When the occupant returned and sat down, the ink would shoot all over his socks and shoes. The technique was very effective, and I later reused the same principle in high school with chocolate milk cartons.

My friends and I started shooting paper wads at each other with rubber bands. I developed a paper wad with a straight pin protruding out of it that would stick in wood when shot. Girls were wearing bras now, and those less endowed would pad them. We suspected one girl named Deanna of falsifying her chest cup size, so we pooled money for the winner who could prove it. Many would bump her and try to feel her chest, but I won the pot with my paper wad and straight pin. I shot her left breast, and it stuck. She walked around for an hour with it stuck in her while we followed and snickered. They awarded me the money pool.

I had graduated Cub Scouts and became a Webelo and then a Second-Class Scout. I was good at picking locks at the school gym where our meetings were held. We were left alone for an hour sometimes, so I would open up the ball closet. By the time the scoutmaster returned, balls were everywhere, and we were playing a violent version of dodge ball. I never made First-Class Scout but did win a ribbon at the winter Klondike derby. As part of the competition, each participant had to build a sled, cook food in the forest, tie knots, and start fires in the snow. We were each given two wooden matches for the day. Many never got their fires started. I was a master fire starter from childhood, so I didn't have any problems. I made my stew in a coffee can, tied my knots, and got my sled through the obstacles. I had the second-best time and completed all the knots, so I earned my patch and ribbon. Unfortunately, my lock skills (picking the door lock on the ball closet) got me kicked out, and my Scout career was finished. I asked for a patch for ball liberation, but that just ensured I would never be allowed to return.

Dad had got Mom pregnant with my first brother, Page, who was born December 25, 1960. Earlier that year, he thought a summer vacation with Lauren, Mom, and I would be good for the family, so he bought a motor boat and hitched it to the family station wagon. We went to Lake of the Ozarks in Missouri. It was a hot drive, and as we arrived at our destination in the afternoon, we pulled up to the dock. We all had our swimsuits on, and Lauren and I ran to the end of the dock and jumped into the cool lake water. Mom was sticking out with Page at four- plus months along, so she was just walking slowly. Dad, however, got swept up in our frolicking in the water, so he jumped off the edge of the dock too. Unfortunately, he didn't swim and never learned. While Lauren and I splashed each other, Dad was bobbing up and down, finally realizing he couldn't swim. Mom alertly saw the problem and dove in (with Page inside her) and hauled Dad to shore. It was a good thing that he was okay, and the incident gave me a new respect for water. Ever since that day, I've been much more observant at pools, rivers, lakes, and oceans. I was able to save the life of my middle son Bob, my friend Joe's daughter, a woman in a Montana river, and some old guy in La Jolla, California, from drowning.

Later that summer, I was swimming at the Dolphin Club in Homewood, and a girl my age invited me home to her home nearby. She went to Flossmoor Junior High, which was right next to Homewood, and she was quite attractive. I walked her home, and we went downstairs to the recreation room where she taught me to kiss; to me, she was great. But we never talked much, and she had a line of boyfriends waiting for her favors. Still, I really appreciated the extensive instruction, whatever her motive. That evening, I walked home on air. This was a beginning of a real sexual awakening for me (although I never had complete, actual sex until I turned twenty or an ejaculation until eighteen).

Other than photographs or family, the first naked girl I saw was at a retreat for confirmation at my church. We had to drive up in the woods to a campground with log cabins. At meals, we could not talk and had to stare at things to get someone to pass what we wanted to us. The boys were in one building, and the girls were in another (we were all eighth graders). Both groups were housed on the second floor, pretty high up. There was a small balcony separated by about seven feet with a twenty-foot drop to concrete. One kid brought fireworks, so I was helping him blow up frogs for a while, and then we walked back to the dormitory. On the way, I looked up and saw girls in their window taking off their clothes, but I was at a bad angle to see anything. When we arrived back to our building, I went out of the dormer up top and foolishly jumped to the other balcony and made it. I looked in the window and got to see the girls giggling and putting on their pajamas. A couple were totally nude and unassuming, like they were showing the others that their breasts were bigger and they had their nether region hair. I was dumbfounded but pleased and the next day made sure all the naked girls I viewed the night before received my undivided attention. They were passed whatever they looked at immediately by me in spite of the retreat ban on talking. I can be "real religious" when properly motivated.

It was colder now, and my cousin Lee and I would go to Isaac Walton League Park to ice skate. We would mostly speed skate and do quick side stops. As soon as we got there on one particular day, I hit a patch of rough ice speed skating and went over backward, saving my head with my left hand on the ice. I completed the fiasco on my left side and severely hurt my left wrist. I told Lee, and he thought I was trying to spoil everyone's day with a fake injury. I toughed it out for a couple of hours, and on the walk to Lee's house, it really hurt. When we got there, Aunt Kay had to cut my glove off because my wrist was so swollen. It was broken, and I had to wear a cast for six weeks more. Mom was still pregnant with Page, and she called to Dad Christmas morning to leave for the hospital. Dad uttered his immortal line: "I've got to start my pants and put on the car."

My cousin Lee and I got to go on a spring break vacation with Dad and Uncle Page (Lee's Dad) for our upcoming middle school graduation. We drove to Florida in early April and got to watch the Chicago White Sox and the New York Yankees play during spring training. Dad was impressed with Chicago, but Lee and I were Yankees fans then and got to meet Roger Maris and Mickey Mantle. It couldn't have been better timing in April 1961, because that year they had the homerun competition and Roger Maris broke Babe Ruth's record of sixty, while Mantel was close behind with fifty-seven. We later went deep sea fishing, and Uncle Page got seasick and didn't catch anything. I didn't catch any trophy fish but got a lot of big mackerel that we enjoyed cooking at Page's dad home in Clearwater.

Our classmate Chic S had an after-graduation pool party to officially end our junior high clique before high school. Many boys and girls from dance class and sports were there. We finished swimming, and the girls went to a bedroom to change for our last dance. One of the girls, Chris, answered the door with a towel around her, recognized me, and then screamed and dropped her towel. While revealing her large dark bush, I noticed several other girls I knew sans tops and many totally naked. I was stunned with the view, and I swear no one closed the door for several minutes, as they were all screaming and making a fuss. This was my finest moment at the pinnacle of junior high. A couple of years later I asked Chris about the moment. She just said they thought it was the Chic's mom at the door and didn't know why it took so long to close the door. I thanked her, and she smiled.

CHAPTER 3

High School

When I was a freshman in high school, we had girl gangs, as well as boy gangs. The older girls with gang attitudes would pick on younger or weaker guys. They would jump them when they were alone and "pants" them (remove their trousers and shorts) and then laugh while they ran home. The girls would keep the pants as a war trophy (reminiscent of panty raids in college). I got it once in junior high when I was more than a mile from home in the suburbs (Homewood). I still had my powder blue sweater on but nothing except socks and shoes below the beltline. I started running (my ass was turning pink from the cold fall day) and saw some people walking toward me (housewives), so I jumped a waist-high privet hedge and stood on the other side. I stayed there freezing with my arms folded across my chest as they slowly walked by, and I politely said hello. When they had passed by a safe distance, I started running again. I never did get the pants back, so I'm sure they're in some war memorial to high school memories for someone.

Anyway, back to freshman year. I was pretty bright in math (algebra in fifth grade), so I was in mostly honors classes. (We had basic, intermediate, advanced, and honors classes.) I had taken astronomy, which had a lot of advanced math with angstrom values and magnitudes. Girls mature faster than guys do, and this senior girl in front of me was always ragging at me because I knew all the answers, and she was into her social life and gang of buddies more than anything. She would do what she could to embarrass the immature freshman. Our instructor was the chess team sponsor, and I was the number one player so we had a good relationship. That made it even worse, and because of her poor grades, she hated Mr. M. After six weeks or so of verbal abuse, I was getting tired of being obsequious (wussy). I decided to strike out, even with my junior high experience still seared in my brain from two years earlier.

She sat in front of me. In those days, girls had to wear skirts and blouses, and boys wore pants and dress shirts. Her dress hung down the back of the chair. (Do you remember the original The Parent Trap with Hayley Mills?) I didn't have scissors, but I had a safety pin, so I pinned her dress and slip up to her belt loop. Girls in those days carried their books in front of them with their arms clasped around them. When she got up, you could see her semi-sheer, white, laced panties and butt perfectly. She walked down the hall with her two friends on either side, acting very important as usual without any clue to her situation. Homewood-Flossmoor was a big high school, and while changing classes, many students are in the hall. Well, she had a real following that day; I think half the freshman and sophomore boys were late to class. Just before she got to her next class, one of her friends noticed and told her about her skirt being pinned up. The snickering hit home, to say the least, and she was totally embarrassed and miffed. It was fun, but I was now subject to reprisal and worried. She didn't come to school the next day, but the following day she showed up. I knew if I talked to her she would read my fear and emotion, so I decided to write her a note. I said: "If you don't leave me alone, next time the punishment will be much worse." (If you're going down, Bravado helps your image.)

Apparently, she came up in her own mind what "punishment" could be worse and she stopped the harassment and never browbeat me again. It's usually better to be lucky than good.

Dad was a pain in high school, and it wasn't until I was twenty-five that he finally got much smarter. As a matter of fact, the older I got, the brighter he seemed. Anyway, for Christmas 1961, Page was a year old, and Dad got me a new ten-speed made in Japan. It didn't even last six months before some pin in the gears broke. We couldn't get a part for it, so it sat in the garage up on some hooks. Dad constantly badgered me about it, and whenever he decided I needed a lecture, it was about how I never took care of anything, just look at the hardly used bike rusting in the garage. For years, I received inner ear abuse over this lemon from Japan. I could spend all day cleaning the basement or the garage, and Dad wouldn't say a thing, but if he saw a broom not replaced from the day's ordeal, I was told I never put anything away. Dad had pegboards in the garage with little metal hooks to hold up the various implements, so if any were missing, it would be painfully obvious.

He surprised me one day when I was fourteen (probably feeling guilty for all the browbeating he'd given me) and told me to back the car out of the garage. I was elated at this great opportunity to prove myself and be "grown up." The new 1961 Buick Electra had a 445-cubic-inch engine in it (close to seven liters by today's standards). It was a beautiful tan convertible and had an automatic transmission. The gearshift then had a difference from today's automatics in that reverse was at the end and not second for choices of gears (then, it was ordered as follows: P, N, D1, D2, R; now, it's ordered: P, R, N, D, L). When a car is cold, the choke automatically kicks in and gives more gas until the vehicle gets running better. I, being a novice with no training whatsoever, easily started the car. I, unfortunately, did not place my foot on the brake before I began to move the gear selector toward reverse. It hit D1 first, and with the choke on, the car leaped forward into the woodpile at the back of the garage. The impact buckled the back of the garage and ruined the new Buick's front grill. I was mortified and received numerous unflattering retorts professing to be parental guidance. I was summarily grounded, and the damn bike was brought up again!

Finally, after months of ridicule, I was graciously given another opportunity to back the car out of the garage. I was now bolstered with renewed vigor and imminent success possibilities for this opportunity to display my care and knowledge of propelling an automotive vehicle. I got in, adjusted the seat and mirror, and started the Buick. I deliberately placed my foot on the brake; I was not going to let the car escape my control this venture. I deftly placed the car in reverse, felt the transmission engage, placed my right arm on the seat, and looked out the back window over my right shoulder (like I'd seen my parents do many times). I slowly crept backward, watching for children or animals in the driveway behind. To my untimely demise, as I adjusted the steering with my left arm and continued to look out the back window, the left bumper caught the left side of the garage right where the garage door goes up and down. My world crashed around me, and once again, I was grounded and heard the bike story. I'd had two solo attempts at driving, didn't even get all the way out of the garage, and had two accidents. Life is so cruel sometimes. Driver's education was still more than a year away, and I was doomed to walking or getting rides from my parents and hearing about my abilities to care for a bike and crash cars in the garage.

While I was grounded, I could go to school but had to stay in my room other than that. Idle minds are the devil's workshop, and I'd get an assembly line running. I had a Daisy pump BB gun and was an expert shot. (I practiced a lot.) During the week when I was going to school, I'd take a piece of toast with me and spread it on the front lawn outside my bedroom window. Our house was a tri-level, and my room was on the ground floor. If I stood up, the ground outside was at chest level, and the windows would wind out a few inches above the ground cover. I set the toast out where I would get a good field of fire. On Saturday, I would still put the bread out but would return to my room and continue my war with the evil blackbirds, sparrows, and suspicious winged creatures of other species. One morning I shot a rather large blackbird, but my gun wasn't powerful enough to kill it so it limped squawking to neighbor two doors away and across the street.

That neighbor was in her thirties, very much a busybody, and always discussing propriety and moral values. I went back to bed in my undershorts, and she came over a half hour later and rang the bell. No one else was home, so, half-awake, I went upstairs in my briefs that were just barely hanging on. I opened the door, and she started complaining about the bird and then noticed I was hardly wearing anything. She immediately stopped and gasped, turned red, looked three times, and left. Well, you'd think I was a rapist or something. Anyway, after that, she only called my parents to complain. She had moved in to the G's home, who was a homebuilder. A couple of years earlier, he had left his bulldozer out front, and I got it started and accidentally drove it through their flower garden out front. No one was impressed that a lad so young could operate heavy equipment. (I didn't mean to aerate the flower garden with a bulldozer track, but I was labeled a vandal. I remember reading about the vandals who sacked Rome in the fifth century. I could identify with them. The Romans would conquer and "civilize" a smaller country, but when they got their butts kicked, it was a sack. The people who won were vandals, and coincidentally, Mrs. G was Italian.) The house had bad karma for me I guess.

All through high school, when you missed a day of school, you had to bring a note from home. I had the same girl write my notes all four years. Janet dated my friend Pat and had awesome handwriting. She eventually married my cousin Mike B who was killed in a car wreck at age nineteen. Even if I was really ill, I threw Mom's notes out and had Janet duplicate them. In the hundred days I missed sophomore year, I lost to death seven grandparents, three uncles, two aunts, numerous cousins, and even some siblings. I concocted every contagious disease known to mankind. If anyone ever put them all together, I was the unluckiest kid on the planet. When the report cards came out, I had good grades. I always had someone get my assignments for me, because I deliberately applied myself to make up for all the shenanigans I was pulling. Sophomore year was my best year for grades in high school. One day I wanted to leave early (I was bored) and went to biology lab and put a stink bomb (made from sulfur so it smelled like rotten eggs) in the air ducts. I was a total hero with the few who knew, because we all got to go home to avoid the nauseous stench.

In the summer of 1962, my brother Jim was born. He had long dark hair and a prune face reminiscent of Winston Churchill. I turned fifteen a few weeks later and had two brothers to babysit instead of one. Lauren had a back operation, so I got the brunt of the child relief for Mom.

Boobs were becoming a big focus in my life, and the girl across the street (Robin) had a great pair and liked the attention. She would hide my softball in the center pocket of her pullover. I would have to search her for it, and low and behold, I rarely found the ball but always found her breasts. I was in a strange relationship. I really didn't fancy her, but it was fun to roll in the grass with her and feel her up. She encouraged it often, and I usually responded. Men are such beasts (but are easy to trick).

Randy was dating a friend of mine named Sandy, and her friend was my old spark Aleida (who I later found out had jilted me in my early years for my own cousin Lee). She even lived behind Lee across the field in our town. She had sex with Lee when we were fourteen, and Lee never said a word till we were eighteen. He was very skilled at keeping secrets. I was going to meet Randy and Sandy at Sandy's house, and Aleida would be there for all of us to fool around. I didn't realize she was sans hymen status and looking for action. I was cutting through backyards to get to Sandy's house when I jumped a tall fence, and a huge German shepherd dog accosted me full bore. I couldn't escape. As he leapt, jaws gaping for my flesh, I could only think of one thing to do. I shoved my hand down his throat as deep as I could, and the dog immediately stopped, gagged, and coughed. I fell backward into some of his dog shit from the impact and quickly got back to my feet. He looked at me with soft big brown eyes, smelled his own odiferous feces upon my body, and started wagging his tail. I hesitatingly patted his head and jumped the other fence. I got to Sandy's a mess, and she and Aleida immediately started to mother me. They took my pants and shirt to wash and gave me a stupid girl's robe while they puttered around the laundry room. Randy wasn't there yet, so Sandy gave us space. Aleida was getting hot, but I was so bummed out with the dog crap, almost being eaten and wearing girl's robe, that I missed my opportunity. She even unbuttoned her blouse and kissed me to cheer me up (and it did a little), but I was too naive to realize the extent of her offer. Randy had come, and my clothes were done, but Aleida was no longer interested and left with Randy and Sandy to go home.

The word sophomore comes from Greek Sophos mores, meaning wise fool. When I was fifteen, it fit me perfectly. Out of the 180 in school days required, I only attended eighty during the 1962–63 school year. The system in those days was to take attendance in homeroom and put the note out on the door for the dean's assistant to pick up. I, being the know-it-all guy, stole a blank pad of those pink slips. I would copy everyone's name on a new sheet except mine (or later have a crony do it) and replace the slip in the door. Then I would sneak off the school grounds and hitchhike ten miles away to Glenwood stables and ride horses all day till two thirty and hitchhike back and take the bus home. Mom always wondered why my pants were dirty on the inside leg and toward the bottom. If it was a warm day, I would ride without my pants in just my shorts. She never said anything about my shorts and must have expected guys to have dirty shorts. One day I was racing through the forest (I rode English saddle with double reins) in my undies, and I came on a Girl Scout camp. I was halfway through the clearing before I realized it was occupied. The girls saw me and started screaming, and their leader came running after me like I was some kind of rapist or violator of young girls. I tore through the camp at breakneck speed, knocking over the garbage and trampling their lawn with hoof prints and flying pieces of sod. They were all chasing me with whatever they could brandish from branches to pans. I figured I was fortunate to get out of there alive.

On the weekends, I was a trail guide for the "tourists" and would brush down the horses. I didn't ask for money, and they never charged me for "exercising" the horses during the week. One time I was riding a sixteen-hand horse (very large) and was beating this mare named Goldie in a race by a half a length when she bit my left love handle, drew blood, and bruised me pretty bad. I had a riding crop in my right hand, and I cracked her across the forehead to release her grip on my body. About two weeks later, Goldie was hit by a car while acting up with another rider, and they had to put her down. A week after that, I took a bad spill on Prince (the sixteen-hand horse). Nothing was broken, but I was a mess with imbedded cinders, hurt muscles, and bruises. I stopped riding after that and have only ridden a couple of times since.

I made the wrestling team in the winter and was second-string at 145 pounds. The next higher weight had too many good athletes, so I had to keep my weight down. When Reavis HS came to Homewood-Flossmoor, they put me in so our number one starter wouldn't get hurt. Reavis won state in many positions that year. I began in the upright, and the guy threw me off the mat and into the wall, leaving me with a chipped tooth. I came back, and he got a takedown and a near fall. When I started on top, he escaped, and I had another near fall. He never pinned me, but I couldn't control him and lost the match badly. Coach noticed I never got pinned, but I was just an average wrestler. We did have one match where I just went dead weight. I let my body just go limp when the guy grabbed me. He couldn't support all my weight, and I fell on him and ended up with a record twenty- four-second pin.

Homewood-Flossmoor was completely Caucasian students when I attended, and I had little contact with African Americans other than Sam at work. The first time I had to wrestle a black student was in Kankakee. I started to laugh, and he almost pinned me. Coach Lombardi was worried. I tried to explain that he smelled so different (they used depilatories instead of shaving so they wouldn't get bumps). When he began to sweat, his skin got really greasy. The coach was getting really mad, so I settled down by the third period (I was down eight to two) and finally pinned the guy. Coach was happy, but I was still feeling strange. I ended the season winning one over half my matches, but I was never pinned so I felt good. I had a rough time keeping weight, and some days ate only oranges for energy before the weigh-in for the match. If I was a pound or two over, then I had to jog until I made weight. The next year I went out for tennis, because I knew I wouldn't be able to make weight anymore.

Randy had just turned sixteen and wild (moving up here from Texas). He didn't have a license either, but we all pined for the day we could drive. I told my folks I was going to the movies with Randy to see Elvis in Kid Galahad. My dad dropped me off at the theater, and as soon as he left, I jogged over to Randy's house. We quietly pushed his mom's car out in the street and started it down the block. Apparently, we (Randy, Pat, and I) were pathetic thieves. Randy's mom called my dad and told him. We thought we were big stuff in the Oldsmobile driving fast on the I-394. We had a BB gun with us, and we would go really fast coming up on a truck and shoot out the taillights and race down the highway. We had the needle buried at 120 miles per hour, and then a Corvair Spyder Monza passed us like we were standing still. It was like when the nurse would hit your erection with a pencil during a medical exam; we just went limp.

Randy took me back to the movie theater, and I snuck in through the back door where I had a buddy put gum in the lock. I saw the last ten minutes and asked a guy sitting there what the movie was about so I could encapsulate it for my parents. Thinking how slick I was, I sauntered out of the theater looking for my ride. Dad was there and looked surprised to see me come out of the show. I didn't think much of it and thought I had all my bases covered. Dad (almost sarcastically) asked how the show was. I began my encapsulated rendition when he interrupted halfway through my dramatic presentation.

He said, "I walked up and down the aisles looking for you with the usher and a flashlight."

I knew I was toast, and all the lies in the world wouldn't save me. I had lied before, but this was the first time I'd been caught. My facial expression must have born witness to my demise. Dad took my head with his palm and, not unlike a basketball, dribbled it on the passenger window. He repeated countless slanderous statements that were lost in the pain of discovery and the loss of faith and trust my parents had for me.

I decided I needed some new pets. We had an awful dog called Peppy, who was a small, black toy French poodle. Mom spoiled him, and the dog was in serious need of psychotherapy. He would only eat broccoli and chicken livers. (Now, how Mom discovered this is beyond me, for I would have never hit upon that food combination for a dog.) Peppy did most everything wrong and nobody cared for the dog but

Mom. This was a bonus for me, as it was a respite from personal criticism and a focus on Mom's dog by Dad. I was 15 John F. Kennedy was president, so I think it was an attempt for showing we had class and were also a part of Camelot.

One day, when Page was a little less than a year old, Peppy left a "package" on the pristine living room blue shag rug. It attracted Page, and he crawled over and placed the animal excrement in his mouth for a taste. I happened to observe the consumption at the exact moment Page attempted to ingest the feces. His face was first pleased at his new discovery, but then a scowl and finally a serious frown appeared. I thought it was so funny I fell on the floor at the entrance to the living room from the kitchen. Mom and Lauren ran out as I explained the reason for Page's displeasure between out-of-breath laughs. They carried him excitedly to the kitchen sink to torture the curious lad. As they began to wash his mouth out with soap and water, Page began to cry. I was still on the ground laughing, and they both began to kick me as they said how Page could die. While still laughing hysterically, I would say, "What a crappy death." And they would kick me some more. I later asked why they didn't kick the dog, but Peppy got away with being a dumb animal. He constantly messed up their "restricted" living room, but Mom just cleaned it up and said nothing. When Peppy was eating his broccoli and chicken liver, no one could get near him without getting nipped. He was very protective of his food. When Mom and Dad left on vacation, I gave Peppy dog food, and he would never eat it. I refused to give him his regular meal, and the food got hard on his plate. Lauren finally gave in after four days and fed him his chicken livers (the dog was looking peaked).

I went and bought two mice that I named Nikki and Charlie. Page wore these Dr. Denton pajamas (the ones that zipped up the front and had the footie built in), and I put Nikki and Charlie inside his pajamas. He had diapers on underneath, but the mice crawled all over inside, and he laughed and giggled the whole time. I took my mice back and put them in their cage. Page went upstairs when Mom called, and she was going to get him ready for bed. I heard her shriek upstairs, so I naturally ascended the stairs. She thought Page had measles because the mice had left tiny red marks where they climbed around on his skin. I assured her Page was fine and brought the mice up to show her how much Page loved the mice. When I reinserted the mice, Page lit up with laughter and giggles, and Mom was placated. Mom then got a weird voice and started to curl her hands up. She said, "Nikki and Charlie are coming to get you," and began tickling me around the throat and chest so I would be laughing also. She doesn't even tickle well, but the whole act got me going. She still does that to this day. Moms are great!

I was 15, school was out, and so Randy, Pat, and I decided to run away from home. Pat was a neighbor diagonally behind us. I left a note with my mom explaining how I was going to strike out in the world and make it on my own. We planned to caddy at the golf course for a while to earn traveling money and then hitchhike down to Florida. There we would get "easy" jobs working on fishing boats and live the good life. Pat wanted us to camp by Dolphin Lake Country Club in the woods because it was by his girlfriend Janet's house. We lived in the bushes and slept in an old tree house. The first day we all caddied and made five dollars each. The second day Pat didn't feel well, stayed away from work, spent ten dollars of our pooled money on a pink button-down shirt, and spent the day with Janet. Randy made five dollars, and I had doubles for eight dollars. Randy left us for good the third day, and Pat worked a half round (nine holes) and then quit for good. Unbeknownst to me, Pat was charging food for him and Janet at Dolphin Lake to his mom's account. His mom put out a police report on both of us, and we were arrested in a day or so. I was returned home from the police station.

Dad was disgusted with me for worrying Mom and disrupting our lifestyle once again. He told me to put on my suit and pack my bag. Dad wasn't big on discussion in those days, so us kids just followed instructions or faced certain death. He came back a short time later and gave me a lecture about feeling my oats and doing things the "right" way. It turned out to be self-justification for the "lesson" he was going to teach me. (Years later, during therapy for divorce, my shrink thought my parents were horrible for allowing this to happen, but I thought it was an opportunity and didn't have a problem with it.)

This trek to Denver began with a lecture, a round- trip bus ticket, and twenty-five dollars in cash. I still had seven dollars left from caddying in spite of my friends, so my bankroll was thirty-two dollars. Dad put me on a bus to Denver because I knew no one there I could sponge off of. I tried to explain about Pat and Randy but was told I had to take responsibility for my friends' actions. Dad was a light switch with no middle ground—only black and white. Dad was judge, jury, and executioner, besides being the lawgiver. Negotiation and compromise were for weaklings and had no place in our society. Unfortunately for me, I was always wrong, and he never was. Dad was an excellent source for learning tenacity, which, in the long run, is more successful than any other method of accomplishment I can think of.

The bus ride took more than two days, stopping at every Podunk station. I traveled with some soldiers, and we sang songs and played cards. I had a great time until we stopped at Denver. I got off the bus at two thirty in the morning; the bus left with my "buddies," and I was alone in unfamiliar territory. I saw a sign that read: "Kenmore Hotel Rooms $2.50 and up." I figured that was something I could afford. I had close to twenty dollars left and figured I could last a week if I was really careful and ate sparingly. The room was adequate with a sink and a pay AM radio. I learned to put a quarter in and unplug it to keep the timer from running down. The bath/shower and toilets were common (shared) for the floor. It was an unsavory lot, but no violence erupted during my stay. I did have to use the stairs; Denver is the mile-high city, and if I used the elevator, my nose would bleed. I went downstairs, and the first day I wasted a couple of dollars riding public transportation around the city so I knew where things were. I found locations on a city map and figured out what bus route was the closest. It made the next six weeks easier. I tried to get a job, but in 1963, you had to be sixteen to get a Social Security card and fourteen to get a work permit. I wouldn't be sixteen until late August, and this was early June. So how was I supposed to survive? By lying, I told the Social Security office I was born in 1946 instead of 1947, and they bought it. Today you always have to prove it with a birth certificate, but back then, they took your word.

I got my card and was able to get a job bussing tables in my hotel at lunch for eighty-five cents an hour and 10 percent of the waitresses' tips. The waitresses ripped me off, and I was lucky to get 2 percent. I didn't make waves, and I got my lunch for free. The next day after work I went to another restaurant called Duffy's Shamrock, home of the Irish coffee. I told them my experience at Kenmore, and they hired me for ninety cents an hour and 10 percent of the tips. (The waitresses still ripped me off but only for half.) I worked over the dinner hour, and they also fed me a meal. I now had an income and my meals. I'd make three to four dollars at lunch and at least five dollars at night, so I was getting ahead in the world. Some days I brought home ten dollars, which was better than doubles when I caddied. I met an Asian girl (American born) at Zekendorf Plaza wee putt, and we started dating. I took her to see The Nutty Professor with Jerry Lewis, and later she saw me win the Plaza wee putt tournament (ten dollars and free wee putting for the year). I got to be in a Route 66 television show (They taped me as I walked pass the bench where the actors were sitting and talking by the plaza.), but never received any royalties. Today they have to pay you, but then you volunteered and were paid only if you spoke or had a contract. Things were good, and I wore my suit one day and even got into my first X-rated movie. It wasn't very good but I was proud that I accomplished an "adult" endeavor.

Tragedy struck the fifth week of my lark. I ate a bad tomato at a Walgreen's cafeteria and got a case of ptomaine poisoning. I lost all sustenance to the toilet, and then the porcelain princess wanted more. I was down to yellow bile burning my rectum, while yellow bile burned my pallet. The worst was that it was simultaneously not unlike two hands wringing a damp dishcloth for the last drop of moisture. I convulsed and suffered for several days, unable to think or eat. When I took water, it would start again.

Having a "key" skill of bussing tables didn't save my position at either location, or someone who could at least show up quickly replaced me. I was out of money, and my spirit was really broken. After the bill was paid for my room, I had five dollars left. I still had the return ticket Dad bought me, and I proceeded to the bus station.

In my family, the tradition was whoever went on a trip brought back gifts for the kids. My brothers were little, and my sister was fourteen so I stopped and spent the five dollars on presents, not thinking about the length of the return trip. I had a couple of Tarzan paperbacks to amuse me, and I was set. The trip home was horrible. The bus was crowded, and I had a very heavy black woman in the seat next to me. She competed like a weed for more ground, or, in our case, seat space. I was starting to at least feel numb from my bout with "dish rag death" when we stopped for food. I had no money, and we still had two more days to go. I quickly learned to get water and put ketchup in it with salt and pepper. Then, before the waitress would pick up another customer's dinner, I would take crackers, kale, parsley, or whatever was left on the plate. I finally made it home, but I'd gotten no sleep and was very hungry. I was crumpled in my suit, had a sallow skin color, and had circles darkening under my eyes.

When I entered the house, Dad looked up from his paper and smiled. He said, "How'd you enjoy the world, Son?" A retort was out of the question. I didn't even eat and just went to bed for twenty-four hours.

The summer wasn't but half over, and I realized I was coming of age for a boy—the age we all focus on, sixteen and a driver's license. I had already passed the driver's education written part during the second semester of school, but I still had to take the driving part. I quickly got set up at summer school but had missed the first day. Coach Schmidt (my wrestling coach) was teaching, so I felt comfortable. He foolishly let me have the wheel, and we struck out on Governor's Highway (four lanes with a speed limit of fifty-five). I was cruising in the right lane at about sixty miles per hour, and Coach wanted me to turn left about a block and a half up. I quickly swerved to the left lane and hit the brakes with great control but a fast deceleration to make the turn. The whole car shuddered as a semitrailer missed us, swerving from the left to the right deftly avoiding killing us from the rear. He couldn't even honk until he was half a truck length past us. Coach looked like I did when I returned from Denver, and I immediately had to switch with another driver.

The rest of driver's education was fine, and the state troopers came to give the test on exactly my sixteenth birthday. I had my mission to pass, and Coach asked for my learner's permit in front of the state trooper from the DMV. I said, "What permit?" Again, Coach looked like I did returning from Denver. He said, "The one you had the first day of class." I, of course, replied, "I wasn't there that day." Well, after much commotion and grief for poor Coach, I finally got to test. I was so pumped that I peeled out on the tires when the trooper said, "Let's go!" It was the only three points I lost, and I was a valid Illinois driver at last.

My first wreck driving with a license was shortly thereafter and one of the few that was not my fault at all. I was in Dad's beautiful Buick in front of Dixie Square Mall in broad daylight. I was in the left lane stopped behind a car also waiting to turn into the mall. I had my signals on, not thinking about anything much when a car driven by another kid didn't see us and slammed into me and pushed me into the car in front. The kid was sorry and got a ticket, and the driver of the car in front claimed whiplash. Our car was the worst for damage because both the front and back were destroyed. Of course, the bicycle in the garage was brought up by Dad and then came the comments about how I have the "Midas touch" in reverse and I'm irresponsible, etc.

Unfortunately, sometimes you get what you ask for. I was driving my sister downtown in Homewood shortly thereafter but in the 1963 Pontiac Safari station wagon. We were a two-car family, and I guess you have to spread it around. I was inching up to the stoplight (even though it was green) behind a slow bus in heavy traffic (for Homewood). The car was in drive but just idling on the choke for gas. I was casually watching the huge bus in front of me, and a beautiful girl with white hot pants (short shorts then) was walking on the sidewalk to my right. I was daydreaming about her until I slammed into the bus that had stopped to pick up a passenger. His rear engine door was bent, and the headlight covers on the Safari were pointing up at a forty-five-degree angle. Once again, I heard about the bike, but this time, I was grounded and lost all driving privileges.

The first girl (Mavis M) whom I ever "seriously" dated in high school was four ten with curly light brown hair, quite cute, freckles, a little plump, and well endowed. We went to Turnabout together first semester of our junior year (where the girl asks the boy to a formal dance and dinner). I went to Homewood-Flossmoor High School on the south side. I was nuts about her but made the classic mistake of putting her up on an unreachable pedestal. I was sixteen and she was fifteen, and she didn't know how to drive but wanted to learn. I was willing to teach her even though I'd only been driving a year. She was so short she couldn't reach the pedals with her toes, so I foolishly (and wantonly) let her sit on my lap to steer, and I worked the gas and brakes. We were driving in Chicago Heights going to the Tivoli restaurant, and she didn't see the turn. We doubled with another couple and had my dad's new Buick Electra. We ended up crashing into the car in front of us through my assumptions and her inexperience. We never did get to dinner, and because of her age and the fact I was so enamored with her, I had to take the whole rap. I got a ticket from the police, experienced my dad's wrath, and was grounded for six weeks. At the end of six weeks, I went to a party with her. She was drunk as a skunk when I got there, so I protected her, got her to her home, snuck her in, and got her into bed so she wouldn't be busted. She never knew what I did. She left the next weekend for Florida and didn't come back for a month. Next time I heard about her she was out of school and pregnant from some guy in Florida. I was crushed.

My junior year at Homewood-Flossmoor I'd had the encounter with Mavis first semester, but after Christmas, I was attracted to this brunette with big brown eyes and powder blue angora sweaters. She had a locker next to me and would stare deep into my eyes with this come-hither look. She was a junior also and dated the elite Kingsmen weight lifting team at our school. I would talk to her occasionally, and she would listen so intently and stare with those big brown eyes. I finally was so entranced that I asked her out. She enthusiastically accepted. Her name was Judy, and she had a gorgeous shape and appeared to be very receptive. I then started to think any one of the Kingsmen could kill me. My sophomore year I wrestled at 145 pounds, so I was maybe 160 and five nine by this time. I didn't get my growth spurt until my freshman year at college, when I finally shot up to six three. I was looking forward to the date, but like all new ventures with the opposite sex, I was naturally apprehensive. It was early 1964, and downtown there was a new movie called Goldfinger that I really wanted to see. I had my dad's station wagon (I didn't get to drive the Electra much after wrecking it with Mavis), I wasn't grounded, and I had an interesting date.

I picked her up, and she was dressed nice, as I was, to go downtown. It's about forty-five minutes from Homewood to the loop in Chicago, so I had the radio on and we were talking about school and each other as we drove down the Dan Ryan Expressway. (I was still a virgin at this point and didn't lose my silver bullet until I had just turned twenty.) She was sexually confident, and I'm positive she was more experienced, having dated the testosterone kids from the Kingsmen. Anyway, we were listening to the radio, and "Louie" was on. I had my right arm around her and was driving with the left when she reached down and started rubbing my crotch. I was so startled that I froze, but I kept my head and didn't wreck the car. (I didn't need to be grounded again.) I didn't know what to do, but I was very uncomfortable with this new development. I moved my right arm down to the small of her back, pulled it out, and went under her extended arm to knock it up free of my crotch while pretending to adjust the radio channel and volume. She backed off, and we got to the movie without too much sexual stimulation.

It was very crowded, and we could only get two aisle seats. She was seated across the aisle and one row back from me. She didn't want to sit there; she wanted to sit on my lap. I really wanted to see the movie, so I made her sit over there, and she was very displeased with me. She sat on the other side of the car on the way home and didn't say a word as I tried to discuss the movie. I took her in her house, and she wanted a kiss goodnight, which I felt was okay. She was a very good kisser, and I was breathless in no time and grew bold. If you ever saw the movie The Graduate, she was Mrs. Robinson. I was Dustin Hoffman with the older woman (even though Judy was the same age, she was by far the more mature). I reached up and caressed her left breast with my right hand, and she never missed a beat on making out and her tongue never quit. She moved me downstairs to the pool table, climbed up on it, and hiked her skirt up. I was instantly shocked back to reality staring at her white panties. I apologized and told her I had to get home, or I would lose my driving privileges and be grounded. I ran out of there and went home and never asked her out again. It was too much, too fast; she obviously needed a man. Looking back, I have to laugh at myself, but it's all part of growing up.

I had a Jewish friend Jim R who was smart but very sheltered. His dad was a metallurgist, and Jim had to report everything to his parents even though it was boring. He could never get a date, and the girls thought he was a real dork. When he got excited about something, his eyes would seem to bug out under his powerful glasses. He walked on his toes, so instead of a gait, he had more of a sine curve up and down. He was really cheap with money until I got him a date, and then you'd think he was Rockefeller. He couldn't do enough for the girl but didn't even get a kiss. After our double date, I thought he needed a reputation to get some action. I was misguided by my imagination, but nevertheless, I proceeded with my plan.

Painting a water tower was daring and something everyone would talk about. So I told Jim if we could paint HF-65 on the Flossmoor water tower, we'd be heroes and he'd get kissed. He foolishly bought in, and I got the spray paint and began the long climb with Jim trailing. Unbeknownst to me, Jim had acrophobia (fear of heights). Halfway up the tower, he froze in stark terror and couldn't move. I go the rest of the way up and painted our legendary logo. It was then I noticed the Flossmoor Police Station many blocks away. (I should note it was broad daylight.) I see men in blue looking back at me and rushing to their squad cars. I quickly started climbing down, and I could see them rapidly cutting through the residential areas to get at us. Jim was still frozen. I could have ditched him and escaped via the prairie, but he was so helpless that I couldn't. I talked him down a rung at a time and made him look at my eyes and not down. By the time he touched the ground, two squad cars were waiting with several officers. We were taken to the station, and Jim had to call his parents. It was like he got the electric chair. He was grounded and forbidden to ever see me again (probably a good and appropriate punishment). My Dad told the police to leave me in jail it would do me good. Incarceration didn't disturb me by this phase in my life. Police were always trying to teach me a lesson with fear and it had worn off. I just went back to the cell and asked what was for dinner. My mom eventually got me out. All the police knew me by my first name by now where it was almost embarrassing.

Later in the semester Dad got called to Washington, DC, for a National Association of Plastic Fabricators meeting, and Lauren and I got to go. Dad was going to be the new chairman, and we could visit all the sights. I'd never been to the capitol before and was naturally curious. The cherry blossoms were out, and I had images of George Washington cutting down trees (even though the capitol was Philadelphia when he was president). Lauren and I were so enthused we climbed the Washington Monument four times (898 stairs) just for fun. Her body cast was in the past, and she was finally feeling her oats. We met Hubert H. (in an elevator) who was a senator from Minnesota and speaking at Dad's convention. He shook my hand in the elevator (and would say he was "pleased as punch"), but his hand was cold and clammy. He had body odor, and his suit was gray and all lumpy. I was very disappointed meeting my first senator.

I remember at one restaurant we went to Dad got Yankee pot roast, so I got Southern fried chicken. It was just after we'd seen the Lincoln memorial, so the Civil War must have been on our minds. I met some local kids there and went driving around with them singing a favorite of the area called "Bad to Me." I also got to ride English saddle in a Maryland park nearby, so it was a fun trip.

Dad was grooming me for manhood whenever he got the opportunity. I was paid two dollars to mow our lawn, but everyone else in the neighborhood would pay four or five dollars for the same size yard. If I borrowed the car, I had to wash it and fill it up with gas. Now, admittedly, back then gas was in the twenty-four cents a gallon range, but Dad liked V8 cars, and they ate gas. Two dollars wasn't enough to fill the car and go on a date, so I improvised resources. I took my two dollars one week and bought a siphon kit. Whenever I needed to fill up, I'd drive Dad's Buick to a parking lot, find a car with gas, and siphon it over. It was great, and I always had plenty of gas and money to date. Unfortunately, I was in a subdivision, and some guy saw me and complained to the police. The police got there when I was leaving. I denied any knowledge, but they recognized me (being a prior customer so many times). When I got home later, my parents were up and disappointed again. They said the police had just left and were waiting there for quite a while. There went my siphon kit and my gas money.

I had to come up with something, so a buddy of mine (Ken) suggested we go into business to raise cash. We were both skilled in lawn care, and he worked part-time at the Southgate Pharmacy, so we developed a marketing plan. One of Ken's neighbors wanted his lawn cut for eight dollars. I did it for Ken because he had to work and found out the guy was a printer by trade and made business cards, invitations, etc. I told him if he would make us a box of business cards, I would cut his lawn for free. He agreed, and I told Ken. Ken liked the idea and said we could pass them out at the pharmacy. We made the cards to say C&D Expert Lawn Care, using the initials from our last names. We included our phone numbers and all kinds of small print that suggested we did landscaping, rototilling, and spraying in addition to grass cutting. It worked fabulously. When we showed up on the job, the people assumed we worked for a big outfit and were just the help. When we had to do rototilling, we'd rent the necessary equipment and build our cost into the price. Our parents' mowers were getting some hours on them, and Dad wasn't into it. I went to Sears and got the cheapest push rotary mower with the widest cut (twenty-four inches) plus a ten-dollar service contract for a total outlay of forty-five dollars. Dad's mower was self- propelled, but we didn't want to pay the extra money for that type of model. The mower ran every day, and I was not into maintenance then. We paid for a mower, a rake, a grass edger, a pressurized sprayer, and various clippers. The service contract for ten dollars paid for itself ten times over. We had the mower in the service center once a month for hitting wires, not changing oil and burning out the engine, replacing the blade, etc. At the end of a year, I brought it back for a tune-up, wheels, and blade. When the technician returned it, he was glad the contract was over. That was the first summer I ever made "decent" money. Ken and I each had a few hundred left when the season closed.

Erv (the father of the girl who played hide the baseball with me) came to one of our block parties. I was fascinated with him, as were the rest of the neighborhood because he would eat the cob after he finished the corn. He even ate other people's cobs after they had eaten their corn. He really liked consuming cobs or entertaining us with his antics. Either way, he was great for a different viewpoint. When we had block parties, the whole neighborhood would attend, and we would drink, dance, and be loud. Lauren and I would polka to the music, and I loved to go fast. We would go so fast that we would knock everybody off the dance area. Another neighbor, Irv, would get loaded and wanted to fight me (or anyone else available). He was a nice guy sober, but after a few beers, the testosterone went wild. If he was really toasted, it was hard to get him to stop being aggressive. I just had to keep away from him. Beating up a neighbor is a no-win situation even if he's at fault.

I was babysitting Page and Jim, and Page got an erection. He was naturally curious about it, and I tactlessly told him he had a big boner. Mom and Dad had a dinner party a few nights later with some politically correct Goody Two-shoes, and they all dressed up. Mom made a great dinner. Entertaining was an art form her whole peer group participated in. They were all very proper and polite (unless they had too much to drink) and solved both local and national problems with their conversations. Page came running down the stairs naked to join in and excitedly (in front of the guests) said, "Look, Mom. I've got a big boner!" Well, you'd have thought I ran over their dog deliberately. Everyone knew where Page got the language and attitude, so once again, I was in the doghouse. Almost twenty years after that day, I saw ET and laughed at the kid saying his brother had "penis breath" at the dinner table. It definitely brought back this memory of Page.

Senior year, the fall of 1964, I took the gym class for the hard cases (hoodlums and ruffians)—not because I wanted to be with these meat-knobs but because it was just before lunch, and if I hurried through the showers, I could get to lunch ten or fifteen minutes early. It was a poorly organized class with the vermin from all the other gym classes in a common repository. When they played basketball, they didn't dribble and they knocked down the weaklings and stomped them. They sat on each other's shoulders to shoot the baskets and non-players would interfere. I was used to their cheating and lopsided teams. But one day I saw this dung-head blond guy out on the wrong side fighting back. He was a new kid from California by the name of John IV. The Irish always pretended to be a dynasty and numbered their kids for each generation. After knowing them, I figure the families drank too much and just weren't creative enough to come up with new names. I decided to join in on his side, and after the game, I found out he liked to play military board games (Gettysburg, Tactics II, D-day, etc.) like I did. Neither one of us had found anyone before, so we pretty much played with ourselves. Our new friendship allowed us to play these games like they were designed. Fifty years later, we're still best friends.

In those days, we would go to the beach and camp out to play Afrika Korps half the night. John also showed me a valuable skill. It was shooting bottle caps like a Frisbee by snapping my fingers. I passed this valuable skill down to my children a generation later. I already could spray saliva silently for several feet from under my tongue by emulating a yawn. John told me it was called glicking. I worked for hours in the mirror perfecting the skill. I'm sure Mom wondered why the mirror was always spotted. Small skills are important, especially to people with childlike minds like me.

I met another blond, Tom B., a rich Flossmoor kid whose dad was a corporate lawyer. They had a huge house in Flossmoor's best area, and he wanted to go drinking. I wasn't a drinker at all and had never done anything but taste one of my parents' drinks or champagne at a wedding. He stole a bottle of his dad's best scotch, and we went to the Dunes (beach) in Indiana thinking we were cool. I hated the taste and even put it in Coke, but it was still terrible. I didn't even get high and did not understand all the fuss about drinking.

In June 1965, I graduated in the bottom half of my class (just below midpoint of 620 students graduating). We had four levels of classes, Basic, Intermediate, Advanced, and Honors. Computing GPA and class standing in the sixties did not adjust for level, of course, only the actual grade received. I took all honors and advanced classes because I was told they were for college preparation. My ACT math scores were in the top 1 percent of the nation (I received a score of thirty-five out of a possible thirty- six), and my verbal score was twenty-nine for combined ACT of thirty-one. I wasn't miffed and proceeded to graduation with a positive outlook. My folks asked me what I wanted, and I replied "a nickel- plated 357 Colt revolver pistol."

For graduation day, I had bought the biggest aerial bomb I could find in the nearest state that sold good fireworks. After commencement, I quickly went out into the lot and lit it between parked cars. There were lots of police around, so I quickly had to blend in with a crowd of people twenty-five paces away. It made a loud "whump" sound to launch the bomb, and it went a hundred feet in the air before exploding like a megaton bomb. Everyone stood paralyzed at the sound and gazed at the smoke. We (me and my buddies) were, of course, ecstatic at the success and impact on the students and parents. The police scanned the parking lot and harassed nearby people when they found the launch hulk between the cars but couldn't resolve the perpetrators. Cherry bombs and M-80s (a quarter stick of dynamite) weren't illegal in the

United States until 1968, so fireworks and I were no strangers. Illinois restricted types you could buy.

We would blow toilets up in gas stations and vending machines off the walls. Pyrotechnics are the devil's tools.

During the summer, I got Sweetie my dog, which was one of the best animals I ever owned. She was swollen with worms and had a potbelly when Mom and I first saw her in the litter. Her ears didn't stand up, and she was half toy collie and half German shepherd. She looked like Rin Tin Tin with short legs. I trained her with a bag of potato chips. She would sit, lay, roll over, stay, and not eat anything unless I made a kissing sound with me mouth and snapped my fingers. She would catch food midair, but if she missed, even if it was steak, she wouldn't touch it until I gave the command. Page and Jim were little guys, and when I'd babysit, I'd set up arena combat.

Mom and Dad entertained on the weekends, having friends and business associates over for a fancy dinner and drinks. The living room had very nice furniture, and the kids were never allowed in unless company was there and we were introduced. I would take the couch pillows and cushions off and make ramps and forts for the kids. Sweetie, Page, and Jim were given the blunt kitchen dinner knives, and I took a sheet and knotted one end and remained on my knees. The boys would assault me with their knives, and Sweetie would stay in reserve till we locked up. Then she'd get excited and join in, biting my arm or leg in mock battle. When the boys attacked or retreated I would whip the sheet out and wrap their feet by whipping the knot around them then pulling, and they'd go down on their rear ends. We'd trash the living room in no time with everything disheveled. When Mom or Dad's car hit the driveway, we'd immediately rush to straighten everything up and then go in the kitchen and pretend we were coloring or something else. Sweetie would still be hyper when Mom would come in, but I think Mom thought the dog just was glad to see her.

John, Joe B, and I went to work at dear old Homewood Cabinet Top. We were bummed with the job and decided to be dickheads and cheat on the time clock. Whoever was working punched the others in.

That way, we were able to work less for a bigger paycheck. It worked well for a month or so, but I was living with the president of the company, and he was getting smarter as I got older. He finally confronted me with the time card that showed I was punched in and working on a Saturday when Dad knew perfectly well that I was in bed snoozing at home. It was hard to deny. He told me that my cheating him put a big knot in his stomach. Well, I felt like shit; I had screwed up again. John and I never got our paychecks that week or what was withheld, so Dad wasn't hurt financially, but the fact that I was willing to cheat him really bothered both of us. It's interesting; Joe B was never caught and kept on working there till college. When Dad asked me if John was involved, I said yes, but he never asked about anyone else, including Joe. I didn't want to lie to Dad, but then there's the code of friendship; you don't drag someone down without a reason.

Joe went to Blackhawk College and ended up in the FBI. I probably put him in to a career of undercover work after his successful time card adventure. John still kids me and Dad about where his last paycheck is from Homewood Cabinet Top. I always tell him that I just talked to Dad, and it's in the mail with interest for thirty-five years.

After losing our jobs, John and I had time on our hands, so we played games at his house in Flossmoor. One day his stepsisters, Pat (who was our age) and Judy (who was a year younger), had over five or six biker buddies. John and I decided the neighborhood was polluted enough, so we went out to confront them. We didn't have any real weapons, so we came out brandishing hollow plastic/rubber bats for Whiffle ball. We figured the bikers were so stupid they wouldn't know the difference. We were right, and they cleared out quickly, much to Pat and Judy's disappointment. Appearances are deceiving, and a positive mental attitude can change things.

CHAPTER 4

College

During my freshman year (1965–66), incompetence reigned as I attempted to care for myself. The first weekend I did laundry I washed my new maroon University sweatshirt with my underwear. In those days, everything was white. My T-shirts and undershorts came out a pretty pink. The pinks faded each time I washed them, but it was hard to not be kidded in the dorm sharing with four guys.

Paul, Lynn, and Lenny were my roommates. Paul was like a light-haired George Harrison, and Lynn was his own man and had reddish-brown hair and dark glasses. Both were slight of build and short. Lenny was a big, blond farm boy studying engineering. He wasn't quick, but he wasn't stupid either. Paul was always moaning about his girlfriend and what travesty she was committing on their relationship. Lynn was always scheming and owned a 1954 Ford with a straight-eight engine and overdrive.

Lynn and I would play pinochle and eat pizza until the wee hours; Paul would leave and study at the library with his girl and then come back later and complain; and Lenny would go to bed early and get up with the chickens.

One night we were all up except for Lenny. It was two o'clock in the morning, so we changed Lenny's clock and woke him up for his eight o'clock class. We told him he was going to be late and flunk engineering. He got dressed, got his books and coat, and walked out the front door. We were on the third floor and watched him leave in the dark, take three steps, and stop. He looked around, pieced together the swindle, and looked up at the room where we were peering down. He looked pissed, and we quickly ran out of the room and hid on the fourth floor. When we came back an hour later, he was asleep. He was wise enough not to pay us back, as between the three of us there was too much deviousness. I later found out Lenny hated Native Americans and Jews, so I had to bait him again. When we were alone, I told him how much I liked him as a person and wanted him to come to my bar mitzvah. His part in the ceremony was to escort my Sioux Indian mother down the aisle.

He got very sick and didn't know how to handle his prejudice. He tried all kinds of excuses to get out of it. When I finally told him the truth, he was much relieved. Maybe later in life he could reflect on his myopic viewpoint.

I was in ROTC (Reserve Officer Training Corps), which was required for the first two years of college. If you went on to be an officer, then you were paid seventy dollars a month to attend class and were required to do two weeks of full-time summer camp. I wanted to be an officer in the Army, so I got straight A's and joined crack squad drill team (where you spin the rifles in parades) and the University rifle team. I was quickly nominated to Pershing Rifles, the military honorary fraternity. The rifle team was interesting, and we trained to fire at a pinhead at fifty feet. It was with open sights, but you had a spotter scope on a separate tripod to see where you hit. I shot in the mid-nineties (one hundred was perfect with ten shots at ten targets hitting the pinhead for a full ten). Our best shooter shot ninety-eight consistently, and I drifted between second and third.

I also became very good at spit shining shoes, and after a few months, I was doing other people's shoes for fifty cents a pair. I could burn shine for a quick finish and then spit shine the top level for depth. To burn shine, you light the Kiwi black polish until it melts. You put the lid back on to put out the fire and then take a cotton ball, dip it in the polish liquid, and quickly apply it to the shoe. After it dries, you take a woman's nylon and buff it out.

My roommate Paul was complaining so much I figured he needed a perspective change to appreciate what he had. I took a .22 bullet and pulled the lead out. I replaced it with toilet paper and put it in my pistol. When he came in, took off his shirt, and began telling of his girlfriend's lack of appreciation, I told him I was fed up. I said he didn't deserve to live and should be permanently shut up. He looked scared as I brought out the pistol and aimed it center mass. When I fired, he lurched backward, feeling the sting of powder and toilet paper. The look on his face was total disbelief as the situation came to his reality. It took him a good five minutes to realize he wasn't hurt. Then he was pissed and said how rotten I was, and I asked him how he felt about his girl now. I told him you live by comparison, and different viewpoints allow real comparison. I should have considered an acting or psychotherapy career, but I was still a math major at this point.

In South Dakota, they had rodeos. Being a city boy, I was attracted to the concept. At the college, there was a sign-up for the wild cow-milking contest, so I decided when in Rome, do as the Romans. I had never milked a cow or even seen it done properly. I went to the rodeo, and when it came time for the contest, they put a number on my back and a Coke bottle to hold the milk. The first person to bring back milk was the winner. They let the cows go in the middle, and like idiots, all of us charged them with our Coke bottles. I tackled the first "cow" I saw and knocked it over. The back of it was a couple inches above my waist, so it wasn't a big animal. When I reached underneath this frightened animal, it had a penis not an udder. Well, the announcer said, "That poor boy has himself a steer; he must be from back East!" No words rang truer as the crowd roared at my ignorance. I got up, and the steer rolled up and walked off quite indignant.

I got to the next cow (I checked this time) and started to yank on her teats, and she was very perturbed with me. After much shifting and pulling, I finally got a tiny drop out, but it went on the outside of the bottle. The cow was mad at my ineptness by this time and was trying to kick me. The announcement came over the intercom, and some local person had won with a half bottle of milk. My roommates were teasing me and got me to go to the greased pig contest. I figured I might as well get the full baptism of country. I couldn't get close to that pig. He was small (less than 150 pounds) and could move so fast. Many guys tackled the poor critter, but he would scoot right out of their grip. I dove and touched him once but never got my hand on anything I could grab. Two guys finally hit the pig from opposite sides, and it was a little stunned for a second so a third guy was finally able to pick it up and won the event. I was sore all over and filthy with all kinds of manure and dirt on me. The smell was so bad after I showered that I did laundry to get the smell out of the room.

Lynn pledged Tau Kappa Epsilon, and I tried to pledge Lambda Chi Alpha (I was a legacy with Uncle Page) but wasn't asked after I set the record at their all-you-can-eat rib dinner. They must have felt they couldn't afford me when my pile of bones topped the other prospects. (God, could I chow them down.)

Lynn talked me into pledging Tau Kappa Epsilon second semester. I had an unofficial audition in October where they got to see my potential as a total pig. I had a guy buy me a pint of one hundred-proof vodka (Smirnoff Silver). I got a bottle of 7UP from the vending machine and mixed a drink. It had little taste, and within a half hour, I had consumed the entire pint myself. I had never been loaded before and couldn't understand what all the fuss was about. I was telling my roommates about how alcohol had no effect on a true and brilliant mind when I arose and, for some reason, my feet didn't work right. All my motor skills were impaired, and I couldn't figure out why.

I went across the hall and knocked on the floor counselor's door. He was a senior and the starting quarterback, and when he answered, I told him he was a pussy and I could easily defeat him in a fistfight. I swung on him and missed by a mile; he promptly gave me a just deserved gut shot. I went down windless, and my roommates picked me up with one arm on each shoulder and walked me down to first floor and out on the sidewalk. I could still talk, but my legs, arms, and brain were failing fast.

I asked Paul to take out my dong so I could pee, but he refused and I wet myself. A car full of girls pulled up to my slovenly self on the curb, and I shook the two guys off, leaned over, and said, "Girls, I want to fuck each and every one of you!" I then passed out, falling backward before even getting a reaction to my question. That's the last thing I actually remember until the next evening, more than twenty-four hours later.

What Lynn and Paul later told me is that they got Lynn's Ford and put me in the backseat. I almost drowned in my own vomit in the rear wheel well. They took me to the TKE house where Lynn had pledged and hosed me down in the alley while the TKE actives jeered. October in South Dakota is chilly, but I apparently had enough antifreeze to not mind. I had alcohol poisoning so bad it took three days to heal. When I first woke up, Lynn was playing Johnny Rivers "The Seventh Son" over and over again. It was shear torture, and I had no usable verbalization skills to defend or attack. I was covered in bile and could hardly move. Everything hurt at once, and I don't remember ever having that much pain except when I was in Denver at age fifteen with ptomaine poisoning.

I slowly crawled down the hall to the showers (it felt like fifty miles). When I finally got to the shower, I was so exhausted and mentally imploded from the alcohol poisoning that I could barely reach up to the shower knobs. I foolishly flipped just one, and ice- cold water streamed over my face and down naked body. I didn't have the energy to scream and just lay there and took it like the world was over and nothing mattered. Fortunately, someone finally came in. I pleaded for hot water, and they complied. Forty-five minutes later, I rose to my feet and dried off the best I could. I walked very slowly back to the room and changed the sheets. I didn't even have the energy to tuck them in before I sprawled back on my bunk. I couldn't hold anything down for two days and finally emerged from my room on the third day. I could hold down 7 UP and broth, so I rejoined the living, vowing an empty promise of never doing that again.

Lynn was from Canton, South Dakota, and knew a red-haired girl from his high school (Mary) whom he was going to hook me up with.

He talked to her on the phone and then gave it to me, and I introduced myself to her. She wore geeky glasses but was slender and had a nice figure. I thought she looked great at the time and was excited about a date with her. I was eighteen, away at school, and ready for my first date out of state. I spent more time than a woman getting dressed up in slacks, a shirt, a sweater, and a tie. I was to pick her up at her dorm at seven o'clock that evening. I arrived fifteen minutes early and called up to her room. Her roommate said she wasn't ready yet, and I was early. I patiently waited till ten after seven and called again, but there was no answer. I called again at twenty after, and her roommate answered and said she had left. I called up again at seven thirty, and the roommate said she was sorry and explained Mary had left a half hour ago. Reality set in, and I realized I had been stood up. I was all dressed up and had money to take her out for a nice dinner at the Charcoal Lounge, which was the best place in town. I decided I deserved a good meal and went by myself.

Charcoal was a twenty-one bar. (South Dakota law was 3.2 beer for nineteen-year-olds, and for everything else, you had to be twenty-one.). So, I sat away from the bar area at a table. The waitress was polite and gave me water and a menu and returned a short while later. I ordered a T-bone steak and salad with a Coke. She then asked me how I'd like my Coke.

I was confused and asked her to clarify. She replied, "Do you want it high or regular?"

It finally sunk in. I told her I'd like it high and then closed the menu and gave it to her. I forgot I had the tie on, plus I was alone and not with a bunch of buddies. She brought me the Coke with some whiskey in it. I sipped it knowingly and with my best suave and debonair look. If I'd had a mustache, I'm sure I would have twirled it. The salad came, but it wasn't a salad like back in Chicago; it was just a wedge (a quarter of an iceberg lettuce head) with French dressing spilled over it. I ate it anyway, and the waitress asked me if I would like another drink. I said yes and asked for something I heard about on TV called a grasshopper. It was not that great and was green with a funny mint taste. Every time the waitress came back, I would try something else. I enjoyed my steak and had a martini for dessert. I then hit on whiskey sour drinks, which I thought were tasty. It was getting late, and I decided to go and paid my bill. I tipped the waitress too much and got up. I still had to walk past the bar with all the stools, and they were getting ready to close. I was really tipsy and began a zigzag pattern of walking to dodge any torpedoes. As I approached the bar, I slipped to my right and grabbed a stool to steady myself. I fell to the floor, knocking over many barstools in the process. Everyone still working was concerned, but you can't really hurt a drunk. They helped me up, and I somehow made it back to the dorm with a meandering pattern of locomotion. I was hung over the next day, but it was just a headache and groggy feeling (not like the first time). Looking back, that was the best thing I could have done to set me up for all four years. Everyone that worked at the Charcoal Lounge knew me and saw me inebriated. I was never carded there all four years of college. I was carded at the nineteen beer bars and at other places but never at the Char bar. My senior year I came in for a free drink on my birthday, and the owner noted that you only received a free drink on your twenty-first birthday. When I produced my ID, he almost died after having served me liquor the three previous years.

Freshman year was the only time I went home for Thanksgiving. After that, every year I went to someone else's house in South Dakota or Minnesota. When I went home Christmas, I noticed how short Dad had gotten. My senior year of high school I was five eleven, and by the time my freshman year of college was completed, I was six three, which was four inches in a little more than a year. My pants all looked like I was ready for high water, and most of the time you could see the tops of my socks.

In January 1966, I pledged TKE. My grades for my first semester of college were 1.12 on a 4.0 system, or a solid D average. I flunked freshman English. It was at four o'clock on Monday, Wednesday, and Friday, and I had eleven cuts. Students were only allowed six. I had a B+ in the class and aced the final. My teacher was from Berkley, California, but wasn't liberal even though he had a bubble top MG, a beard, and granny glasses. I knew I was a bad kid for cutting his class so much, so I actually devoted a couple of hours to studying for his final. When I finished writing in my blue book, I walked up to him and turned in my test. I was the first one finished. He could see the pride in my face when I turned in my masterpiece and took it from me. Without opening or perusing the contents, he boldly wrote an F on the front and told me I had eleven cuts and had failed his course. He explained how this was for my own good to get good habits and explained that the classroom was just as important as my creativity. I told him that there was no way I merited failing the course. My command of his subject was, at minimum, a B and with this brilliant final probably an A. Unfortunately, my pleas and logic fell on deaf ears, and I was doomed to a poor GPA and ineligibility to activate in a fraternity, which required a C or 2.0.

A pledge is a lowlife doing the bidding of actives and acting obsequious as often as possible in their presence. As a pledge, your lot was to clean and be humiliated, although the frat had a wonderful health club atmosphere and you got to do push-ups and other muscle-enhancing exercises often. I was too interested in social activities, and despite my potential and top ACT scores, I only achieved a disappointing 1.8 GPA for the second semester. I had to start studying and going to classes. I had only studied on Sunday nights from ten o'clock until midnight for all my classes, so something had to change my sophomore year if I wanted to get out of permanent pledge status. It was depressing to see the other pledges be activated while I was still a pledge. I did get to meet an interesting guy named Roger G. One of the TKE actives called him Rudy Zoom Boots, because his middle name was Rudolph and he had some Cordovan dress boots with zippers. I changed it to Zoomer, and Roger had a new nickname that stuck. Roger had lost one of his arms in a tractor's power takeoff when he was ten. His twin brother, Richard, carried him home two miles. Roger made a great comeback and even started on his high school basketball team. When not being the star, he was shy about his arm being gone, so he went to Minnesota to get an artificial limb. They made him learn how to use it even though he only wanted it for cosmetic reasons. If his right arm was hurt, he could grab things and drink with the fake arm. Roger lived off campus in a trailer and cooked his own food. He came from a farm, so he could bring in his own beef. He'd take a hunk of beef and throw it in a roasting pan with water and cook it till it was brown all the way through. It was like every cut of beef was pot roast. Roger got to go to school (including law school), and his twin brother Richard got the farm so he didn't get college.

Roger said he liked to hunt, so we soon became friends in spite of him living off campus.

The Summer of 1966

I got a job in a boxcar factory, and it was a death trap. They'd had so many serious injuries that the safety manager had almost as much power as the CEO. I was tired of Dad's Homewood Cabinet Top Shop and his anti-nepotism, so I thought higher wages and a change of climate would do me good. I doubled my wages to two dollars per hour but had to work from five o'clock in the evening to five o'clock in the morning. I had enough money to buy my first car—a 1957 Chevy two-door. I put new seats in it, a rebel license plate, and an AM radio. It was green and white with three-on-the-tree and a small straight six-cylinder engine. I was a god.

We were paid every two weeks on Thursday night, and the Friday after payday I was one of the few people who showed up. Most of the workers were white trash hillbillies, and I fit right in. They brought white lightning in their thermoses, and we went out for beers and shots at 10:30 p.m. lunch break every night. We could get in six shots and five drafts in the half hour allotted for lunch. I remember teaching them The Beatles song "Yellow Submarine," and we would come down the aisle at work in our hard hats, arm in arm, singing "we all live in a yellow submarine..." We thought we were the Rockettes with our leg and arm moves and droning voices.

Dumb luck kept me from being killed there several times. A twenty-ton overhead crane chain hit me, knocked me fifteen feet, and split my hard hat open. I woke up in the infirmary with the what-happened look on my face. Another time I was pulling air hose across the tracks, and someone moved the trains up without the customary warning. The hose was cut, sending me into a pile of heavy metal gears. I acquired some nice bone chips in my right forearm plus minor fractures. One guy fell off the roof of a boxcar in the gears and was paralyzed for life from the neck down. They gave him two hundred thousand dollars, and everyone but I was impressed. I knew mathematically it wouldn't last or be enough for a guy in his late twenties.

My best friend John aspired to greater heights, as he had just graduated from high school. Even though we were two weeks apart at birth, John decided to go to high school on the five-year plan and not rush it. He would be attending Coe in Cedar Rapids, Iowa, in the fall. He got a job with migrant workers picking tomatoes and other vegetables. I think it was so he could brag about being a farmer when he arrived at Coe College in Iowa in September. John also ran away from home, and being the adventurous lad, he camped down the block from my house in a prairie. He could sneak over for a shower or food if destitute and could stay away from his mom. Actually, John saved my life one day when his mom (Maggie), while in a drunken stupor, took me for a negative influence in John's life (Fancy that!) and tried to stab me with a butcher knife. She would have hit me in the solar plexus had John not grabbed her arm at the last second only inches from my body. I didn't think she was serious, but John knew better. Maggie was not into chicanery whatsoever.

When Mom and Dad went on vacation, I "watched" the house. John came over immediately, and we began to empty beer cans. Both of us are builders, so we decided to build a wall around the fireplace. It took more than ten cases of Falstaff, which was a cheap beer, to accomplish our worthy mission. Unfortunately, Mom and Dad did not agree to the merits of our construction in the pristine living room. Some people have no appreciation of true art and bona fide creative thinking.

I took my five-year-old brother Page shooting. We went to some railroad tracks by the quarry west of town, and I taught him to shoot pop bottles with a.22-caliber rifle. He was very pleased with himself once he learned to line up the sights, squeeze the trigger, and watch the pop bottle shatter.

My Sophomore Year, 1966–67

I went to college early with my new car and drove eighty miles per hour on I-80. The speed limit was seventy then, so I was fortunate not to get stopped. The Chevy vibrated at high speeds, and the engine, which was nine years old, had never been driven faster than fifty. It was a 235-cubic-inch, six-cylinder engine with no oil filter. I had to change oil every thousand miles. One of my fraternity brothers, Jim H, lived near Rapid City and invited me to visit before school started. Jim's dad was the postmaster in the town of Blackhawk. It was interesting that the back of the house was the post office.

Jim worked at one of the tourist gold mines in Keystone, near Mt. Rushmore. He loved suckering out-of-state people with whopper lies and could usually pull the lie off. Some of his favorite stories included the jack-a-lope, which was a horned jackrabbit, and fool's gold being valuable and nearly gold. He was good in his presentation and eventually became a state senator (what a surprise, considering his skill set). We took out the three-on-the-tree shift and put in a three-on-the-floor. I couldn't afford a four-speed transmission, so linkage conversion was enough. We also took off the muffler and tailpipe all the way to the manifold. I took the hood off the car to work on the manifold connection better and started it up sans exhaust system. Well, it was so loud, and a blue flame went up the windshield, I couldn't, in good conscience, not to let my fellow man benefit in my discovery. I drove it downtown to Rapid City sans hood at dusk so the blue flame could be seen for blocks and the engine heard for a mile. I thought I was too cool for words with my bad-ass '57 Chevy with the loud engine and the blue flame. I was fortunate not to have been cited for disturbing the peace and being a menace to society. The next day we replaced the hood and exhaust system, but I replaced the muffler with a cherry bomb (for less back pressure and a little more noise). When I drove it back to school, it now got up to ninety-five miles per hour before starting to shudder.

I moved out of the dorm at Julian Hall and into the TKE house even though I was only a pledge. I was determined to get better than a 2.0 so I could be activated. I actually studied more than once a week and received passing grades. I managed a 2.2 by the end of the semester and was able to go through hell week. While I lived in the TKE house, the price of my meals went up compared to the dorm, so I didn't have as much money. What was worse was they did not serve food on the weekend; Friday lunch was the last meal until Monday lunch. They never served breakfast. Being a mighty hunter from youth, I decided to bring home the bacon myself. I had a .22 Colt pistol single-action six gun (had to cock the hammer to fire not just pull the trigger). I also had a .22 Remington automatic rifle and a 20-gauge pump shotgun. If I had enough money for shotgun shells, then the 20-gauge would be my meal ticket; otherwise, the .22s would have to do. I got a weekend job (sometimes during the week at night) at Charlie's Pizza delivering and making pizza. They had a pressure cooker (broaster) there, so whatever I shot, I could cook up in the slow times. I would drive out in the fields of South Dakota, and whatever moved was lunch. I've had squirrel (nasty), possum (yuck), grouse (awesome), pheasants (my mainstay), Canadian goose, partridge, and rabbit. I even shot a raccoon, but after the possum and squirrel, I didn't even try it.

If you shot a coyote and brought the lower lip to a farmer, he would give you a box of shotgun shells. I only killed two during my whole four years at college, but when I did, I ate well, because I could hunt birds with the shotgun. Ruffled grouse was the best eating. They ran really fast, following each other with the one feather sticking up on their heads. I'd shoot them mostly on the ground, but with the pistol, I'd get one at best. They're smaller than a chicken, and you need a good sized one for a meal. I was out with the shotgun one cold day in early November and saw a Canadian goose coming in to land on a pond. I led him with the 20-gauge and smoked him right on the nose. He went down like a ton of bricks and hit hard in the center of the pond. I didn't have a dog and was really hungry, so I stripped off my clothes and waded out in the freezing water to collect my prize. The bottom of the pond was mud, and I sank in, so I had to breaststroke out even though the water was only four feet deep. I swam really fast and got back to shore in world-record time. But by the time I ascended the pond bank, I was mid-thigh in mud and bright pink to my neck. I used my T-shirt and underpants to wash the mud off and dry off. I then put my clothes and jacket back on. When I got back to Charlie's Pizza, they were really impressed. I was just relieved I was going to eat. We all indulged in broasted goose, which is like an all-dark-meat turkey. It was a feast.

Charlie's occasionally cost me money when I delivered to the girls' dorms after hours. A girl who'd been out drinking and wanted munchies after curfew would call Charlie's for a delivery and say Beede Hall, fourth window from the west on the north side. I knew to go around and deliver to a window, and someone would open it to receive the pizza. Usually there was a tip involved because of the special delivery. Well, I went one night, and this cute girl was drunk and had on only a boy's shirt, and it wasn't buttoned. (I never did see her face, so I really don't know if she was cute, for my eyes never even made it above her neck.) I didn't even collect for the pizza, let alone get a tip (except for a visual tip). When you make eighty-five cents an hour, a four-dollar pizza shoots your night's earnings. Women do fascinate me, and am I easy...

To further enhance my income, I noticed a lot of people required identification for going to the nineteen or twenty-one bars. I decided to focus on white-collar crime for additional income. I took my Illinois driver's license and Photostatted both sides. I did the same to my draft card. I then took a damp pencil eraser and removed all the numbers. I carefully redrew any light lines and used whiteout where necessary. I then re-Photostatted the blank identification card, and I was ready for business. I sold new identification for ten dollars a set, which included both an Illinois driver's license and a draft card. I typed up the cards and plastic-coated them. They sold like hotcakes, and in no time at all, South Dakota had more licensed drivers from Illinois than from South Dakota. I'm sure I violated federal and state laws, but it also accelerated the collection dollars of state and federal liquor taxes. I guess at the time I figured it was an almost symbiotic relationship between the government and me. I know I invested all my profits back into the liquor industry.

I drove to Bruce M's home in Minnesota for the Thanksgiving break. My Chevy had snow tires on the rear with studs, and I was pretty confident driving in any weather. We hit snow going to Minnesota on the back road to Bruce's, and I foolishly didn't slow down. Everything was fine on the snow-packed surface until we hit a stretch where a farmer's sewer pipe went under the road. The heat had melted the packed surface, and we went into a slide toward the ditch on the right. My passenger window didn't stay up all the way unless you wedged something in it. The window was down maybe three inches when we careened sideways off the road, leading with the passenger side. The snow from the ditch streamed in the three- inch opening and caused a blizzard in the car with zero visibility. I don't know how we missed obstacles like signposts and trees, but we came to a stop unscathed with the front of the car aimed where we'd been. Bruce had his hands dug into the edge of the seat with white knuckles. He couldn't talk, and I just got us going really fast in the ditch and popped up over the hill to get out. I drove to his house like nothing was wrong until he decided to communicate verbally. Bruce was very disturbed that I wasn't disturbed. I told him that I was spared for a reason, but I couldn't imagine why he had been. He began to think and get out of his shock and finally started to smile again. Sometimes people forget to thank providence or luck, but it's part of the mix of life too!

Bruce's sister was still in high school (she was probably sixteen or seventeen) and was a cute redhead with freckles and a nice figure. She took me up to the hayloft and was experimenting with her sexual attraction and tried to make it with me in the hay. She hadn't known me even fifteen minutes, and she had her blouse off and was going for my pants. I kissed her and got her glasses fogged up, but there was no way I was going to get involved with a fraternity brother's high school sister. Her hormones must have been popping that day, and she finally left me alone after I explained my situation. Bruce and I had a good time there, and the whole family went to see a newly released film called Dr. Zhivago. I had read the book by Boris Pasternak, and it was confusing because I think the lead character had four different names in the book. After we finished watching the movie, we went for coffee and I explained the movie to them for more than three hours.

The next day we got to do farm stuff that they hated, but I was fascinated. I got to shuck corn and even neuter pigs. Pigs are only granted six months of life. The farmers fatten them up till they hit 210 pounds and then sell them for slaughter. A sow is a female and a boar is a male, but when they give the boars a vasectomy, they become pigs just like bulls become steers. The operation took place outside on an elevated picnic table. The "pigs to be" are smaller but really fast. (Who could blame them?) All the non-boar candidates are herded together and, one by one, hoisted up on the table. As small as they are, I had to give it all I had to hold them down when they were cut. They threw the "balls" to a waiting army of cats who had acquired a taste for this semiannual delicacy. When we finally sat down for a meal, I was famished in spite of the cats' voracious appetite.

Bruce got us local dates—not gorgeous but fun. We had a great time dancing and drinking and were driving on some back road when we slid off into another ditch. We weren't going fast, and I told Bruce this should be old hat to him. The girls were fine, and the only problem we had was being stuck in the ditch. We tried to push out and drive out (with three pushing and a girl driving) but to no avail. We got back in to the car to stay warm and ran it for a while. It was four o'clock in the morning, and we were running low on fuel even just idling. I left Bruce with the girls, and I walked to the nearest farmhouse about a mile away. Even though I could see the place, it took twenty minutes to walk through the snow. I knocked on the door, and a wonderful farmer and his wife answered. I explained my dilemma, and the man got his coat and boots on and took me to the barn. He had an old tractor with a crank to start it. He got up on the tractor, and I cranked. We got it started in five minutes. I threw some chains over my shoulder and hopped up on the hitch above the power takeoff (the power takeoff runs implements pulled behind the tractor). It was breezy, and I stood up considerably higher than the farmer who was driving. We got back to the girls and Bruce just in time, because the car had run out of gas. The girls were cold, so Bruce and I got under the Chevy and hooked up the chains while they stayed in the car. We had one of them steer, and the tractor pulled us right out. We pulled the car back to the farm, and the girls and Bruce went in the house for coffee and breakfast while I rode six miles on the back of the tractor to town to get a can of gasoline. We got the gas from a friend of the farmer and came back. I primed the carburetor and put the rest in the tank. The girls and Bruce were done with coffee and breakfast, so we fired the car up, thanked our gracious hosts, and took the girls back to their homes. At least they had an alibi with the farmer if they needed it for their folks.

Guys can be real shits sometimes. I took this petite redhead out who was less than a beauty. I had a car and thought I was important. I took her to a fraternity party, and we played Gotcha, a board game where you custom-make the cards. The object is to spell the word gotcha, and you collect the letters like property in Monopoly. It's a drinking game, so if you make any mistakes, you chug some beer. The rules were flexible to allow for different playing levels. We had many different chance cards and would use the ones appropriate for the players. The card could say "kiss the person on your left" or "chug." (We always sat boy, girl, boy, girl.) Another card might say "all boys with boxer shorts chug or prove it." It didn't matter if you had boxers on or not as long as you dropped your pants to prove it; then you didn't have to chug. My date would show me her tag from her shoulder strap when the card said "all girls with bra size 34B or larger chug or prove it," while the rest of the girls opened their blouses or lifted their sweatshirts. It was snowing out, and we drove a mile out of town to park after the disappointing game. I wanted to make out and pet, and she wanted to know me for a couple of months first. I got mad because I wasn't getting anywhere, and she was lucky just to be with the "great" me. I told her to get out and walk back to school if that was her attitude. I probably still harbored some hatred from being snubbed my freshman year by a redhead. Fortunately, she was dressed warmly enough, and to her credit, she got out and made it back okay in spite of my behavior. Sometimes you can be so full of yourself you don't even see others around you.

Sometimes being a shit is okay. I went to an exchange for pledges where we met pledges from a sorority and danced or conversed. We dressed up in suits and were supposed to be on our best behavior, and the girls had on dresses and used their best manners. We danced and talked with each other, and it was more like a political event than a date. We were supposed to get to know each other, and we were on display as a potential future member of your respective Greek house. It was polite to always dance with someone if she asked, but two dances in a row weren't required unless you wanted to. It was a nonalcoholic affair, and our housemother Rachel was the chaperone. Rachel was always on me for some protocol mishap. She was a teetotaler, so I had to be careful with alcohol around her or face disciplinary action.

We were having a good time at this exchange, dancing and talking, when one of the girls started to "shoot her beaver" at me, which is when a girl crosses her legs repeatedly for attention, allowing her underwear to show for effect. This was not accidental but deliberate, and as I was the only one across from her, I could not help but notice. I stopped talking to the girl I was with and excused myself. I went to the washroom and did the breath mint thing and combed my hair. I came back and sat alone at a different angle, and sure enough, this gal turned toward me and gave me another beaver shot. She wasn't wearing a girdle, only white panties. I was impressed, and she was attractive, so I figured why not talk and dance with her a little. I went over to converse, and she rudely blew me off in front of this girl I had been talking to earlier. I didn't even bother to ask her to dance and went on to someone else.

This other girl I was with had a good personality, and I was having a nice chat with her when this beaver-shooting girl started on me again. She was talking to the girl I was with, telling her what a bunch of losers we were and that they should all leave early. My friend politely explained the rules of an exchange, and we went off dancing to another part of the room. My partner wanted a drink, so I told her I would fix a special punch bowl up for those in the know. I retired to the kitchen and dug up some Everclear alcohol and some Real Lemon reconstituted juice and whipped up a punch that was thirty proof (15 percent alcohol by volume), although the alcohol couldn't be tasted at all. I placed it behind and to the left of the "safe" punch and told my partner only to clue in her buddies who needed a jolt to get through the social function. Well, after I made the third punch bowl, no one wanted to leave, and everyone's panties were showing, including the housemother's. Girls weren't crossing their legs anymore; they were spreading them like a guy would sit. I don't think I'd ever seen so much hose and underwear at one time before. The girl who was teasing and rejecting me earlier was now stable and friendly. She got pretty trashed, so I took her and the girl with a personality home. After I dropped off Miss Personality, I got to thinking about the helpless beaver shooter. I decided to be a dick and teach her a lesson. I reached under her skirt and removed her panties and put them in my jacket pocket. I took her to her dorm and got some girls to help get her to her room. The next day I was ready for her. I was in the student union, and true to form, she was with friends and started to snub me. That's when I pulled her underpants out of my pocket and tossed them to her so her friends could see what they were. She looked surprised, and I told her she'd left them in my car the night before after the exchange, and I wanted to make sure she got them back. She got really red in the face, and I quickly turned around and left before she regained composure and could question me further. She never verbally bashed me again (at least where I could hear) and was too embarrassed to ever ask me what happened.

I loved my '57 Chevy, and I drove home at Christmas to see the folks. Zoomer came with me, as he'd never been to Chicago. Dad was disgruntled with me and told me I owed him $150 for car insurance. I didn't have the money, so he sold the car for exactly $150 so he'd be paid back. The car was sold in an hour. I was crushed, and my transportation was gone. I took Zoomer downtown in Dad's car, and he got whiplash from looking at all the tall buildings. He was a true bumpkin, gawking at all the sights (kind of like me at the farm).

We played strip poker with my sister and her friend Ruth B. We won, and the girls then cheated. They took off their clothes but put a blanket over themselves first. Zoomer still got a kick out of it. He even dated my sister a couple of times. I always hoped they'd hook up, but he had other destinies in life. When the holiday was done, Dad got Zoomer and me a rental from Hertz to drive back to school, as it was too late for public transportation. When it was Zoomer's turn to drive, he missed the turn at Des Moines and started us down to Kansas City. An hour or two had passed when I awoke and discovered the mishap. I redirected us and then took over for Zoomer. We were running low on gas and were near a town called Grove, Iowa, when we pulled off I-80. It didn't have any stations open, and we were running out of gas quickly, so I pulled into a local airport. No one was around, so we pulled up to a pump and put ten gallons in the car so we could get back to school. It was airplane fuel ninety-seven-plus octane (premium was ninety-three, and regular was eighty- seven). We flew back to school, and I parked the rental behind the TKE house. It snowed during the night, and the next day I was supposed to take the car twenty-five miles west to Yankton to the Hertz dealership. I tried to start it, and it would hardly run. When I floored the gas pedal and turned the engine over, the car barely chugged along. Even after it started, it just slowly chugged, and I noticed black ooze coming out of the tailpipe all over the white snow. I called Hertz, and they apologized and came to tow the car away. I'm sure the high-test fuel cleaned out all the buildup in the engine. I never heard from Hertz again.

The semester was over, and because I finally had the grades, I would be activated. The actives called the pledges over to the TKE house, and we had to stay for the week. I was already living there, but the rest had to bring suits and work clothes. We were assembled in a lineup and given poles as tall as we were. On the poles we carved our chapter name (Theta Eta) and our scroll number to be (mine was 109). We were called "froads" throughout hell week, which was a cross between frogs and toads. We were "lower than whale shit in the deepest part of the deepest sea." Because I'd been a pledge so long, I knew that hell week would be tough with little time for rest. I got myself a bottle of multivitamins with iron and called myself Iron Man for the duration of the week. We were required to go to class in suits every day and then return directly to the house for harassment and chores. We got to sleep between five and six o'clock in the morning if we were lucky, because the actives took turns keeping us awake with various duties.

They gave us a card to get the signatures of ten certain girls. The card was attached to a string that went over my necktie and down inside my clothes and was then attached to my privates. When a girl signed it, she would unknowingly be tugging on my personals. Some girls who were pinned to actives knew and would come up to us, pull on the card, and say "ding ding" with two tugs to tease and let us know that they knew. I became very protective of the card after a girl jerked it hard to sign it. If I'd been smart, I would have cut the string in the middle and refasten the break with a rubber band. That would have been a nice shock absorber, but who knew? That was a tough day to say the least. We also had to make our own underwear for the week out of burlap from potato sacks. I took my sack to the Laundromat and soaked it in Downy fabric softener for several hours before washing and sewing up my burlap undershorts.

Another wonderful pastime for the actives was to give each of us an egg to put in our shorts and make us break it when we missed a catechism question on TKE history. Working with eggshell and goo in your shorts is quite uncomfortable. Why did we do it? I guess to see if we could complete the struggle, the knowledge that we only had to do it once, and knowing we could make others do it several times. That kept us sane enough to complete the arduous trek. By the third day, I was crazy from lack of sleep and constant harassment, so I decided to fight back a little. I unscrewed the light bulbs in our stairway and put mop handles through the banisters. Anyone sneaking up on us in the night would be tripped, and we would wake up in time to pretend to work. The ruse worked, and after I had done in two actives, we got our much-needed respite. Unfortunately, I fell asleep against the radiator and striped my body with blisters. Not only was I tired and sore, but I was disfigured as well.

We also had to eat dinner in unity. We couldn't talk, and our right hands were lashed to a froad pole and we weren't allowed to use our left hands. We were only allowed soup with a teaspoon and had to eat square, meaning the motion of our right arms had to make a big square. Together, we filled our spoons, raised them straight up to mouth level, came back to our mouths, and sipped the teaspoon of soup (or what was left of it) before dropping straight down to bowl level and finally straight out to the bowl to complete the square. If one person was out of sync, then, of course, your soup would spill, and you'd have even less to eat. We were allowed ten minutes for lunch, and I don't think we got much more than 5 percent of the soup in our mouths.

We weren't allowed to talk to girls, but they would smuggle candy to classes for us and cover for us if we fell asleep in class. Women are great when guys are in trouble or in pain; the nurse in all of them comes out, I guess. At this point, we weren't allowed to even go steady with a girl, so most relationships were in secret. I didn't have a regular girl then but had many friends who understood my plight and would contribute to my success.

At one point, the pledges were split in to four groups and send out on a scavenger hunt. Among the items on the list were a used Kotex and bras and panties signed by the girls who gave them to us. We had to count all the windowpanes in the Armory and had a list of inane items to obtain. We bought a Kotex in a girls' bathroom, and Frank Armstrong hit himself in the nose to bleed on the sanitary napkin. The only problem was that out of ignorance, he bled on the wrong side. Fortunately, the actives were just as ignorant and didn't catch our faux pas when we turned our booty in later. We sent one guy to the Armory to multiply and add up all the windows, and I went to the Pi Phi house for underwear. (They were the beauty queens of the six sororities at USD then.) They had been hit by the Phi Delta Theta fraternity the night before. One girl had lost fifty dollars in underwear, and they were in no mood to give up anything. I went to the Chi Omega sorority next, because they were the second cutest but they tried harder. I convinced them to give up their older underwear and sign it so they would be famous hanging in a guy's room. One of the less-endowed girls brought another girl's bra with a larger cup size and signed it as her own. She told me it didn't hurt to advertise, and I laughed and told her she had a great attitude. We were the only group that obtained all the treasures, so we didn't have to clean up after the hell week party.

One night we had to do a fire drill. This consisted of the froad leader wearing a heavy fireman's helmet and getting down on all fours. Each following froad grabbed the ankles of the froad in front of him, and we crawled up the stairs to the third-floor bathroom. The bathroom had no lights on, and we could barely see with the outside light reflecting off the translucent window. The actives were dipping something into the toilet, but I could tell it was a pan inside the toilet because the steel ladle banged the metal side. They put bananas and vinegar in the water to make it seem like the toilet, and we filled our mouths with the liquid. Next we crawled back down the stairs (three flights of stairs to the ground floor) and went to the fireplace. The actives had built a roaring fire, and we each spit our mouth full on the fire, which lowered the intensity of the flames but didn't put them out. We then proceeded to crawl up the stairs for another mouthful. After the second time, I noticed the actives putting lighter fluid and paper in the fire as we left. Before we reached the top floor, I called a halt and told the others to wait to spit until we were all at the fire and we would do it as a team. We did just that, and when I got back down, the fire was going pretty good. When we all spit on the fire, it didn't quite go out, so I quickly urinated on the fire to finish it off. The actives couldn't believe it. After we failed at everything (according to the actives), we were finally initiated and given beers. The formal activation and ceremony was performed later by a national from TKE. Upon completion of hell week, we got to paddle the active of choice. It was an honor that was usually given to the guy who pissed you off the most during the week. Because of my size and strength, they were worried whom I would pick for my paddle. I chose the nicest guy who never bothered anyone and was a great mentor just so he would get the honor of the toughest paddle. Dan was in ROTC, was a great student, and was going to be an officer in the Army. When I hit him, he was in pain but took it well and was the hero of the party.

Rushing, or meeting prospective members, is an important part of a fraternity, because without new recruits, the organization eventually dies. We had our second semester rushing to do. We had a poor turnout. I played cards with a good kid named Paul R. I took all his money from him and gave him beer, and all my fraternity brothers told me we were rushing and I should return his money. I told them it would be an insult to Paul that his money wasn't really at risk. Of the twelve guys they rushed, Paul and one other guy were the only pledges.

Paul became my little brother, and I was his mentor through his probationary period. He was an attractive guy, kind of like Jason Priestley (the guy with the sideburns on Beverly Hills, 90210). He was just eighteen and had a lot of emotional issues with women (like we all do). One girl he was particularly fond of was leading him on. He would take her out all over (he even had a car) and out to the bars, dinner, or dancing, whatever she wanted, but she would still cheat on him even though they were going together. She finally dumped him, and he was crushed. Being an asshole and as a big brother, I decided retribution was in store for her. We had our elections for officers, and I won social chairman hands down (mostly because no one wanted it, and it was a lot of work). We only gave two dollars a month for social dues, so I said I'd take the job if they would double the money. They went to three dollars (which is less than a hundred a month for thirty actives), and I still accepted. This would come into effect in the fall when we came back to school.

I asked the girl who dumped Paul out just after the school paper came out with the new officer announcements. She was a social climber, and I was an active and an officer so I was "good" dating material with the potential of a fraternity pin for her chest. I planned to trash her, but I didn't know exactly how at first. I decided on a movie, and that was our first and final date. We had a Coke to share and popcorn. I then decided on grossing her out. I took my thumb and penetrated the bottom of the popcorn box and then unzipped my pants under my coat and pulled out my penis. I slipped the popcorn on top of my coat and then pulled the coat away and inserted my now erect penis into the popcorn box hole I had created. We ate the popcorn, and I was hysterical inside while remaining pokerfaced outside. It took a while, but we got the popcorn down and she finally found her surprise. She was confused at first and didn't know what it was as she carefully felt it all around. When she had her hand all the way around it, I looked at her. She was still confused, so I wiggled it with a contraction. She looked into my eyes with shock, so I raised my eyebrows three times in quick succession as I continued to contract. She finally shrieked and stood up with the full realization of her actual predicament and ran to get a cop or an usher. I quickly got myself back together and then followed her out. She was ranting to anyone who'd listen, and I told her not to worry and that everything was okay. She didn't want to talk to anyone else then and left the show in a tizzy. I felt like Paul was avenged, and I never saw her again. Who says men don't have a sensitive side?

Being social chairman elect, I had to work with the existing social chairman to see what he did before I took over the following school year. I decided it was a social fraternity, and we were going to be social. The house currently had one party a month, and it was usually held at the fraternity house to save money. Booze was purchased in South Dakota at the state store, so they paid too much. I would rectify that when I took over in the fall. We had to get the most out of our few dollars, and after all, college was all about learning to manage available resources.

Fighting when you'd been drinking was the norm for the area residents. I was not particularly interested in fighting but learned when I was young not to back down. In the long run, a beating was better than turning tail and running; besides, I wasn't very fleet of foot, so I'd be caught anyway. Unfortunately, when I'd be out with a few of the fraternity brothers, they'd run for help while I'd hold off the antagonists. I actually got to like it a year later at the Pleasant Pheasant bottle club a couple of miles out of town.

I bought some sock garters and thought I was really hot. The garters looped over the top of my calf in back and hooked to the sock in front. I began wearing them with shorts and got a lot of attention with the ladies. It was warmer out, and after a winter in South Dakota, warm weather brings craziness. We started coed water fights. We made giant slingshots that could propel large water balloons for more than a block, and a bucket or hose worked just fine in a pinch. I got so involved in a water fight with the Chi Omegas that I broke my little toe on a cement curb while charging a group of warring babes. When I stubbed my toe, it broke sideways. When I saw the doctor, he said there was nothing that could be done for a broken toe. My toe is still crooked from that fateful day in the spring of 1967. I have to say that at the moment I did not quit fighting but heroically stayed until all the girls were well soaked before I sought succor and aid.

Gingivitis is a social disease of the gums that is usually passed by kissing someone else infected. As I was a social chairman, I must have felt it my duty to contract a social disease. By this time, I was drinking and osculating (kissing) with many females, so I don't even know who shared the disease with me. I remember my gums ulcerating and being reminiscent of calf's brains growing on the roof of my mouth and halfway down my teeth. I couldn't consume solid food and drank mostly to forget about it. The gingivitis did not go away and instead got worse. The roof of my mouth became mushy, and I could move it with my tongue. I promised myself I would get it looked at as soon as I took a test in political geography. I passed out on the way to class and woke up in the Vermilion hospital. I had lost about twenty-five pounds during my social disease period.

While in the hospital, I met Bobbi, a nineteen-year- old local girl who was a little overweight, blonde, and filled with personality. I enjoyed her visits even though she painted my mouth purple with some antifungal liquid that made me look like I had no teeth. She tried to draw blood from my arms and failed several times. She started to feel bad, and I told her she could take it from my upper thigh if she wanted, which cheered her up. I was incarcerated for three days as they tried to eliminate the disease and rebuild my nutrition. I went out with Bobbi several times after that and even took her to our spring formal, but she turned out to be a prude with sex, and at this point, I was a salmon swimming upstream looking for the mating grounds. Bears, river current, and rocks weren't going to slow me down.

I had met this girl right at the end of my sophomore year named Ruth W. I finally got a date with her, and her home was in Yankton, which was twenty-five miles west of campus. I was still a virgin, although many girls had excited me by this time. School was almost out by our second date, and we'd barely kissed. I didn't have a car because Dad had sold the Chevy at Christmas, so I was in the backseat double dating with a fraternity brother.

A guy's job was to try everything and feel everything. All moves were hearsay from other guys, and in reality, you were on your own with these sketchy guidelines. It was tough to be masterful when you were a novice, but I always believed you should run it up the flagpole. If they saluted the flag, then everything was okay. I usually started kissing a girl and then worked to her neck and then French kissed her. If all was positive and she was responding, then groping began from the back under the arms to the breasts in front. After that, it was unbuttoning the blouse or raising the sweater to caress her brassiere. If that panned out, I would then go for the hooks in the back (a talent many guy practiced) in order to release the breasts for serious petting. I didn't know what happened beyond that, because that was as far as I'd personally been. I'd seen naked girls and all their genitalia but had never touched or experienced up close the magic of the lower female body.

Ruth didn't respond to anything after the first kiss, so I had to change tactics. I knew she liked me, but I didn't seem to be turning her on. (What's a guy got to do?) I knew what the salmon felt like swimming upstream to mate. I was still struggling swimming and banging my head on rocks with no real gratification. This time, I decided to go under her dress instead of the standard top-down methodology of the past.

I just kissed her and ran my hand between her legs, and surprisingly, she kissed back hard and almost choked me with her tongue. I really didn't know exactly what to do with my hands, but I knew I had a new powerful tool in this relationship. I determined by feel that she had on hose, panties, and a girdle. (A girdle did not cover the crotch back then. It was elastic and went around like a tight skirt with snaps that hung down to attach to nylons.) As I touched her panties, they were very warm and damp, and her kisses increased proportionally in passion to the amount of time I spent caressing that area. I was still clueless, but I knew I was where I wanted to be and was doing something right. I slid the panties to one side and felt pubic hairs for the first time.

The couple in the front seat wasn't doing as well, but I couldn't slow down or miss this once-in-a- lifetime opportunity. When my middle finger caressed her labia, it relaxed and spread, and I felt real body heat for the first time. I pressed inside of her with my finger, and she convulsed. It was a little scary, and she moaned like an ill person. The people in the front had forgotten their issues and were starting to concern themselves with our relationship. I was impressed with the reaction my finger obtained each time it entered in deeper and with the reaction if I curled it up and touched a rough area inside of her. But I was growing concerned with her convulsions and moaning and the other people, so I withdrew my finger and replaced her panties back over the coveted place. I had never smelled a woman before, and my finger now reeked of this curious odor. It was a little reminiscent of fish, and I thought again of the salmon mating ritual. She was very friendly when I took her back to her dormitory and gave me her home address and phone number for the summer.

Because beer was 3.2 percent alcohol instead of 6 percent for nineteen-year-olds, it was necessary to chug it and drink twice as much to get loaded. Unfortunately, you would have to regurgitate and then drink to get high. If you drank right after that, you could usually get fairly well inebriated. My buddies and I were always having barf contests, which was a strange form of male competition. We had prizes for the highest vomit, so someone would puke out the window. Then, not to be out done, the next would throw up from the attic, then out on the roof, and finally climb up the chimney and stand on his tiptoes to toss his cookies. We also had a prize for the best toilet stuff (getting into the toilet), and someone actually threw up underwater in the toilet. Our dormer was freezing, and I got the most unusual by throwing up in my ski mask while sleeping. In the morning, I had to peal it off and remove the waste from my eye sockets before I could even see. On the pillow next to me was a perfect piece of cake-like regurgitation that was rectangular in shape from exiting via the ski mask mouth hole in the freezing cold. I also got credit for best bank shot when I got Jim H off the wall from the top bunk down to his lower bunk. We had Frank, who was chugging out of a pitcher of beer and threw it up right back into the pitcher, and it wasn't even warm yet. We had our best chugger (fast drinker) do a whole bottle of wine, pass out standing up, and fall on his head. We dragged Gilliam into the Litzelman room (the TKE house living room), and his head was swelling up where he fell. He then proceeded to spout a perfect geyser like a whale from his mouth straight back down on his face. It was truly an amazing sight to behold.

I had no car. The school year was over, and it was time to go home. My parents sent me money for a plane ticket, but I was so tapped for cash that I had to invest it in beer so I would feel better about my cash-poor position. It worked, and I had a good attitude again but still no way to get from South Dakota to Illinois. I decided hitchhiking was cheap, and I still had five dollars for food, so it was the open road for me. The Land of Lincoln seemed only a hop away. We didn't have Polish suitcases (plastic bags) then, so I put my dirty clothes in my bed sheets and made a big Santa Claus bag to throw over my shoulder. I had bought a pint of Canadian Club whiskey for medicinal purposes and had a .22 Colt Frontier Scout six-gun for any emergency.

I began my trip, and it took me four rides to get to Fort Dodge, Iowa, which is still in northwestern Iowa. I found a trucker there with only the tractor, and he was heading for Detroit. He asked me if I could drive, and without thinking, I said I could. I gave him my bottle of CC and had to ask him how to get the tractor in reverse. My Chevy was a stick shift, and I learned on a Rambler stick, but it was different in a big truck. I had a clutch and air brakes, so I took it slow and let him drink. I learned how to drop the shifter to the next layer of gears and skip the lower ones since I didn't have a trailer on the back, and pretty soon, we were on the interstate. After the trucker emptied the bottle, he passed out, and I proudly flew down the highway. By the time I got to Mom and Dad's, it was five thirty in the morning, and the birds were just starting to tweet. I pulled into the driveway with the big rig and woke the trucker up from his drunken slumber. He was really paranoid and hadn't a clue where he was in this residential neighborhood. I calmed him down and gave him instructions on how to get back to the interstate. I think he was pleased to be only five hours from his home. Dad was up and let me in, but he hadn't seen the truck. I just took the Santa Claus bag to the basement and went to bed exhausted from my big trucking night. My grades for the term were a disappointing 1.8 on a 4.0 scale, which was equivalent to a D+, and I was on academic probation again.

The Summer of 1967

I wrote Ruth in June to tell her I was coming to visit her in Yankton on the way to California. My best buddy John was from California, and he wanted to visit his dad in Malibu. I felt it was a good travel opportunity. Neither one of us had any money or a working car, so I hit upon a plan inspired by the classifieds. A drive deal was offered where we paid gas, and the company gave you a car to drive to California. When we arrived, they would give you seventy-five dollars. They would give us a week to make the trip, and we had to be at least twenty-one year old. Well, I was still only nineteen in June, so I had to fake it. I wore a suit and got the deal in downtown Chicago. Some Chicago salesman had quit an LA firm, and they didn't want to pay shipping to get the new Pontiac Bonneville back to the offices. I had a week to drive it there. John and I now had the means to travel, and I could indirectly prove I was twenty-one because of the legal agreement. We packed some food and bathing suits for the summer and a dress suit just in case. We headed west full bore in our big car and even bigger attitudes.

Our first stop was Ruth's house. She was in the southeast corner of South Dakota, and beer age was only nineteen, so we had a double purpose for stopping. I went in to see Ruth, and John took the car to invest the majority of our meager funds in liquid libation. I was ready to sexually experiment with Ruth, but her parents protected her, and I was stifled again. I did get some promising kisses and some quick feels but not the exploration I had anticipated. She was totally in control, and I was off base. I felt curiously jilted and continued my trip with a less-than-positive feeling about her. I didn't know if I did something wrong or if she had someone else. Ruth seemed to delight in my confusion and offered no help whatsoever. True communication is difficult in early romances, and for some, it never does bear fruition even after marriage and in later years.

John had come back, and we had three cases of beer and were set for a fun trip. We hit a cop just east of North Platt, Nebraska who pulled John over for being incompetent. He was so tired he was wavering on the road, making mild S turns. Upon inspection, he found the beer prominently displayed in the back and promptly confiscated it all, much to our chagrin. I wasn't nearly as tired, so I drove, and the officer let us go. I'm sure he had a nice party with our beer. We trekked on, disappointed that we were continuing on sans beer, but Colorado was only a few hours away. In Colorado, the legal age for buying Coors was eighteen. When we got to the mountains, we had shorts on, and there was snow everywhere. We got our Coors and had a snowball fight in the Rockies. We drove by a ski resort and saw these people sitting on one side of a ravine. We had stopped to relieve ourselves, we were semi-loaded and they were disgusted. Fortunately, our funds were rapidly diminishing, and we couldn't afford any more beer. We hadn't eaten in a day, and we didn't want to waste our last food—a quart jar of College Inn Chicken and Noodles. We drove through Colorado stopping in a ghost town to look around and then proceeded into Hanksville, Utah.

We decided to go to Las Vegas, which was the "quickest" shortcut, and noticed a town called Boulder, Utah. It was in southern Utah right near the Hell's Backbone ridge of mountains. We drove on hardtop and then dirt roads, and near a ranger station, we saw a broken sign that we thought pointed the way to Boulder. We discovered later that a broken part said "Top," as in "Boulder Top Mountain," not the town of Boulder, Utah. As we proceeded up on this "road," we had to get out of the car and push rocks out of the way and drag tree branches off to the side. The road wound up the edge of the mountain and at the top narrowed to a goat path maybe eighteen inches wide. Someone had the audacity to put a sign up that read "Primitive Road Ahead," and John and I had to laugh. We then tried to turn the Bonneville around, and it collapsed into a soft shoulder. We pulled all our stuff out of the car and tried to push it out but to no avail. It was still early in the day, so we decided to descend the precipice on foot and try for the ranger station by the sign. I took my .22-caliber six-gun and a bandoleer of ammunition, but first, I took my Indian blanket and cut a hole in it and wore the blanket like a Mexican serape. I had plaid shorts and sneakers on with the blanket and bandoleer. John looked a little better with a jacket, T-shirt, sneakers, and jeans.

We climbed down the rest of the day and found a stream and the ranger post just before sunset. That's when we noticed the broken sign and discovered we were going not to Boulder but up to Boulder Top Mountain. As luck would have it, the ranger station was boarded up, and we once again had to refocus on survival direction. We were tired and traveling down the road we'd come down early in the morning when darkness set in. John had been out for football at Coe College the previous semester, so he was still in pretty good shape, but I was destroyed. We could hear coyotes, but it was pretty quiet in southern Utah after dark. Off to the north we could see lights, but they twinkled. I'd had enough education to know that atmosphere makes it twinkle, and until you can make out a shape, it's pretty far away. We kept trudging along, but I felt I was done. I told John to keep on walking and said I would stay there and shoot my pistol every once in a while so he could find me when he got help. He finally agreed to my pleadings and was leaving me slowly, but then the moon went down.

John quickly came back and explained he had night blindness and couldn't see if there was no moon. I had to lead, like it or not.

My legs were becoming numb, and it wasn't so bad pushing on after a while. We weren't going to win any races, but we were steadfast in our resolve to get somewhere. All of a sudden, I could make out a windowpane instead of twinkling light. I was excited. It was still small and a long way off, but it was real. The road was winding like a snake toward this window, and I was growing impatient after a while. I made a serious error, forgetting why we were there in the first place, and decided to take a shortcut to save us some distance. We went down a hill, and I could hear sprinklers going. The cattle were down in this gully, and they pumped water at night for them. There were little tufts of grass up high and crevasses filled with ice-cold water. It gave John and me an instant charley horse when we accidentally stepped in one of the crevasses. Now the pain was mounting, and John was a physical wreck besides being blind. I could see, but I was a total loss myself. It was the like a death march from then on as we put one foot slowly in front of the other. We finally got out of the gully and slowly ascended the far side.

We were at the edge of Bicknell, Utah, a small town north of Hell's Backbone Ridge. We were going to sleep a barn but decided to follow our guiding light. It turned out to be the window of the local library in a woman's house. When we knocked, she came to the door. It was about four thirty in the morning, and we were filthy. She appeared to be paranoid as she looked at me with the blanket, pistol, and bandoleer. I'm sure she thought Pancho Villa was raiding too far north. She offered no assistance but said we could rest in her garage. The word rest sounded so good that we did the death march some more with a zombie twist and made it to her garage. It only had a little more than three walls and a partial roof. The floor was mud but felt like modeling clay, and when we laid down, the floor gave slightly. We didn't care and lay side by side on the muddy floor. John was a sleep in a heartbeat.

I couldn't sleep at all. I just stared up at the hole in ceiling and spaced. I felt those little brown slugs you see when you lift a rock crawling in my hair, but I didn't care at all. I probably stared for an hour and a half, and then it was light. I could hear someone working across the street and talking. I slowly started to push myself up, forgetting John was right next to me sleeping soundly. My left palm was firmly in his stomach as I pushed my full weight up. To say the least, it was a rude awaking for poor John. I didn't have the energy to apologize, and he didn't have enough to complain.

I said, "Let's go," and we took another half hour just to walk across a drainage ditch and the road. It was maybe fifty feet away with a three-foot deep ditch. The guy across the street was a saddle maker and an ex-Marine, so John liked him immediately, as John's dad was also a Marine. The guy was wonderful and made us cowboy coffee (where you boil water and throw the grounds in), which is messy but warm. He also overcooked us eggs, but we were so grateful and started to feel good with the resurgence of basic blood sugar. We didn't have any money to spare, so the Ex- Marine and his friend got us in a pickup truck, bought us five gallons of gas, and drove us forty-some miles back to our vehicle. It was covered with snow, still stuck, with our clothes and things all over the ground from when we tried to lighten the load the day before. We picked up our wet stuff, brushed our suits off, and hung them in the back. The Bicknell boys yanked out car out with a chain and turned us around. We thanked our saviors profusely and resumed our journey.

Our spirits soaring from our near demise and resplendent resurrection, we took off to Sin City—Las Vegas. When we crossed from Utah to Nevada, it came to our attention that there was no speed limit except around cities. Well, what a mistake for late teenagers, we buried the needle and arrived at Las Vegas at just over 120 miles per hour. When we arrived, we were still disgusting and gross. We pulled into a gas station and filled the car up. We bought some McDonald's hamburgers and had twenty dollars left between us.

We were in the gambling capital of the free world, so we decided to invest our money in the three fates (Clotho, Lachesis, and Atropos—one to spin, one to wind, and one to cut the thread of destiny). We took our suits into the bathroom at the gas station where we took clothes off and washed up in the sink. Some guy came in and saw two naked nineteen-year-olds washing side by side out of the sink. He didn't use the restroom at all and just quickly turned and got out of there as fast as he could. We laughed and finished our much-needed body cleanse. We put on our suits and ties and headed for Caesar's Palace. John took ten and I took ten to make us solvent again.

John went to the slots, while I headed to the blackjack table. I was steady playing and very cautious. I had read a book about bet management that my dad had purchased and applied it to my play. John was broke before he had completed two drinks. (In those days, if you were playing, drinks were free, and the minimum bet was two dollars.) He came to me, borrowed some chips, and returned to his slots. He kept doing that, as I would win while he would lose. When he hit eighty dollars, I told him enough was enough, and I realized I had half my money bet on one hand. (It's easy to forget that it's money when you play with chips.) I added it up, and I had another eighty dollars out on a bet and eighty dollars in front of me. I lost the hand and decided to survive and leave. John was getting antsy not being able to play, and we still had to drive to Malibu. We left with eighty dollars and were okay once again.

John said he'd drive, so I took a pillow and leaned up against the passenger window and started to go a sleep. I was drifting off when I heard a swishing sound to the right of my head. I opened my eyes and saw the reflectors that are off the shoulder on the expressway just outside the window, one after another. I looked over at John, and he was fast asleep. I yelled at him to wake up and tried to steer the car back on to the right lane and off the shoulder. John was stiff, and the wheel wouldn't move. I was shaking and yelling at him by this time, and as he woke up, his grip relaxed. At seventy-five miles per hour, we went sideways on the expressway. The tires made a lot of noise, but we weren't hurt. Both of us felt lucky after the near miss. I drove until the adrenaline wore off from the close call and then pulled over in a pass in south central California to rest. We hung out there exhausted for a couple of hours and then drove in to LA and west to Malibu on the beach.

John's dad lived near Chuck Connors (a baseball player and actor), and the beach scene was awesome. Poor Chuck later lost that beautiful home in a California mudslide. I always loved water and had swum in the Atlantic and Gulf but never the Pacific. John and I went to the beach and watched all the bikini babes. He told me about body surfing, and I was game to try. The red flags were out to indicate severe undertow and huge waves, which were a definite danger. The waves were twelve feet over our heads sometimes, and where the water would crash was only be a couple of feet deep with lots of suction and sand removal under our feet. (This is the worst point of undertow and the strongest pull.) John said since he was the California big kahuna, he'd show me how it should be done. John proceeded to swim out beyond the breakers by diving under just before the wave broke and holding on to the bottom until the pressure was past his knees toward the beach. He then swam to the forming area to ready himself to catch a wave. He chose his ride and began to swim with the wave toward shore, get in the crest, and take his drop, and then he'd ride on top of the foam in to shore. When he was in the crest, the wave didn't curl and break right; it walled up on both sides and threw him into the sand headfirst in about two feet of water. It skinned his whole face and shoulder with giant scrapes like floor burns from basketball. The bruises were red and sweating drops of blood. He crawled weakly up on to the beach and lay on our towel after his ordeal. I said to him, "Could you show me that again? I didn't quite catch it all." John groaned, unappreciative of my sarcastic wit for some unknown reason.

On the last day, we took the car back, and the company in LA gave us the seventy-five dollars as promised, but they were pissed because the oil hadn't been changed in a long time. We left and went back to the beach by Malibu. One of the big new songs was the Door's "Light My Fire," which played often on the juke box at the beach hut. There was also a club we attended off the pier called the Cheetah, which was a dance club environment.

I was still white (I peel easily and never brown) and decided I was going to get a tan. In those days, the rage was putting iodine in baby oil to burn deep. I tried and fried and then baked and flaked to no avail. After I burned and peeled several times, realization set in that I wasn't ever going to tan. I got drunk and threw up in the living room at John's dad's house and was banished permanently. I had to get a job, or I was toast. I started selling Encyclopedia Britannica door to door with The Book of Knowledge. I did okay at first, but the people I was given leads on were poor married folks with one or two kids and another on the way. I didn't have the heart to make them feel guilty and buy books for their kids' education when they didn't even know the alphabet song yet. My boss didn't appreciate my merciful outlook and retired me early.

I was broke and not near John anymore, because I couldn't afford rent in his neighborhood, so I had my suit on looking for work. I had exactly one dime to my name, but I looked okay. After looking all day for work, I dropped in to a nice bar to see if I could drum up some drinks. I sat at the bar and started talking to this guy in a suit with a flattop haircut who was sitting next to me. He began buying me drinks and hung on my every word. After four or five drinks, I was feeling pretty good, and this guy put his hand on my right knee and began rubbing my inner thigh. I didn't think anything of it at first, but after he persisted, I looked at him quizzically and then looked around and realized the place was all males. I'd heard about gay places, but it never occurred to me I was in one. Thinking about the situation—him hitting on me, the place I'd inadvertently picked to drink, and the fact I was still a virgin with women—caused me to begin to laugh. He took it all wrong and thought I was laughing at him and looked really hurt. I didn't mean to hurt him, but I knew it was time to go, and others were picking up an ill feeling. I left and began to smile again out in the light of day. A panhandler came up to me begging for spare change, and I flipped him my last dime like I had a million and walked on laughing at myself and figuring this guy could probably buy and sell me ten times over. I knew it was time to leave California, and my folks graciously sent me a ticket to fly home to Chicago. John would flunk out of Coe College the fall trimester and would enlist in the Marines at Christmas time.

When I returned home, it was late July. I got a job downtown working in bulk brick sales for Illinois Brick. I lied and said I wasn't going back to school. Why else would I be applying so late? They bought it, and I had a decent-paying job the last six weeks before school. I was now a commuter and a full-time suit. Working in the Loop in Chicago is uplifting and depressing, depending on your mood. That many people can get you down, but the pace is exciting and gets you moving.

In early August, I went with my sister to a coffeehouse. They had games and hootenanny-type music ("Michael Row the Boat Ashore" and "Puff the Magic Dragon"). I was chatting with Lauren and one of her friends, and I glanced across the room and spied this utter vision of loveliness. She was five feet five with dark hair, a curvy and busty body, and a heart-shaped face. My jaw dropped, and she looked at me like she was trying to figure out what was wrong with me. I couldn't stop my ridiculous stare. It lasted for a few minutes until I woke up and rejoined the conversation and stopped thinking about it. I found out later she was a friend of John's younger sister Leslie, and she wanted to know what I thought about her. I told Leslie she had a "nice bod," which miffed Madonna, who would become my future wife. When confronted by Leslie, I said that I'd never talked to her and didn't know her but thought she was attractive. She wanted to know about the girl I was with, and I told her it was my sister.

Madonna waited at the coffeehouse every night for three weeks until I finally showed up again. When I walked around the corner, she was sitting on the front stoop of the place and later said her stomach did a complete flip-flop when she identified me. We talked and played this Chinese game called GO, and I asked her how old she was. She told me eighteen. She wasn't going to be sixteen until October but had heard me say to someone that I wouldn't date a girl unless she was eighteen.

She was eighteen every year on her birthday for the next three years. She was four years behind me in school (like John, she wanted a year of bonus education) but only three years younger in age. We went to the old Aurelio's in Homewood, and she was talking to me or listening a lot. She was partially deaf and would look and listen extra hard and conveyed a genuine interest that was quite attractive.

One of Lauren's friends (who liked me) came to our coffee house Phyllis M. (I couldn't date my sister's friends no matter what, although I did try with Phyllis for a while). As soon as Madonna detected the interest, the claws came out, and she took her foot out of her shoe and gently ran it as far up my pant leg as she could. It was stimulating, and I had two competing for my attention, which was confusing. I took Madonna home and kissed her goodnight. She was an excellent and passionate kisser, and a goodnight kiss would last an hour and seem like only a minute. We went out several more times, and she let me feel her up but I couldn't touch her pants. She was worried about herself, so when we dated, she later wore a girdle, figuring it would be too hard to take off. I didn't even consider it then, and she was in high school despite being "eighteen," as she had told me. She wanted to come to University for homecoming and I told her that it might work out. I was getting closer to going back to school and started writing Ruth and was listening to that song by The Box Tops called "The Letter." I told Madonna I was leaving for school on Labor Day even though I wasn't leaving for another week. She called the house looking for me, and I was so pissed when I answered (basically, she caught me lying) that I told her it was unladylike to call a guy and not to ever do it again. She wrote me at school, but other things were a foot.

My Junior Year, 1967–68

When I got back, Ruth was glad to see me and told me about her boring summer with her parents in Yankton. I told her more about the California trip, and we started dating. She was more than passionate when I touched her, and either Madonna improved my kissing or Ruth was hit hard by her hormones. I think she wanted to be with me more. I took her downstairs in the TKE house to a room where we could lock ourselves in and not be bothered by housemothers or fraternity brothers. I started to kiss her, and she was ready and squirming. I figured this was the time to go for it, and all my fraternity brothers had said how wonderful it was. I was dying of curiosity, so I went for it. I understood what was supposed to happen. I knew I was to put my penis in her and move it in and out, but I had never done it. I didn't have the guts to admit I was cherry to my date, and she had told me that she'd never done it but had an accident on her bicycle when she was young that ruined her hymen (what a crock). I figured I'd be the teacher, so after I got her girdle off (which was like skinning a pheasant and didn't take long), I started to finger her. I was hard but still didn't know how to get it in where my finger was, so I replaced my finger with my thumb and slid it in on top of my thumb. Now, she was far from tight, and it was like putting on your galoshes without putting your shoes on first. She was warm, and I managed to only slip out twice when I got too aggressive. When I was getting really interested and close to ejaculation, she told me to pull out and not go inside her. I complied as I got close to getting off; I dribbled on the couch, my dick was cold in the air, and it wasn't the great experience I imagined. I was very disappointed after waiting twenty years to just dribble on the couch in the cold air. I had her get dressed and took her back to the dorm. I came back to the TKE house, and a Peggy Lee song was in the back of my head called "Is That All There Is?" I was depressed. My fraternity brothers were talking about sex as usual when they got back from their dates, and I can remember thinking they hadn't had any sex, or they'd know how terrible it was.

I was social chairman, so I began to plot my budget. I only had three dollars per man per month to work with and get parties going. If I invested all of it at one time, buying just liquor in Omaha, Nebraska, I would have enough goods for a party every week instead of once a month. I had to improvise for the rest of the accouterments like food and decorations, but that was the challenge. I planned a party a week.

At first, it was easy to just have some alcohol and have a kegger (beer party) in the woods or in the basement of the TKE house. People require variety to stay amused, so I had a toga party.

It was the same basic format of a keg of beer and some records to listen and dance to but with the twist that you had to wear a bed sheet or you and you date couldn't come. The girls got in to it more than the guys did. Engineering was not USD's strong suit among the student body. Girls and guys came in flimsy and ill-conceived designer originals that barely lasted a single fast dance. Pinning the top of a toga to a bra strap is not going to last in a fast dance. We were drinking heavily, and many girls got their first taste of stripping in public whether they wanted to or not. I was quite pleased with myself, and the exposure we achieved campus wide was marvelous. Most of the girls wore white underwear, and everyone in attendance could attest to that fact. There were probably a dozen broken bras that night, a new low for fraternity frolicking.

I had my bubble busted the following week at the fraternity meeting when my party was officially denounced as debauchery, which led us to campus ruin and expulsion from the fraternity system. What better press could you get? Expulsion for a wild party is a social chairman's dream. Now whatever I did would be a campus legend. All eyes were on me, and the students waited. Everyone wanted to be in attendance in case it was the party of the year. People make happenings work, and if they think it's great, well, then it is. I decided that because the dress code of the party was frowned upon, why not use the outfit for decoration? I decided on a TKE mattress party. How much more flagrant can you be?

I went downstairs and brought up all the bed sheets. I tacked them to the ceiling, forming cubicles for each couple. The cubicle held a mattress to recline on with your date. The sheets only reached to about eighteen inches off the floor. If you lay down in your cubicle, you could see everyone's feet dancing or other couples reclined on their mattresses. I borrowed the backup jukebox from Southgate Tap, and we had a great time. It wasn't nearly as rowdy as the toga party, and no one had sex on their mattress; it was just the idea of a mattress party to frost the powers at large. Of course, it was the talk of the campus for the next week, and everyone was "disgusted" and swore to uphold moral decency by eliminating the vermin that caused such upheavals. I was told I was on very thin ice, and so was the fraternity if I continued to have this type of social activity. The bonus was everyone was interested in our "borderline" dismissible parties.

I invited the president of the university to come to my next party, the monster mash, in honor of Halloween. I was careful not to have beer but did have "special punch" set aside from the other punch in case the university people sampled it. At this stage, getting a date for a TKE function was easy. Everyone wanted to be there just to see what I came up with next. I decided to be bad (of course) but with a twist and make them think I was good. I went to the school of medicine's gross anatomy laboratory and obtained an arm from one of the donated cadavers. It smelled like formaldehyde, so I had to clean them up some. I put the left arm extending out of the piano with some angel hair on it, and I told everyone it was Zoomer's arm coming back to claim the body. I made up gray cardboard tombstones for everyone I knew who'd be there (with supposed actual dates and reasons for their deaths in the future). All the reasons were because of something current in their life. For example, one of the guy's girls would never have sex with him even though they'd been pinned for two years, so his death was because of blue balls. I put water troughs behind the tombstones and dropped dry ice in them to get the fog effect on the Litzelman room floor. We got to dance in the fog, and it even traveled down the stairs to the basement. The university people came eventually, and one even remarked to me that I should have got a better arm for the piano because the one I had looked too unrealistic. I agreed and started to laugh but was careful not to get too carried away.

I was still unhappy with my sex life to date, and I began to focus on another approach in my quest for gratification. Undaunted, I decided I needed professional help. Something was wrong, so I'd get it ironed out with hookers in Sioux City, Iowa. I talked to some guys from the area (it was only twenty-five miles east of college), and they gave me an address on lower Fourth Street. I was to say, "Blackie sent me," as a password. This was something I was going to do out of curiosity, and I felt I needed to learn a skill for future relationships. I was totally clueless, but with books and practice with a professional, I was determined to master the art of love. I went with a buddy from Chicago who was a year younger than me. Rob was a tall guy with an average build but had severe acne. His dad gave him a Corvette to take to college, but he was always drinking and chasing women and later flunked out. He never even got a C average, so we couldn't activate him in the fraternity.

After giving the password, we were each taken to a separate room. Mine had a sink, full-sized bed, a small closet, and a chair. An attractive blonde came in and introduced herself as Honeydew. I don't think she knew how ignorant I was and asked me to drop my pants. She went over to the sink to run water, and I had taken my pants down. She came back and told me I had to drop my shorts too, because she had to inspect me. (I later found out that was for threefold reason—first, to establish control; second, to check for obvious venereal disease; and finally, to make sure I wasn't a cop.) At this point, I was sure she knew I was ignorant. I was embarrassed to be standing there naked from the knees to the waist with her fully clothed, but I figured when in Rome, do as the Romans.

I wasn't excited at all and felt like Ethel (all guys name their penises) was a turtle trying to get back in its shell. She stooped down to look at it really closely, and I can remember thinking that she must be really careful about VDs, which was a good thing. She carefully used just her index finger and thumb to lift Ethel up and peruse the bottom side. She then started to caress/stimulate me up and down with her hand, grasping like you would a tennis racquet. I was frozen in fear, waiting for what I was supposed to do. She then told me to give her money. I don't remember if it was five or ten dollars, but I reached for my wallet in my pants at my ankles. After the money exchanged hands, she instructed me to take off all my clothes and said she'd be right back. By the time she returned, I was naked. She kept looking at my loins, I'm assuming to see if I was erect yet. I felt strange standing naked in front of a total stranger who was still totally dressed. She then pulled her dress over her head. She had on heels, a bra, and nice-looking panties on but no slip or hose. She again visually perused my loins and realized I was not getting hard. I wasn't even thinking about sex. At this point, I was wondering what I was supposed to do next.

She quickly removed her bra and panties, and as she walked toward me, I was fascinated that I could see right through the top of her thighs. She was thin enough but had a large pubic bone, and I could see the bed behind her by looking right below her pubic hair. She had a nice shape, and everything jiggled in the right places when she walked. A lot of women today don't jiggle after working out so much, and they don't wear skirts or dresses anymore. It's a changing world.

She walked to the sink and produced a pan with warm, soapy water. She squatted down and douched her vagina in front of me so I could see she was clean. Honeydew then came over to me and had me hold the pan just below my scrotum. She then began to wash me and play with Ethel at the same time. I looked at her body up close, not even seeing her face but visually feasting on her breasts and vagina. Ethel was not along for the ride and tried to drown herself in the bottom of the pan. Honeydew kept trying to raise an erection but finally took away the pan and dried me off. She then quietly asked, "What would you like?" But I didn't know what I liked. She then volunteered at my silence, "Would you like half-and-half?" To me, that was something for coffee, but I eagerly said yes. At least I'd made a decision. She had me lie on the bed, and she sat down and began to give me head. Well, that woke Ethel up. She was sucking but flicking her tongue very rapidly on the tip as she went up and down, and I finally started to realize why I was there. Unfortunately, I didn't stick with the head, and she mounted me on top now that I was erect.

She wasn't hot inside as some women get (maybe from all the douching or not being naturally turned on), but she gave it her best Oscar performance for excitement. I found myself wishing she would shut up with all the easy verbiage. As I started to move with her, she grabbed my balls and squeezed them to get me to come, but it just felt uncomfortable. I think she did it a little too hard. She finally gave up and said "time's up" and dismounted. I hadn't ejaculated and still felt weird. I talked to Rob when he came out, and he said how great it was and how he came in the pan while she was washing him. I can remember thinking at first that he'd missed the best part (head) and then thought about it and realized he had gotten off and I hadn't. I thought about it all week and went back the next Friday.

I was learning, but I wasn't getting it right yet. I got a different girl the next time and dropped my trousers and shorts on cue. This time, when she inspected me, I got an erection when she began to play. I gave her the money and took off my clothes without her having to tell me. She returned, and I felt very grown up and experienced. She tried to tease me while undressing, but I wanted to get to it. She finished drying me off (and at least Ethel wasn't drowning herself), and we started to the bed. Instead of asking me for half-and- half, she said, "Do you want to go around the world?" I was lost again. Curiosity got the best of me, and my desire to learn surpassed my desire for pure head. I replied yes.

This time, she got on her back, and I had to give her head. Now I knew I had to use my lips and tongue but where and how presented a problem. I was a student but also a teacher as evidenced by my first sex with Ruth. I couldn't ask (which is stupid, but guys can't seem to ever ask for directions), so I dove right in. This was an opportunity for an up close and personal visual inspection of the vagina and my first oral lesson. Her vagina probably needed a fifty-thousand- mile checkup (figuring the average penetration is six inches, so in and out would be a foot, and then 5,280 thrusts would be a mile), but I didn't care. I licked her like my first ice cream cone and then spelled the entire alphabet with my tongue. She seemed to enjoy it, but I had no base of comparison and didn't trust reactions from a paid player at this point. Her vagina had hardly any smell or taste (probably from all the douches she'd given herself).

I then proceeded to mount her and slam her missionary style. I was determined to get off inside her and practice my technique so I didn't slip out so much and have to reenter. She was warmer inside than

Honeydew, and I wanted to take as long a stroke as I could without popping out. This girl was only trying for an Emmy award, so it wasn't quite as distracting. When she grabbed my balls, swinging them into her rectum with a crack (making a curious popping sound), she was gentler. I came within a short time. The second I released, she said, "That's it." It was very empty, and Ethel was out in the cold. I could understand later why women want a hug afterward and are disgruntled when the man leaves right away after ejaculation. I now felt ready to return to the collegiate world rearmed with knowledge and skills (at least comparatively speaking).

Miss Ruth and I got hot and heavy after this, and sex became quite enjoyable. I quickly got into it, and my mission was to find a place. (Guys need a place, and girls need a reason.) I didn't have a car my junior year, so we had to be creative. It would get cold outside in South Dakota, so that was over with quickly too. I was so possessed with libido one night and couldn't find a place. I thought I was going to explode. I never used to have these emotions, and it was uncomfortable when I started to lose control of logic. At the TKE house, the room where we first made it was already taken. The kitchen had a swinging door with a small glass window in it, and the center of the kitchen had a big wooden chopping table made of butcher block maple approximately three feet by three feet. Ruth told me as I walked in that she had a girdle on, and it would be inconvenient. The swinging door had only made one cycle and the girdle hit her knees. The butcher block was getting a workout in no time, and Ruth, for all her coyness, was in seventh heaven. I could hear people outside the door talking, but no one came into the kitchen. We finished, and with her hair and makeup destroyed, Ruth decided to call it a night.

Ruth was always "working" it. I later found out the only reason she came to college was to get married. I had just found out my Grandma Clara (my mother's mother) had died, and I was feeling bad. My mom had said not to come home, as there was nothing I could do. I tried to get Ruth's attention, but she said she had lost both grandmas and it was no big deal. I really cared for Grandma Clara and used to meet her downtown in Chicago (she lived north; I lived south) and go to a movie and lunch with her. Grandma was always worried about her weight and said no goodies, but I would buy buttered popcorn and in the show she'd always sneak some. She was always good to me, and I missed her pleasant attitude.

One day Ruth and I were riding in a car, and she started complaining about something I didn't want to listen to and then started crying for no apparent reason. I had a headache from all this and said, "Don't give me any of that crap." She immediately stopped crying. She then began babbling and asked me how I knew she was faking it, because no guy had ever caught her faking her tears. That little outburst told me a lot about her motivation, and I began to take a new attitude to this woman. I was still upset about Grandma Clara, and Ruth told me she was pregnant. I began to worry about that, and being a typical dung head, I never thought to take that possibility in to question. I tortured myself for a week until her roommate Nancy came up to me and told me Ruth had gotten her period. I waited for Ruth to tell me, but I finally had to confront her about it after two dates. She said yes, she had gotten her period and had meant to tell me, but it had just happened the day before. I didn't bother to tell her what Nancy said.

I began reading Mickey Spillane books (Mike Hammer, private eye) and began to treat Ruth poorly. I was amazed that she only responded more. Why do girls like the bad guys? One night we were locked in the missionary position in the backseat of a car under a streetlight. As I was penetrating her, I could clearly see her face, and she was really enjoying the experience. Her arms were over her head, and her armpits were exposed with a five o'clock shadow (not freshly shaved). As I went slowly in and out and she was writhing with her eyes closed, I wanted to her expression change from pleasure to whatever, so I licked her armpit. Her whole body cringed with repulsion, and she was totally out of the mood. I then proceeded to turn her on again just to see if I could get her off. It took a minute, but she again got into it, and I got her off. I'm sure this was an evil power trip, and I was doing this just to see if I could, but at that point, I didn't care about her that much. I guess the curiosity of how much power I had and what I could control was of more interest than the person I was controlling. I was probably cheating myself by just continuing the relationship, but who was to know?

I would go to the football games for fun and release. We were not allowed to drink on the college campus at any time, but everyone would sneak in flasks with their favorite hard liquor. We had our TKE bell down on the field. It was mounted on a Civil War–like cannon caisson with wooden wheel spokes and painted cherry and gray. When the coyotes would score, we would pull it out on the field and ring it madly. We had paper cups we got from the concession stand, and we mixed our drinks in them. Drinking was acceptable as long as you were cool and didn't draw attention to it. I, alas, was always the center of attention. The local police had to clamp down on any indiscretion committed by the students.

Well, as I was pushing out the bell at halftime, the flask fell out of my pocket. It was quite visible from great distances on the football field. We rang the bell, and upon returning, I discovered it so I picked it up. I looked to the stands, and everyone was watching. I could see the police moving toward our area from every part of the stands. When we got to the sidelines, the police arrived in masse and began the usual interrogation. The flask was empty by this point, so the police pointed to our paper cups and said to bring them along for evidence. I (with much bravado, considering the large audience) kicked over the three glasses and was hauled out to the police area amid cheers and jeers from the crowd. I had the officers release me halfway out and turned back to the crowd and took a real "hammy" bow (kind of like a maestro), and the crowd roared and cheered. The police had had enough at this point and dragged me away, again to more cheers and jeers. When we arrived at the station, my partner in crime was a Lambda Chi whom I didn't want to get in trouble with and an underage student, so I gave the police one of my fake identification cards that said I was twenty-one. It turned out that he was only twenty, so now I was being charged with contributing to the delinquency of an underage minor. How ironic for the master of falsified documents to be busted with being old enough by virtue of his fake cards? I eventually paid my way out of it and was proud of my forgeries being so successful with the local law.

The TKE bell was constantly being stolen, and we would find it miles away in some field or on the roof of some home. We chained it to our frat house flagpole, but it was still an object of desire. I decided I'd had enough with the Sunday pickup of the bell two counties away, so I set a trap. I built a bomb with gunpowder and coffee cans. I packed the powder in tight and then took a lamp cord, stripped the ends, and wound them together. I inserted the exposed wire into the powder, drilled a hole in the powder can for the cord to go through, and sealed it with candle wax. I dropped the coffee can into a bigger can and filled it with water. I covered that can with a bigger can and set it on the ground near the bell. I didn't drink that Friday night and took a nap early. I got up at midnight and waited by the closest window and wall socket with my electric cord to plug in. I cracked the window enough to hear outside but didn't dare to look outside in case someone was looking for a guard. I waited about two hours, and sure enough, I heard struggling, whispering, and a light ding from the bell followed by shushing. I plugged the cord in, and the house lights that were on dimmed dramatically. A loud but muffled explosion ensued with much pandemonium. The water insulated most of the fragmentation, so no one was seriously hurt, but many of them (four, I found out later) were cut up by the outside can. There was a six-inch hole in the ground with just the bottom of the expanded coffee can. The rest of the pieces were scattered everywhere. No one ever even attempted to steal the bell again after it got around how it was booby-trapped.

Zoomer and I went hunting, and I went to his house after homecoming. He lived in the country out on a real farm. They were beef cattle ranchers but grew corn to support the cattle. They also had some milk cows with the automatic suckers you put on the teats of the cow. This made sense to me after my rodeo experience milking a cow freshman year. They also played music for the cows. I was told it comforted them, and they produced better if they listened to what I called elevator music. They thought my comment was funny (of course, to them, an elevator was to store grain not raise people in buildings). When Zoomer worked around the farm, he got rid of his artificial hand and put a hook on instead. He looked like a badass biker with a strange and horrible weapon in his left hand. For him, it was functional to grab a bale of hay or drag a bag of something around, where the old spring-loaded rubber hand was just cosmetic.

It was just after harvest time, so there was a lot of work to do. They had picked the ears of corn, but they were in the corncribs and had to be further processed. We took pitchforks and loaded the ears on to a conveyor belt that took them up to a mobile machine. It put the cobs in one pile, the corn kernels in a chute going to an open truck, and the rest was silage. I've seen silos my whole life but didn't know what they were for; I just assumed they were for corn. Well, they're for the corn stalks chopped up. That's what they call silage, hence the name silo. The farmer loads it up with a conveyor after it's been field dried. On one side of the silo there is a cylinder that houses a ladder that can be used to climb up the side of the silo. Zoomer climbed up this cylinder, and I saw a switch at the bottom I assumed was a light. I turned it on to Zoomer's dismay as it dumped silage all over him in the cylinder. I shut it off, and fortunately, he was still okay but very dirty.

I then went up the cylinder myself and looked into the silo. At the top of the silage was a huge floating fanlike machine that took up the entire diameter of the silo. When I had turned on that switch, it activated that floating machine (it floats on top of the silage) and began scooping out silage and pushing it out to the cylinder. As the silage is used up, it moves down the silo. We climbed down, and I got a wheelbarrow and put in under the cylinder. I turned on the fanlike machine for a couple of seconds and shut it off just as it started to descend the cylinder. About a third of the wheelbarrow filled up, and then Zoomer had me throw a coal shovel full of oats over the silage. I repeated this twice more, and the large wheelbarrow was full. I proceeded out to a gangplank-like structure that ran through the cow pens. It was a structure of wooden planks maybe two feet wide with a fence on either side and openings every three feet. The cattle didn't pay any attention to me. I guess because I was an unfamiliar person. I went to the end of this gangplank (about half a football field long) and dumped a third of the wheelbarrow's contents and then backpedaled six feet and dumped another third. By the time I dumped the last third, every cow in the place was my best friend.

Their heads came through the openings everywhere, and I had more than 135 feet to get back to the barn. It was scary the first time, because all these huge cattle heads were knee high looking for chow. I learned to fight my way back, dragging the wheelbarrow behind and trying not to hurt these docile creatures. Of course, the farm people thought it was funny that I was so polite to their product. For me, the cows were like pets, but for Zoomer's family, the cows were their source income. I quickly got the rest of the herd fed once I had the technique down, but I was still gentler than the locals.

We had a little time after dinner on Saturday, so Zoomer's dad said he would sponsor a cat hunt. He meant he would pay for the ammo to shoot the barnyard cats. Unlike Bruce's farm, they didn't like the cats. The cats hunted in packs like wolves and killed anything they could. They were not tame cats but totally wild. We saw about a dozen of the cats tearing a rabbit to bits about a hundred yards from the barnyard, so we quickly got ready. We took our shotguns over and had a field day. When we hit the cats, the fur literally flew. When we opened up on the hunting pack, it looked more like Fourth of July fireworks going off. It was just the multicolored fur flying in the air. We each shot off a box of shells, so we harvested the cat crop pretty well, and Zoomer's chickens and barnyard small animals could breathe a little easier.

I went to church with Zoomer on Sunday at a country Orthodox Lutheran church. There were probably thirty in the congregation, and they all took communion from a common cup. At my home church (Flossmoor Community Church), we only got grape juice in communion, but they had the strongest red wine I'd ever tasted. The minister offered the cup, the parishioner took a sip, and he quickly wiped it off with a rag soaked in alcohol. I don't know why he bothered to wipe it as strong as the wine was, but it was a ritual. It was nice that communion could be indulged by the whole congregation in a matter of a few minutes.

Ruth had to go home for Thanksgiving but wanted to get with me first, so she suggested I go to her roommate's home, and she would meet me there Friday. I didn't want to go to Illinois, so I agreed. I rode with Nancy to her West River farm/ranch and met her parents. They had turkeys and chickens. They had horses (Western saddle only), and we decided to go out riding with some of the local cowboys. I had my 357 Magnum Colt with me, so I felt like a range rider even though they treated me like a city slicker. The locals gave me the chubbiest and slowest of the horses. I really had to work to get her to gallop, and I think the horse had gone through menopause ten years prior.

The local boys left me in the dust, so I decided to show off with my Colt shooter. A jackrabbit got up in front of my nag when I was at the fastest canter the horse was capable of generating. I pulled the pistol and fired from my shoulder almost like I was throwing the bullet at the critter. To my total surprise, it fell over with a hit at the top of the fore legs. I was still in shock as I pulled up next to the rabbit, and then the locals came up from behind talking with each other rapidly. As soon as they were next to me, I lowered the gun barrel to my mouth and blew the smoke away slow and deliberate like and without glancing in their direction. And then I put the pistol away. I was careful to never take it out again and fire it in front of them. I knew I could never recapture that moment, and they had it coming. I pretended everyone from Chicago shot like that and it was just a matter of fact happening in the Windy City.

We went home, and I still had those guys talking to themselves. We ate, had a few beers, and watched the local TV. I retired to the bed downstairs in the basement, which was next to a sink and a meat freezer. We were all tired and went to bed before midnight. We also had a big day ahead with Thanksgiving. A little while later I heard someone coming down the stairs; it was Nancy in a lime-green baby-doll nightgown. I was confused but pleasantly surprised as she unabashedly jumped into bed with me. Sometimes it's really better to be lucky than good. She was lonely and knew I was, and Ruth wouldn't arrive till Friday night. It was amazing. Nancy didn't ask for a commitment or for me to dump Ruth and was just content to enjoy the moment. I was easily tricked into passionate lovemaking. What was more remarkable was the next morning Nancy's father came downstairs to the freezer, got something, threw it in the sink, ran water over it, and went back upstairs. He saw both of us and never said a word.

I got up and went hunting with him, because he had a deer tag for his county. We went with his buddies in a pickup truck riding around Marlboro Country. He gave me a 12-gauge with slugs, and he had a .30-caliber bolt action. We stopped at a valley, and on the other side was a nice herd of deer maybe forty yards away as the crow flies. I whipped up the shotgun, marked my target, and squeezed off a round. The slug dropped to the bottom of the valley not even twenty yards away. I fired again holding the barrel twelve feet above the deer, and the round didn't even make it halfway up the other slope. The slugs turned out to be ten years old and were paper that had gotten wet before. The shotgun was useless unless I threw it at the deer. I was in the back of the truck with Nancy's father, so I figured I'd let him get it since it was his tag.

We came around a bend where the edge of the trees was fifty feet away. There were several deer only halfway to the trees, so we stopped. Nancy's dad fired at the closest one and missed. The deer jumped but came toward us. He reloaded and fired again, and the deer was bummed out just from the concussion we were so close. He ran toward us about eight feet behind the truck, and then I really could have killed him with the shotgun by throwing it. I smelled the kill, and I was disgruntled with all the incompetence at this juncture. I took the gun away from him and told him to sit in the truck with his shotgun shells.

We came on top of another hill, and there was a herd of deer there also. The other two guys fired in to the herd and got nothing. I got out of the truck and saw a deer crouched down in the bush. I aimed and fired, and the two-point buck got up and started running. I couldn't believe I missed it at less than a hundred yards. I dropped the rifle and ran with my bowie knife to the right of the hill, while the deer went left. We met in the middle, and I felt like Tarzan as I stupidly leaped on its back and brought the crazed buck down. I grabbed its neck with my left hand and sliced the deer's throat with my right. I thought I was the most macho guy in the world at that second. Those few seconds in life where you know you're the greatest human being that ever lived are rare and wonderful, but like the deer's life, they are also quickly fleeting.

I turned the poor dead deer over, and I had blown his heart wide open with the rifle. I don't know how it ran, but that's probably how I was able to catch it running. I was never superfast and surely couldn't ever outrun a deer, even downhill. We field dressed it, put the tag on, and threw it in the truck. Nancy's dad was elated with his meat, and life was good for him. I found out later he really had poor vision and hadn't shot a deer in years. Maybe he never even saw me in the basement, but I never asked him about that.

We got back to the house around nine o'clock in the morning, and Nancy's mom wanted me to kill a turkey that she would bake for Thanksgiving. I had never done that before. I started out in the barnyard, and of course, the turkeys wouldn't let me get anywhere near axe range. I had my .22 Colt with also, so I whipped it out and shot a good-sized turkey right in the head. It ran around for a while just like a chicken does and then flopped over. Nancy was impressed that I used only one head shot, but I explained you live by comparison, and shooting a moving grouse in the wild is a lot harder than a dumb tame barnyard turkey.

She decided to help me decapitate the fowl. I had my new Florsheim leather penny loafers on, and I didn't want to get them dirty. I placed my foot on the turkey's neck, and Nancy grabbed the feet to stretch the neck as I started to bring the axe down. She was a little too exuberant, and as I followed through with my chop, her tugging inadvertently pulled my foot to the right and under the axe. The axe penetrated the outside of my new shoe and cut me deep between the baby toe and ring toe. My loafer filled with blood where you could see it on the socks below the outside ankle point. I was hurt but more upset because my new loafers were ruined. I finished knocking the head off as Nancy was apologizing profusely, and I told her not to worry. We went in to the house and took off my shoes and socks. I cleaned the wound with peroxide and butterfly bandaged the wound to close it like stitches before covering it with gauze. I threw the shoes out (the left was perfect, but the right was cut and soaked to disfigurement). I put my boots and new socks on but did not tie the right one. I went out to the garage to help Nancy's dad with the deer and turkey. The deer wasn't that big, and we strung him up to the rafters with a metal coat hanger through the Achilles tendon. We got the hide off him and butchered the deer up and threw the roast chunks into the sink with salt water in order to soak the game taste out. We then took the turkey and began to pluck it. That was real work. I had it finished before noon, but my hands were sore after so much time with needle-nose pliers. We had dinner late, but it was interesting consuming the fowl you had killed earlier. That was the first and last time I'd ever killed and cleaned my Thanksgiving turkey.

Nancy spent another delightful evening with me, and her dad came down in the morning to check on the deer and take it out of the salt water. I got out of bed and chatted with him but had to hobble around. My foot was sore by then and quite bruised. I took it light and kept ice on it. Ruth came up and slept with me the next two nights. Nancy's dad came down the next morning true to form, but I was in bed with Ruth and not his daughter. He said nothing, fooled around in the freezer, and went back upstairs. I never had the guts to ask him what he thought about me and the girls. I do know he was happy with his "free" deer meat. With vacation over, Ruth and I went back to school with Nancy on Sunday. It was weird driving with two women whom I'd just slept with, who are roommates, and who both pretended not to know about the other's relationship with me. I didn't bring it up, and we just talked about school.

I went out shooting with Zoomer, and I gave him my Remington .22 automatic rifle because it was plastic and easy to shoot one-handed. He had a bolt- action and had to tuck it under his chin or between his legs when he wanted to cock it. We went out in his new beautiful Pontiac GTO that his Dad had gotten him. We were doing road kill from the car, so Zoomer was loading his new acquisition and I was driving. All of a sudden the gun went off in the car, which scared the willies out of us in such a close environment. Zoomer looked at me sheepishly as I pulled the car over. He knew he screwed up, and it had discharged through the floorboards of his new car and then fortunately had ricocheted off the highway and away from the car. I doubt if he ever told his dad, because he was about to graduate and go law school the following fall. It was a small hole, and sometimes things are best left unsaid. We went out drinking later, and he took me to a guy who was giving IQ tests. I don't remember it well, but Zoomer told me I scored so high that the guy's statistics were garbage for his hypothesis. He was amazed I did so well, especially since I was under the influence.

I didn't do so well under the influence on my Russian history final. I had a C on the midterm and an A for the classroom presentation. My speech was on Napoleon's invasion of Russia. When we got to the battle of Borodino, I began drawing the troop movements on the blackboard. I noticed the first move of the Russians looked like a six, so I showed the French movement as a nine and chatted to the class. I told them in summation that "through a series of gross maneuvers, Napoleon won." I then circled the sixty-nine on the board. It took a minute, but I got a big laugh and then finished the speech. The class was on Wednesday night from six to nine during prime drinking time. I forgot the final was the night in question and had been in a beer fight with some girls at the Southgate Tap. Someone asked me if I had Russian history, and I said that I did, and they related that the final would be taking place momentarily. I quickly rushed to class in my beer-soaked TKE sweatshirt without anything to write with or on. (In those days, you brought a blue book to class to write your essays.) Fortunately, the girls were well prepared, and I mooched a pen and a blue book. I was given the test and wrote one paragraph on the first question before nodding off. When I woke up, forty- five minutes were gone, and everyone was busily writing. I was sick to my stomach, so I left and went to the bathroom without even asking permission. I barely made it in and was throwing up in the urinal when the teacher arrived. He said he was sorry and left me to my misery. I completed my mission, went back to class, and turned in my one paragraph. Everyone else was on his or her second blue book when I left. The professor must have taken pity on me and thrown out the test, because I still got a B for the course.

Ruth was taking elementary education and had to take the classes she was going to teach. She told me toward the end of the semester that she was flunking sixth-grade geography. It would ruin her college career, and she was worried. I told her I would take her final for her and get her an A so she would get a C for the course. I stupidly went to her final, signed in as Ruth, and took the final. Fortunately for me, they didn't check student identification then, or I'd have been thrown out of school. It was mostly girls in the test, but no one said a thing. I got her an A, and they even gave her a B for the course. Ruth whined a lot, and I had no confidence in her as a human being, so I figured it was time to move on. She wasn't really broken up about it, so I must have been a right decision. She was quickly dating an independent (non-fraternity) guy who was several ranks above me in ROTC and a senior. No grass would ever grow under Ruth's feet.

In the fraternity (Tau Kappa Epsilon), we had a complicated way of defining relationships, which the women then absolutely subscribed to. A date was first, and if you wanted her to feel special (like the most important of your dates), you gave her one of your TKE sweatshirts. If you wanted to go steady, then you gave her a lavaliere (a necklace with TKE suspended from it). The next step was the big one when you gave her your fraternity pin. This was engaged to be engaged (before a ring but a solid commitment). The next step was the rock (engagement ring). The women wanted to be pinned, serenaded, and achieve social status with their name in the paper. Women were in love with being in love.

I decided to be a player. The player days culminated when I stupidly pinned three different girls simultaneously, and they even lived in the same dorm. I borrowed two of my fraternity brothers' pins and was a total cad. At the university, the campus paper only came out on Thursday, so all announced pinning the company had to be in by Wednesday morning. I would break up with each of them on Tuesday for some lame reason and re-pin them on Thursday, Friday, and Saturday nights. This would save the embarrassment of campus knowledge via the paper and save my fraternity brothers the hassle of the sweetheart sing. (For the sing, we would all go to the place the girl lived with candles and sing sweetheart songs outside her window.)

Girls fascinated me, and I started to push to see what they would do. They were so in love with being in love, and being pinned was the goal almost more than the person they were dating. I would make up "secret" rituals, and they loved it. We had to be pinned at the Southgate Tap upstairs on the left cup of the brassiere with two or more witnesses. They would whip their top up in front of a couple of my frat brothers and stick their left breast out to receive their reward. Eventually, all this chicanery caught up with me (deservedly so). The girls saw each other in the hall on a Sunday or Monday and began talking about the guys they were pinned to and discovered to their chagrin they were all pinned to the same idiot. They called me over and confronted me, and I knew I was toast. One of the girls flushed my pin down the toilet, one threw a pin at me, and the other wanted to stay pinned. The pins were very expensive, and it cost me a month's worth of summer wages to replace one of my fraternity brother's pins. I decided then I was not created for subterfuge, and I would stick to board games and not play romantic games. Relationships are too complicated by themselves to add anything else, and if you're honest and it fails, you can still live with yourself.

I know I'm partially demented, and this funnels externally with my sense of humor. Zoomer would not wash his fake arm. It had a pocket that fit where his armpit was, and it smelled when he took the arm off. I told him about it and asked him to wash it, but because it wasn't noticeable with the arm on, he wouldn't take the time to clean it. The next night when he hadn't washed it, I took a pen and wrote him a note that said, "If you don't wash me, I'm leaving home for good!" I then put the pen in the hand of the arm and left the point of it on the exclamation mark's period. When he didn't wash the arm the next night, I took it and hid it. He went to bed a lot earlier than I did, and I slept in so he came and woke me up whining about his arm. I told him I heard the arm mumbling about finding a responsible master and saw it leave around two o'clock in the morning, hitchhiking eastward.

He was upset because he would have to go to class without his cosmetic adornment. I had put the arm on the skull of our fraternity pin symbol that hung below our bedroom window. When Zoomer was walking out, I hailed him. He looked up to see his arm on the skull's head. He quickly returned and refitted his pseudo-appendage. He did wash the arm finally that night, so the next morning I got up early and lit a cigarette and put it in the arms hand and had it sticking out of his closet when he got back from the bathroom. There was never a doubt who the evil perpetrator/transgressor was in violating the arm's normal hands-off motif. A little later our house president was having a hissy fit over how clean our rooms were, so I had the arm visit his room. I had string run all around, messed everything up, and had shaving cream everywhere with the arm holding the shaving cream can hanging out of the President Rich's closet.

I had to give a speech on a famous quotation. It had to be less than three minutes, use a visual aid, and be something the class remembered. I also had to illustrate the point of the quote. I was out partying the night before and forgot to do the homework (typical dung-head guy). I woke up late (imagine that), realized my dilemma, grabbed a pair of my underwear, and stuffed them in my pocket before racing to class. When I got there, the class was already in session, and I received the cold "nice of you to join us, Mr. C," line from the teacher. He then criticized the prior speaker and admonished the class for their lack of creativity.

He asked me for my outline, and I quickly scribbled one line on a piece of paper and went to the front of the class. I got up in front of the class and said, "Brevity is the soul of wit!" I pulled out my underwear, held them up to the class, and said, "Be Brief!" Then I sat down. The class was stunned and thought I was going to get back up and continue the monologue. I, of course, had nothing more. Slowly, the brighter ones realized it was over and started to laugh, and pretty soon, the whole class was roaring. The teacher gave my one-line scribbled outline back with the note "A+ A one-time function. N'est Pas?"—which is French for "You understand?" I ended up with a 3.0 for the semester and a B in every course, and everyone, including my parents, fainted. They were so used to my underachieving that they didn't know how to act when I made the dean's list.

I was at the student union, and people were playing chess. I was pretty good, so I trashed five guys in quick order. One of them turned out to be on the University of South Dakota chess team. He asked me to play a particular guy, so I did and beat him. But I had to think more than I did with the first five guys. I found out he was the number-one seed on the chess team. He wanted me to join, but I didn't have the time. We had a chess team from Moorhead State come to USD, so I agreed to play. I won every match and beat their number-one board and their coach.

My mom (when I was five), Mr. Cl (my junior high chess coach), Mr. Mosevich (my high school chess coach), and Mr. S. (a neighbor who was really good and played European masters) had all had a turn at my chess instruction. I also studied it for classic openings (king's gambit, Berlin defense, etc.) for a couple of years. I was no master, but I could hold my own. I did beat Bobby Fisher in a round-robin. (He was playing sixty people at a time in the mid- seventies at Governor's State University, and I was one of two who defeated him. He beat fifty-five and had three draws. I have no doubt in my mind he could destroy me on the chessboard one to one. In a round- robin like that you don't have time to plan more than a complete move ahead, whereas I could plan two moves ahead while he was elsewhere. After the victory over Moorhead, the chess team wanted me to go with them to all events. I told them I only wanted to be a substitute and didn't have time for full-time status or road trips.

They went on their next gig without me and lost, so to their credit, they kidnapped me for the next away match. The match was an all-day Saturday tournament at the University of Minnesota. I was out drinking and carousing on Friday, and on my way home, they stopped me walking and offered me a beer. (I really needed another at two o'clock in the morning.) I got in their car and woke up with daylight.

I was in Minneapolis. I was hung over, and they brought me to the tournament. The first game I was pathetic and would make my move punch the clock, and my head would hit the desk. The adversary clock, and my head would hit the desk. The adversary would wake me up, and I would quickly move and pass out again. I think I lost in twenty moves. My team all lost, so we were in trouble. They took me out to lunch and got food and a Coke in me. I woke up, and we went back.

I then beat one school's top seed, so I got a match with "the man." He was the University of Minnesota's top seed, and he was great. We made fourteen moves without even a pawn loss. He methodically pushed me back off the board, so anywhere I moved, I would lose more than I would gain. We played with chess clocks. Each player had fifteen minutes on his clock. If your flag dropped, you lost. It didn't matter how much ahead you were. When you moved, your clock was on, and as soon as you moved, you hit your clock, which started the other player's clock. He can think, but he wants to think on your time so he moves quickly and hits his clock so yours starts. I knew I had to change the pace of our match, because this guy was way better than I was. I deliberately made a bad move and took a pawn with a major piece to destroy his insurmountable wall. I hit my clock, and he sat up straight for the first time and really studied the board hard. I began to plan my retreat, because as soon as he discovered the ruse, I would be doomed. As he pondered the situation in confusion, his coach and nonplaying teammates surrounded him in silent awe. I had to act like I was on the brilliant coup of a lifetime and had hatched a magnificent counter to his unstoppable attack.

He pondered for five minutes until one of his buddies told him about the clock, and he began to act. Our game went into high gear with lightning moves and much destruction on my side as he began to power me out and hit his clock quickly. I used my troops like flak to slow his attack and scrambled to keep my king safe. He killed all of my men, so I only had a naked king, and he was ahead by a bishop (that I threw away) and two pawns that could be promoted to queens. As he harassed my king with his bishop and king, he drove his pawns across the board to become a queen. He got one and made one move to check me. I quickly moved, I hit my clock, and his flag dropped. I still had seven minutes left, and I had beaten the all-state champ. He was livid with the loss and wanted a rematch immediately. I told him maybe next tournament but suggested that he practice his time management. We ended up with a trophy for third place in the tournament (my early loss cost us second), so the team was elated. The college had its first chess team trophy. It was by far the best match I'd ever played, and I decided to quit the circuit on that high note. I never played in university competition again, although later I did hustle chess in bars.

At Christmas, I returned to Illinois by hitchhiking as usual. I met Madonna, who was in a hurry to see me. We went out, parked, and made out and got into some heavy petting. She offered herself up for sex and had lied to me that she was eighteen as she had done each year. (She was only seventeen at the time.) She was still a virgin, and I was tempted but had a mental problem with having sex with an "innocent" woman. When I wouldn't copulate with her, she later told me that her attitude changed about premarital relations, and she decided to wait for a while before having sex. The next night I took her out again and was mad at myself for not taking advantage of the situation. I tried the same stuff, but she refused me and I became even madder.

A couple of nights later she was babysitting somewhere in Glenwood, and I showed up. She had put the baby to sleep, and we got in to the owners' booze. We got completely naked and danced around the house. I held her upside down off the floor and gave her first oral sex. We didn't have sex, but we made out and fondled a lot. I was going back to school soon, so I asked for her underwear and she asked for mine. I gave her my briefs, which she put on along with her skirt and blouse, and I put her stuff in my jacket and got dressed. She passed out, and I left, driving like I was in a ship avoiding enemy torpedoes in an erratic zigzag pattern. She was still passed out when the people came home. They had to drag her to their car and have her parents put her to bed, and I'm sure they had to wonder about the men's underwear she had on. She was never asked to babysit there again.

The college decided to raise money, so they put on an ugly man contest. Each dorm and fraternity could enter a man, and people would vote by putting pennies in big jars. Only pennies would count in the total tally (I have no idea why pennies only if they were trying to raise money), and half of the money would be split with the winner. The jars were placed in the student union, and each participant would walk around all week in costume and solicit votes (pennies). Each contestant's picture was going to be in the student paper, so I wanted an unusual outfit or concept. I opted for concept and became "the Whistler." I cut a sweatshirt out to emulate a hairline. It had sideburns under my arms and a Beatle-like cut at the top of my chest. I took cold cream and mixed dried tempera paint in it and painted my nipples blue to look like eyes and created luscious red lips around my belly button. I then drew a nose above my navel, ears on each side by the sideburns, and eyebrows above my blue eyes (nipples) to complete the visage. I wore a sweatshirt (the same color as the one I cut up for a hairline) over the face, and no one knew I was in the contest. Everyone else wrecked their faces to look like bums or pirates and wore corresponding outfits.

When I wanted to get money, I would raise the sweatshirt, which would cover my face and arms; plus, it looked like hair on top of the head of my face (belly). I didn't speak, but I moved my belly in and out while I whistled the school's fight song. My navel went in, making it looked like a mouth, and the lips around it were pursed like they were blowing, so the face actually looked like it was whistling. The guys would roar and give me money, and the girls were grossed out and would pay me to leave them alone. I was by far the front-runner until corruption set in. The Lambda Chi house decided they wanted to win the trophy, so they went to the local bank and bought $150 in pennies and stuffed their jar. The contest ended in two days, and there weren't enough pennies to get from students to make up the difference. Even if I collected enough money to cash in, all the local pennies were gone. I met this new student from Scarsdale, New York, and he said he could help me. He fronted me $200 and a ride to Sioux City, Iowa, if I would replace his investment and split the pot with him. I agreed, and we drove the thirty miles to Iowa and purchased the pennies. We didn't drop them in until the last minute. It looked very close, so Lambda Chi approached me and said the escalation of pennies was ridiculous and demanded the trophy. I told them I would give them the trophy, but I wanted the cash and forty extra dollars for the insult. They agreed, because they weren't trying for the money at all, just making sure they got a trophy for their fraternity house. I withdrew from the contest prior to the ballot counting, and they won. There was about $900 collected from everyone, so we got $450. I gave Bob from Scarsdale his $200 and $125 from my share. I got another $40 from the Lambda Chi house and made $165 for the week. (Jobs on campus paid less than a dollar an hour then.) Bob also told me my eyebrows had grown together and got me to pluck the center out. I wasn't comfortable about it, but he was right. I was starting to look like a Cro-Magnon, so I was glad I listened to him.

I got a job at the Southgate Tap as a bouncer. The bouncer sat at the front door and asked for identification to make sure the place was protected in case the police would check up. Actually, it's to the advantage of the business to let underage people in because it leads to greater sales and more profits. The disadvantage is in the fines or closure for being caught. Having me guard the door was like having a fox guard the chicken coop. One advantage would be my expertise in spotting fake identification, but I really never had the heart to use that power given the fact that I was such an abuser of the system. I was a junior, and one of my skills was the ability to spot freshman girls. They would come down to the Tap and try to get in without identification. If we were busted and they didn't at least have some sort of credible identification, the establishment would be closed. I had some attractive (but too young) girls try to get in to dance and drink. They had no purses and claimed they had left them in somebody's car. I told them I needed two forms of identification, and this one girl came up close to me, showed me her breasts, and asked if they would do for her two pieces of identification. I had to admire her resolve, and after a minute of contemplation on the shape and size of her weapons, I decided she could enter the establishment. I whispered to her that if the police did show up, she was to leave by the back door through the kitchen as rapidly as possible. I'm too easy.

I've always had a special pride with my ability at games, knowledge, and trivia. In the sixties, there was a show on Saturday afternoon called College Bowl. Different schools were academically challenged with pop-up questions, and if they were correctly answered, the team got a chance at a bonus question. The pop-up question was given to the first one who hit the buzzer on his desk. If you hit it too soon, you wouldn't get the whole question, so timing was everything. If you got it wrong, then you paid a penalty. I went to the competition with three of my fraternity brothers. Whoever won would get to go on national television for regional college bowl action. I was good, and I really wanted to be on TV with the program. We had our local match, and I was in seventh heaven. My team members were slow, but I didn't care because I could do it without them if necessary. It was fast and furious, and we won an opening round and then proceeded to the finals. I answered two-thirds of our questions, and my fast hands got the drop on the other team's buzzers. A toss-up question was worth only ten points, and a bonus question was worth twenty-five points. My team was upset with me, because I was hitting the buzzer so fast they couldn't keep up. I explained that even if we missed every other question, the bonus was worth twice as much and then some, so we'd be way ahead of the other teams.

I guessed and won at some really outrageous questions like, "What's the Hottentot word for antelope?" and I hit the buzzer in record time and said, "Gnu!" Everyone was amazed, but it was the only weird word I knew for antelope. I also got the question, "How many species of mushrooms are there?" It was a fill-in-the-blank toss-up question where everyone got to respond. We were last to guess. The first team said 100, the second said 350, and the third said 1,000. I just said 1,001 and effectively won, because the answer was 20,000 and we were closest. One question I challenged the organization on was, "What war first saw jet planes in combat?" They should have said US jet planes but didn't, and I said World War II with the ME-262. They ruled me wrong and said it was the Korean War with the Saber jet, and I argued their source. They said it was the World Book Encyclopedia, and I've never trusted the World Book since.

We got down to near the end, and Craig, our English major and team captain (decided by overall grade point), got a toss-up question right. Our twenty-five- point bonus question was, "What is the capital of Australia?" We were behind by five points from the lead team, and this was the last question. I told my three teammates I knew this one, and we were all set. I told them the answer was Canberra, and Craig and another team member said they'd never heard of Canberra and thought it was Sydney. The other team member thought it was Melbourne. I told them it didn't matter what they thought; I knew the capital. Then the third guy changed his vote to Sydney from Melbourne. Craig said the three of them had outvoted me, and Sydney was going to be the response. I told him voting had nothing to do with the correct response, and they were making a big mistake. I said half of their majority thought Melbourne was right and if they said Sydney, they would cost us an appearance on national television. They refused to listen, and Craig (the captain who had to respond to bonus and group-decided questions) told the judges Sydney, and I didn't get to go on television. Some people never get the vision; others see it and can't execute. I guess I got to see it and had the ability to execute it but was blocked by those who never see. I never spoke to any of them again.

I was out early drinking on the east side of Vermilion at a place called Taco Town. I was low on funds and was looking to hustle some beer when in came Ruth, whom I haven't seen in several months. She was still dating a senior ROTC officer named Jim and was driving his car. She had moved out of the dorm and was living in the trailer park. She started buying me beer and showed me all the money Jim had given her and her engagement ring. After a few pitchers, she said she wanted to take me for a ride in his car, so I agreed. We bought a six-pack and went to her trailer. I told her I was glad things had worked out so well for her, and then she wanted to have sex. I accommodated her, and we had a really nice roll in her finance's bed. She gave me a speech about being bored with Jim and said she wanted to come back with me, but I declined. She was hurt and upset, so I left, but I wished her the best anyway.

The Summer of 1968

I worked for my stepdad again at Homewood Cabinet Top but out in the shop. I basically loaded the custom tops for local delivery and helped the drivers set their deliveries up for the day. One of the drivers was dating a married secretary, and he was also married. So, we double-dated and went to a motel with a pool out on Governor's Highway. The pool was by the main road, so we got one room for the four of us. I brought Phyllis, who was still very interested in me, but I had a hard time because she was a friend of my sister. We were in the room drinking and making out, and we could tell the driver and the secretary wanted the room for what it was intended for. So, I asked Phyllis if she wanted to go for a swim. (It was summer.) She said she didn't have a suit, and I said I didn't either but suggested we go skinny-dipping. She surprisingly agreed, and off we went.

I stripped down quickly and got up on the diving board. The pool lights were off because it was late, but on the diving board I could see the highway clearly, and they could see me. I did a flip off the board and swam over to Phyllis at the shallow end. She was acting shy and covering up her huge breasts. (She was dark haired, five four, and slightly chunky, but very curvy and attractive.) She had a large, dark bush I could see even though it was under a couple feet of water. I don't know why she was covering her breasts up, and I didn't ask. I just went over and hugged her and gave her a nice, long kiss. I think that made her more comfortable, and we began to play in the water. We never had any sex or even petting, just kissing, although some of the kissing was serious. We goofed around for an hour and then wrapped towels around ourselves and went back to the room where the driver and secretary were passed out in different beds. We woke them up. The guy was worried because his wife would find out, and the woman was really worried because it was after midnight and she was going to be in trouble with her spouse also. I took Phyllis home, and the light in the front room was on at her parents' house. It was after four o'clock in the morning by now, and her dad was still waiting up. I really liked her dad and felt bad. I tried to take the blame for it, but he didn't even want to talk to me. Phyllis was looking like a bad kid, not a free spirit who just skinny-dipped in a motel pool. Her dad and I would become friends again later, but for now, I was a despoiler of women and children.

I was going to be twenty-one in August, so two weeks before my birthday, I threw away my fake identification. I'd been drinking in bars for years but figured I shouldn't chance an arrest now that I was so close to becoming legal age. Well, as soon as I did that, I was thrown out of every place I'd previously drank. I couldn't believe that no one would serve me. My confidence was shot, and even though I'd been to the places before, my lack of identification verification must have shown through. Again, irony sets in after three years of cheating the system. I took it for granted that I could get served anywhere and now I couldn't get a sip in my own back yard. I also dated Madonna (my future wife), but I only considered her as a date at this point and was still thinking about returning to USD. We would go to movies and make out a lot (she was a wonderful kisser), but nothing more.

My Senior Year, 1968–69

The fall of 1968 was my fall from college. I had brought my cousin Lee, who never graduated from high school, with me to college. He had "slipped" through the system by going to junior college part- time and accumulating a GPA over 3.5. We were only six weeks apart in age and had known each other from birth. Lee was manipulative and easily got through the system at USD to become a full-time student. He loved sociology and psychology and majored in social psychology. He got a trailer near the campus, but the propane leaked profusely, and Lee always looked groggy. I used to yell at him to get it fixed, but he refused for whatever reason. So, when I visited him, I would open the door, throw in a lit match, and watch the look of shock appear on his face before closing the door. He would be really bummed out and start complaining, and then I would tell him to get the gas leak fixed. We finally found him passed out in the snow from the gas, and he had to go to the hospital. He was a hard case. He would borrow my car, take a girl to a motel, and run out on the bill. I would get the car back and a call about an unpaid bill that matched my license number. He would lie and deny it, but the description by the night manager would match him and his current girlfriend perfectly. I was drinking heavily at this time and cutting classes. I would sleep in late. The sun bothered me when it shone in the window, so I painted my windows black with Rust-O-Ileum paint.

In addition to my cousin my sister transferred from Northern Illinois University. She had a boyfriend named Bill K who was coming to visit her. He needed a place to stay, so I hooked him up at the TKE house. I was glad to see her with a date, although I had gotten her dates with several of my fraternity brothers in the past. At the time, I was hoping she'd get laid and lighten up a little. Bill moved in, and coincidentally, Lee's brother Mike also came up for a visit. I got a spot for Mike to stay at the TKE house also. Everything was going great until twenty-five dollars of mine disappeared. I spoke up for my guests as the scandal unfolded, and I knew Mike would never consider lifting my money because I'd give it to him if he asked. With Bill, I assumed if my sister liked him, he was okay. Mike thought it was someone else and beat on him to no avail. It turned out to be Lauren's guy Bill. I met him later in a bar after they broke up, and he apologized but never repaid me.

I saw Ruth one last time. I went out to Beresford (small town six miles east of campus) to drink at Wimps with a group of friends. Ruth was there with her Jim and two other couples. She was quite pregnant and hadn't been able to see her feet since mid-July. She looked at me and then my date and suddenly grew considerably louder and began having the best time of her life. She even got out and danced to a fast song. I called the waitress over after she sat down and sent Ruth a drink. I gave the waitress a tip and told her to tell Ruth "name it after me" when she gave her the drink. Well, the waitress did, and Ruth became unglued. She started throwing things everywhere, and her group had to physically remove her from Wimps and take her home. My comment must have hit too close to home. She wasn't enrolled at school for the fall term, and I don't know if she ever came back. But, she had her man (and a child too), so I hope everything worked out for her.

To enable my alcohol consumption, I took a job as a houseboy for the Alpha Gamma Delta sorority. I had to bus their tables, be a lackey for all kinds of jobs, and clean up the kitchen. For this, my meals were paid for, so I could use the money for the bars. It was fun showing up early to work, because I always caught some girl in her underwear (or they let me catch them; I could never really figure that one out). On one school day, I took one of the sorority girls out dancing and drinking at a local bar with Lee and his date. As we were slow dancing, I was kissing on her neck and wondered if I could spell my initials in hickeys on her neck. I then proceeded (to her delight at the moment) to write a large T on the right side of her neck and then a C on her left side. We were trashed by this time, so I took her home. We had just kissed not anything else. The next day I got a call from the Alpha Gamma Delta house that my services were no longer required. I asked why, and the woman on the phone said it was because I had mutilated one of their members. I had just got out of bed, and three thousand students already knew what a bastard I was. I found out the hickeys stood out like a sore thumb, and the girl was wearing a turtle neck and heavy makeup to hide them. You could read the TC all the way across the room. It was some of my best artwork ever.

My sex life had been lacking for a few months, but everything was about to change. After my expulsion as houseboy, I was banned for dating by the sorority council as an unfit and immoral date. I was finally there! Nothing better could happen to you than being banned for immorality. The cutest sorority girls were all over me. Everyone wanted to take me out of town and be ravaged by me. I would not be an acceptable date at any formal or homecoming event. Oh darn— there would be no pomp and circumstance, only sex in sleazy roadside motels for poor me. Some weekends I would have two dates on the same night, and I was such a pig that I'd use the same motel room. I began to feel like I was a college course that all the cute girls had to complete before graduating. They each had their own style, but surprisingly, these cuter girls had little experience—maybe one or two intimate boyfriends over time. Doing them doggie style or in a bathroom with their rump on the sink and a leg on each door of the vanity was a new and exciting event for their diaries I guess. I didn't get attached to any of them; it was more like hunting and just bagging the limit.

Of course, if I wanted to go to a formal, I could bring an independent, but never a sorority girl. I asked this independent, Judy H, who was six foot one and I just knew had a pair of high heel shoes. She was a big, curvy, farm girl but not fat. I could tell she hadn't dated much but was willing to learn. I met her for some beers and a dance out at Taco Town and asked her to the fall formal. She immediately accepted, and I was to pick her up around seven o'clock Friday night. I was a total pig with this unfortunate woman. I got ready for our date with my best threads but decided to stop for a quick one at a local bar. I arrived to pick her up three-fourths loaded just before nine o'clock. Her roommate came down to talk, because Judy was done with me. She had been ready at seven and started to call the fraternity house at seven thirty. By eight thirty, she had given up and undressed after spending all day on hair, outfit, makeup, and whatever. I said, "Well I'm here now if she's willing to give it a go." The roommate told me what hole to crawl into after she found out I wasn't late for any good reason. Undaunted, I returned to the familiarity of the local pubs to imbibe in the golden nectar.

I was still the social chairman and looking for creative ways to utilize my meager budget. I met with the president of Burgess Hall (a senior named Elaine H) to plan an independent/Greek street dance where we split the cost. I set up the place and blatantly lied about the costs of beer and music. My philosophy was to distort it enough to get them to pay for the beer and band from their half, and we could have a party for free. Dastardly dude that I was, it worked, and the trusting, honest, and really nice Elaine was taken in my silver-tongued deviltry. I momentarily felt guilty, but I quickly drank myself careless and was over it. The street dance was at the local park in a parking lot, and Elaine and I showed up early to get everything ready. I got the band set up and the keg tapped, while she set out cups and snacks. The fraternity showed up reluctantly, and the girls were herded to one side of the parking lot. After a couple of beers and several dance songs, no one had begun dancing, and the party was looking bad. I grabbed Elaine, and just the two of us began dancing, first fast and then slow. Then, finally, a couple others dared to dance, and pretty soon, all were dancing and having a good time. I had only purchased one keg and the band for an hour and a half. The band and the keg ran out quickly. Those who struck it up had dates for the rest of the evening, and the rest went home.

Elaine and I hit it off pretty well, and I took her out for another beer and then returned her to her dorm before midnight. Elaine was slender with light-brown hair and was majoring in mycology (the study of mushrooms). She was already working on her master's in some courses even though she hadn't officially graduated. She was someone to admire; she came from a poor, large family and worked her way through school with scholarships and lifeguarding at the public pool. She was an introvert but very industrious and caring, almost saint-like in character. I was her antithesis, and they say opposites attract. She was very interested in me, but she kissed terribly and had absolutely no sexual experience at all. I couldn't fault her, and I was at a dilemma as to what to do with her. I felt like a flame, and she was an innocent moth; in retrospect, it was probably her best protection from me. I would go out with her and get her trashed-on beer or whatever, and she never complained. She was just glad to be included. When she was sick and throwing up, I couldn't believe how polite and delicate she was. I don't recall any woman ever throwing up as dignified and quietly as she did. She was so good that I felt almost evil just by comparison, even if I wasn't doing anything bad.

We began to date off and on quite regularly. She loved making out with me, but I started feeling like I was this terrible influence in her life. I gave her a sweatshirt, then a TKE lavaliere, and finally pinned her and then took it back. I made up some communist propaganda about why I couldn't be pinned to her, and she was hurt but didn't complain. It felt more like a reward that she earned than deep love or biological lust. She was willing, but I never felt any heat. She turned out to be my lab monitor for biology, which was part of her scholarship requirements, and it was weird being in a class (not the lecture hall) where she was in charge. We each had to give a lecture to the class on a biological function. I did mine on the reproductive system of the Homo sapiens male. I knew I could pull it off if I stuck to technical terms and did not laugh for any reason. I drew a huge penis on the blackboard with a scrotum, gonads, and the correct plumbing attachments and a small stick figure of a girl. The audience was jovial to say the least, especially since everyone knew me by this time. I described an interlude where the girl removed her clothes, excited the man, and caused an ejaculation from oral sex. I drew an exorbitant amount of sperm that coated the stick figure to the total demise of my audience. I was the only one not laughing, and several students were off their stools on the floor.

I was out drinking, again, and I stole my own car. I was driving home totally three sheets to the wind, and I ran out of gas. I left my door open and got out to flag a cop down. I told him the car was out of gas and explained that I would get it the following day. I walked home and went to bed. The next morning, I arose and looked out the window to see my car wasn't where I usually parked. I always left the key in the ignition, so I figured someone was joyriding. I could not recall any of the prior evening's events, so I waited for an hour and then called the police. They began to investigate, and I went down to the station after they called in the afternoon and said they had impounded it. I gave an eloquent speech about the incompetence of the police department, unnecessary harassment of university students, and the lack of real crime control. I told them about the sorry state of these United States when criminals could run rampant, unchecked, by the powers paid to protect the good citizens of the community. When the afternoon shift got there, they related my participation in the car theft and reiterated that the only crime was in my mind. I paid the impounding fee and quietly left with my hat in hand and tail between my legs.

A bunch of the football jocks were drunk one night and came by the fraternity house and began to throw beer bottles through the windows. The flying glass cut both Ron F and Bruce M. I got upset at the audacity and affront of the action, so I went into action mode. I ran upstairs and grabbed my 20-gauge pump shotgun and threw seven shells in it. (I had removed the plug in the tube.) I ran out the front door into the front of the crowd of fifty-some people. They weren't intimidated, so I picked an open spot on the ground in the light and fired a round. The grass flew up, and they knew I was serious. They began to disperse rapidly down Main Street. The street had arched elm trees overhead, so I fired a round into the trees over their heads, so they could hear the lead shot whiz through the leaves. When I did that, they accelerated their running considerably and ran through yards. In their haste in the dark, they got into clotheslines, ran into birdbaths, and fell over all sorts of objects. They did far more damage to themselves than I had intended. Some of them called later and wanted to talk to the "asshole with the gun," so I answered the phone. I received a lot of threats about getting my shotgun placed in my rectum, so I said, "Come on over. All I saw last time was elbows and assholes, and it would be nice to meet you."

My attitude was changing, and I was starting to get a chip on my shoulder. There was a bottle club just a couple of miles outside of town we called the Pleasant Pheasant, because you could always get a drink there. The off-sale liquor (state liquor stores sold bottles only) closed at eight o'clock, and on-sale (in the bars by drink only) closed at one o'clock in the morning, except Saturday it closed at midnight and no liquor could be sold on Sunday. They got around the law by charging admission and calling it a private member club. You couldn't have beer but could buy mix in a glass with ice. You then put your bottle in a paper bag on your table (almost like a roaring twenties speakeasy). If you showed up after midnight, they would sell you a bottle of Kessler's blended bourbon under the table so you could still participate. This was not a college bar, and the clientele was primarily local farmers and their families. I had a bad attitude, and so did they. Like the old John Wayne movies, we decided to take it outside and battle it out.

The first night it was pretty fair, and I think I got through seven guys before I hit the ground for the night. I woke up with the birds tweeting and gravel in my face. My car door was open, the keys were in the ignition, and the interior light was still on in the gray of dawn light. The next time I went in they were more prepared, and I only got through three guys before someone finished me off. The last time I think they were getting tired of my attitude, so when I raised my right hand, someone from behind grabbed it. When I raised my left, someone else grabbed it, and then the guy I was fighting began to pummel me profusely. I didn't get anyone that night. When the birds were tweeting at the gray of dawn and I was picking the gravel out of my eye sockets, I noticed my back, rump, and ribs were sore. Apparently, someone decided to dance on me (a local Fred Astaire wannabe?) and kick my ass. I decided the John Wayne tradition sucked, and it was time to forget drunken brawls.

My cousin Lee told me about a girl who came over to his trailer to party. He said she was an eighteen- year-old freshman virgin who decided she'd been one too long. One of the guys at Lee's party had brought her, and she asked to use Lee's bed for cherry destruction. She then proceeded to have this guy deflower her so she could get on with a college sex life. I was very impressed at the time with her attitude and wanted to meet her. It turned out her name was Leslie K, and her father was the state's attorney. Unfortunately, I was going with Elaine, so I declined an introduction at that time. I filed her name away for future reference.

I had heard all the girls talking about a Jean Dixon prediction that in a small Midwestern college, an axe- wielding man would murder eight girls in a sorority with Alpha and Gamma in its name. I was dating the president of the Alpha Gamma Delta sorority and knew they were scared about it on the particular week it was supposed to take place. They had a cop stationed downstairs in the living room. I, like an idiot, called her up on her private line in my normal voice and said; "If you don't get that cop out of there, I'm coming over with an axe and killing eight of you." I thought it was funny, and they didn't. I was to be kicked out of school and sued unless I volunteered to leave myself. The school administration said I violated phone use and would be prosecuted by Ma Bell unless I took some psychological exams. They had a resident shrink who administered the inkblot test, and I approached it like a game. They would show me an inkblot, and I would look at it and decide what the overall theme of it was. (Later, you had to show where it was.) Then I put an imaginary chessboard over the drawing and divided it up in to sixty-fourths (A through H along the top and 1 through 8 going down the side). Then I could tell the shrink what I saw in c3, e5, etc., and later point it out to him. This process usually takes the shrink fifteen to twenty minutes to finish with a normal patient. I had him writing for almost three hours. When they came back with the report, they said I was probably brilliant but would most likely run down the street with my shirt open slaying old ladies with a butcher's knife. I foolishly listened to these pseudo- psychiatrists (as did my parents), and I dropped out of school for my "own good" and went to a local shrink in Illinois.

My new shrink's name was Fe, and after a quick interview, he said I had to be admitted to a hospital immediately. He couldn't do it. I had to sign myself in, and then he had the power over me until he said I could leave. (Understand that I couldn't stop treatment once it started. He was totally in control.) I was checked in to Our Lady of Mercy in Dyer, Indiana. In the late sixties, they still did electric and chemical shock therapy. It's kind of like erasing your hard drive and reinstalling the software. (This practice was eventually outlawed by society.) He put me in total wacko lab with the real space cadets (a ploy to get me to totally focus on him as my savior). They called it intensive care.

We all had tan pajamas and lived in tan rooms with tan curtains. We had a day room with puzzles, and each morning they would bring us each a cup of coffee. This one patient would take his coffee and pour it on the floor and then take off his pajamas and wipe it up naked. The nurses would admonish him, and he would go bonkers, yelling and screaming. They would have to restrain him in a bed with leather wraps. Now this was every day, so you'd think they would stop bringing him the coffee; he never drank it anyway. My roommate Tony was this older Italian guy who was Mr. Victorian of prim and proper. He was a decent chess player, so I at least had some entertainment. I used to think he was fairly okay, but I caught him in the stairwell with this girl who could barely talk and had the blank eyes. She had a huge rump but was very slender from the waist up. She and Tony were hugging, but Tony had his hands around her and was squeezing her buttocks like Mr. Whipple does Charmin. He was drooling all over her shoulders and making some strange animal sounds. Everybody has their thing I guess, but Tony didn't live up to his own standards. He was being given electric shock therapy two to three times a week, but I guess some things can overshadow brainwashing. It's not legal now, but in the late sixties, you could use electricity or chemicals to brainwash someone, and then the hospital would use religion to fill the void after destroying the brain. We had nuns in the place to provide any and all mental programming. They would come for Tony around nine o'clock in the morning and wheel back a total space cadet around eleven o'clock. The other vultures would hover around until they brought his lunch and steal him blind. (Tony didn't seem to mind.) For fun, about ten minutes before the shock crew arrived, we would tell Tony, "Guess what day it is?" And then go on to tell him he was going to be brainwashed. By the time the guards arrived, he was ready to fight, and we had our own Friday Night at the Fights show. I met a guy in there who was a heavy drug user, and he told me all about LSD, Jimson weed, etc. I asked my shrink why I was there with all these whacked-out people, and Fe finally released me to Open (which had more freedom) and apologized with a lame excuse about how there wasn't enough room in Open for me. He began to place me in group therapy, and I got to know other dysfunctional people.

After moving to Open, we didn't have to wear tan pajamas all day and could have regular clothes. We could move around freely but couldn't leave the hospital. Downstairs there were pool tables, crafts, puzzles, and playing cards. Davie Jones was my friend there but was a foreboding character with a reputation. We played pool, and I found out he was in for drinking violence. He was mad at his girl and threw a heavy, padded armchair though her parents' front picture window. It took four cops to neutralize him when his girl's parents called in the violence. Alcohol had supposedly set him off in his environment.

I got a call from Phyllis's father, and he said he heard I was in lockup and asked me if he could do anything for me while I was incarcerated. I told him I could use a pint of Vodka, because it leaves the least amount of odor on your breath. He came over and smuggled a bottle of one hundred-proof Smirnoff Silver into the hospital (nuthouse). I couldn't put it in my room, so I went into the elevator, jammed it between floors, and opened the escape hatch on the roof. I left it up there so I could access it when needed. I had a nice talk with him, and he was worried about Phyllis and her boyfriend Walt up in Madison, Wisconsin. I told him that when I got out, I would look in to it for him. I got Davie the next day, and we went to the elevator. We jammed it between floors, and I opened the top and brought down the vodka. Davie couldn't believe it, and we quickly had a few ounces apiece and put the bottle back. We got off the elevator in the basement and went to the craft room, and for the first time, he went in. Davie had lost his cloud of doom and was a happy camper. He actually made some leather key chains and a wallet. I told him he didn't have a problem with alcohol, just women.

My shrink, Fe, began group therapy. We were the players, and he was the playwright. I watched in fascination to see him strip everyone bare and tell their inner most secrets and fears. He would browbeat the people to tears and then be the loving soul when they broke down and cried. He expected to be admired and revered by the men and loved completely by the women. I knew at that moment the only way to get out of this abomination was to emulate him. If I acted like him and looked like him, he'd have to say I was mentally okay. I began to grow large, bushy sideburns just like the pseudo-doctor. He had begun working on his law degree, so we talked about torts or contracts for casual conversation. In the group, I was as relentless as he was in getting to the other person. I would hug when others broke down but was careful enough to let him intercede if he wanted the credit. I became his little helper and his shadow.

The time flew by, and I saw some weird things but the only one worth mentioning was an attractive new girl I met in the elevator. She was five eight and maybe 145 pounds and had long light-brown hair. She had on a puffy-sleeved, plaid dress and black shoes with short, white socks. I don't know her name, but she had a good figure and a nice but blank face. I always wondered if the nuns were reprogramming her after shock therapy or if she was spacey naturally. As we descended to the crafts in the elevator, she was making polite conversation about God or the weather when she began to slide down the corner of the elevator in a squatting position. She didn't bother to take off her white panties, which I could see clearly in her squatting position, and began to urinate. She got some on the back of her plaid dress and soaked her panties and the elevator floor. She never stopped her conversation or indicated that she had a problem of any kind. When she was finished, she stood up and walked away from the puddle. We got to the craft floor, and she walked out and past me to the areas, and I distinctly smelled asparagus so I figured she liked vegetables. Later I learned it's one of the few vegetables you can smell in urine. I don't know if that was a cry for help or if she was just bananas, but it was different.

I asked Fe at the group session if I could get some time away to see my parents at home, and he said he'd think about it. I played it cool and went on with my therapy-for-others bit. At the next meeting, Fe decided it was okay and said I could sign out for an extended weekend. I didn't tell my folks and decided to see Phyllis and Walt up in Wisconsin for her dad. She was going steady with Walt but dumped him one night a week to search for someone else. I told her I was coming up and that on Friday we could do whatever Walt wanted, but on Saturday we were to be alone. Walt was beside himself and wanted to know what we were going to do. (He was very jealous, and for good reason.) I told him it was nice to meet him and we'd go to the bars or whatever he wanted and to not worry about Phyllis because I would take care of her Saturday.

The next night we went out to places where Walt couldn't check on her. He was smothering her, and she was feeling the pressure. I didn't want to have her as a girlfriend, but I knew she needed help with Walt. We went out drinking and had a good time dancing, but when she wanted more, I had to cool her down. I got her home about four o'clock in the morning, and Walt was bummed. He didn't know what had happened, and I didn't tell him anything. I just put Phyllis to bed and crashed with her. I left early the next day and figured she could tell Walt whatever she wanted. If she wanted to distance herself from him, she had me as an excuse, and if she wanted to get closer, she could make up with him. I went and briefly visited my folks to their surprise and then returned to the nuthouse. Next group therapy, I was in top form trashing and then helping my fellow inmates.

We had a guy who was fairly normal but had a hang-up with money. He would pretend the world was okay until he had to pay for something. He would flip out over the cost of whatever it was and start pacing and complaining almost violently. The rest of the time, life was good. I asked him if he wanted to get out of the hospital, and he said he was perfectly content to stay. I then remarked how much per day or even per hour it must cost to stay there, and he started to boil. His arms started flaying and he was very adamant. I grabbed him and gave him a bear hug to stifle the convulsions and whispered in his ear that if he wanted to save money, he had to get out of there, and to get out of there, he had to get a grip on his money hang-ups. After a few minutes chanting about money savings and squeezing the breath out of him, he finally decided to calm down and save himself. I don't know if the money motivated him (probably) or if it was my "grasp" of his problem, but he did begin to work with the group at solving his problems and not just be content to stay. With that success, Fe decided to release me and just do office visits. I was his mini-me with sideburns and psychotherapy. I was released, and at the next appointment, I told Fe what I had done (growing the sideburns and acting like him so he couldn't say I was a problem), and then he went nuts. He said I was his only failure in fifteen years of practice (which I sincerely doubt) and how horrible everything was. I didn't care, because by getting out, I was allowed to go back to college.

I called Elaine back at school to tell her I was out and asked if she wanted to spend Christmas in Chicago. She had never even been out of South Dakota, so she was enthusiastic about the visit. I sent her a plane ticket, and she was coming the day after Christmas. Dad, in the meantime, was having problems with the whole nuthouse deal. He decided we should all get away and go to Puerto Rico for the balance of the vacation. I told him about Elaine coming, and he said no problem. She landed at O'Hare airport, and we had to take her shopping for summer clothes. We bought her a bikini and various outfits to wear in warmer climate. This was a totally unexpected shock for her, as she was planning on Chicago for ten days and now was heading to Puerto Rico. Given her background, I'm sure it was like watching a major weather front move through when my family did something. You have no real input; just watch the storm break and hope everything is all right.

The family took off for Puerto Rico (Mom, Dad, Page, Jim, Lauren, Elaine, and me). Page was eight, Jim was six, Elaine and I were twenty-one, and Lauren was still nineteen. When we got there, we stayed at the El Dorado Hilton (just west of San Juan) for the first night. It was a neat hotel with a saltwater pool, a regular pool, and a cove with ocean beach. I think Elaine was still in shock, and she bunked in with my sister. Mom and Dad had a room with the boys, and I had my own. I figured that was opportune, so if Elaine and I decided to go at it, we'd have a place. Everyone but me was tired and went to bed, so I put on a short-sleeved white shirt, some shorts, and sandals and decided to meet the people. I spoke no Spanish but was good at charades. I walked into the trashy neighborhood and got a beer. I learned to say quiero (key-yair-oh), which means "I want," and point at it. I could say beer, ice, water, yes, good, thanks, and such in a matter of no time. I would really pay attention to the person speaking and get the major emotional part of what was being said and just reply yes (si). I don't know if they were talking about home improvement or their wives cheating, but I went along, and there were plenty of people who wanted to chat. I would go to the jukebox and play a song. If everyone started singing, I would remember the number (B5) and play it again later. If no one responded, then I knew it was a loser and did not play it again.

I went to an area guarded next door, and it turned out to be an illegal cockfight. It was a small arena, and I was surprised that hardly anyone was sitting in the first row, so I foolishly grabbed a seat. I watched with intent as they brought out the first "contestants," and the money began to flow around the room. Certain people held money between their fingers in a specific order, and lots of negotiation was taking place. I didn't understand it, but it was obviously who would win or score the first bloodletting. As the fight ensued and the blows were tallied, the money changed hands. I began to be showered with blood and began to understand why the front row was vacant. No women were allowed inside but waited outside for their men. After the match, I went with several of the guys back to another nearby bar where they served food. It was meat and potatoes cut into small, bite-size pieces and skewered with a toothpick. It tasted fine, and I ate with them and drank into the wee hours of the morning. We were out front when the dawn came, and I was watching the cockroaches crawl over me. They were friendly, and I had names for them in Spanish, so I knew I'd had too much to drink. My compadres were fading fast, so I walked back to the hotel and crashed.

Later that day we took off for Mayaguez on the west side of the island. In route, we saw a horrible accident where two police officers had run into the back of a truck with their squad car and had been decapitated. We stayed at the Hilton in Mayaguez, and it was a gorgeous spot. Every day we had a light rain at two in the afternoon for a half hour to cool everything off. I would sit poolside and drink during the rain, and they served a pineapple freshly cut that tasted like strawberries. They had a nice high dive, and my folks got a great picture of me midair doing a one-and-a-half flip. We went deep-sea fishing the third day, and Dad rented a nice cabin cruiser. Everyone (Mom, Elaine, Lauren, Page, and Jim) got seasick and wanted to go back after an hour. Dad and I drank India beer, which is a local brand, and decided to go back out since we'd already paid for it. We caught lots of mackerel and some grouper and had a great time.

I had been out with Elaine a few times but had gotten no action. I figured the next day was New Year's Eve, so we'd be together then. I later found out my sister got involved and told Elaine if she slept with me I would never respect her and she'd lose me. I ended up dropping Elaine after this in favor of Leslie. I felt a full relationship required sex and that it actually binds you together. New Year's Eve brought us an exciting time. Elaine, Lauren, and I had dinner and drinks provided by the hotel. There was a big dance, and this Puerto Rican gentleman was hitting on Lauren, so I was happy for her. He sat down with us and started drinking. We were having good conversation and enjoyed dancing when this guy asks all of us to go to his place. I didn't want to go, and neither did Lauren or Elaine. We told him we were having a great time, and it was silly to travel somewhere else. He did not want us to stay there, so he threatened us with a loaded, .25-caliber automatic pistol. This guy took on a whole new light, so I stuffed a steak knife up my sleeve for future use if necessary. I decided to drink him unconscious.

We began to do Puerto Rican toasts and drank to everything imaginable. My adrenaline was high, and I didn't feel a thing. After an hour and a half of toasting revelry, he finally passed out, and I got the manager. I showed him the weapon and explained our position, and he disposed of the man and his gun in whatever manner he thought fit. I wasn't interested in pressing charges, just getting free of the threat. After he was gone, we breathed a lot easier, and I put the steak knife back. Elaine was hesitant about spending the night with me, so I took her back to Lauren's room and bid her good night. I figured it was her feelings and didn't realize how Lauren had sabotaged the relationship. Elaine and Lauren had to get back to school before I did so they left first. I told Elaine she was free to date whomever and that I was moving on. I returned to school a few days later. I really admired her as a person but really did not know what to do with her.

After returning to school, I was not a happy camper and went to the TKE house. One of them had turned me in and caused the incarceration at the nuthouse and cost me a semester of grades and credit. When I came back, the traitorous fraternity brothers were scared. They didn't know what I'd do, and they'd seen me in the past take on the football team single- handedly with the shotgun, so they plotted to be rid of me (probably with some justification because I couldn't trust them). They proposed to eliminate guns in the fraternity. (I was the only hunter living in the house at that time.) I was also to be installed as sergeant of arms (officer) before I was forced to the nuthouse. They had a meeting, and I was the only one on the ballot for the office. I was told I wasn't allowed to go to the meeting for elections, yet everyone else was for the other offices. I was the only one on the ballot, and I lost. They changed the procedure and voted yes or no (like for judges in the national election). I couldn't believe what they did.

As they broke for a while and I ascertained their plot, I decided to wage psychological war. I quickly went and brought to the living room my guns, cleaning kits, ammunition, wooden matches, and a can of gasoline. As they returned to vote on the gun issue, I opened the gas container so everyone could smell the fumes. I sat on the chair, and as they passed by, I was cleaning the guns. When their little minion informants came over to inquire what I was doing, I said, "If they vote against guns in the house, I'm starting the place on fire and shooting anyone who tries to escape the flames." This freaked them out, so they had a secret ballot. I put all my stuff away while they were down doing their worst. The issue was tabled for a later meeting.

Later that night I was having a few drinks, and the vigilante committee decided to take measures into their own hands. I had obviously scared them earlier, and it was payback time for me. Ten of them, led by Dave H (who my cousin Mike had hit), were going to thrash me into total submission. As they approached me cautiously, they began to talk tough. Dave was particularly vocal, so I told him he was going to be destroyed physically even if no one else was hurt. He slowly receded to the rear and became less vocal. I replicated the tactic on others, and they too receded until no one was left to confront me. In the finality of it, no one was even shoved or touched. I had even less respect for my "brothers" and decided to reacquaint myself with dorm life, and the Teke boys breathed easier. The fraternity thing died for me that day, and it's interesting to note that the house died too. Within a few short years, it burned to the ground and was never resurrected again. I visited the site in the summer of 2000, and sadly, there is only a stone with a bronze plaque commemorating the location.

When I moved back to the dorms, they put me in a room with Jim C., who looked a lot like John Denver. He was very well mannered, trustworthy, cute, and cautious. I found him safe to be around, which was a nice change after the politics at TKE. However, I don't think he felt the same about me. I was still an accident looking for a place to happen and a naturally chaotic piece of the cosmos.

I decided to pursue Leslie K and asked her out now that I was no longer a Greek and living in the dorm sans social commitments. She was a short, dishwater blonde with sparkling eyes and a slightly plump but curvy exterior. She was a couple of months older than Madonna but had a quick mind and humor. I knew sex was a driving force in her life, and after Elaine, I decided I needed a wanton hussy in my life. I took her out and parked, and after some heated necking, I went for the copulation. She was willing, but in my haste and desire, I had trouble keeping my little guy inside her. She sensed the frustration and brought a swift end to our pandering. I was really pissed and promptly took her home to her dismay. Women sense passion, and frustration without fruition is not necessarily bad. I was understandably depressed and took fault in my inability to complete the act. She still was interested and really enjoyed me, so the next outing we got in the backseat and took our time. She wisely told me what she wanted and had me play with her breasts and extend foreplay, and by the time I mounted her in the back of the Buick, she was on fire. That exited me (as passion is definitely contagious), and we had a great session with her repeated soaking of my cloth backseat. The badly stained seat was an embarrassment and a badge of honor at the same time. Giving someone pleasure was very fulfilling for me as well.

We became inseparable and like two monkeys in heat. For one particular "glorious" moment, I didn't want to take her out to the boondocks to copulate, so I foolishly parked in the student parking lot behind her dorm on campus. It was cold in South Dakota at night, so we let the car run with the heat on and steamed up the windows quickly with our hot passion. It was warm inside, and we were both naked in the front seat. My undershorts were on the top of the seat, and a flashlight peered in through the passenger window while I was in the saddle with Leslie. She was naked underneath me, and I knew it would be a "mental" problem for her to be caught with her drawers down. As I arose from her to answer the policeman at the window, I grabbed my shorts and quickly covered her face so the probing flashlight could not identify her visage. I rolled the window down, and the officer made inane comments and tried to see whatever he could. She was absolutely frozen with the undershorts in her face, her breasts spilling over to her arms, and her pubic hair glistening in reflection of the light. I asked him what he wanted very sternly, and he said, quite meekly, to go farther out of town next time and then left.

Leslie was understandably mortified, and I wasn't going to get to finish lovemaking that night. I later calmed her, stating that because of my shorts no one knew it was her naked in the car. She didn't buy it at first, but I told her the story of John Quincy Adams bathing in the White House pond. He was a large man running late one day, and the ladies were out walking with the parasols spinning on their shoulders. He only had one small towel to get back to the White House, and it wouldn't cover him completely. His feeling was it would be embarrassing for the president of the United States to be caught with only a towel to cover his privates and part of his body. President Adams' logic dictated that he should cover his face and walk naked (but unidentified) through the ladies to the White House. It caused quite a stir in those days, but it worked. No one was the wiser unless they read certain historical memoirs. This helped Leslie a little, but it was a good week till I got her naked in a car again. She was argumentative (as I was), and after three months, we had broken up.

We met at Taco Town a little after the break up, and she started to talk about women's superior abilities. I bet her sixty dollars that she couldn't walk sixty miles in twenty-four hours. Leslie felt she could do it, so I drove to Sioux Falls and clocked off exactly sixty miles. She left at noon Friday and had until noon Saturday to win. She was very courageous and headstrong but made a serious error by selecting loafers as her walking shoe of choice. I drove back and forth throughout the day to monitor her progress, and she made about four miles per hour. At that rate, she would complete the bet in fifteen hours. The only rules were she had to walk the middle of the interstate and couldn't take a ride. If she got off her path, it was on her own time and didn't count for her total mileage. I parked off the road in Canton, approximately forty miles along the way, and she walked a mile out of her way to get to my car and sleep a few hours with me. I made her walk the mile back to the interstate, so she added two miles to her total.

At fifteen minutes to the deadline of noon, she was still five miles away from her final finish point, but she was at the southern end of Sioux Falls. I left and drove back to Vermillion, selfishly confident and smug in my victory. She called me back at the dorm, announcing that she had won the bet. I told her no she'd lost and had obviously cheated, because she was still five miles out when I left. She said she didn't want to discuss it at the moment and told me I should come pick her up. Being a total bastard, I said, "No, I won't pick you up. You should walk back." My roommate Jim felt sorry for her and drove to Sioux Falls and returned her to the college.

Her feet were crippled for a week with huge blisters from the loafers. She did walk fifty-seven miles, and had she not slept with me those few hours, I think she would have made it. Her tenacity was awesome! I admired it but would never admit it to her. She refused to pay the loss entirely and let me have about half of the money. The rest I had to spend with her on dates. After a date or two, I told her to keep her money, and I sulked away. It didn't last long, for she turned up a couple of weeks later with a pregnancy.

Gary E, a good friend and fraternity brother, had gotten his girl pregnant the year before. She was a gorgeous Doris Day-type girl and didn't want to have the baby their junior year, so they decided to have an abortion. Gary was premed, so he tried to scrape the womb with a coat hanger. He inadvertently killed her, because she got an air embolism and had a weak constitution that no one knew about. Gary was sent to prison on manslaughter charges. It seemed so unfair, because he really worshipped her and would literally do anything for her. He even wanted to marry her, but she wanted him to finish medical school and felt it would ruin his chances if they had a family early. Unfortunately, someone had to pay, and he did inadvertently cause her death no matter what the intention. He eventually got out and is now happily married with children out East but has nothing to do with the medical service profession.

I was worried I would be in the same mold, except I had already broken up with my "mistake," and now she was returning with an issue I couldn't refute. We got the tests from the doctor confirmed, and Leslie refused to consider an abortion (and after Gary's ordeal I wasn't about to go for a "custom" abortion). Her dad was the state's attorney, so I was worried. It turned out he didn't want to meet me or cause any issues. Leslie was leaving school at the end of her freshman year to have my child in December 1969. I was getting messed up fast and needed something, anything actually, to escape my reality. Leslie told me of her father's lack of interest in me, but she still wanted me to be with her. I told her it was pointless to marry her since we'd already broken up before the knowledge of the child's existence and in spite of her protests said we should go our separate ways. She would only agree if we would have sex one more time. I reluctantly agreed and got us a room at the local motel. It was the worst sex I ever had in my life. I might as well have screwed a raw piece of liver. That was the last time I ever spoke to or saw Leslie. I often wondered what the child looked like and what she and Leslie were doing. By this time in my life, I needed an outlet, and the new world of drugs (introduced at the nuthouse) looked like a good plan and a way to leave my troubles behind while experimenting with a new medium.

I met some guys in the art school who had some pot. They said it was great, so I took it, and Jim and I decided to experiment. There was a new album to try it with by The Beatles called Sergeant Pepper's Lonely-Hearts Club Band, which I figured was appropriate. We lit up and played the music and drifted off to fantasy land. It was good pot, and we even got visual colors from it. Jim enjoyed it too but was apprehensive about a loss of control, while I was eager to ascend higher levels of "enlightenment." I fell in quickly with a local band that seemed to have good drug connections. I went to a party in a loft over a store that I had passed a hundred times and never realized anyone resided there. There were about twelve of us druggies in the whole town. (The population was more than six thousand during the school year and less than three thousand over the summer.)

During the first half of 1969, drugs were not popular in the Midwest. Most of the action was in California. We smoked a little, and I got so ripped I became stupid. Now the other participants were not considered bright by society, but on drugs, they were fine. I was the stupid one, and the ridiculousness of it delighted me. I laughed and grinned at my own personal "insight" and at their ability to control the drug (and my lack of ability to control anything). After a few hours of nonsense, they told me to meet them the next night for a trip. I agreed, and we met on campus the next night.

Jethro was the bandleader, and he gave me a small pill that looked like a child's aspirin. When I inquired as to what it was, he told me LSD (also referred to as acid). I was impressed. They were all taking it, so I decided to pretend to take it and just hang out with them and see what effect it had on them. I carefully saved my precious "trip" and followed them around most of the night. Through trial and error and by watching reactions, I learned a lot about the drug. They would be very interested in anything you wanted to show them. Emotion was not to be expressed (they had enough for a hundred people), and questions were long roads to nowhere. A question would lose them, so I just learned to let them dig (they would visually see whatever on the simplest things) and talk in a monotone voice. The attention was phenomenal when I told stories in a monotone. If I talked excitedly, they were confused or even paranoid, and if I asked questions, it took me an hour to bring them back to a good trip. Simple card tricks were a delight, and they were like gentle children who really appreciated attention. I shepherded my flock all night, and no one got hurt or flipped out.

After eight hours, I was beat, but some of them still wanted to continue. When the sun was up, I left to go sleep and told them I'd see them at their concert in a couple of days in Sioux Falls. That Saturday I drove to Sioux Falls to watch their concert, but I really wanted to try this new drug. When I arrived and parked my Buick, I dropped acid for my first time. It was lunchtime and a nice spring day. I walked around for twenty minutes, and nothing happened, so I figured it was a joke. Jethro's band was playing. I started to watch, and the music sounded good. He then played the Rolling Stones' "Jumping Jack Flash," and I started to really feel it. I was digging on the band. Jethro knew I was wasted, so he was giving me all kinds of looks no one else noticed. By the time the song was complete, I was starting to see lots of colors everywhere. Color trails came off my hand as I moved it. It reminded me of steam off a hot object in winter, except the steam was colored like a rainbow. If I focused (maintained), I could keep it together and only see trails. I sat down in front of the band and looked at the pavement. It was ordinary black asphalt, but it started to separate if I stared at it. All the action began if I just stared (like in a daydream). It was like a mini-earthquake in slow motion but with more color. If I was focusing or moving, I just saw trails, but if I stopped to daydream, all kinds of stuff happened. The visuals became amazing, and cartoon objects arrived from anywhere. I'm sure I was there only a couple of hours, but it seemed like weeks. All my senses were heightened, and I was like a kid in a candy store for the first time.

I began to experiment with my new "powers," and the world was renewed. My smell was enhanced, so when a woman walked by, I could smell at least three things. I could smell her perfume first, then her vagina, and then usually something like baby powder, shampoo, or bar soap. With others, I noticed the body odor or some offensive food. I stopped the smells and then focused on hearing.

It was a county fair atmosphere, and for South Dakota, a pretty good crowd was in attendance. I could listen in on many conversations at once. I could comprehend fifteen conversations at one time all around me. I then experimented with touch and found I could feel different textures on a blade of grass or even my scalp. I began to touch many things, appreciating the difference in texture and subtle softness that each object offered. I didn't eat anything, but I had a drink from a park water pump that tasted and felt great. I had to pump this old green handle, and there was a small green box that would pressurize and squirt the water in a constant stream for a minute while I sipped the water. It was warm at first but quickly changed to a comfortable cool. The water came from a well but tasted good (not like the sulfuric tasting well water I had at home as a kid). I was so into the moment, a one-minute drink seemed like a half hour. I felt I could distinguish the minerals in the water by taste as they passed over my palate. It was hard to maintain, because I was so astounded by the beauty in everything. I could literally be happy playing with shit. For some fool reason, everyone was leaving this beautiful place, so I decided to go with the flow. I got into my car and began the sixty-mile trek back to college.

Driving on acid is an experience I would not recommend. I was fine at first and could maintain the images, but as time wore on (maybe a mile on the interstate), I tended to daydream. The second I spaced out, the psychedelic images would take over. I finally found a solution as my brain went in and out of control. I invented a little man who sat on my left shoulder. He drove the car and watched the road through a small porthole in the windshield. For me, the highway was gone, and cartoon telephone poles went to the sky. He drove the car all the way back at about forty-five miles per hour (in a seventy-five mile per hour speed limit area), so it took a couple hours to return home. I saw all the ends of the universe while he drove. There were brilliant colors with lots of depth and then no depth whatsoever (two- dimensional, cartoonlike background). I thanked the little man when he finally parked the car and got off my shoulder. He walked away, and I've never seen him since. I walked over to the campus chapel and went in. There was something fascinating about God when I was ripped in His house. I could really feel Him, and I could understand the Native Americans using peyote and mescaline to get in touch with the spirit world. The color part lasted about eight hours, but the effect on my brain, value system, and outlook were considerably longer.

Because of this experience, I began to pay attention to the protestors against Vietnam more on the television. Apparently, so were other students, and they focused on the ROTC department as a symbol of "the establishment." I was walking around campus and discovered a discussion group of hippie aspirants sitting on the lawn in a semicircle. One of the girls had short blonde hair with a headband on and school clothes. It looked odd to see her with the hippies while dressed in a yellow tartan skirt with a lacy white blouse. She looked out of place somehow. We began to talk, and a solid attraction ensued. She was a year younger than me and clearly desired intimacy.

We walked to her trailer arm in arm, and we were alone sitting on her bed. She kissed me once and pushed me gently on my back. Then she undid my pants and pulled them halfway down to expose my ardor and kissed me there ever so gently. I said and did nothing, fascinated by her approach. She left her tartan outfit on and only raised her skirt and pushed her white panties to one side. She mounted me and was very soft, damp, and quite warming. She moved slowly up and down then leaded forward to nibble on the bottom of my ear, and I could feel her breath upon my ear. I was quite motivated at this point and was no longer just fascinated. I fought a hard-uphill battle till release and was a sweaty mess. She got composed fairly quickly, smoothed out her dress, and said she had a class to go attend. I said great and left with her to go to campus.

The May Day ROTC program parade was the next day, so she asked me to wear a red armband on my left sleeve. She gave me this red scarf like item that doubled as a headband. She would be in the stands protesting. The next day I tied it on my green outer jacket just before we started. She saw me as we marched by and got very excited with the others shouting, "hell no, we won't go," and other protest chants. After the parade, I was called into the commandant's office, and he was pissed. I got the whole humiliation of having him cut the brass buttons off my jacket. He would have broken my sword if I had one. My hundred-dollar a month stipend was stopped, and I had to clear all my stuff out of the armory. He didn't even ask why I did it. Had I graduated that June, I would have been a second lieutenant, but it was not to be. I lost my IIS student classification deferral from the draft and was immediately reclassified 1A. My life and aspirations were rapidly changing. My grades were still okay, but the A in ROTC had turned to an F with no appeal. The summer was upon me. My life was now subjected to a disciplined and hard-nosed draft. When I got home, Dad said to leave. I was three times seven (age twenty-one), and he was done. I did what any other lad would in my position… road trip!

CHAPTER 5

The Psychedelic Summer Of 1969

I was homeless, jobless, and looking to buy/share/sell drugs, so it was time to go to the promised land of California. I had my '63 Buick Le Sabre, so I just had to get enough money together to make the journey. Drugs were becoming fun, and Madonna's brother was one of the biggest dealers at Homewood- Flossmoor High School. We would speed and smoke together and even did LSD once. Her dad was having a rough time with Madonna's mom. The fights were constant. The children adapted, and when dinner was served, they would quickly grab their plates when one of their parents would scream and jerk the long table up to ruin dinner. One time during the summer, the window was open, and the neighbors were out on their patio when the screaming began. The table went up, the kids quickly grabbing and then holding their plates on their laps, and the roast flew out the window, bounced on the grass, and ended up at the neighbor's feet. Family drama at Madonna's house was always high.

I was fascinated at the constant drama and violence. Her dad did not like me living there, especially with a lock on her bedroom door, so he took it off while we were gone one day. Madonna's mom went ballistic on the dad and kicked him out for good. Madonna and I were happy and making love the next day when her mom walked in on us through the unlockable door. I didn't stop my humping, although Madonna was frozen in anticipation of a scene or grief. Her mom had put her hands over her eyes and was making strange noises while she muttered almost apologetically that dinner was ready. I had not slowed my movements on the bed and observed her mom peeking through her fingers. It was then I then stated, "I'll be up as soon as I get my nut." She gave a highly indignant "oh" and slammed the door as she stomped back upstairs. I had to find another place to dwell before leaving for California. Drugs were on my mind, and I had an inherent curiosity about what they would do to me and for me.

Madonna and her friend knew a guy named Chuck that lived on the other side of the quarry. He moved around a lot and didn't pay taxes or have any ID. He was eccentric with gray, unkempt hair and had a home I could stay at until it was time to go. Madonna had another acquaintance named Rick who wanted to go West and score some grass, and my friend John's brother by marriage, Curly, wanted to visit his mother in San Diego. Both were also acquiring funds for the journey. While I was sleeping there, Madonna's friend came over and wanted to stay overnight and had stated she was scared of some guy. I didn't care, so I said okay. There was just the one bed upstairs, a double, so I told her she could stay with me. I wasn't interested in her and thought she was a little timid. I got into bed with just my undershorts on, so she did too. I don't know if she expected me to attempt to have sex with her or not, but I just went to sleep. Madonna came over the next day, and I told her the tale. She seemed upset with the girl even though nothing happened. I think it put her in the mood, though, and we had our first sex there. It was time to go after a week there. I managed to save a couple of hundred dollars (gasoline was thirty cents a gallon or less at that time), and the other two travelers (Rick and Curly) had maybe sixty dollars between them, so we took off in my 1963 Buick Le Sabre to seek our fortune in drugs and to have a great adventure.

Madonna gave me some speed she got from her brother, and we headed west. I had work done on the car before we left at a standard oil station. I had them redo the cooling system, and they needed to put on a new water pump. Just outside of Joplin, Missouri, it fell off, and the fan hit it and drove it into the radiator. We pulled into another gas station with everything smoking in the front. I shut off the engine, and some mechanic came out of the car bay screaming, "Don't shut it off!"

I was out of the car by then and started to get back in (the car was still running with engine run on) as the car engine sputtered and locked up. The Buick would need extensive repairs to operate, and we were in a hurry. The owner of the station had and old 1959 Nash Rambler station wagon he offered to trade me for the Buick. It burned oil and had a hole in the radiator, so we had to bring water with us and add a quart or two of oil every time we filled up with gas. The Rambler had three spare tires in the back, because the tires were so bald on the car. On toward evening, Curly wanted to drive. I was tired, so I agreed. He took some more speed, and off we went.

We were in Oklahoma in the middle of nowhere when Curly wigged out. He was babbling and had lost control of reality and the car. I slowly got him to pull off the interstate and stop the car. He left the car and went to the nearest hill. He climbed to the top and stared at the stars until first light. Rick was worried but managed to sleep in the car. Interestingly, the Rambler seats folded flat front and back to make a double bed or just one side a half bed. I talked Curly down from his wild fantasies and fears and got him in the car. Rick was the only one who'd gotten any sleep, so I told him to drive. The car had a slush box transmission with no clutch. To start it, you pulled the gearshift toward you and then shifted your gears. I had only been napping for a half hour when Rick pulled over. An old gray-haired guy was on the side of the road in the ditch. We got him in and gave him some food, and he came out of his stupor. He was dirty and disheveled from sleeping in the ditch, and he needed to go to Clair, Texas. I found it on the map and discovered it was only sixty miles out of our way, so we figured we should get him home. When we pulled in and let him off, we saw that the town was dusty and had few people like the movie *The Last Picture Show*. Even the gas stations looked dilapidated. I saw no entertainment and no recognizable eating establishments. We quickly moved on. Curly wanted to see his mom in San Diego, and my Great-Aunt Ella (Grandma Clara's sister) was in La Jolla.

The next obstacle was the Rocky Mountains. The Rambler was a flatland car with a leak in the radiator that we had to fill twice between gas fill ups. In the mountains, it was worse going uphill. On the side of the road every ten miles or so, there were rainwater barrels, which we needed desperately to keep the engine cool. When we finally got to the top and started down on the Arizona side, it was a relief. Gas mileage was great, but water and oil were not so good. I still had to add a quart of oil at every fill up. Now when I started to accelerate, smoke would come out the back tailpipe. The engine rings were worn badly.

Rick and I dropped Curly off at his mom's, and he looked like he needed mothering. That was the last time I saw John's stepbrother. We drove northwest to La Jolla, which was a very nice area with plenty of money. Aunt Ella owned a hotel, and lifestyle went up a couple of notches for Rick and me. She gave us her friend's place who was touring Europe for several months. Aunt Ella was short, chubby, and very explicit on what she wanted. When you used the sink, all water had to be removed and the metal polished. Beds had to be made, and no messes were allowed. She was smart, eighty-one years old, and a great canasta and bridge player. (Twelve years later, I would visit her deathbed and ask her for her advice over her ninety-three years of life. She answered, "If it hurts, rub it.")

Rick and I separated during the day to scout for drugs to buy and use. I went to the beach and on the way saw a surf/scuba shop. I rented a mask, fins, snorkel, and Hawaii sling spear. I was a fair swimmer, so it looked like fun, and maybe I could bring home dinner. The spear was seven feet long and had surgical tubing attached in a circle at the base. To use it, I put my hand at the farthest point from the spear base in the tubing. The spear went in my hand like the fat end of a cue stick, and I pushed it back by moving my hand closer to the sharp end of the spear. The tension from the base to my hand increased the farther I pushed it. When I released it, the harpoon/Hawaiian sling would lunge out ten to twelve feet in front of me in the water, but the tubing was still attached to the base, so I could pull the fish back. I found it hard to miss, but it was necessary to get within twelve feet of my victim.

Rock bass were not that accommodating. I had to take deep breaths and swim around the underwater reefs to surprise the fish on the other side. I did and got a beautiful rock bass more than two feet long. I was semi-exhausted, and then I saw these huge golden fish that were fat and maybe eighteen inches in length. They were easy to kill and just looked at me. I quickly killed three, but the energy of youth was fading in the ocean currents. I had a simple stringer and had my bass and the three golden fish on the rope. I swam back to shore convinced the people would think I was the world's greatest fisherman. I collapsed on my beach towel, exhausted, and then heard the people talking about me. "Someone should call the police or game warden."

Apparently, I killed the garibaldi gold fish, which was protected to the tune of five hundred dollars each. Adrenaline kicked in, and I quickly left the beach. As I crested the cliff, I tossed the stringer of all four fish back in the Pacific. The rock bass was legal, but I didn't want to be implicated, so they all returned to the deep, and I had no fish dinner that night. I decided I liked the climate and would stay a while, but Rick was interested in scoring a kilo of good pot (2.2 pounds, which is also referred to as a "key") to bring home.

While Rick continued his search, I went to get a job. College kids were a dime a dozen in California then, as tuition for residents was paid if you went to a state school. Aunt Ella was tiring of our crazy hours, so I knew it was time to move. I found a position that didn't pay much, but company gave me a bed and living area with a pool table. It was an ambulance company that shared a California Highway Patrol (CHP) contract with the famous Bay City ambulance of Hollywood fame. I received minimal training, and the rest was on the job. We (all ambulance people) had our shirts with the company logo, which was a red cross, and some pull-on engineer boots (for speed dressing). We slept there six days and were off the seventh. I was now at Aunt Ella's only one day a week, while Rick still stayed there full-time.

On my first day off, I went to Aunt Ella's. Rick and I were both unsuccessful obtaining drugs, so we decided to go to Mexico's Tijuana. The Rambler made it but was now using two quarts of oil per fill-up. We shopped around, tried the chili, and had some drinks but found nothing. I did buy some homemade car-tire sole sandals and a real portable cigarette roller.

We were on our half of the month for CHP at Pacific Ambulance, so more emergency calls would come at night. (Note: The bread and butter of ambulatory services is the pickup and delivery of invalids/ geriatrics and transport to the hospital and back). I had just turned twenty-two when I went on a call for an evening crash up in the mountains. Some guy had flipped his Toyota and was dying in the car. The firemen were trying to free him from the car with a tire iron but without success. (This was before Jaws of Life were standard issue.) I could see the guy was not good through the windshield, so I asked for the tire iron. I smashed the windshield (to everyone's surprise) and dragged the guy out of the middle through the windshield. He got some minor cuts but was still breathing. My partner and I got him on the gurney and into the emergency crash rig. I knew he was serious, so I didn't even take time to turn on the AC. I just braced my back against the roof and began heart massage and resuscitation. We were going full speed down the mountainside to the nearest hospital, which happened to be a private Catholic hospital. We made it, and he was still alive and kicking. The administration asked for his wallet, but they didn't see an insurance card so refused to let him in and be stabilized. I was crushed and hauled the man back to the ambulance for a half hour ride to the county hospital, which would take everyone. Five minutes from the hospital he expired. My whole world felt like a dishrag just wrung out and lying there. You can't become emotionally involved, or the job will sap everything out of you. My partner offered me my first cigarette, and it made me dizzy. It was a Camel filter, but they were hard to find, so I bought Camel straights. I was up to a pack a day in no time.

The next big mission was a motorcycle wreck where the guy hit the front of a Pontiac. We had to pull parts of him out of the grill and place them in a bag. I had to give him resuscitation even though he was never coming back to life. Only a coroner or doctor could declare him dead. We put him in one of the overhead spots (a crash rig has two overhead prone positions and two bench spots with a gurney down the middle). He had a female passenger who flew over the Pontiac and into the weeds. She was understandably disorientated and had been punctured by dry weed shafts on her right side. Her flesh looked like hamburger hanging from her arm and neck. The top of her head had a minor laceration, so blood ran down her face, which made it look worse. I cleaned her up and put compresses on, but she seemed okay physically with no broken bones or deep puncture wounds. She kept saying to me, "I want a piece," which impressed me. After all, she just lost the guy and thought she was going to follow shortly. I thought she wanted to have sex with me before her imagined death and was going to accommodate her. Fortunately, we got to the hospital before I executed a mercy fuck. It turned out that as she got better on the way in, she was asking for a priest. I really could have been indicted even though I had good intentions.

I had one "fun" encounter with an elderly patient we moved from home to hospital. He would wait until we picked him up and would then crap all over the poor attendant who had his legs. It would ruin the target's pants and boots. He would then laugh hysterically at the victim's demise. My partner took his head, and I had his legs. I watched his eyes, and when I saw him about to release, I quickly threw him back on the bed. He messed himself, his hospital outfit (open back), and his bed. I called the nurse, and he was cleaned up while we waited. He was not happy at all that his trick was thwarted.

When I got back, I called my cousins, and they wanted switchblade knives from Tijuana. Rick and I went back the next week to look for drugs again but first went south of Tijuana down to Rosarito Beach. There, druggies used STP a very powerful hallucinogenic that you need a caretaker for (like opium dens), and you were placed under a palm tree in a vegetative state for four months. I'm sure some never returned to reality. We found a guy to hook us up with a pot salesman north of the border. He gave us some "gold," and we had a great time walking the beach and wondering about the STP guys. The next day we drove back to Tijuana, but first I rolled some pot into a Camel-like cigarette and took a pencil and wrote Camel on it in an arch shape just like my regular

Camels. We got into Tijuana and found the knives. We each carried one for fun, and the Mexican police (who were following) stopped us on the street. They were looking for a bribe (I didn't know this) and went right to our pockets where the switchblades were waiting. When we didn't offer money, they took us to the Tijuana jail. The merchant that sold us the knives got his wares back to sell to some other unsuspecting dummy. I had a fifty-dollar bill in my shoe for emergencies that I'd forgotten about. Had I remembered and bribed the cops ten dollars each, I would have been released (no switchblade, though) and not had to suffer needlessly in a foreign jail.

Rick and I were separated, and I was put in a holding area with mostly Mexican prisoners. I'd been strip-searched already and given my stuff back. In American prisons, they take your clothes and give you outfits for felonies. Lo and behold, my special Camel- like cigarette was still in the cigarette pack. I observed the trustees sweeping the floors but looking in everyone's eyes. You're in prison, and who do you trust? Usually, the answer is no one, but I had a huge joint of pot, and this was the spot and time to trust everyone. I lit up the Camel-like joint. No one was fazed at first, but the smell of "gold" was overwhelming, and then all the tough guys were worried they'd go down with me and we'd be busted immediately. The truth was, no one had ever done it; only trustees (also prisoners but trusted) were around. I enjoyed every puff as I got wasted and the colors rushed over my eyes. Finally, one guy asked for a hit, and then they almost fought over the remainder of the joint. Soon it was gone. and I told the last guy to swallow the last bit. Not all had partaken but enough had to ensure trust from them. I'm sure someone ratted, but I had no repercussions from the epiphany of the moment.

Jails suck, but I had to put my thoughts elsewhere. The rest of my day was a pleasant blur. My cell was three bunks high on two walls (six to a cell) with a cement floor with a drain in it and an empty two-pound coffee can with a cardboard square over it for odor control. We had no toilet or sink, and the "bunk" was a piece of sheet metal that flexed a little when someone laid on it. It had a few holes in the sheet metal that I thought were for ventilation until the afternoon "sanitation engineer" came by to clean up. They took the coffee cans and emptied them in a vat and then brought a fire hose up and sprayed the cell and inmates. This served at our shower, I guessed. I looked out the bars and could see there were three floors. I was on the second. Girls were also there but not in with boys, just in our view. They knew it and would flash their privates incessantly. I don't know if this was for fun or future business, but they seemed to enjoy tormenting the boy prisoners. The only ones who seemed to use them were the trustees, who would get head for cigarettes or a snack they would sneak to them. That evening we got two drunken Marines who vomited all over the bunks on the other side of my cell. I never thought I would enjoy the hose guy the next day, but he soaked them and their bunks well. I wisely took off my clothes and wadded them up by the front door frame, and he hosed me off too. It was cold, and the girl who was flashing across the way watched so I pointed at her and winked before I dressed. She smiled, but we never met again.

I was there three days and then decided to pay my way out. There was no trial date or lawyer, so you had better know someone on the outside or have your own means. I asked the trustee to see a guard and said I wished to pay my fine, and off I went. It was two hundred pesos (twenty-five dollars), and since I had fifty dollars, I paid for Rick too. He was not happy or grateful, so he must have had a bad time in there. He went back to Aunt Ella's, and I returned to work after missing three days. I explained the jail time and apologized, and they allowed me back. (I don't think they could find a replacement quick enough.) I returned to Aunt Ella's the next week to find Aunt Ella very unhappy. I liked Aunt Ella even though she was a taskmaster; she was honest and forthright and my grandma's sister. It turns out Rick robbed Aunt Ella's friend's room and took all her coin collections, which were worth hundreds of dollars. Rick then went back to Chicago. I found out later he went to Madonna and told her I said bad things about her and was cheating with other women. He told her he saved us from jail and suggested that she should go out with him for a boyfriend. I did manage later to get Aunt Ella some of the friend's money back when I worked at National Steel, but I'm sure the couple of hundred didn't pay for it all. I never saw Rick again.

My original Beatle look haircut was getting longer, and I was growing a mustache. I went to a Jefferson Airplane concert, and by 1969, they were quite popular. I bought some acid cut with speed and prepared for the entertainment. I sat down on the grass by these two cute girls with flowers and granny dresses and some interesting blouses. One of them had these fantastic silver-cast buttons. She saw I was interested, so she let me touch them. I started ever so slowly to unbutton each one. She had no bra on, but it wasn't about the sex for me, only the beautifully crafted buttons. I had them all unbuttoned when her boyfriend came back. He was about to bash me against her protest until he saw my eyes and knew I was anywhere but there. He took her away to another part of the stadium, and that was okay. The band started to play "Go Ask Alice," and Grace Slick (the lead singer) had a Girl Scout dress on with the awards sewn on, but it was unbuttoned all the way down. We were close together writhing to the music when people collapsed on me, banging their arms into my head, and I passed out. I woke up at sunset, and there might have been twelve of us left on the grass. It was just *wow* or *far-out* . . . It's hard to remember exactly. Pacific Ambulance was becoming more distant to me. I learned things that would help me later in life, but the work was getting boring, and they did not like my metamorphosis. I was first a seeker and then an observer, but I also liked to experience. I found acid to be very beneficial in experience. Eight hours was like a week when you were on it. My powers of observation and absorbing sound were awesome. I was still feeling the echoes of an acid trip on a Monday morning when we got an emergency call not too far away. It wasn't our turn for CHP, and we were washing the regular ambulance, so my partner and I grabbed the crash rig. Four cars had an early- morning road rage session, and all hit head on. No other emergency vehicles responded (it was during the shift change for regular city), so we brought the backup driver with the wet ambulance.

Eleven people were hurt badly, and several were critical. The other ambulance refused to take more than two and loaded them in the back and left for a half hour drive to county. That left me and my partner with nine "customers" to cart to the hospital. Triage is not that hard if you observe. I put the five most serious on the stretchers, two on hangars, two on couches, and one on the gurney. I crammed one medium-hurt guy at the front of my back rig area and tied him upright with rubber tubing. The three least in jeopardy I stacked in the cab with my partner, which is not allowed, and tied the two seat belts around the three upright to keep them stable. We raced off to the county hospital. As we unloaded, many ER aids gawked at what I had done. All eleven made it, even the most critical. But pressure from the hospital, Bay City (whose turn it was for CHP), and the ER workers all trashed my boss, so shit runs downhill. I know we would have had at least one dead body, but I felt it made up for the one we lost to the Catholic hospital refusal.

I was let go a couple of weeks later, but before I left, we had another serious CHP call. This time it was just two cars with multiple passengers. There were a lot of shocked people to comfort and a crazed young mom who had a slight head wound from hitting the windshield. We had a second ambulance coming, so we had to settle the shock on the victims. The slightly wounded mom needed to quit flaying aimlessly around and screaming. I whispered in her ear, "Help me help them." She was still upset but quizzical. I took a folded blanket out of the back and shook it out. I came over to her, handed her the blanket, and asked her to fold it. She became very quiet and took the blanket I'd handed her and slowly began to fold. She was no longer hysterical, and after carefully folding the blanket, she brought it to me. As I placed it under one of the more battered patients, I said, "Thanks. This really helps the breathing." She squatted off to my right and watched (maybe waiting for more instructions) but ceased to be a negative force.

I had to sell the Rambler and get it out of Aunt Ella's garage. She needed me gone. The stress of my life was a little hard on her. (She was eighty-one then and did live to ninety-three, so I'm glad I respected her wishes.) The car was in bad shape, and the rings allowed too much oil in the combustion chamber. California had just put in smog laws and had its own emission standards. I was in a nice section of town up by La Jolla Beach and Country Club when a beautiful blonde girl in a white, convertible Alpine Tiger (very fast) pulled up behind me. When I took off from the stop, I could not see her in the mirror through all the black and blue smoke. She was still there coughing when I rounded a corner two blocks down. A day later I got a smog ticket and was deemed a health hazard. I traded the car for the cost of the ticket and grabbed my Illinois plates.

At Aunt Ella's, I packed a Boy Scout knapsack with all my worldly possessions and started walking. I wandered around for a day or so and called Aunt Ella to see how she was doing now that I'd cleared out. She invited me for lunch, and we went to the Beach and Tennis Club. I was getting thin, and a good meal was welcome. We had just sat down when some guy over sixty collapsed with a heart attack. It was like never leaving Pacific Ambulance. I rolled him over on the floor, checked his airway for blockage, and breathed into his mouth while holding his nose. I then gave him fifteen chest pumps and then breathed into him again. All the people watching were in shock and totally frozen in time. I grabbed the closest person and said to call an ambulance. I went to work for another twelve minutes (it seemed longer), and who came but Bay Cities, the outfit that complained that we took their CHP call. I didn't care anymore. The guy survived, and La Jolla Beach and Tennis gave Aunt Ella and me our lunches for free. That was the second to last time I saw Ella (the last was on her deathbed in 1981). I felt good about the day, but I was still homeless and jobless.

I had my tire sandals, hippie Persian rug jacket, and blue jeans. My hair was long enough to part down the middle. I used a headband to keep it out of my eyes and mouth. It would be another six months before I could sport a ponytail. I wandered south from La Jolla at night down the beach and by some cliffs. It was night and getting much cooler, and I needed a place to sleep. A small cave appeared at the edge of the sand and cliff, so I headed in to investigate. It was shallow, maybe eight feet deep and three to four feet in diameter. There were no signs of any animal life, so I figured I was okay. I had enough sand to be comfortable, and I was exhausted. In the wee hours, I got a rude awakening. It was very cool and salty in my mouth and eyes. The Pacific Ocean had visited, and instantly, my world had changed. When the next wave receded for a moment, I quickly gathered my knapsack and slogged through the following wave down the beach in the dark to a spot where I could climb up the cliff.

I was cold and wet with nowhere to go, so I visited an all-night Laundromat. No one was there, so I took off all my clothes and proceeded to wash and dry everything, which all fit in one load. I was sitting there naked and waiting for the dryer to complete when an older woman came in to do her laundry. We never spoke, and she did hers while I finished mine. I got dressed and left with my pack. I'm sure she had a story to tell when she got where she was going.

I forgot about my search for drugs to deal and use and focused more on the moment. I hitchhiked to Oceanside and met someone in a coffee shop who needed a boarder. It is a Marine town near Camp Pendleton. I couldn't afford to be there long, but it would do until I picked up my last paycheck at Pacific Ambulance. This group liked downers Nembutal, Seconol, anything to depress your brain. Someone would put on five long-playing albums, and we would sit in a vegetative state for almost three hours. We didn't sleep, and we had no pain. My brain was so slow. I was a searcher and observer of life, and these people slowed my journey down. I listened to late- night broadcasts either interviewing or analyzing the acid guru Timothy Leary. He had a cult of LSD followers (and other psychedelics), and I liked his take on authority. He was a psychologist from Harvard but had gone his own way.

Balboa Park was a great place to enjoy the world. I dropped some purple haze (named for Jimi Hendrix's song) and began to drift and observe. I came upon a picnic area with a variety of people, and all were instantly attuned to me. It was a busload of disabled children and adults with a driver and another person (woman) to watch over them. She seemed more interested in the driver. Well, I hit it off with the children—immediately, and we were playing games and just goofing off in general when the couple decided to take us to the museum. The group was amicable, so I went with them. I think the group had been there before. I am a history buff, and once we got inside, this storyteller motif got into me and I began history lessons with personalities and how they lived and died. When we got to the airplane exhibit much later, the couple said the group takes a long time there (airplanes actually hang from the ceiling).

The driver and chaperone left me in charge and said to meet them back at the bus. I saw the group with their mouths agape and then looked up again at the actual planes. I started to make engine sounds, and they naturally followed me, everyone making a different sound. I put my arms out like a plane and began a serpentine route around the room. After I "flew" once around, they all followed in glee with their arms out, following me like a conga line. After a few times around, I noticed the other visitors were watching us and not the exhibit, and some were irritated, so I led them on. We cruised the rest of the museum with a fast walk, our arms stretched out and our engines on full. Our planes were out of gas when we finally got to the picnic tables by the bus, and everyone was quite stimulated. After a brief rest, the driver and chaperone wanted to get them home, and naturally, they didn't want to go. They just wanted to sit by me and enjoy the moment. I had to hug all of them finally to get them on the bus, and we waved for ten minutes. I remember thinking how nice and pleasant they all were.

A week later I went to the park, but the group wasn't there, so I went to the zoo. San Diego Zoo is one of the largest in the world, and it's impossible to see everything in a day. They do have a wonderful sky cable car like the ski resorts that crosses over a large part of it. It's a wonderful view but not up close and personal with the animals. The animals are in their natural environments and seem to enjoy their life in spite of captivity.

About six acquaintances and I decided to road trip to a festival back East. Woodstock, New York, was a long drive, and we had plenty of hallucinogenic help to wile the hours of driving away. Someone had a beat-up pickup with some poles in the back and a canvas shade roof. There was a side wall on the bed of eighteen inches and a broken tailgate tied up. We pooled our money after we bought drugs and began our journey. Unfortunately, we all dropped (driver included), so our trajectory wasn't east but eight hours of meandering south. We woke up in some Mexican ghetto on a hill with adobe sides and partial roofs with locals everywhere. I met a good contact for pot but had no money after our spaced-out journey. It took two days to get back to San Diego by hitchhiking. I saw the Woodstock VHS tape years later and was sorry I missed it, but at the time, no one cared. It was all about the present.

On the hitchhike home, a guy picked me up just inside the US border and bought me a hamburger. He was a businesslike man with an agenda. He handed me a key ring with sixty-four keys. The keys were all GM and were the masters for all GM cars. He said if I joined his group, they would be mine. I would find the right key for the car and drive it to a specific location. If I brought them two cars, then I would get the third one "clean" for myself. If I didn't want a car, they would pay me two hundred to three hundred dollars each time, depending on the vehicle. They went to junkyards and bought wrecked car titles and VIN numbers. They would match as close as possible to the stolen one (for example, a 1965 Chevy would be the VIN number for a stolen 1968 Chevy) and get a clean title and matching VIN for the hot car. Of course, the VIN is stamped on the frame as well, but it requires some effort to read it if suspected. I thought about it, but being jobless, I could not afford to maintain a newer car let alone risk it with the law. I declined a turn at grand larceny.

Vietnam was going strong, so I figured it was time to get some employment. The shipbuilding industry was south of San Diego by the harbor. I applied for an apprentice pipefitting course, and they took me. It was almost four dollars an hour to start (minimum wage was around a dollar or so then). After I finished my apprenticeship, the pay would go up again. A lid of grass was then dollars, so I was in the money at last. Pipefitting was dangerous on the ship. Someone would drop a hammer or pipe from above, and I could be crippled for life. When you're young, you don't think about the dangers, and I've been really lucky.

Benefits didn't start for thirty days, and I only made double the minimum wage to start, but once I got my union card, I would receive benefits and four dollars an hour for wages. (Chicago pipefitters were paid twice as much, but it was very controlled who got in and when.) All training was on the job, and an occasional safety meeting was thrown in for fun. I saw others there with long hair and beards, while in the world of office work, long hair and beards were taboo. This looked promising.

With my first paycheck, I bought a Ford "woodie" wagon from the late fifties vintage. It had some issues of vibration and poor gas mileage, but it didn't burn oil and had California emission controls. I slapped on the Illinois plates that I'd saved (mistake), and I was mobile for work. I found a place to live in the old grand section of San Diego on Twenty-Second and K. It was an old mansion that had been converted to rentals. This guy named Jim had gotten out of the Navy and needed a roommate. He rode a ten-speed, played guitar, and was a gentile guy. The home was less than two miles from work, so I could walk if my car failed. I was finally substantial.

The new place had a back with an elaborate fire escape. The various renters sat on the stairs and chatted. On the top floor a unit down from me, two guys shared a place, and next door was a cute girl. The girl was madly in love with one of the guys, and the other guy was in love with her. The first guy was gay and wanted to break in his roommate, and it became an endless triangle of desire. I think when they drank or smoked weed was the only time they didn't plot against each other for the affection of the one who didn't want them. It was entertaining after work to sit out on the fire escape and listen to the hate and unrequited love like a reality soap opera.

I went down to Tijuana for some drinks and to watch strippers, and this woman lowered herself in a basket with cutouts on to a guy with a hard-on. It looked painful more than sexy, so I chalked it up as cultural differences. On the way back across the border, I was pulled over. My Illinois plates were on the Ford and listed as stolen or lost by the owner of the Buick I'd traded in Joplin, Missouri. In Illinois, the plates stay with the owner, but in California, they stay with the car. It was a Saturday, the charge was a felony, and no arraignment was available until Monday. They took my steel-toed boots because they were considered a weapon, not a safety feature. The cell was a considerable upgrade from Mexico's, but it was still a waste of time. On Monday, I was put on a double chain gang where our stocking feet were handcuffed to one chain and our arms to another. It was quite awkward, and we had to work together or fall. There were more than a dozen of us shuttled to the court. I watched the proceedings to get a sense of the court's justice and just told the truth to all the questions. I discovered the problem, told of my employment, and was fined and released. As soon as I was out, I called work and explained. They were not pleased but told me to return to work the next day. My boot socks were ruined, but I still had my job.

Shipbuilding was like my industrial job making boxcars in 1966, only bigger. To start, they put me at the pipe shop cleaning up and then trained me to make large flange plates. They gave me an electric power sander that looked like a giant handheld drill, but the end had a bit that was full of small cards of sandpaper. They spun very fast and cleaned metal parts well before fabrication. It was all metal except the business end. I had taken some barbiturates and was very mellow while cleaning the castings. My sander shorted out and began to spark seriously, and the voltage felt quite nice in my depressed state. I noticed everyone staring at me in shock, and I thought they knew I was having a good time on my drugs, so I dropped the sander. Well, several of my contemporaries were worried about injuries, but I stated I was okay. They said my hair went straight out and up, and I looked like an avenging angel or something. I assured everyone I was fine (and very glad not to have tipped my hand about the drugs), and the next day I was moved to the drill press full- time.

This wasn't a hard job, but I had to pay attention to the drill bit and keep it cool with the oil and speed, or it would break. I was to lift the eighty-pound plate, place on the press, and set up the drill. The first pass was small holes to correctly position the drive guide holes. Next pass was larger holes in the guide holes, and then finally smooth bolt holes through the plate. I had to use oil on the bits and drill very slowly. The previous drill press guys were getting two completed plates in an eight-hour shift. By the third day, I was doing four plates a day (with no drugs) and decided to see how many I could do in a shift. I got a girl to get me some black beauties (an upper used by pregnant women, so I knew it was safe) to accelerate my processing. The next week I was able to comfortably (on drugs) complete a plate an hour. Now no one had ever done more than four plates, so to management, I was a hero, and to the union, I was a suck up.

Management quickly moved me to the pipe shop where all pipe less than eight inches was bent to a blueprint spec. Pipe longer than eight inches was bent on the floor and was mostly nickel steel. I had copper, nickel, and iron-steel, each with a separate procedure. Copper had to be annealed (preheated) before bending and needed a dildo-like ram inside so it wouldn't flatten out. This old guy who ran it made it seem more complicated than it was. There may be several bends and offsets on a particular drawing (kind of like a bicycle handlebar), but the rise and run had to be accurate, or it would not line up with the bulkheads on the ship. He showed me the tools and how to do it on his Ouija-like board, but again, Speedy Gonzales (me) thought it ponderous and inefficient. I saw that the correct angles could be figured out quickly using trigonometry. The length requirements were known, and if I imagined the pipe in triangles, I could figure the angles quickly. The pipe shop was more than two months behind in production fabrication, so this guy had a lot of overtime offered to him and held the pace for the yard. I was his student for the rest of the week and tried to show him the faster way, but he was not interested.

We were working on a large Navy LST (landing ship transport) project at the time. I went out at lunchtime to enjoy the sun, but it was a little too hot. I saw an open door on a six-inch turret gun and went in to get some shade. Inside was an armed Marine guard, and I was treated like a potential saboteur. It was my bad, so I was more careful after that confrontation. On the way back, I was walking sideways on a wooden skid, and my foot slipped partially over the side. It was only a couple of inches, but my soul stayed on top while my ankle touched the ground. The ligaments snapped, and I was limped the next couple of weeks with a pressure-wrapped foot.

My pipe bender teacher went on a two-week vacation the following week, and I was in control. I found it fascinating to use my math skills in a practical application and began to attack the pile of backlog. It came easily for me, and I rapidly knocked the pile down. When he returned, we were all caught up and slightly ahead on the requirements timeline. My bosses were ecstatic and wanted me to go nonunion expediter on salary. I would have to get a haircut and shave and wear short-sleeved white shirts, so I declined. They pulled me out of the pipe bender area and set me up in the assembly area where I took my bent pipes and welded hardware on them like flanges and nipple connections per drawing specs. I had to use cutting torches, welders, and grinders. The blueprints and assembly reminded me of my old model-making days as a kid, and it too was easy. In quality control, I think I was only rejected once for one of my pieces. Work was going great, but the union people were now hateful toward me and actually told me to slow down. I began to distrust the union and dislike their tactics. I kept to myself as much as possible from then on. I felt like a classic hero to zero.

My Ford wagon was running well but surprised me one day on the freeway. I was in the middle of a seven-lane (going each direction) stretch of highway during afternoon rush. We were all moving information at fifty-five miles per hour when my hood blew up and blocked my vision. Now, if I tried to turn off, slow down, whatever, I would hit someone. Instead, I got up out the driver's side window on my elbow while keeping my right tiptoe on the gas pedal. It seemed like an eternity with death waiting for a wrong move in my very awkward stretch, but after fifteen minutes, I managed to get over to the right side in spite of the horrific, speeding traffic. On the side of the road, I finished removing the hood and threw it in the back.

I dropped some acid the following weekend to get some positive observations. I decided San Diego State University campus would be perfect. I wandered the columns and grounds, appreciating architecture and nature. I thought of Madonna back home, so I borrowed some chalk from an art student and began to write and draw on the sidewalk. It took a couple of hours, and when I was done, I wrote her address on the top of the section of walk and asked a passing student for a stamp. I cleared out a spot in the upper right and stuck the stamp there. To this day, I'm still positive that it was never delivered.

Not complete with my acid trip, I went to the student facilities for a nice shit. I had never shit on acid before, and maybe all the squatting and sitting to draw on the sidewalk got me stimulated for the dump. It was unbelievable in sensation. I could feel the entire turd in my lower track and the muscles contracting to spur it forward and out. My sphincter could assess every crease and lump as it slowly egressed from my rectum. I had chills going from my lower gut building like harp music, up my spine, to the base of my brain and back. When the turd dropped, a water droplet came straight up to kiss my rectum good-bye like a gentile bidet. I'm not sure how long this took, but the sun was low, and it was time to go home.

I enjoyed LSD and dropped twenty-eight times in my life, most times lasting at least eight hours of wonderment. When I learned to control the wild colors and fantasies, it became about power and abilities. I moved from a child full of fantasy and colors to an adult capable of manipulating others and updating my skills to perfection. Hippies called the controlled people heads, and we had the power. Heads could walk into a bar and pick up a girl with no possibility of failure. Your balance and mind power was phenomenal. The only enemy was you, and we called this paranoia. I could get myself fed, laid, high, and transported with no money and with total strangers. Interestingly, I never got into a fight during this period. Aggression was controlled, but so were most of the other emotions. After a while, I found I could control the other drugs just the same, so it didn't matter if it was booze, pot, speed, or downers; I was still a head.

My fellow dopers and I were curious one afternoon about gossip that the cooking spray can oil Pam was a cheap high. I had to investigate, so another guy and I got a couple of cans to try it out. We heard you were supposed to inhale it quickly and hold it (like pot) and then slowly release. This was an immediate auditory attack, and everything was like a trumpet mute being put on and then released (wa wa wah). The colors weren't as strong as LSD, but we made up for it with a screaming yellow zonkers show. (The candied popcorn called Screaming Yellow Zonkers was named for this phenomena). To a clothesline stretched across the yard, we attached plastic bags (like the ones your suits come home from the cleaners in). Every eight inches we knotted the plastic until it reached the ground. We would light the bottom, and as the flame it hit the knots, it would flare and create interesting black, yellow, and orange bursts of flame. This was very attractive to someone partially stoned.

I had smoked weed with many people, but this one guy who I gave one of my ambulance shirts to wanted to do acid with me. I went to his home near the beach and found him painting artwork. He quickly changed into the shirt I gave him (covered with oil paint), and we got on his scooter as we took our drugs. It was a Honda 50, which was very small for two grown men, but it was fun. When we started to peak, which is the most intense part of the high, he drove through a school bus lot where rows of them were parked end to end. The rows were about thirty-six inches apart. Black, yellow, and glass was exhilarating at twenty miles per hour. We weaved through all the banks of busses and then drove on 101 Ocean Highway. The air and beach really made for a great trip.

There was a free concert at Balboa Park, which turned out to be a group I already had the 8-track for called Canned Heat. I asked my roommate Jim if I could borrow his ten-speed bike. He agreed but gave me a lock to wrap around the bike at a sign post. I enjoyed the exercise and got to the park when it was half full. I was pleasantly stoned on some good weed and ready for the tunes as I locked up the bike per Jim's instructions. I walked around the lot observing, and maybe thirty-plus Hell's Angels showed up. They were quite noisy and trying to be as intimidating as possible. I watched curiously, and they were very meticulous with their bikes, parking them perfectly parallel to each other maybe a foot and a half apart on a leaning kickstand. As unclean and unkempt as they were, their bikes were the opposite and immaculate. They marched up to the entrance and left one small guy behind to watch the bikes. He was down on one end talking to some girl, and my curiosity got the better of me. I had built large dominoes setups to fall with the knocking over of just the end piece. I lightly pushed over the first bike, and lo and behold, all but the last two went down. The little guy talking to the girl freaked out and ran to the big guys to tattle on me. I walked over to an entrance on the left side of the concert auditorium and four bikers, followed by six more, came after me. I chatted with a cop at the entrance and then walked down the far aisle on the left. I sat down near the front there with a wall a couple of seats to my left. I felt eyes burning through the back of my head as the concert began. Halfway through the show, I was standing and digging the music when I heard a whizzing sound from behind and to the right of me. It just missed my right ear and burst on the wall. It was a half-full quart bottle of cheap whiskey. I knew there was no reconciliation for my misdeed, and I needed to disappear.

The concert came to a close, and I quickly walked up the left staircase and onto the stage. The stage was open in front with doors on the left and right with an opening in the back. The crowd helped, but I figured the Angels were doing a blood oath on me. Behind the stage left wall were four fifty-five-gallon garbage cans. I quickly closed the lid on three and got into the forth, which had the least stuff in it. I left my lid half open so people could look in and place some garbage on me. As the crowds exited, I could hear the clanking thud of the motorcycle boots with chains on them. They were moving quicker, and over a fifteen-minute period, three different guys looked in my trash can and threw a lid off one of the other ones. One guy even dumped over one of the trash cans, but I remained sequestered. I stayed in there until I heard the motorcade take off an hour later. I still waited until dusk and then left. The place was empty, and I walked out to the empty parking lot. There, crucified on the signpost, was Jim's bike. It died for my sins, and I felt terrible. I walked home and told him what happened, and he was crushed. I offered to pay, but he moved out before the following week was over.

I needed a new roommate, and the one I got was named Hobey. He was a gregarious guy with short hair and glasses, but he liked drugs and had great energy. He was a bit of a con man too. I fed off his unending energy, but he had a downside. Hobey would borrow money for an "emergency" and never get it repaid. The last time I saw him he borrowed my Ford wagon and didn't secure it when he returned. It rolled down the hill backward and hit the neighbor's house. What made it worse is the poor black woman who lived there was on the toilet when it happened, and it knocked her off and broke the porcelain water closet. Fortunately, she wasn't hurt seriously, but her dignity and house both were. When I returned from work, Hobey was nowhere to be found, and my car had been impounded. This would come back to haunt me later.

I made a new acquaintance named Dennis who had a scraggly blond beard and long hair. He wore a cowboy hat, but it was more flat, and he had a beige, rough leather jacket with the fringe hanging off the long sleeves. He had dumpy suede boots that were a cross between a moccasin and a cowboy boot. We were goofing around, and some female began to stalk us. She was like five nine; had blonde, short, curly hair; was a little chubby; and was wearing a print summer dress. She was spaced out but was fascinated with me. She thought I was the Protestant standard depiction of Christ. She was older but not brighter. Dennis got all excited, but she seemed to like my look, and I was uncomfortable with it. When we got to the house, she wanted sex and got naked right away. She wanted me, but I think anyone would have done. She kept calling me Jesus and other religious things. I did have a short run with her, but it was not even lust and was totally unexciting. I declined and got off, and Dennis quickly mounted her with a Southern glee. I think for him it was extended masturbation, and I took a quick shower. One of Dennis's other friends was there watching, and when Dennis culminated his efforts, this guy jumped on. He seemed to be the best fit for her and had some honest lust at least. The woman still looked depressed after the encounter but had a slight smile toward us and slunk away into the night.

I met this beautiful brunette in a Howard Johnson's on my next "trip," and I started to peak looking into her eyes. Her companion said to her, "What did he see?" She replied, "Whatever he wanted." I guess that about sums up drugs. She loved the attention and was moving stuff in her VW van, so I came along to help, just digging on her. I got into carrying stuff, and pretty soon I had most of the stuff on my shoulders. One of the guys was impressed with my ability and asked if I wanted to be a part-time roadie. He was the percussion instrument guy (not the drummer) in a band that opened for some other band I'd never heard of. I would carry instruments and speakers and set up the cords, mikes, and wa-wa pedals and then wait until it was over and pack it up back into the vans. They would pay me in weed and wine, and I didn't mind. The farthest I went with them was to LA, but as they got more gigs, I didn't like the long weekend travel and then having to go back to work on Monday. I had one more encounter with the brunette, again on drugs, but this time, it was mescaline, which is a natural psychedelic from the peyote plant. It was used by Native Americans in their spirit encounters, so I thought it was appropriate to take this girl to her church on it. She took some and loved the idea. We started to get colors as we arrived at the church. It looked like a typical church from the outside, but inside the pews were facing the center, and the pulpit was off to one side. The pastor was in casual clothes just like us. There were twenty of us in a square array with the pastor in the middle. Being ripped was fun, but when the sun hit the stained-glass windows, I really felt like God entered the room. We talked about love, God, and individual splendor. It was very peaceful talking to God, and by the time we were coming down, it was getting dark.

I got with Dennis again. He wanted to make a big score and buy a kilo of gold to sell in San Diego. I remembered that this was why I had come to California with Rick and Curly months earlier. I agreed, and we drove across the border at Mexicali in the middle of the state. We were trying to find the guy I met when we did the Woodstock misfire. It turned out he was in Tecate, which was closer to San Diego.

We drove there and somehow found him and got more than a kilo of grass. Tecate was so poor there wasn't even a US border town when we crossed. We took these back roads and came out in the San Diego suburb of Bonita and then drove home. Dennis quickly got baggies, and we split up the stash. Dennis immediately cut his half of the stuff with oregano and who knows what else.

We went to the plaza where the Navy guys hung out. San Diego was a big port town, so we had lots of customers. When you have good drugs, you get money fast. Dennis didn't get the repeat customers like I did. We left the plaza together, and about a mile away, all hell broke loose. We had six police cars hit us from all sides while we were crossing railroad tracks. It was about dusk, and the gumball lights on top of the police cars were pretty cool. Dennis decided to struggle, and they quickly found more than a pound of grass that we hadn't sold yet. I was willing to talk, and they went easy on me. I gave them a story about Dward Farkwar selling the pot to us. He was Enial Bellini's second cousin who lived on Silver Strand… and the cop was busy writing everything down. Another cop (much more astute) was listening and came over to beat on and slap the cop writing everything down. He then motioned for me to get in the squad car. Everyone was laughing except Dennis and the duped cop. Dennis got a court-appointed lawyer who was worthless, and I used my call to phone Dad. I explained the situation and that I was up for two years of hard time for sales and possession. Dad said he would help this time but not to ever call again in similar circumstances. The lawyer was Jewish and awesome. He boiled it down to just cause. The person who tattled had no ability to determine what the "green vegetable matter" was, and the police just went and arrested us with no investigation. If the green vegetable matter was given by a Navy guy to the police and tested, then I would be guilty and get two or more years for sales and possession. Today with all the legal marijuana it seems petty, but back then, it was a serious crime (interestingly, not unlike prohibition in the twenties and thirties).

Dennis and I were exonerated, and as I left the courtroom, I ended up in the same elevator as the district attorney who had just prosecuted us. He was very angry with me and said he would get me for this flagrant violation and then noted that I was a hopeless criminal. When he told me that justice would be served, I stated, "It already has. Can I have my green vegetable matter back?" At this point, the other assistant district attorneys had to physically restrain him. I never did get my pot back, but at least I was free again. I never saw Dennis again.

I missed John's wedding to Mellie while inside, but it was just as well. I never liked her, and the only reason I tolerated her later in life was because John wanted her. John stayed married to her for 30 years and finally divorced her.

I owed dad $2,500 for the lawyer, but I somehow managed to keep my job. It seemed like all my paid holidays and vacation days were used in jail time. All my assets were depleted, and I now hitchhiked everywhere. I needed to get out of the Twenty-Second and K house, so I went to a club and dropped acid.

It was amazing what I could do with a drug if I wanted. I could funnel the music through my body and dance very strange (being strange/different was important back then) while still moving in perfect rhythm to the beat. When I sat down, I began to focus on different conversations all around the place. My auditory sensors were quite acute, and I was fascinated with my new power. I then heard the sound of a pool table on the other side of the club and went to investigate. It was a beautiful table with other people playing but not very well. I watched a couple of games and then got my turn. My brain was like a computer, and I could see all the angles. I could not miss, and this was my first Zen experience. I was the ball. I played shape (figuring where the cue ball would be after the current shot), cut awesome, and even bank cut. Before I finished, I was double banking and making shots way beyond my usual ability. Between pool shooting, listening, and dancing I was getting very popular with the hippie girls.

The straight girls were also trying to get in but had many conflicts. When you're stoned, you can focus an extreme amount of attention on a woman. They all love attention and just want some love. The expression of "love the one you're with" held special meaning then, as did "free love" and "peace." Free love meant no strings attached, and peace was also misconstrued as "piece of ass." Sex became spontaneous with one look, even shyness slipped away, and nudity ran rampant. I had a couple who had just met stay the night, and they "got it on" while on the floor next to my bed. (Two years later in Vietnam, I would be the porn star.) I was curious about the expressions as they continued their floor dance of love. No one seemed to mind. Girls and guys wore no underwear, and thin granny dresses showed pubic hairs in the sun. Women's breasts and armpit hair hung out everywhere. This was a great time to be past puberty.

I met Darcy at one of these meeting bars. She was more responsible than most of my peers and had a good job at a bakery. She was tall (five ten), had brunette hair that hung down to her breasts, and had a nice figure. She was like Dennis (more violent and with a quick temper), but she was great to me. I loved kissing on her when I was stoned, and she was aggressive too, having no issues grabbing and stroking me. My memory has her close to Minnie Driver in overall looks. I went home with her and stayed. She rented a small house in El Cajon. She had a '65 Chevy Malibu, so in a pinch, I could get a ride.

The first week I was there she put her younger sister in the hospital by throwing a heavy glass ashtray into her back as she was trying to escape Darcy's rage. Darcy felt bad about it for a week. We had other couples crashing at our place, but we were the only two whoever worked. Rent, gas, and food took the majority of our earnings. People always were visiting, smoking, sexing, and just having a good time. Pot was expensive, because everyone got the munchies, and all the cupboards would be bare. Darcy could bring home day-old baked goods and bread, but we were always running out. I figured we supported on average ten people a month. One couple was with us four months without contributing anything but conversation.

We had an awesome Mazola party in late 1969. We had pot with pine tree mixed in for Christmas spirit, and I brought a tarp home from work that covered our living room floor. We moved the furniture to the kitchen and bedrooms, and everyone got naked and poured oil on themselves. It made sense then, and the sensations from the acid, female bodies, and slippery oil, well, it was out of sight to use the expression of the day. It took two days to clean the place up, hose the tarp down, and get everything clean and back together. It was a great time, and many asked about it later.

I don't think I was volatile enough for Darcy, and she loved her peaks and valleys. She was always upset about something, and I was unaffected, which made her even angrier. While she was at work one day, I decided to provide some entertainment and hung signs on strings from the ceiling. Each was a poem or message from me that meant something. I stressed how she could not commit to a relationship and that it was okay, but for the last string in the kitchen, I made the mistake of hanging a whole raw chicken from the grocery store with a note attached that simply read "Darcy." She went ballistic being called a chicken and went after me with an electric cord. She hit me very hard across my face, and for the first time, she saw my anger. I did nothing except take the cord away from her hand, but when she looked into my eyes, I saw deep fear in her soul. She ran out the door and down the street, and I didn't see her until the weekend. When she came back, she had a semi- straight boyfriend with her (ostensibly for protection), and she made sure she kissed him in front of me. She told me to move out. I was fine with it, although the New Year was upon us. I had a few days off, so I hitched to Tijuana and bought some LSD. It was bad and had too much speed in it, so I began to drink. It didn't matter how much; I didn't come down. When I finally returned to El Cajon, my few clothes and possessions were on the lawn. I waited.

When she finally returned from work, she seemed calm and gave me a pillow and blanket to sleep on the small screened porch out back. I thanked her, and the next day she let me in to take a shower. (In a bind, I could take one at work.) I could see the handwriting on the wall, but she complained about this other guy and had moved on to even another.

I felt I was an observer, and it was her life I had intruded on, so I voiced no complaints and just slept on the porch.

It was 1970, and the car crash at Twenty-Second and K into the house had resulted in a US marshal serving me at work. I was off the day he came, but I found out the next day. The bosses were understandably finished with me. Now I had an outstanding warrant on me, and I knew it was time to leave. I had my last acid trip in kind of a funk. I didn't see a lot of action and held it together to analyze and think. I had been on drugs for a year, and I looked at the people who had just started feeling joy and wonder. Then I looked at the paranoids, and lastly, I looked at the Timothy Leary types who had done it much longer. I decided it was no place to be and knew I needed to move on. Whatever a drug gives you it also takes away. If booze takes away your pain, it also gives you a hangover. Pot stimulates you but then slows you down, while downers mellow you out but later you can't sleep.

I explained my work situation and new direction to Darcy. I knew she cared about me but didn't know what to do with me. I waited until my final paycheck was ready at work and quickly invested the proceeds in LSD. I took a piece of Double mint gum and filled where the gum was with LSD on baby aspirin. I mailed it to Elaine in South Dakota and told her to put it in her freezer until I hitchhiked there. Darcy cut the bottom seam of my jeans and sewed red triangles with some designs to make them look like bell bottoms pants. She was very teary and quiet when I hugged her good-bye and stuck my thumb out in front of her house. Afterward, I pulled the thread out and sewed the remainder of my baby aspirin LSD in the seams. If I decided to sell some, I could pull a thread loose and then tighten it back up. I called one of Darcy's friends before the anniversary of our Mazola party, but she said Darcy went north with some other guy to Canada and was pregnant. I don't know if it was mine or not, but I think a baby might have calmed her passions down.

I only had a couple of joints on me, and I put them in the lining of my self-made poncho. I smoked one hitchhiking out of El Cajon and got a short ride to nowhere. I saw another guy hitching, so I shared my next to last joint with him, and not long after another short ride, I was still hitching with him. The police in some small town picked us up. (Long hairs always got hassled in those days.) We were searched and thrown in a cell for the night, but at least they fed us. The next day we were let go, but I lost sight of the other guy.

I still had a wake-up joint left in my poncho, so I enjoyed the morning and got a ride south of Flagstaff, Arizona. I was hitching north at the city edge, and a Flagstaff cop picked me up. He drove me for less than an hour but to the other side of town going east. He told me to get out and keep going. (Twelve years later when I saw *First Blood* with Rambo, it was a flash of this moment when the cop dragged him through town, except he went back.)

I got my next ride from a Hopi Indian and his family. It was an old pickup truck, and I was in the back with the dog and kids. They let me off in the middle of nowhere at dusk. They went north into the reservation, and I was by two houses on old Route 66. There was a small sign that said Two Guns, a short rail fence, and lots of sand. It was getting dark, and no one was on the road. I spent a half hour searching for wood and managed enough for a small fire so travelers could see me. I lit it when it was completely dark, and it was nice, because the desert is very cold at night. Someone drove past but didn't stop. Then one of the houses opened up, and a semi-crazy guy came out ranting. He told me he was the fire marshal and wanted to see my fire permit. I had none and explained my plight. He was also the proclaimed mayor and police chief of Two Guns, Arizona. I had to move on and put out the fire. The only thing remotely burnable was the rail fence twenty feet away; everything else was sand and highway. I needed the fire for anyone to see me, so I slowly separated the wood as he stormed back into his home. It was almost out fifteen minutes later when some hippie types stopped and picked me up.

The hippies were going to a commune outside of Albuquerque, New Mexico, near the Laguna reservation. We first went to pick up someone in one of the suburbs before heading out to the commune. The home was nice (one of the hippie's relatives), and they fed us well. We crashed on the floor and couches, and in the morning, we got showers and breakfast, which was wonderful. We loaded stuff into the van, and then it was off to the commune. Structurally, it was unsound, and even the outhouse wasn't a big step up from a cat hole. They had several gentile guys there trying to plant a crop, but mostly they were interested in growing pot. Some of the girls were attractive but in need of bathing. They had farm horses that were usable, but their housing was not much better than my self-built childhood tree houses. The girls were a little better than the guys on working and could cook if they had something to work with, but they were content to smoke and talk. Granny dresses were the outfits, and free love was the rule. I helped with the carpentry and made one hovel stable and leak proof and repaired an outhouse. There was a nice stream nearby, and I wondered if a flash rain would flood them out.

They weren't planners, and the only success they had was growing pot and trading for necessities. I didn't want to stay permanently if I was going to be the only engineer and repairman. Interestingly, most of the people were from middle-class families. As I was preparing to hitch-hike to Elaine in South Dakota, several members approached me about staying. I was offered a horse, a choice of two women, and my own hovel to fix up. I was to be the commune's carpenter, but I declined and thanked them for the offer. I had no way to contact them, so I never found out how they fared. I suspect a good portion returned home, but who knows.

I hitchhiked uneventfully to Denver. It had changed since 1963 when I lived there, but it was nostalgic for me on my travels. Two rides and little sleep later, I was in Lincoln, Nebraska, and turned north to Dakota Territory. I didn't get a ride for more than fifty miles, but many would stop to run me as far as they could. I had Elaine's off-campus address, and she was living with her friend Jan. It worked out well for them, and I think Jan was shyer the Elaine. They were both excited to get a boy to stay with them now that they were grad students. Elaine had my Double mint gum in her freezer with all my LSD intact. I still had a dozen left in the seam of my pants, which I removed and put with the others. I gave the girls my clothes to wash and repair, and they were worried and giggling at the same time. I took a shower and walked out still naked. Elaine tried to cover me up, and Jan was blushing. It had been a long time since I'd seen women like this. I think they were seeing their first naked nonrelative male, and it was a lot to absorb.

The next day the girls went to class, and I went to campus to peddle my wares. It was very conservative on campus, and people still wore ties to class. I went to the art school first to see what was happening. The girls offered their bodies for me to paint or explore, and the boys offered me pot. This guy offered me a kilo of pot for some LSD, but it was weak compared to what I used in California. I agreed if he could get me some heroin. I traded most of my LSD for a kilo of pot and a couple pops of smack. We went to this guy's trailer, and they dropped the acid and began their trip. I was no longer interested. I took a cookie sheet, some wine, and a bowl. I put the pot on the cookie sheet and mixed the heroin into the wine. I took half the pot from the sheet pan and put it in the bowl. I sprinkled half the "herowine" on to the pot and mixed. Next, I spread it over half the cookie sheet and repeated for the last half. I baked at two hundred degrees to get it to set and not burn. My "herowine" pot was ready for market.

I was like a major drug dealer at this point, and everyone wanted some. I wanted to get going at some point in time, but the people needed me (weird). I gave away two joints for two different groups to try. That was all the marketing I had needed. I was still in the trailer and met this cute little hippie wannabe. We had sex in the trailer, in her car, on a table, and in the girl's bathroom. I think she was using me to complete her college bucket list before I left. I didn't mind being used. I found the best of the pot on campus and traded some of my specially treated stuff at three-to- one, so now I had more pot, and the heroine-loaded stuff was gone.

I found Zoomer, my old college roommate and friend, in law school. He wanted to try some pot, so I took him to a gathering, and he got wasted. He couldn't move, so I did exercises in front of him to motivate him, but he could only smile. He was a bright and religious guy, but this was not for him. He's still a friend today.

I returned to Elaine's to shower and clean up before my road trip would recommence. She got rid of Jan and decided to check my interest level or hers. This time, she got naked, lay on her couch, and got my curiosity up. She was thin but shapely and offered herself to me. I teased her a little, kissing her all over, and when I kissed her labia, she went stiff as a board. She could say nothing, and maybe I should have continued, but it just seemed wrong still, so I lightly kissed her lips and got dressed. I wished the best for her, but someone else would have to deflower her. I heard a decade later the she moved on and was married. I'm sure she made someone very happy and is a great wife.

I got to Mom and Dad's around Easter. I had traveled a month and a half from California with four dollars and some acid only to return with four dollars and half a pound of pot. Who said bartering was dead?

I came into my parents' house, and Mom was glad to see me. Lauren was at college, and Dad was at work. Page was impressed with my visage, and Jimmy looked at me and said, "You don't have any underpants on." You could see through my pants in places from the burning metal holes created at National Steel. Dad was very conservative with a flattop and wanted to beat up long hairs whenever and wherever he saw them. When he got home and saw me, he went out into the backyard and threw up. It felt good, and I cut the beard one day and the hair a few days later. It was fun to shock everyone then. The longest hair in 1970 in the Chicago area was the Beatle cut, which was very risky. Opera stars looked at my long hair with disdain. Wherever I went, everyone stared. I then cut it back to a Beatle cut until I went in the service later that year. After the hair was cut and the beard was gone, I was socially acceptable again. I didn't know why it was like that; my great- great-grandpas all had long hair, and short hair was only for little boys. It was fun torturing people with it for a few days.

Madonna did some drugs, and her brother was the largest drug dealer at the high school, so I gave them the pot to sell. I made four times back home what I would have gotten in California. It had been a couple of months since I'd done LSD and a few weeks since I'd smoked any pot. I started to get paranoid, illogical paranoia where I thought the "heads" were plotting to bring me back into the drug fold. I knew I needed help and direction there, and when I changed my address for the draft again, I decided maybe that would be something I would consider. I stuck to booze in the meantime and got jobs like storeroom clerk at the racetrack. I learned to bet only in the rain on mudders (horses that ran well in the mud) and go place or show. I never won a lot, but I usually won and stayed ahead.

Madonna and I got an apartment on the south side near Dad's company and the train station. She worked downtown as a secretary and file clerk and rode the train to work. The neighborhood was tough white trash, so I needed to make a statement or be swallowed up. One day when a bunch of the local tuffs were chatting around a car hood, I shot a squirrel in the tree above them, and it fell right on the hood. It jumped around for a few seconds and had a real hammy death where it slid off the hood with a blood smear trail while one paw reached back for the higher part of the hood. They broke up their meeting and quietly disbursed. Next, I wore my pork pie hat with a black shirt and white tie and dark suit. Under the thin suit coat, I had my grandfather's Colt 45 in a shoulder holster. It was huge and stuck out well for a concealed weapon. I never talked to anyone, but they all knew me. My door upstairs (we lived on the second floor) didn't lock and had a window in it, so I set up my Marlin rifle aiming at the door with a visible string going to the doorknob. If someone opened the door, the string would go slack, but it looked like a dangerous trap. No one ever tried to come in while we were gone, even the landlords when we didn't pay our rent.

Madonna got a hearing disability scholarship at Kishwaukee College and got to stay at a university dormitory. My cousin Lee moved in, but he had no money and was selling copy machines to small business. I still had a Bank Americard checkbook with nice preprinted checks. I would only use every fourth check with the fancy Hope graphic on it. The landlord would come to the apartment with the bad check, and I would ask him to give it to me. I'd then offer another check with both months' rent. I'd tear up the old check and write a new one twice as big, and he would leave but with justified concerns. He would come in while we were gone, so that was another reason for the rifle and string trick. I also posted the legal tip of the day from the *Tribune* that said landlords were not ever allowed in the apartment when the tenant was gone except with permission. The next month he came I had his new check taped to the window outside and he ripped it off, leaving part of it there. I then posted a law about two exits being required, pointing out that the second-floor apartment was in serious violation of the law.

Lee finished us when he fired his 9mm Beretta, and it went through the wall into the adjoining apartment. The bullet penetrated the wall and missed a baby's crib by a couple of feet and cut a groove in their sidewall. The police came, and Lee had stuck a piece of gum in the hole, which I never understood. The police said several had complained of gunfire and the neighbor had been shot at inside. We said it was some guy Bill on a Kawasaki 500 motorcycle, and he had headed south toward Homewood. The three of them wanted to come in and search, but we asked if they had a warrant. The three little pigs left, but we knew they were plotting against us. A short time later, the landlord's partner came over with an investigator's badge—what a mistake. 'We both rode him into the ground for the fake badge. We were horrible, making innuendos about his family's health. He couldn't wait to get out of there. I'm sure when I moved out in August, they had a huge party. I only lived there four and a half months, but it had to seem like a year.

CHAPTER 6

Army

Basic Training

My draft lottery number for August 29 was thirty-two. They were taking up to 150 that day, so I was doomed. I had been in ROTC (Reserve Officer Training Corps) for three and a half years in college, and when I put a red armband on my uniform to protest the dead in Vietnam in the spring of 1969, they kicked me out and notified my draft board. I was a problem child, and I had an attitude.

I had legally dodged the draft for a year in California by changing my address and sending the forms in every time the draft notice came. Their own paperwork choked them, and if I moved and supplied a change of address every two or three months, I wasn't in violation. I had finally moved back to Illinois and decided to stop dodging the draft. I went in for a physical wearing a pork pie hat (like everyone wore in the forties and fifties) and didn't take it off. The facility in Chicago had every draft dodger and crook you can imagine trying to get out of service. They dumped sugar and blood in their urine, had other people's blood and urine, and took all kinds of different chemicals to screw up their tests. The visit with the shrink was a joke; everyone was acting crazy or handicapped. When the doctor listened to my heart, he couldn't have heard even one beat it was so quick. When they told me to bend over, drop my shorts, and spread my cheeks, I pulled the sides of my mouth and laughed. When I was to be weighed, the guy directed me to jump up on the scale, and I did— just as high as I could. It jammed the scale needle at 320 pounds. No one else could get weighed. It didn't matter; everyone was being certified. After I passed, I was instructed to return for induction in November. I told them that I volunteered the draft and requested that they send me in late August, so they did. I just wanted to see my cousin get married.

The nine weeks of basic training was very interesting for an ex-hippie with an attitude. I came in August 1970, and Vietnam was starting to wind down and would be over in three years. I had my twenty-third birthday in basic training, and it wasn't pleasant. I was the platoon guide and had come in an E-2 because of all my ROTC. Everyone else was an an E-1.

Being the boss is a lonely job in basic training. I had ROTC, Pershing Rifles, the Rifle Team, and Crack Squad in college to fall back on, but comrades were few and far between. I was very conscientious. When Drill Sergeant Odom was explaining how to respond to the command "Dress right, dress." He told the troops to put up their right arms and look right, and I stopped to correct him and explained it was the left arm when you looked right. He told me I was insubordinate and not to correct him, and I stated that according to 22-5 (the Army drill manual), the proper way to do it was with the left arm. He went ballistic and took away my platoon guide status and gave me a week on KP (kitchen patrol).

KP involved getting up at three thirty in the morning to work in the food service at the mess hall until nine o'clock at night. The most hated job was pots and pans. All that the job entailed was washing huge, greasy, baked-on pans all day. The other feared job was cleaning the grease trap (mostly due to its horrendous smell). I was, of course, given both due to the status of my latest demotion. The grease trap was cleaned with a hospital mask on, and I had to open up a metal box in the pipes, use a ladle to empty it, and then replace the top. It looked like a breadbox in size and shape, with a tapering pipe coming out of each side. I removed the top and quickly emptied the inner sauce. With that disposed of, I decided to really clean it, so I meticulously scraped the inner walls and then used a Brillo pad to shine the metal. Next, I used floor wax to seal the metal walls and got the sergeant so I could show him my brilliant cleaning job. He came and inspected it and was really mad. Apparently, they liked to use the trap as a punishment weekly, and the way I cleaned it, the grease trap would not be repugnant for a couple of months. Another gesture of excellence on my behalf fell short. The week's KP gave me another benefit in getting to know the regular kitchen cooks and permanent staff and whom to trust.

As soon as I returned to the barracks from my week of KP, I made a lot of friends. People tend to gravitate to principle and the underdog. I was also armed with mess hall knowledge and would apply it soon. I went out to the rifle range and sighted my weapon perfectly for two hundred meters and cleaned and oiled the internal working parts carefully. The range had targets like silhouettes of men at various ranges: 50, 100, 150, 200, 300, and 400 meters. At each increment, the target got bigger. For example, at 50 meters, the target included the head and neck, while at 400 meters, the head to waste was exposed. If a round from the M-16 passed through the target, the vibration would cause it to go down and count as a hit.

To qualify and get my marksman badge, I needed fifty percent hits. There were also sharpshooter and expert levels at approximately 70 and 90 percent hits. I had shot for my college rifle team and had been an avid shooter most of my life from slingshots to bows to BB guns. Hitting those targets was easy once I set my hold over and under. (My zero was at two hundred, but the Army had most recruits set their guns to one hundred.) The close target I had to shoot way short, but for the four-hundred-meter, my holdover wasn't too much. We went out for practice on qualification, and I never hit one target. It was a new record for the Army. Ten magazines (two hundred rounds) and not one hit. My drill sergeant called me Bolo C, trying to intimidate me. I had actually shot small pebbles to either side of the target to mess with them. You'd think they would have caught on that I never even hit a target accidentally. If they had seen my sighting in paper target and the tight pattern, maybe then they would have suspected. I only made it twice more to the range. Once was without sights at night (automatic fire), which I loved. Fortunately, I didn't get swept up with it, or I'd have gone Infantry. I fired expert with only half of the ammo required at night and helped a buddy who was having trouble qualifying with the rest of my rounds. At night, you look over your sights with the stock at the base of your neck. If you shot short of the target, the round would ricochet dirt and gravel into the target, so additional hits would register. They said to use three round bursts, but I really enjoyed the feeling blazing half a magazine or more. During the other daytime qualification, I did get a hit, but I think it was a ricochet or someone else's gone wild. My one hit caused the drill sergeant to go ballistic and volunteer to give me extra training. I declined, telling him I was getting the hang of it and how I had improved my score from last time. Then I suggested that maybe I should only fire at night and on automatic, as I had done so well there. He was still mad because he was measured on how we all shot, and I was looking bad for his record.

The drill sergeant took us to chemical warfare training. It was a joke to us, but in the unlikely event of a nerve gas attack, I knew to use atropine to save my life (if it was available). I smoked Marlboros at the time, and smoking was rewarded in the service with low prices and smoke breaks. We were next taken to the gas chamber and ordered to put on our gas masks. The drill sergeant was talking but I knew he'd be up to no good, so I took one of my Marlboros and broke off the filter. I took out my knife and cut it in half and then took the paper off the outside of my two pieces. I wet them with my saliva and shoved one up each of my nostrils. The drill sergeant set off several CS grenades (like a tear gas that waters the eye and nauseates the stomach) and then told us to take off our masks. We did (except the drill sergeant), and everyone but me left rapidly. I was very careful to draw air in through my nostrils and exhale through my mouth. The drill sergeant set off another CS grenade, but I kept breathing. My eyes were watering, but I kept them to little slits. He finally couldn't understand why I wasn't coughing and foolishly took off his mask. He began to get sick and ran out. I waited another two minutes for full effect and sauntered out. Everyone was depressed and gave me terrible looks but didn't know what to say. The drill sergeant just glared at me. I told everyone I was immune to CS and couldn't understand why any of them had a problem. After I got some heat from friends, I showed them the trick. They were relieved and laughed because I suckered the drill sergeant into taking his gas mask off.

We had a PT (physical training) test, and I did well on everything except the mile run (with our boots on). I could run a half mile but would have to walk and get a cigarette for the next lap. The last lap I would lope along at best. My time for the mile was nine to ten minutes, which was pathetic by any standard. To improve my performance, the drill sergeant made me a road guard. I was outside rank in the second row of a four-wide formation. When we double-timed between destinations, the road guard ran ahead to secure the cross traffic and then ran in cadence (but in place, not advancing) while the formation passed. As soon as they all passed, I would have to run really fast to catch up to the front and my position. I got the opportunity to run a lot. It worked, and eventually, my time was less than seven minutes for the mile, and I ran the whole mile. I never got to six minutes, which was considered perfect, but I was more than adequate. I also lost a lot of weight, and I could take my ex-belly skin and hide my belt for 225 degrees around my body. I did max all the other skills, including run, dodge jump, grenade toss, and low crawl and was especially good at the overhead rungs.

We then went to combat training. We had bayonet (archaic, but if you're out of bullets?), hand-to-hand judo, ambush, and pugilistic. The first two were uneventful, but ambush got me thinking. The drill sergeant took you out in the woods. A group of four walked with two BB guns (we had to share, because there weren't enough) down a path in the woods and were ambushed by snipers, one by one. Then, at the end, you walked into a clearing and got shot by four guys in cheesy forts. I told the other guys I had a plan, and knowing me, their eyes lit up. I told them to walk down the path slowly, talking and smoking. I took one of the guns and swept out left in the woods. In no time, my guys were shot and tried feebly to return fire. I located the sniper, came up from behind, and using my many years of bird and target shooting, I pelted the poor lad until he was begging for mercy. (The inner thighs were the least protected, so I concentrated fire there.) He surrendered, and I tied his hands up and sent him back to the start on his honor. I picked up his gun, and he had four spare tubes of ammo. (We were only given one in the gun that held about fifty shots.) I armed another one of my guys and replaced the other guy's tube and my own. I kept the other full spare and let them keep the partials.

At the next sniper, it was the same deal as before. Now we were all armed, so we had a chance at the ambush. I told them that this was boring, and we should just destroy one guy and verbally abuse the rest when they saw what happened. We got to the clearing, and I had everyone attack and shoot the heck out of the guy in the middle left. He screamed in agony, threw his gun down, and ran away literally crying. We told the rest to surrender, or they'd get the same, and they all did. We were the only ones who totally defeated the ambush, and the drill sergeant was mad because we didn't follow orders and stay on the path. I told him the others stayed on the path, and I was the only flanker. Instead of praise for individual initiative, I received another day of KP. During the nine weeks of basic training, I was on KP twenty-two times, which equaled more than one-third of my cycle time. I should have gotten a crossed knife and fork medal.

While on KP, I learned how to make applejack from apple juice, yeast, and sugar. It was alcoholic in about three or four days. It was nasty, but it did the trick. I would volunteer for pots and pans, the job every regular KP trainee hated the most. I analyzed all the jobs, and I knew I could scam it the best. If you were diligent and cleaned the dirty pots after breakfast, the cooks would just mess them all up again, but if you dogged it, they would rinse and reuse certain ones they liked, and you wouldn't have to wash them a second time or even a third at dinner. I would get the water so hot that steam would rise everywhere and I could barely be seen. Then I would light up a cigarette (a major no-no without permission) and set it on the sink top backsplash and lean over in the steam and take a drag without using my hands. One time the mess sergeant came back and asked me whose it was, and I lied and said some officer left it. He put it out, and I lit another as soon as he was gone. As soon as dinner was done, I would bust my ass and clean every pan perfectly. I knew they would not mess the pans up that late and wanted to get out themselves so they could drink on base. We'd be done cleaning up and GI the concrete and tile floors (soap and water and then hose it all down and mop up) by nine o'clock in the evening. GI means Government Issue and they always had their way of doing tasks. I decided to sell my services in KP.

We made ninety dollars a month at E-1, and maybe I made $110 as E-2 for the two weeks I was in charge. I would take someone's KP if they'd pay me twenty dollars on payday (too many took me up for ten dollars). Many still hated it and were willing to make the deal. I also loaned money three-for-five and offered IOUs in poker. When the first payday came, I was at the front, so after I received my pay, I stayed behind the officers, opened my book, and collected in excess of four hundred dollars.

The next month we got our first on-post leave, and all the money was loaned out the week before payday three-for-five (borrow twelve now pay twenty on payday). Because they'd be able to buy beer and goof, it was all loaned out in twenty minutes. I knew the drill sergeant wouldn't let me go, but I had plans. I took one of the guy's KP, so he could imbibe. I charged twenty dollars and a favor for the occasion. I had noticed that the CO had put a keg in the storage mess hall refrigerator. A sixteen-gallon keg had a cork in it, and you needed a tapper to control the flow. I had no way to tap a keg, but from the guys who didn't get a leave I took their canteens. I got about ten canteens and went to the keg. I slammed the cork in and used a milk hose from a five-gallon milk box to direct the flow to the canteens. Unfortunately, I did not have a way to stop the flow when the last canteen was full. I closed the refrigerator as the beer flowed and ran to the barracks.

Stolen officer beer is the sweetest beer in the world. There is something exciting about forbidden things; I can't put my finger on it, but it's a natural high sometimes. We were playing five-card stud and drinking beer in the barracks. I had the best stud hand of my life and made hardly anything on it. I had an ace in the hole, and my first two cards turned up were aces, and everyone but one dropped. My next card was an ace, and no one was betting but me. I probably made two dollars among five guys. The platoon guide came in and suspected us of drinking and smelled the beer. We could whip him, so he ran off to tattle to the drill sergeant. I took charge, and everyone quickly chugged their beers, brushed their teeth, rinsed the canteens, and put root beer in them. He came back, and we weren't playing poker anymore. Instead, we were playing fish, and the canteens were full of root beer. The drill sergeant was suspicious but had no evidence and yelled at the platoon guide for being incompetent. A week later, the CO went for his beer and opened the refrigerator and flat beer poured out on to the floor. He was mad and called a special formation and stated he knew who the perpetrator was, but he was going to give the persons a chance to confess, which would be easier on them in the long run. Nobody came forward, and I knew he didn't know, because he used the plural case, not singular.

We went on a forced march (twenty-five miles) one day and into the night. I had dumped my rain gear out of my backpack and made room for a can of sterno, a six-pack of Coke, and some Baby Ruth candy bars. We marched at a rout step (longer than a normal stride) for hours, and everyone was thirsty. We were a few miles out from our bivouac area, and I traded a Coke for a full canteen of water. When we arrived at camp, everyone (but me) was dying for water. I traded a sip for rain gear, another for a tent half, and another for more sterno. I sold the Cokes warm at a dollar each (I'd only paid fifteen cents), and those guys were selling sips at a quarter each. I took the extra tent half and made our pup tent very large. Ordinarily, each man carries a half of a pup tent and then everyone crowds in to a small area. With the addition of another half joined at the top of each, the width of the covered area was considerably greater. The tent looked more like a grocery box than a pointy little triangle. The sterno gave us warmth, and the Baby Ruth provided energy. We were kings of the hill in our heated condo tent.

I had KP the night after the on-post leave (for another twenty dollars), and after I got back at nine o'clock, I was in the latrine taking a leak when the drill sergeant came in very inebriated and took a leak next to me. He told me how much he detested me and how I was wasting a fine opportunity the Army was providing. He left, and I went upstairs to much commotion. One of the guys was bleeding in his top bunk and holding his nose. Another was rubbing a welt on his arm. Two of the drill sergeants had gotten drunk reminiscing about the older and tougher Army. They went through the barracks and were hitting trainees while they were sleeping. I told everyone it was illegal, and they couldn't hit you. We could see them in another barracks pounding other troops across the compound. The next morning at formation, four people were called out. The guy with the bloody nose, two guys from another barracks, and I were the chosen few. The CO, XO, and drill sergeants took us to the CO's office and began to question us about the night before. I didn't know why I was there, because no one had hit me, but I stayed quiet and listened. They did not bring in everyone hit only the guys with bashed faces and me.

The drill sergeant said I was one of the abused trainees, and he thought he beat me up in the bathroom (wishful thinking probably). Well, the CO said he wanted to keep his dirty laundry at the company level and not bring it up to battalion or brigade. I noticed all the troops were nodding their heads. Soon the CO stopped talking to the other troops and looked and spoke to me directly. He asked me for input, and I knew he was worried about me trashing his good name and record. I said that I was often punished for my indiscretions, and it would only be fair that the sergeants received equal treatment. They were all nodding now, and the trainees were stunned and listening. The CO noticed and quickly dismissed the other trainees and had me stay. He obviously recognized true leadership potential even if it was negative. I said I didn't want to destroy these fine enlisted men's careers, but this type of behavior could not be tolerated. Ordinarily, something like this would bust an E-7 and E-6 down to E-1 and maybe even include stockade time. The sergeants were starting to turn green, and the officers were nodding again. I asked if I might suggest a possible recourse, and everyone immediately nodded and assented. I said that they needed an Article 15 (temporary discipline that was removed from your record after a year if no reoccurrence), forty-five days of extra duty, and pay fine to equal two months' salary. I stated that they obviously had too much time on their hands and too much money to get in this kind of trouble. The CO looked stern at the sergeants and said, "Is this agreeable?" in his nastiest tone. Like little kids hoping not to get a hard spanking, they nodded appreciatively.

Pugilistic training was another classic training moment (my daughter's verbiage). This and live grenade toss were the last of the combat training. (We still had lots of drilling and army discipline training. A pugil stick is the length of a rifle with padded ends. Our stick had hard rubber ends with a fiberglass stock. It was hard and durable. The training was to simulate hand-to-hand fighting, and we were given a beehive-like hat, a crotch protector, and hand protectors. You could thrust with your stick, and if you touched a kill zone, the match was won. You could also beat the person up by using the other end like the butt of a rifle. I had a natural skill at this and primarily used the bayonet and first strike approach. I quickly defeated my entire squad, platoon, and company.

For the next level of competition, all the company champs fought at the battalion level, and the winners moved on to brigade championships. At battalion, I was winning all my matches, usually in less than two minutes, until I came up against Gabe, a six-foot, six-inch, lanky black man. The troops made a circle around us, and we fought in the middle. Gabe was taller and had a longer reach, but we were about the same weight. I figured he'd have leverage, and I would be concentrated strength. We started to circle each other. I made a feint and followed up with a quick kill barely touching him with the bayonet end at the heart. If a bayonet had been there, he'd have had his heart opened. I stopped the match and turned to my drill sergeant and looked at him through the beehive screen in the helmet. Gabe then blindsided me with a rifle butt hit to the helmet. It rang my bell, and I was totally disoriented. I shook it off and looked at my drill sergeant, and he was laughing, shucking, and pointing at me. I got another slam to the helmet that knocked me back several feet. I got blood-red mad. I was mad at the breach of rules (I'd already won), I was mad because I was blindsided, and I was really mad that my drill sergeant was laughing and encouraging the cheating.

I turned to face Gabe, and he was grinning ear to ear and getting ready to bop me again. I was going to finish this now and took my weapon like a baseball bat and struck the left outside of Gabe's knee just as hard as I could. The knee broke to the inside of his stance, he screamed bloody murder, and he crumpled over like a building being brought down with dynamite. I leaped on his chest and began to use the bat like a crop in a horse race whipping from side to side, striking around his love handles and watching him unable to scream for lack of breath and writhe silently with slight gasps on the ground. The drill sergeant and some others pulled me off of him and said, "It's okay, T. You won and are going to brigade championships."

I threw the pugil stick down and said, "No I'm not! I'm a conscientious objector, and I'm not fighting or hurting anybody anymore!"

The drill sergeant wanted me to calm down and recant my decision, but I was adamant. They hauled Gabe away, and I never saw him again. I never went to brigade championships and never picked up a pugil stick again. They made me low crawl up a hill and back and stand at attention all day, but I refused to cooperate. I then refused to carry the rifle, and they made me carry rocks to make up for the weight loss. I got sent to KP again and wasn't granted a base pass, but I didn't care. I passed my PT test, and the drill but I didn't care. I passed my PT test, and the drill sergeant was pleased but still bummed at Bolo me and the not shooting. He couldn't get my score up if I wouldn't fire a rifle. On the day of the Brigade Rifle Shoot, I told him I decided not to be a conscientious objector anymore. Sergeant Odom was happy but then realized the most I ever hit was one out of two hundred. I picked up my rifle, hoped the sight was still set okay, and marched to the range. The first two hundred I never missed once, and I wished I'd had a camera on Odom's face when his jaw dropped. I stayed on with the rest of the qualifiers, and we fired again. The rest of the troops had to wait. I ended up in second for the whole fort; some Mormon kid beat me for first, but the shot I missed I still think went through a hole already in the target. My whining notwithstanding, we did get the silver banner for our guidon flag.

When we marched back, the CO was so happy to see the silver because it makes a difference for his promotion. When he found out it was his "little problem child," he wasn't so happy. He called me in his office for a conference. He didn't even mention the victory and told me I wasn't going to graduate. He had my records on the table. He said I didn't complete the live grenade toss (I had KP that day) and that I would be recycled into the next training term. I told him that was just great, and I hoped he would be my company commander once again. He looked shocked and took a stamp out of his drawer and stamped expert on the grenade throw evaluation and said to get out of here. I don't think he wanted to even take a chance on getting me again. I got orders for chaplain's assistant training beginning with clerk's school at Fort Dix, New Jersey, and then Fort Hamilton, New York. I flew to New Jersey after graduation and began my clerk and jeep driving classes at Fort Dix.

When I arrived in New Jersey, my sister told me her college friend from South Dakota lived in Riverside. I got a hold of Pat C and took a bus over the weekend to her house. We had a good time chatting, and I noticed her Dad was a captain in the reserves. She gave me one of his captain's bars to mark the day, and I thought nothing about it. When I got back to the fort, they issued us winter clothes even though it was barely fall, and one of the items was a helmet liner that looked like a Korean War vintage. It had the little furry bill and earmuffs, and you could wear it up in lieu of your regular fatigue baseball cap. It looked like a communist hat when worn up, and I put the captain's bar in the middle front. With fatigues and a field jacket on, no one could tell me from a real officer. I decided to play. My ROTC experience allowed me to fake it properly, and I had noncommissioned officers throughout the base reeling at my commands. I was ordering cleanup details and picking on the littlest defects to abuse these poor men. I didn't even think about personal risk for myself. If I were caught impersonating an officer, it would be a serious crime.

Fortune ruled, and I had pulled it off. I never again donned the captain's bars. Those same sergeants I harassed later got me for a work detail and marched me off with others to mop a hall out. I was at the end of the formation as they marched us and did not turn in to the work building but instead kept marching straight and marched to the cafeteria. When the sergeants discovered I was missing, they quickly followed me to the cafeteria. I could see them rushing toward me through the window, so I moved to the food bar. There was an island food bar with drink machines and silverware in the middle, and the ordered food items (like hamburgers, etc.) were on the outside. I stayed crouched on the floor as the sergeants walked around looking in earnest for me. Everyone else could see me but them, and it was obvious I was hiding. No one spilled the beans, and they never found me. I had a pleasant afternoon in the cafeteria just wasting time.

Ernie worked in supply at Fort Dix, and we began to talk about girls. He had a girlfriend down in Wilmington, Delaware, who needed a date for her friend, so I volunteered. Ernie's girl had a white Chevy convertible with her two kids' names on the back right fender, her name, and several spots where old names were on the back-left fender with Ernie's name clearly on top of the old suitors. My date wasn't much to look at, but she was pleasant to be with, and I liked her in-laws. She got me drunk (I loved to be tricked) and took advantage of my kind nature and body. I must have been okay, because she was a happy camper and wanted me to go to a wedding with her. I figured free food and drink, why not?

I spent the day talking to this older woman who turned out to be my date's mother-in-law and the mother of the groom. Things were getting complicated rapidly, so I drank more to clear my view of things. The mother-in-law and I really hit it off really well, and I liked one of her friends too. I took my date to the wedding reception only to get severe disapproval from her husband who had his own date (a much younger and prettier woman). Understand that she knew he'd be there. She had no interest in getting divorced, and neither did he. The husband just didn't expect her to have a date too. When I went out to the parking lot later, he came up to me and started harassing me. He pulled out a knife and pressed it to my throat. Everyone was scared but drunk little me. People were urging me to leave, and I was saying, "This man has a problem, and he wants to talk to me."

I discovered he was miffed because I came to his brother's wedding with his wife and not that I was dating her. He'd been dating his new honey for a while and didn't give a rat's ass for his wife. I was an embarrassment because I brought her to his brother's wedding in front of the family even though he'd brought a girl. It was some kind of hillbilly double standard. I honestly stated I knew nothing of the relationships prior to consenting to the date. As he pressed harder with the knife on my throat, this friend of his mom kneeled down behind him, while his own mother pushed him backward, causing him to trip over her friend onto his back. The mom yanked me in a car with two of her buddies, and the race was on with the tripped son trailing behind. Eventually, the old ladies lost the kid, and we parked in the woods until four o'clock in the morning. I sobered up and realized how close I had come to death. I didn't go back to Delaware again and had definitely lost any desire forever to see a married woman.

When I was drafted in 1970, my future wife (Madonna) was going to college. She stayed in the girls' dorm with the rule you could have any visitors after eleven o'clock at night. I was in Fort Dix in advanced clerical/personnel and jeep training for chaplain's assistant. Madonna's letters were getting very vague, and I could tell she was straying. I hadn't had a leave yet and asked my CO if I could go. He said no, so I asked what would happen if I left anyway. He said I would get an Article 15 (punishment), which would be a fine of a month's wages, confined to post, and forty-five days of extra duty. I told him fine and said he could write it up, and I'd sign it when I returned. He was so upset he threw his pencil box at me and said I had better not try it.

I took off and went to her college and found her there. She saw me in the student union and ran across the floor and slid on her knees up to me and grabbed me around the thighs. We walked around downstairs, and there was an unused band room with chairs. I left the lights off, bent her over a chair, hiked her skirt up, and dropped her panties halfway down. I came at her from the backside, and as I thrust, the chair on the floor scooted, making a slight noise. The faster I went pushing her around the floor, the noisier it got. Madonna is partially deaf, so it didn't bother her much. I, however, was sure the whole school could hear, and there were two unlocked entrances to the room. I pulled her upright, and she got her panties back up and skirt down, and we went to the elevator. We entered the elevator at the ground floor and went to the top (third or fourth), but people would interrupt and get on and off. Finally, on the way back down from the top, no one got on, so I stopped the elevator between floors. I put our jackets on the floor, got my pants and her panties off, and began some serious copulation. It didn't take but a few minutes after all the previous foreplay, and we were a fluid mess. I used my undershorts to clean up the sperm and her secretions from her crotch and mine. We made ourselves presentable, and I pushed floor one and hung my stained shorts on the elevator button plate for floor selection. When we reached the first floor, about twenty students and faculty were waiting for the elevator and complaining. We left the elevator smiling from ear to ear, and as they went in to select their floors, I can imagine what they thought when they found the underwear dripping on the button pad.

I didn't have a place to stay, so Madonna said I could stay in her room. Staying in a girl's dorm for a few days sounded cool, but it was hard, and I had to be careful. Her roommate was bummed but didn't know what to do and had to act cool about it. Going to the bathroom and taking a shower was tough, because the girls had a common bathroom. But unlike the boys, they had individual showers with translucent shower curtains. Boys' showers are like a giant car wash, and you're all together in the same room. Now, I'm six three in height and have hairy legs. I put on a long, white terry cloth robe, wrapped a white towel around my head Carmen Miranda style, and teetered down the hall giggling. Some girls noticed, but surprisingly, most didn't. I made it to the bathroom, and all the urinals had flowers in them. I thought I was alone, and as I started to go to the shower, I heard the loudest fart followed by a groan in one of the toilet stalls. It was all I could do to hold my laughter, and the more I tried, the worse it was. I was brought up that girls were genteel and never went to the bathroom except to powder their noses, etc. This girl had most of my friends looking for work. I managed to stifle myself and got into the shower, and other than mild scalding when the fart queen flushed, it was uneventful. I did the same giggle routine down the hall coming back, but by this time, the few who knew had tattled, and the jig was up. I quickly got dressed and slipped out a second-floor window so Madonna wouldn't be expelled. I went to the local VFW, and they bought us some drinks and then we got a room in a sleazy hotel downtown. We got undressed and decided to sixty-nine a little in foreplay. I was on top with my knees slightly above Madonna's head, and her feet were spread wide and aimed toward the adjoining suite door. It was an older room with the keyhole-type locks, and as I was performing cunnilingus writing the alphabet with my tongue, I noticed about the letter M that there was an eyeball in the keyhole and a shadow under the door that was moving. I don't know who the voyeur was, but I went over and put a towel over the doorknob to cover the keyhole.

Madonna didn't seem upset and just wanted to get back to lovemaking. We finished our sixty-nine and went to straight copulation, starting slow and reaching a vigorous crescendo with me slamming her as hard as I could. When I finally culminated my mating process, Madonna was very quiet and spastically jerking with me still inside her. When she didn't stop, I was getting worried and I actually thought I might have done damage to her with all my passion. Madonna finally came back from orgasmic heaven to my relief (not that I'd want to deprive her of joy, but I'd never seen a multiple orgasm before and was concerned for her wellbeing). Later, thinking about it, I was fascinated by the ability of women to achieve that much pleasure for a sustained period. I left the next day for my parents' house and dinner and then hitchhiked back to Fort Dix.

Stockade

When I returned and reported in, I found out my captain had called my parents and told them I was AWOL (Absent with Out Leave). I was very upset he bothered them, as I was twenty-three and felt it was my life. I didn't live at home, and they shouldn't be worried about my problems. I went in to his office and chewed him out. He was livid, because I was the private and he was the captain. I reminded him that I'd told him before I left I would sign the Article 15 and take the punishment and that he shouldn't be worrying my folks.

I later found out he decided to set me up. Captain L had a drill sergeant push me around, and when I confronted Sergeant. R with his unfair behavior, he said he'd like to fight. He said we would forget about the differences in rank. We went out back and he asked me to take the first punch. I obliged and knocked him to the ground. The MPs were right around the corner, and on his cue, they came around and dragged me away to the stockade. I was treated harshly, stripped, and placed in a chicken wire cage in the middle of the floor in a guard compound inside the stockade. Everyone was walking around me in uniform. I was being treated like an animal, so I made low, guttural noises and then jumped up on the chicken wire and started making loud and obnoxious ape noises. I became this big, naked crazy guy who climbed halfway up the cage, screaming in ape language at the guards. I unnerved them, and they gave me my clothes back. I guess I read too many Tarzan books when I was younger. They processed me into the big house, and I was taken to the compound that was the pretrial waiting area. This was late 1970, and Vietnam was still going on, so there was a lot of prison action.

The Army prison system is their system. You have rapists and murderers thrown in with deserters and problem children. It's scary not knowing what's going to happen and what trials and tribulations you'll face. There are guards in the front of each billet/barrack, but they are two stories and the guards only go upstairs on inspection. There's barbwire on eight-foot fences with two feet of the circular barbwire on top. Guard towers are every hundred paces with two armed guards in each tower. When you march in formation, you half step everywhere. It became almost a rhythmic dance walking half step with everyone else's footsteps. The black men who were free would use the slang "I ain't half stepping, Jim" to signify freedom from the stockade.

The stockade was 55 percent black, 30 percent Hispanic, and 15 percent white. The whites were unorganized and either AWOL's or gay. In those days, being gay was a crime in the Army. The blacks ruled the compound with a Hispanic minority trying to keep as much power as possible. The whites were not interested in power or hardly even in self- preservation. We had one little whiney white guy in our barracks that the blacks took to the showers and sodomized on a regular basis. I think they even had a pair of girl's panties they made him put on. I was determined to survive, and I was not about to be anyone's bitch. Besides, I had hemorrhoids, and I don't think it would have pleasured me much.

The next day I challenged the upside-down sergeant who was in for murder and rape. He was a big, black man who had won his leadership on his crimes and his ability to enforce his rules. The guards came to him when they wanted something accomplished, and he got to decide who got the better jobs. It wasn't exactly a fight, but it was a test of durability or something. We went out into the yard, and there was a clothesline approximately neck high at the lowest point. We played a game similar to volleyball, but we were the only people on our respective sides. We used a heavy basketball and basically pounded the ball off of each other's heads. After a good half hour of abuse and considerable blood flowing, I asked him if he wanted to make some money, being very careful not to complain about the head bashing. He stopped and was very curious, and I'm sure very hurting as well.

In the stockade, there is no money, but everyone is given five packs of cigarettes per week. This is the real source for currency, and at the time, I smoked two packs a day. (I finally quit in 1981.) I told him we could do it playing hearts and that I was a good player and would show him how to cheat, and we could control all the cigarettes. He was swept up, and in a matter of no time, we had several cartons of cigarettes each. The cheating was no big deal. I knew he was no brain surgeon, and neither were the rest of his cronies, so I kept it simple. If I wanted a spade lead, I held my hand with four fingers showing, if I wanted a heart I had three, etc. If he was void, he was to put both hands on his cards, and I would prompt him again. If I wanted a big lead, I had both hands on my cards. Even if someone might have caught on they would never say anything to the upside-down sergeant for fear of reprisal.

I was also the chess champ of my cellblock, which my family always laughed about. I led a peaceful strike that ended up with me being punished by the stockade head officer who was very disgruntled with my meddling in his little world. He decided to try and get rid of me, so he put me on mag duty, which was digging trenches with a pickax in the winter outside the stockade. I had one guard and had to trench the frozen ground. I found that if I swung really hard and let the point of the pickax miss the ground and hit on the top, I could break the handle in about twenty bad hits. I broke the pickax, and the guard would get another handle. He would leave me unattended outside the stockade, while he would get another and sometimes would not come back for twenty minutes. I didn't run, because I figured they had a guard in the bushes with a shotgun to shoot me if I tried to escape. The whole deal smelled rotten from the start, because usually twenty guys went on mag duty not one. And why would they leave me alone? I stayed there and broke all the pickaxes and got to sit with the guard and have coffee the rest of the duty cycle, as they had no orders what to do with me if all the equipment failed.

After sixty days of this insanity, I was finally granted a trial and court-martial. Prisoners had white patches sewn on their sleeves and white stripes down their pants, so they were obvious to everyone. The escort took me to the regular base for trial, and I got to eat in the regular mess hall. When I came in, the respect I received was totally unbelievable. Everyone (officers included) moved away from me. I immediately transferred into my new role as James Cagney in prison, and they all shrank from my view. People are amazing. I went to the front of the line where the cooks gave me the best and as much as I wanted. No one would sit within a table of me, but all stared uncontrollably.

I went to the special court-martial, and they were going to try to give me a BCD (Bad Conduct Discharge), which would have ruined my life in the business world. The worst discharge was the dishonorable (like Walt Disney prominently displayed behind his desk). If you ever watched his show as a kid, he used to come out at the start to introduce the subject. He'd be in his office, and on the wall behind him was his Dishonorable Discharge framed like a diploma.) There was lots of blustering and a list of charges blaming me for everything from Custer's Last Stand, to Dunkirk, and then finally the Alamo.

After they ironed it all out, the judge said, "If you'd been an ordinary recruit, we would have let you go with sixty days pretrial confinement. But since you've had ROTC, we feel thirty additional days confinement appropriate."

So, I was moved to the sentenced compound, but on the way back, I had a gregarious guard who let me buy a pack of Kool cigarettes. They're filtered and not allowed in the stockade, because if you soak the filters in water and put them in some types of locks wet and let them dry the expansion can spring the lock. I didn't want them for that, and I didn't smoke menthols but the blacks were in love with Kools. I came back to the barracks before going to the permanent post trial area, and the guys were playing cards. One of the blacks asked me for a square (cigarette), and I tossed the pack of Kools. They all got wide eyed like in the old movies. I've never seen such a horrendous display of begging in my whole life. It was great. I let them keep the pack, but I told them to share equally.

I moved to post trial confinement (sentenced prisoners) and was treated rough from the get-go. The guards there would wake us up at three thirty in the morning for KP, (Kitchen Patrol), and we worked the kitchen six days from four o'clock in the morning to nine o'clock at night with Sunday off. This one guard would violently shake me, and I told the guard not to touch me and that I would get up by myself. The next morning the same guard grabbed me, shook me again roughly, and said to get going. I told him not to do it again and that I would get up myself. Well, he could hardly wait until the next morning and gleefully ravaged me, so I got up and decked him. I only hit him once in the gut (so I didn't break my hand), and he went down breathless. Several guards jumped me, and I found myself in DS (Disciplinary Segregation) with all the hard cases.

I had a tiny cell to myself with a toilet (no seat and no sink) and a bunk suspended from the wall by a chain. The mattress was one-inch thick at best, and each day I got out once for one hour of exercise by myself and once to shower. I could communicate with the guy next to me if I was careful, and we played chess, dots, and battleship. His name was Eddie, and he was a flaming homosexual and proud of it. I got a kick out of his enthusiasm for his lifestyle. I asked him what turned him or what he could attribute to his moment of questioning heterosexuality. He said he dated this girl in high school who was really small (five feet tall) and petite (ninety pounds) and loved to ride horses. (Ed was about five eight and maybe 145 pounds when I saw him, so he must have been a little smaller in high school.) He was walking with her one day, and she was leading her horse beside him when the horse started rearing up. Ed said she pulled the reins down and inserted her two thumbs in the horse's nostrils, pinched her hands tight, and threw the horse on the ground. He couldn't believe this little girl could throw a big horse, and he was in shock. He broke up with her and left home disillusioned. When he was hitchhiking, a black guy picked him up (who was several years older), and he broke him in to the gay world. He said he was never happier. He would go to the Hippodrome dance club (I assumed it was a gay club) with tight pants, and all the boys would be drooling over his butt. He finally got drafted and was thrown into DS because he was shamelessly doing all the boys, and the brass (who didn't know what to do with him) felt he would be safer pending discharge from the service.

There was another guy incarcerated whom I couldn't find out much about. He apparently made my ape in the cage act look like a kindergarten play. I don't know if he was a mass murderer or a loony tune. I always wished I could have talked to him just out of curiosity.

I had signed up for two college courses that came from the University of Wisconsin. One was criminology, and the other was medieval history, which I figured seemed appropriate for where I was. DS was great by comparison to the regular compound. No one messed with me, and I completed the college courses with straight A's in three weeks. What a great way to get a problem student focused. I got out five days early with good behavior and proceeded to my old CO until I finished the BCD fight. I refused to sign myself out of the Army, and they were trying to legally eliminate me. My CO must have felt bad or was really testing me, because he made me payroll guard. I had to carry more than twenty thousand dollars in cash and a loaded gun back to the other officers who divided the money up for individual payroll. (The Army paid in cash in those days.) I did it, and my CO finally spoke on my behalf at the hearing. I didn't get a BCD. But, out of 1,500 sets of orders, only two people were sent to Vietnam, and I was one of them. I guess they figured if I was a fighter, I might as well go to where the action was.

While I was waiting to get orders and leave (and then ship to Vietnam), I was given permanent CQ (Charge of Quarters), which is a glorified night guard position. I was basically in charge while everyone was sleeping. I got off duty one morning and was walking back to my room and found a guy who was obviously disturbed. My philosophy is, no matter how bad it gets, sometimes you just need another viewpoint. After questioning him, I found out he had received a Dear John letter from his girl back home and was taking it very hard. He was trying to decide on the best way to end his life. I immediately decided to offer him an alternative outlook. I suggested that he really make a statement, so there would be no doubt his death was a result of her dumping him. I told him he should slice off his penis and shove it down his throat and die from lack of breath and loss of blood. He looked at me like I was crazy, and his depression over being dumped dissipated. He focused on the sicko in front of him, and I could see further advice was no longer required. Needless to say, he did not do anything stupid and forgot all about a suicide. He never talked to me again, so I don't know what happened to his girl, but he was still around. Some people don't appreciate good advice.

War

I finally got my orders and leave at the end of June 1971. I was to report at Fort Lewis, Washington, on July 23 for briefing and transportation to the Republic of South Vietnam. I had told Madonna that if I got orders for anywhere but Vietnam, we'd get married. When I got home, I told her about Vietnam, and we decided to get married anyway. We got the blood test together; I was laughing, and she was crying. (They had two chairs for simultaneous draws.) I didn't have much money, my parents were against the wedding, and her parents were going through a divorce. My dad didn't even want to go to the ceremony, but Mom made him. (Dad didn't come to the reception.) I got married in uniform, and she had a white street dress. We got married on a Tuesday (July 14, which I picked because it was the French holiday Bastille Day). The church cost ten dollars.

The ceremony was very traumatic for me, but it was something I had to do. When I said the vows, I could hardly breathe, and when I turned around to walk down the aisle, all I could think about was getting outside to the sunshine. Once I was outside, I relaxed again, and my stress level decreased. My cousin Mike was the best man (my brothers were small, and John was out West). We had the reception in Mike's apartment, and I had friends and relatives bring booze and food in lieu of presents. My mother-in-law volunteered her cottage in Michigan but showed up on Friday afternoon with all the kids and her future husband for the weekend. We left for some private time and came back to Chicago Heights. I had to borrow plane fare to Fort Lewis from my sister, as I was totally broke. I told Madonna it was best for us to get married before I left, because she would get extra money monthly being a dependent, and if I were killed, the Army would give her fifteen thousand dollars. I told her not to count on me being loyal until I got back. I went to Fort Lewis, Washington, and got to see Tom H in his summer ROTC training. He would marry my sister Lauren six months later (January 1972) and make a career of the Army, retiring in 1997 as a bird colonel. He took me for drinks at the officers' club on base, and considering my background in basic training there, it had a touch of irony. I didn't see my old captain from basic there, but he was there in spirit.

It was a very quiet flight (Flying Tiger Airlines); some of the people on our plane were nervous, and some were very apprehensive, but all were quiet. We landed in daylight in Cam Rahn Bay, South Vietnam (about mid-country on the coast) after losing a day at the international dateline (coming back, we would do the same day twice). I had anticipated shooting and action, but it was quiet when we landed. I didn't hear any combat noises until it got dark. In the distance, we could hear shelling and automatic fire, but it was far away. It was very hot, and there was an uncomfortable humidity in the air. I would sweat without moving, in the shade. It took a good month to get used to the climate. It was still the Army, with lots of milling around and mustering in formations, but we finally got to a meeting for duty assignments. A tech sergeant (E-7, three stripes up, two down) asked for anyone with college experience to raise his hand. Well, I had college, but I figured they wanted someone for shit removal or kitchen patrol, so I stupidly did not respond.

The orders then came out, and I was assigned to MR1 north of Da Nang at a place called Red Beach. It was called Red Beach because the French retreated there to meet their navy for evacuation, but the navy was a day late. Ho Chi Minh caught the French on the shore and slaughtered them, hence the name, Red Beach. MR1 was the northern-most area in South Vietnam and right next to North Vietnam. Quang Tri, Phu Bai, and Chu Lai were some of the other larger towns around Camp Viking at Red Beach. My unit was HHD Fifty-Eighth Transportation Battalion MR1 and was commanded by Colonel R. We were a helicopter support unit north of Da Nang and south of the DMZ (Demilitarized Zone).

When I saw my orders, I asked why they wanted college people. The tech sergeant said "to do the paperwork here in the rear." I tried to get my orders changed by telling him about my college experience, but it was too late. The orders were cut, and I had to fly up north in a C-130. The C-130 was a cumbersome, propeller-powered, flying boxcar with a tailgate that dropped down so you could drive a jeep down it. The seats were like parachute straps or the material for patrol belts from grammar school, suspended from the ceiling. Everything was flexible, except the seat was like a board. It was a very bouncy ride with villagers and their pigs and chickens. We made it without being shot at or experiencing any engine failure. It was so hot we partially opened the back tailgate to get a breeze.

Water at Camp Viking (Red Beach) was either potable or non-potable. Non-potable water, you could shower with and brush your teeth with but couldn't swallow it. We had purification tablets, but I stuck to beer and pop for fluids most of the time. I was only in country for a couple of weeks, and I got this fungus growth at the top of my thighs. It hurt to walk or move. I went to the doctor, and he gave me some purple antibiotic to put on this disgusting and painful growth. I returned to my hooch (living quarters made with wood, screen, and corrugated tin roofing, all surrounded by sandbags), took off my clothes, and proceeded to pour the purple liquid on my tender crotch. It burned immediately, like putting Bengay on sunburn (I'd stupidly done that when I was much younger), and the only way I could think of to help was the showers. We had makeshift showers created out of old pontoons we had over a wood and canvas structure. We had to fill them with a water truck (non-potable), and they were not heated except by the sun (and not cooled), so morning showers were the coolest. It was still morning (not that it would have stopped me), and I streaked to the shower with the purple crotch. I jumped in the shower, turned it on, and laid down on my back with my feet spread toward the sky as I allowed the shower to rain relief on my sore personals. Someone else walked in as I was experiencing comparative bliss, looked at me, and then abruptly turned and left. I learned from that point on not to wear briefs. They were the cause of the fungus in the warm, damp climate. I never wore underwear again until six months after I was back in the states. I never got the fungus again.

We did not have toilet facilities like in the states. We had a large sewer pipe at a forty-five-degree angle buried in gravel to urinate in and outhouses with fifty-five-gallon half drums in them. Under a wood bench with a hole cut in it was half of a fifty-five- gallon drum with an inch or two of diesel fuel in the bottom. Once a week, the Army would pull all the half drums out, place a quart of gasoline on the accumulated excrements, and ignite. The gasoline would start immediately, and the diesel would start with enough heat and burn longer. MI (Many Idiots, or Military Intelligence) had us burn extra half drums in case the enemy was watching and counting our smoking drums and computing how many troops were inside the fort. Vietnamese worked in the fort and would know exactly how many troops we had and where the secret areas were. They probably saw us as idiots wasting fuel on burning crap. I was sitting on one of those benches, and I felt something on my scrotum (which was suspended below the bench and in the hole). Not overly concerned, I slid back to take a look and saw a cockroach the size of my small finger crawling up toward the base of my penis for whatever reason. I immediately freaked, brushed it off, and stood up. My body shuddered at the instant replay in my mind. The rest of my tour I never sat on the bench; I just suspended my rump over the opening and did my paperwork standing up. Everyone who is deprived of normal living has his "hit list" when he gets back to the States. Some want milk shakes, others a steak dinner, mine was a clean, white, flush toilet.

I began to drink regularly, not to get trashed but to be at ease without pain. Everything there could hurt us, and very few things were "good" for us. We dealt with what we had to and tried not to think about the rest. Live for the moment and laugh at the past was our best mental survival. The future was nothing but dreams. When someone got "short" (near his time to leave Vietnam), a person became careful and changed. The future was getting real, and he didn't want to screw it up. One of our favorite drinking songs was by The Animals called "We Gotta Get Out of This Place." We would substitute the word short in at a part where Eric Clapton would yell the same word three times in succession. To this day, when that song plays on the radio, I still yell "short" there, and I don't even know the real word.

We worked sixteen-hour days, seven days a week. We only knew when it was Monday, because that's when we received a huge malaria pill larger than a quarter and thicker. At first, I had to break it in half and take it with water, but later, I could swallow the whole thing raw. I worked first at S-3 which was operations for the Fifty-Eighth Transportation Battalion HHD, which was a helicopter outfit. My combat backup position was door gunner in flight and an infantry guard on the ground. (In case of attack, everyone pulled guard duty and was issued a rifle.)

My rifle skills got me range NCO and all new personnel (officers included) had to come through my check-fire program on the rifle range before they could be issued a weapon. I had an officer who was in charge of the range (Captain M) who was forced there, like the rest of us, and had no military aspirations whatsoever. He would take field glasses and go up on a bluff, while I would run the range qualification. I had my own AK-47 (automatic rifle) and would get up in front of the troops to say, "I don't want to see any John Waynes out here." I would then proceed to fire the entire magazine downrange on full Automatic. I told them they had to fire three-round bursts only and not act like I just had. I always loved being a bad example. If they were officers and it was muddy, I made them fire prone (lying down). Old timers and prior "in-country," I ran through quickly and didn't mess with at all. I also got to shoot up all the old ammo. I would take a three-quarter-ton truck out with some LAWs (rocket launchers), an M-60 machine gun, and five spare barrels. I would have a ball cutting down trees with the machine gun and firing so much ammo the barrel would warp, and I'd have to put in another. I wish I had a nickel for every round I fired; I'd be rich. If I could get up in a chopper (Huey UH-1H) with a warrant officer, we would shoot sharks off the shore and watch the papa- sans (local Vietnamese men) paddle out, cheering to pick up their prizes and food for their families.

One night I was overindulging in mai tais, and we started to get incoming (rocket fire and mortars). I thought it was some of the troops screwing around, and everyone was running like crazy except me. I eventually got to the armory and saw that my weapon (an M16) was the only one left on the rack. I picked it up and brought it along with my gallon jug of mai tai.

I got to my assigned, defensive fire point, and my assigned partner Willie (a black man from Tennessee) was there I could only see the whites of his eyes, and he was rightfully worried. Oblivious to danger in my current inebriated state, I asked him what was wrong and why was so terrified. He explained to me that we were being attacked and could die, and I quickly gave him a drink from my jug and explained that it was probably some of the First Cavalry division screwing around. After a couple of drinks, he started to believe my rap, as I did. He stopped being worried and began to even have a good time. We quickly emptied the jug, and I left him my rifle and low- crawled back to my hooch (living quarters) for more booze. I brought back sparkling burgundy and two long-stemmed glasses so we could drink in style. In the meantime, there were still explosions going on and gunfire. Willie was much calmer, and I realized we were in actual combat, but I still didn't really care. I told him that if we were overrun, we'd shoot till our clips ran out and then surrender and offer the VC or NVA a drink. The only time I fired that night was to shoot down one of our misfired 155 mm artillery flares as it slowly floated over the camp instead of over the enemy. Everybody nearby cheered when I smoked it. We were worthless troops but easily entertained.

For my birthday, my mother and sister sent me a goody package. They had party hats, a dart gun with suction cups, Toll House cookies (in a million pieces), balloons, and the like. I got very good with the dart gun on guard duty and quickly killed more than twenty flies and a spider. We had hooch maids to clean our rooms/shacks, or hooches. They were local South Vietnamese women who did our laundry, mess hall, and sandbag duties. We paid $40 a month for the service, and it was well worth the investment. I did see one of the girls washing my clothes one afternoon. She took Tide soap powder and put it in a puddle in the ground. She then took the clothes and beat them in the soapy puddle. I had seen enough, so I don't know if she rinsed or not, but the fatigues, T- shirts, and socks went on the clothesline for drying. They were folded and back on my shelf in the hooch later that afternoon. I know the sun sanitized the clothes; they didn't smell, and the spots were gone, so I learned to live with the process.

One day I took one of the hooch maid's hats (it was like a straw funnel, point side up), threatened her with the dart gun and told her I was VC (Vietcong) and she was my prisoner. All the hooch maids roared with laughter when I would point the dart gun at them and squat down shorter than they were. My VC impersonation was famous with the girls, and they called me "Dinky Dow," which was local slang for crazy.

I bought a Honda 50 and a .38 nickel-plated revolver with shoulder holster from a guy leaving country. I could get ammo from the flyboys, who preferred the revolver to the .45 automatic. It was for looks only, and I sold it later and only carried the automatic. The Honda was great to get around the base and went maybe thirty-five miles per hour at its top speed. I would ride it around when drinking and dumped it one time in gravel. My arm was a mess with embedded gravel, and I poured some of the Canadian Club I was drinking on it and then put a Kotex on it. The Kotex was a bandage package that was for stopping bullet wounds until the medic got there. It was like a big pad with gauze wings to tie it in place. A few weeks later it started to hurt, and I had the doctor look at it. Under the scab was a rock sized like a twenty-carat marquise-cut diamond. He picked it out, and it left an indentation where it used to be located in my forearm. The depression took a year to go away, and the scar remained for several years. I sold the Honda the next week and moved on to stealing jeeps when joyriding.

I would get assigned guard duty in a tower, and my position overlooked a garbage dump. I had a big machine gun and lots of bullets beside my small arms. We were not allowed to shoot unless shot at—which I didn't think made any sense in a combat zone. Why should I have to take a hit first? —and we had to call in to check fire, or make sure the guns functioned. I saw a lot of rats one evening going through the garbage, so I called for a check fire and wiped out twenty or more with a few bursts. The other tower saw and heard me shooting and flashed their spotlight over to the dump and saw rat guts everywhere. Well, they were just as bored, so they started shooting at the rats that were now eating the previous rats. Pretty soon, we had all kinds of people involved; you'd have thought it was a major firefight instead of vermin extinction.

We were called up every morning very early and watched the dawn break as we got our daily information and special instructions. One morning,

Lieutenant Colonel R (our base commander) was ranting to our formation, and two Vietnamese mongrel dogs got behind him as he was speaking and began to copulate. Well, discipline was right out the window, and we all need our distractions. The louder he screamed to enforce his presence, the more we roared. The two dogs turned from each other and were locked butt to butt, and he finally turned around in the midst of a "get serious" speech. To say the least, he did not feel like commanding the troops anymore and quickly retired before the stigma of the morning became permanently attached to his genre. Captains gave speeches after the morning animal show from then on.

I worked for S-2 (security), occasionally typing the weekly status reports because I could type with all my fingers and could spell better than anyone else on staff. (Actually, when I came to Vietnam, I was a terrible speller. The reports were important and had to be spelled perfectly prior to encryption, so I always used a dictionary to make sure. I did become a good speller, so I'd have to say combat could be educational.) Major C was in charge of my section S-3 (operations), but he was a nervous man and needed to pass his war college to stay in the service and be promoted. He couldn't pass strategy and military justice portions of his required five packages. I told him I'd do it, but he'd have to authorize me a night license for driving. (These were very difficult to get, considering where we were and the combat activity after dark.) My experience with the BCD and court- martial made that a cakewalk, while strategy games have been my lifeblood since age four. In about two weeks, he got his certification and was very happy, and I was a certified night driver. At night, we did not drive with headlights on, only a tiny slit or none at all. I had good night vision, so I was set to travel at all hours, which was an awesome bonus.

S-3 was assigned a jeep, and I was selected to pull maintenance on it. I really had little practical experience on vehicles growing up except for my '57 Chevy, because we were full-service and I had no interest. I got a manual and began to learn how to grease it and change the oil. I had to remove some little cups off the tie rods that looked like flat, black, toothpaste caps about the diameter of a nickel. Inside, there were needle bearings that sat along the perimeter. I put new grease carefully around the inside diameter and tried to set the bearings in one by one, sticking them into the grease. I worked forty minutes on it till a Vietnamese mechanic came over, grabbed the cap, stuck his little finger in the middle, and spun the cap like a manual pencil sharpener. The bearings all stood up perfectly, and it only took him ten seconds. I began to pay more attention to the "little people" and saw real value in them.

One of the other guys (Andy) took over maintenance for me one day when I was at S-2. When he came back, the jeep was smoking terribly. I asked him what happened, and he said he opened the oil cap and didn't see anything there (he didn't use the dipstick to properly check), so he added twenty-eight pints of oil until it was full to the top of the valve cover (a jeep holds four quarts or eight pints). I took the vehicle back to change the oil and felt better about my inability with the needle bearings grease. You live by comparison, so ups and downs can be from varied viewpoints, and even incompetence has a value as a base of comparison. If you're a drunk and want to feel better about your problem, compare yourself to worse drunks and you don't look so bad. I'm sure that's why soap operas are so popular with women in the States. No matter what your problems are, someone else is worse off or uses less common sense.

I didn't speak the Vietnamese language, but I spoke some French (who occupied Vietnam before us), and that, coupled with my skills at charades, allowed me to communicate rudimentarily. The locals usually spoke some Pigeon English (French, English, and Vietnamese slang combined) and had a modest vocabulary. I picked up a few key words and could barely make myself understood. A lot of my fellow troops didn't have a good opinion about the Vietnamese, and it could have cost them their lives. We had a couple of troopers run over a Vietnamese kid in town with a truck, and instead of helping, they mistakenly ran away in their truck, figuring it was "some dumb gook." The Vietnamese had barbwire in their front yards, so when they saw the escape attempt, several of them pulled it out over the road and got it caught in the tire rotation. Enough wire pulled in to jam the truck, and then they threw a lit liter of gasoline in the window to finish our guys off. Understand that this was not a combat situation but more of a neighborhood watch. These were unarmed civilians who may have worked for the Vietcong at night but worked for us during the day. Ordinarily, I would be concerned about the death of fellow troops, but it's important to remember where you are and whose rules you're playing by. I also had to live there and understood it was their country, and we were the invaders (or at least foreigners).

"Slicky" boys were like our high school hoodlums just trying to make a place for themselves. They had two guys on a Honda 50 or moped and would drive up to our jeeps (no doors, keys, or back on the jeep only a roof), and the passenger would try to steal whatever he could and then race off. It could be the sunglasses on your face, your watch, or anything loose on the seat or floor. The poor Slicky boys would not have a bike and would use a local cripple (with one leg) to fall out on the highway. When we slowed down, they would race from cover and get what they could. A lot of our drivers and passengers couldn't handle the pressure and would shoot the kids, wound them, or brandish the weapon. I couldn't and wouldn't (maybe if they were life threatening but certainly not for a pair of sunglasses). At the same time, I was not going to be an easy mark for the local thugs.

Vietnam is temperate, and the coolest I remember it was in the monsoons, but even then, it was still sixty degrees, though we shivered. I drove to the air base by Da Nang (Monkey Mountain and Tan Son Nhut) and swiped one of the big CO2 fire extinguishers for jet fuel fires. It took up the whole back seating area and had a hose connected to a black blunderbuss with a trigger on it. I ran the hose between the front seats and kept the business end on my lap. When the Slicky boys would come to steal from my vehicle, I would slow down to give them a chance, and then when they got close, I'd release the CO2, which was very cold for people who had never seen snow, as well as very loud and intimidating. They would cuss in Vietnamese and once even fell off their bike, but no one was ever seriously hurt. Later, when they used the cripple guy on me, I dropped the jeep into second gear, went off the road, and pretended to try to run him over. Surprisingly, with one leg and a handmade crutch, he moved pretty fast. After doing this several times, the villagers got to know my look and jeep and didn't even bother me. I would even wave when I saw their hideouts, and they would shake their heads. They were a bright people just trying to survive the best way they could. They cared little for politics and took bread from whoever was in town. They really didn't care who won; they just wanted to survive and be left alone. If we'd dole out goodies, whoever got it would become corrupt and overcharge his buddies and be the local lord. If the lord were killed, the person who killed him would be in charge. It was like being a kid again, playing king of the hill. When in town, I would never carry a gun (I kept a .45 in my pocket with tracers in it, but it wasn't visible) and was never attacked. Many soldiers would carry their rifles and disappeared or turned up stripped, wounded, or dead. I was by far the tallest in the crowd, and the average Vietnamese adult just cleared my navel in height (most under 5 feet tall). I was never violated by any of the Vietnamese people (not counting the ones who shot at me in the chopper or on the ground), and I always felt comfortable around them.

I did get into questioning VC one day but not by choice. I was driving through town, and some White Mice (Army Republic Vietnam Military Police) pulled me over and told me to get out. They brought me into an alley with eight people in their black silk pajamas. The ARVN officer took out his .45 and began questioning the first person. He asked him if he was VC, and the guy denied it. Without batting an eye, he fired the pistol into the man's head. It was almost unreal when the body jumped back from the bullet- induced velocity. The front didn't bleed much at the entrance point, but the back of the man's head was a mess of red and gray. The shot man didn't even twitch, and the other seven people froze. When the ARVN officer proceeded to the next person and questioned him, he talked a mile a minute. I don't know what I would have done but being dead sure didn't accomplish anything world shaking. Everyone else there took it like it was a matter of course, like buying a McDonald's hamburger back home. The cheapness of life was stifling over there, and people didn't have a system of individual rights. It's like they were cattle, and if picked, they were slaughtered, and if not, then they could graze and breed. No emotion, just dead or alive. This was conspicuously and curiously close to nature's unemotional life cycle. I felt I was an observer not a participant. What happened by my standards was unconscionable, but by theirs, it was totally matter of fact. The ARVN officer thought he did a great job and got these hapless people to talk for the cost of one bullet. The VC were satisfied that no one else was going to die, and I didn't know what to do. Maybe my presence made it "okay" for the execution to take place, but nothing further was asked from me, and I went on my way. Sometimes life just doesn't make sense.

Driving was freedom, but sometimes clowning when I drove had a price. I loved driving a jeep on gravel. Coming to a corner turn, I would downshift to second, start turning, and jam the gas on to power slide around the turn. It made a lot of dust, and I threw a lot of gravel while sliding at ninety degrees until the wheels caught traction. It was grand fun. One sunny afternoon I came up to the corner (too fast as usual) by the officers' club where there was a seven-foot fence. No one could see around the corner, but I was having a ball and didn't care. I did my patented power slide, patting myself on the back for such brilliant driving skills when to my dismay I saw a bird colonel (one higher rank than our base commander and next up rank is Brigadier General) on the road. It was too late to stop impact, and the jeep's driver's side mirror caught him on his right arm and spun him around counterclockwise. When he hit the ground, the impact knocked his hat and sunglasses off and got his fatigues all dusty. He was in pretty good shape for an older officer and bounced up when I was a block past him. He began screaming and cursing at my poor driver's safety. I didn't slow down (knowing he was okay) and quickly drove to S-3. The visiting bird showed up five minutes later. I had removed my blouse, sunglasses, and hat. My olive drab, green T-shirt had Sergeant Boyle stenciled on it (even though I was only a PFC then). He came in and complained to the major, and I took down all his information for the formal inquiry to bring this perpetrator to justice. I quickly learned he didn't know I had done it or had any clue on who it was. I formed an official investigation team, but the runaway driver was never located. I didn't totally stop clowning, but I always took my time on the blind corner after that incident.

I finally got E-4 corporal rank after passing the NCO (Non-Commissioned Officer) boards. As a corporal (not a technical specialist E-4), I could push troops (command). This made it easier on the firing range and later when I would lead the bowling league convoy. I was allowed to visit the NCO club, and they had a craps table. I was pretty drunk one night and had maybe ten dollars in MPC (military pay certificates) and decided to learn the dice. I still don't know what I did, but I bet along with this big black mess sergeant and won three months' pay from that ten dollars. When I awoke the next morning in my hooch, I had crumpled purple twenty-dollar dollar bills everywhere. MPC twenty-dollar bills were purple and the largest bill, ten-dollar bills were blue and a little smaller, five-dollar bills were red and smaller still, and the one-dollar bill was green and the smallest, which made cash transaction mistakes when you were trashed minimal.

A white E-6 sergeant (who was a lifer) was walking back from the NCO club and was jumped by a group of black soldiers. They tried to intimidate him and then shoved a rusty pole up his rectum that penetrated his bowel. He was forced to retire with only seventeen years' service on a medical discharge. I personally didn't like the guy, but the army was his life, and it seemed unfair to deprive him of his pension. I was walking home with a load one a week or so later, and I always carried a .45 in my pocket with seven tracers in it in case I needed a light show. I also figured tracers were more intimidating than not being able to see what's coming at you. I kept it in my pocket under my blouse, as per usual, and eight black guys jumped me. They were intent on doing harm for whatever reason, and I whipped out the trusty .45 automatic. They were still blustering about having more guys than bullets, and I asked who wanted to be the martyr for the group. When no one volunteered, I had them all line up by a fence on one knee. They had to put their hands out wide and sing "Suwanee" like Al Jolson in blackface. When I had thoroughly coerced them to complete the tune, I put the weapon away, turned on my heels, and walked away. My legend spread fast as a "crazy white boy," and I never had to face my own nationality again in Vietnam.

I rarely had money except what I earned from my business ventures. It was either targeted to soldier's savings, my wife, or the Pacex catalogue for gifts. The Pacex was a duty-free and shipping-free catalogue based out of Japan. It had stereos, jewelry, dishes, silver a veritable Marshall Fields (only at a fifth the cost).

We had a Brownie Troop attached to my church (Flossmoor Community), and I was the only church member in Vietnam. They wrote me custom-made cards in crayon, and my whole group of friends loved them. One in particular was a stick figure of a marching soldier. Inside it said: "Dear Soldier Tom, I hope you don't die." We all thought it was great. I took some of the ill-gotten gains from the crap table and bought brass puzzles for all the girls and a cross necklace made from cultured pearls for the troop leader. I always hoped it made them feel like they made us that special day. Little things become important at the strangest times. Perspective and humor are some of life's most powerful tools.

I was not happy with our mess hall and had purchased a refrigerator for my hooch. I had come in from the field hot one day and chugged a glass of milk fresh out of the machine only to discover too late that it was spoiled. I regurgitated shortly and lost all appetite for the remainder of the day. The mess hall always overcooked everything. Chicken fell off the bone, meat was gray in the center, if not brown, and medium rare to the cooks was an unusual swami Seance. I decided that I worked sixteen hours a day or more, and I deserved better food even if I had to prepare it myself. I rarely went for food at the mess hall but decided I was entitled to my share of the rations. The mess hall was locked at night but was constructed out of a bunch of screens and screen doors. I would walk there late, take out my bayonet, and make an incision by the door to release the lock. I would then pilfer whatever food tripped my trigger. I had two fifteen- inch Sunbeam electric pans with lids I could cook in, and I made the most of them. I didn't steal that often, just when I needed food, and mostly it was just a random act. We had a new guy in-country, and he was following me around. We were imbibing and decided to get some chow at one o'clock in the morning. I went to the mess hall, and he followed innocently. He was dumbfounded when I cut through the screen to gain entry. He followed me in, and we opened the walk-in refrigerator. We gathered up a couple of armloads of goodies. When we started to leave, a flashlight came on with a .45 automatic pointed right at our heads. The voice in the darkness said, "Hold it." It was the sergeant I had played craps with a couple of weeks earlier. I was semi-trashed and didn't really care if he shot us. What was he going to do, send me to combat or the stockade? The other guy was crapping in his pants. He was very nervous, and the sergeant marched us to the CQ. When we got there, he gave me the other bag of food and took the other guy to the office. I was left holding the bag outside. I left and then cooked the chow. I never saw that guy again. I guess they figured I wasn't worth the bust, or he already had his victim to vindicate the robberies.

I didn't stop borrowing things. I would get out of the club at night, and someone's jeep would be there. We would chain the steering wheel to the brake pedal (for all vehicles in a combat zone had no ignition keys). You could drive the jeep straight and swerve a little, but you could not turn a corner. I would drive it as far as I could toward my hooch and then just abandon it. When I was drinking, things just seemed like a good idea at the time.

Just before Thanksgiving, my eye started watering profusely. We were having the local orphans for dinner (not eating them but eating with them). I woke on Thanksgiving, and I could only tell it was light out. My eyes had sealed shut with a crust of sand. I got to a canteen of water and softened up the sand. My eyes were open, but I still could only tell it was light out. I was clinically blind! This really sucked, especially for someone who had never even wore glasses. I got someone to take me to the doctor, and he gave me this brown stuff in my eyes, which reminded me of a camera lens getting mud on it. I didn't feel like doing anything or eating anything. I couldn't even see the little kids. Two days later, with more antibiotics, the pinkeye finally started to clear up. When I could make out shapes and see myself in the mirror, I could see that my eye white was completely red like a fire engine not just bloodshot. They should have called it redeye, but that's already a late-night plane or cheap whisky.

When I went on sick call for a follow up examination, I could see two distinct lines of men for treatment. One line was for all ailments, and the other was exclusively for gonorrhea, the number one social disease the country. We lovingly called it the drippy dick line. It was so rampant that stories of the Communists developing super strains that would kill were circulating. I never saw anyone die of the common clap malady, but I saw a lot of brave men screaming when they urinated. Many guys took "no sweat" pills (antibiotic substitute for penicillin) before they had sex. One guy had a Bactine poster in his hooch, and it had the motto "no sting, no stain." He would do a whore with two rubbers and spray them with Bactine. He never got the clap, but I feel it was the rubbers not the Bactine.

We had four guys in our hooch. I worked at headquarters, Tom H worked the mailroom, and two worked in the PX. This was ideal, as I never had my ration card punched (we were each allowed three bottles of liquor and three cases of beer a month, six cartons of cigarettes, one refrigerator, one fan, etc.) and had unlimited supplies. Tom H got us stuff mailed out quickly, and we got our packages ASAP. Anything to do with operations, I could give them advanced notice. Tom and I hit it off the best, although Jesse, my PX roommate, I saved much later, and we liked creating stuff. When he got the mail from Da Nang, I'd have him pick up basic frozen pizza. We obtained a Red Cross plasma freezer, and with my twin Sunbeams, we made a decent pizza pie. I would procure supplies from the mess hall like dehydrated shrimp, green peppers, and onions and would have my wife send me garlic powder and other spices from the States. We delivered hot pizza and cold beer right to your hooch. The electricity was created from 150-kilowatt diesel generators. (Lights would get brighter and dimmer, and records would go faster and slower, but it was fairly consistent power.) We could create bake and deliver twelve to fourteen pies a night. To say the least, we were the most popular business and mainly served senior NCOs who bid the highest for our services. Once I sold a pizza to an officer for ten dollars when he had a round-eye (Caucasian) date. The materials cost less than a dollar (ninety-five cents, to be exact) but sold for at least five dollars. This went well, but during yellow and red alerts, we couldn't get to town for stock. We then opened a casino with poker, craps, and blackjack. We only made money in poker, and Tom wanted to run it. I kept going with the pizza, and he lost all his interest in cards. He drank too much to be successful in gambling management.

I'd been in-country one hundred days and hadn't been laid. I had told my wife before I left not to count on me being loyal until I got back. I didn't know if I'd make it or not, but I wasn't going to be celibate. I decided to try the Steam & Cream, a local, army- supported massage parlor. It was weird; you went in and had a shower and then came back to your massage table with just a towel around your waist. The girl would massage you, and when you rolled over on your back, she'd reach under your towel, lightly caress your penis, and coyly ask if you wanted a hand job. You would give her five dollars, and she would produce a bottle of Jergens lotion, open your towel, and proceed to jerk you off with her hand lubricated with the lotion. It smelled oddly of peaches. When you came, she would say something in Vietnamese that sounded like "choy duck," grin, and wipe you off with another towel. Then you'd get dressed and leave. You couldn't touch the girls, although some guys dated them and got more, but that wasn't the norm. I knew there had to be a better way for the troops, and I was just the guy for the job.

There was a meeting (shortly after my Steam & Cream visit) for organization of a bowling league. They would convoy down to Da Nang and bowl at the alleys located there. I ran for president of the league, and no one opposed me. Everyone thought I'd slipped, and there must be something wrong with me. Not many signed up (maybe twelve), so we only needed a two-and-a-half-ton truck. I had a license to drive a quarter-ton jeep through a two-and-a-half-ton, and I could drive at night. I took everyone to the alley, and the pin spotters were all manual. We had fun drinking and bowling. If you put the local money in the hole of the bowling ball, the Vietnamese pinsetter would kick over the rest of the pins you missed. It was the only time I ever bowled a three hundred game. On the way back, I pulled the truck over to a local whorehouse outside Freedom Hill. I picked out four girls, gave them helmets and ponchos, and put them with the troops in the back. At the guard station, one of the guards discovered my ruse, and I told him to stop by after his shift and for two bits (a quarter) he could have a shot of leg. I set the girls up in my hooch and kicked out my three roommates. In this way, I had four beds for the four girls. I got them all a good-sized pan of fresh water to douche and a towel. I had to organize the troops. It's hard to keep something like this quiet, but I surely didn't have to advertise. I allowed fifty-two "gentlemen" (no officers) the opportunity for fornication. It was five dollars per guy, and I used a deck of cards. One girl was spades, the next hearts, the next diamonds, and the last was clubs. Ace of a suit went with his girl first, and king went second.

Waiting troops could sell their spots or trade diamonds for hearts. Some used the cards for collateral while playing poker. At first, I sold beer and sometimes pizza, but it got to be too much, so I just concentrated on pimping. At the night's end, I picked the girl I wanted, gave the guard second pick, and the other two waited. When finished, I paid them three dollars per man and saw them safely through the barbwire. I made over a hundred dollars for the night, the women were rich by their standards, and fifty- some guys were happy campers. As my son would say, "pimping ain't easy," but it was a rewarding diversion for all sides.

One of the girls had the clap (gonorrhea), and everyone who had intercourse with her (except for me) had the drippy dick. The only thing I can figure that was different is I urinated immediately after sex. I was stupid and did not use a rubber ever. (I had some lame idea about not taking a shower with a raincoat on.) Some of the men took no sweat pills, and others got the shots, but all of them sang sourly when taking a leak. I proceeded to take the bowlers once a week and pick up the harlots on the return trip, and our hooch was well known to the trip, and our hooch was well known to the Vietnamese women (hookers and hooch maids alike). The hooch maids would tell me I was number ten, and their laundry load was now higher, so I had my hooch buddies come up with some tip money for them and their extra washing time. After that, I was number one again in spite of my new extended occupation credentials. We now had the cleanest bedding in camp. One night I brought a loud and obnoxious whore. She was always complaining, so I went to my refrigerator and got ice cold water. I changed her douche water while she was performing her services to ice cold. When she finished, she jumped off the bed monkeylike and squatted over the provided douche pan. Quickly and without thought, she splashed the icy water toward her crotch. When the coldness struck her warmness, she screamed bloody murder. I fell over laughing, and she knew instantly who the guilty party was and began to chase me with the douche pan spilling water and running naked after me. It was early daylight by now, and people were moving around the compound just getting up. It had to be a sight to see this naked Vietnamese woman really pissed off and chasing this big and laughing American. I finally fell down from watching her, laughing, and not looking where I was going. She pounded me repeatedly, but I couldn't stop laughing. She finally gave up and calmed down and smiled at last. I got the guards and a three-quarter- ton truck and gave the girls a ride back, because it was getting too light for them to go through the wire. She came back again but never again did I have trouble with her. She did get with me the next time and slept the balance of the night with me. She didn't speak much English more Pigeon English, but I could tell she liked me more than she could let on. We never got together after that, and I only saw her with troops once a month or two later, but she looked, smiled, and waved.

My relationship with the infantry regular guards had increased considerably after my cathouse experience. One day, they offered me to take duty in the woman's IRO shack where they search the daily workers for MPC (Military Pay Certificates) and other restricted contraband.

The black market was strong, so MPC wasn't to be given to nationals, only their local currency. Greenbacks (American money) were illegal for even us to carry. I showed up for work from four o'clock to eight o'clock in the evening, and it was a boy's dream. For four hours, I stripped-searched women, checking every orifice. By the end of my shift, I knew what color underwear every woman wore, her cup size, and how much hair she had on her bush. I was amazed that they liked bathing suits (bikinis) the most for underwear. The girls would see an American catalogue, and a flowered "itty bitty bikini" was worth a fortune to them. I guess they wore well for panties and bras. My cut of the MPC take was more than half a month's pay, $188. One of the girls lost fifty dollars during the search, and I felt bad for her. Her husband was an ARVN, and he came up to me later begging, so I returned most of it in local currency. I understood that a day's labor for them was fifty cents, and fifty dollars was a fortune. I never got to do that again, but I'm sure the guards made out well by the war's end. When the government thought the black market needed a lesson, they would change currency and the Vietnamese would line up near our wire with money. We had a day to change our money for the new, and the locals would give us theirs to change, because the next day it would be worthless. We typically charged two for one. We only changed money twice while I was there; the first time I only made two hundred dollars, but the next time, I made more than five hundred dollars. It's amazing how people respond to opportunity.

Once in a while, we got entertainment. Usually it was a Thai band (from Bangkok, Thailand), but once we got a round-eye band from Australia. Well, it was finally Officer Night. These girls held our attention to a stupor. We hadn't seen one in so long it was like we were in a candy shop. They owned the compound, and we would have given them whatever they wanted. (In combat situations, money is almost meaningless, and the present is all that matters.) They apparently knew what they wanted and were getting up to five hundred dollars for screwing an officer. There were only a couple of them; they were beautiful, and they stripped to the buff on stage for a tease and had no trouble emptying the Officer Savings Fund. The officers paid them the big money (half a month's salary or more, depending on rank) plus bought them a nice steak dinner and whatever wine, etc.

The enlisted just leered at them, but they could be with my girls one hundred times for what they'd have to pay (if they could). The band/strippers were pretty good to us, but then again, we were a captive audience. If someone played a kazoo, we cheered. I went out for whores and brought back four to help with the "pressure" caused by the round-eye band. One of the girls wanted to do me, and when she stripped, I realized she had been seriously burned by napalm or something. She had scars from her navel to her mid-thigh. Most of her pubic hair was burnt away (Vietnamese women had much less pubic hair than American women anyway), and I probably stared too long. She got mad that I wouldn't take her on the spot and started to make a scene. There was no way to repair the damage, and I left. I got one of the other guys to go to bed with her, and she calmed down. It was not an intentional hurt, but we really had to be careful, because sometimes looks can kill.

After Thanksgiving, Bob Hope came through for his Christmas (1971) in Vietnam show. We had to convoy down to Freedom Hill for the show, so we did (again, my foresight with the license paid off). It was raining for two days when he came, and we were all on the side of a hill in this runny red clay. If you ever saw the 1971 show, our group looked like Woodstock 1969 all covered in red mud but stoned happy campers. Bob came in a helicopter with his giant face painted like a cartoon on the front of the chopper. He got off with Miss America and some band guys, and they gracefully entertained us slobs. It was great, and I always admired Mr. Hope for making the effort to bring us some cheer. Miss America was beautiful and had her slams set up for Bob, and he had his corny jokes, but it was a day in heaven to us. He was the only one from the States who ever visited us, and as much as we hated Jane Fonda, we loved Bob Hope.

Jane was negotiating with the North Vietnamese and helped get a Christmas cease-fire. This allowed the VC to build up arms and clobber us bad as soon as the cease-fire was over. She was hated more than any other human being in MR1. Fonda should have had to serve in the USO or Peace Corps for two years entertaining the troops to make up for her meddling and grief. I realize she may have had good intentions, but she paved a highway to hell with wounded and dead.

At the base PX, we could order custom-made clothes from Hong Kong. The Koreans had sent ROK Marines to the war, so they had the concession on Hong Kong (even though it was Chinese). A Korean tailor measured me up for a leather coat, green iridescent suit, several custom shirts, two custom tux shirts, and a powder-blue tuxedo with silk accents, cummerbund, and silk-striped pants. I had an R&R planned for Australia but had to change it to Hawaii when I found out my sister was getting married in January. The clothes came just before Christmas, and on Christmas Day I put on the powder-blue tux, a ruffled white with black flower shirt, and spit shined my dress shoes. I was the only person not in olive drab. You could see me for miles in the sand and scrub vegetation. The Vietnamese women all dropped their jaws, and even the officers were stunned. I smoked my cigarettes European style and put on a snobby accent. The ladies were saying, "Me number one. You take me. I love you long time," in Pigeon English if I would pay attention to them.

Shortly after that, the Christmas cease-fire was over, and "thanks" to Jane Fonda's negotiations with Ho Chi Minh), no American bombing took place across the DMZ or Hai Phuong Harbor (the port for Hanoi). The NVA (North Vietnamese Army) brought lots of mortar, AK-47s, and rocket ammo down to South Vietnam, and Russia and China shipped lots of supplies into North Vietnam. The day it was over, I drank too much and passed out in my hooch. A VC mortar crew got close and began walking rounds through our landing strip and nailed a couple of the White da Nang dust-off choppers. (Red Cross helicopters were easy to see in the dark. They were white with big red crosses on them for easy identification.) The Vietnamese were "supposed" to spare dust-off from gunfire. They then started firing and raising it a click and walked the round into our hooch group. Seven people tried to wake me up before heading for cover. The booze wore off around four thirty in the morning, and I looked up to see the stars. The roof was gone, my fan in the rafters was in pieces, and the place was a mess. Everyone then told me what happened and how lucky I was. We paced off the impact, and had they fired one more, it would have been on my nose. We spent the day rebuilding the hooch and piling sandbags. I didn't drink a drop that night and got really freaked out over almost dying the night before. I wrote up a will and didn't sleep at all the whole night, figuring my number was going to be up. The stress of where we were was bad enough but to think about it and know you're going to die is really telling. I knew I wouldn't last unless I could dwell on the present and forget about the what- ifs.

The next night I resumed slow drinking, but I never got trashed again. I would consume almost a case of beer or a pint and a six-pack but over a ten-hour period. That seemed to settle me but not pickle me. My confidence came back, and so did my attitude. We were still attacked with 122s (rockets) from the hills, and I was shot at when riding door gunner in the chopper. On guard duty, the bamboo crossbow arrows would hit the sandbags sometimes (the tips cut like a quill & stuffed with 3 day old feces), and sniper fire was always around, but I never got it again like the fury of that one night. You never want to think about the fragility of your own life in a bad situation; believe me, it doesn't help. Clint Eastwood's portrayal of Dirty Harry said it best: "A man has got to know his limitations." Knowing what you can do to change a situation and knowing when to stay out of it is a really good start on survival.

In mid-January, I got ready to see my sister get married. I had to take a C-130 down to Saigon and hang around there for a jet to Hawaii. We stopped at Okinawa and Hawaii, and then I changed for San Francisco and Chicago. I landed in Chicago the day of the wedding. My cousins Lee and Mike met me with Madonna. I was glad to see everyone, but it was really strange to get back and meet normal people with colored clothes and interests other than the present and survival. My cousins fought in the front, while I reacquainted myself with my wife in the back. They took the wrong turn and went north instead of south. I didn't care and gave them the directions to turn around before we hit Wisconsin. I had my tuxedo with me and put it on for the wedding after we got to Madonna's house. I'd had little sleep, and everything was cold, but I made it to the church and was an usher to seat the people.

Tom and Lauren had a big wedding with all the trimmings. We had the reception at Olympia Fields Country Club, and it was a nice event. I was fortunate to sit with Grandpa Sam, my father's father, and talk with him and Grandma Gene all night. He looked a little jaundiced but still enthusiastic and curious about Vietnam. Grandpa Sam died the following month when I was back in Vietnam. He had received the ICRR golden pass a couple of years earlier, which is for fifty years of service (age sixteen to sixty-six) and got to ride the train for free (sleeper and food too). He was the last Illinois Central employee to earn that honor. I drank steadily at the reception but being used to large quantities in a warmer climate, I was hardly loaded. I ended up driving many people home who could not handle their liquor.

Madonna and I got in late, and I was exhausted and still had some jet lag (after eighteen hours of airtime). I did want to be intimate, but it was strange after not seeing her for more than six months. We talked until the sun came up, finally had sex, and slept. It was a quick four days, and I had to leave and fly back. I told her my two years were up in August, and I'd see her later in the year. I flew in to San Francisco and got off the plane for a short refuel. I asked what time to be back, and they said seven thirty that evening. I went to the bar and consumed several drinks and returned to the airplane at seven thirty only to watch it take off with my luggage. I wasn't bothered in the least, but the airport personnel were very concerned. I told them I'd catch the next flight, and I'd be in the bar, but they would have none of it. They had me on a special flight, and I beat my luggage to Hawaii. The flight from Hawaii to Vietnam was again very quiet. The return travel to Red Beach was uneventful and depressing. I found myself wishing I had gone to Australia instead of home. Getting a taste of the old life and then having to go back to the cesspool was probably the cruelest of tortures. If you ever saw the movie Gulag, they torture the lead actor in prison, and he doesn't snap. They then clean him up and let his significant other visit, and when she gets just close enough for him to see her, they take him back to solitary for more torture. The glimpse of good/normal and the expectation it brings makes the reality of the torture that much harder to bear.

I have a real belief that when your number is up, it doesn't matter who you are or where you are, you're not able to change it. The etched phrase on the Zippo lighter that said, "When I walk thru the valley of the shadow of death I shall feel no fear 'cause I'm the baddest Muther Fucker in the valley," had a lot of meaning for the fatalistic attitude I possessed. Some guys clung to God and prayed a lot, but I didn't. I believed in God like that, but he was like a spare tire in the trunk, and I only brought him out when everything else stopped working. I always figured he had plenty else to do and to screw with him unnecessarily would reduce your chances of him listening when you really needed his ear. I was all about free will and no authority figure; not even God would mess with that. Leaders in crisis have nothing to do with rank. They can be officers or privates. I never asked to be a leader, and if someone was doing a good job, I left him alone. But I've also never followed without questioning the rationale. I would have never been at the Nuremburg trials after World War II if I were a German. (I might have been dead, but I wouldn't have been a blind follower of orders.) When there was a leadership vacuum and a crisis, I usually had little problem stepping up to the plate.

Typhoon Hester (typhoons happen in the Pacific Ocean and hurricanes are in the Atlantic Ocean) was the most damaging of all. We lost nine choppers, all perimeter defenses, most roofs, and numerous buildings to the destructive onslaught of this force of nature. Winds were stronger than 120 miles per hour, and I was out driving when it first hit. The jeep had a canvas roof but no back and no doors. It rained sideways, and the drops stung my face like BBs. I was glad for no doors, because if I'd had them, I would have been blown over instead of just stung in the face. I got back to the base in spite of the weather and secured the jeep. I walked back to the hooch area, leaning forward at a forty-five-degree angle to make headway.

When I got to my hooch, the roof was banging up and down. It was separating from the walls, and I could see sky between bangs. The eye passed over, and it was curiously calm and nice for a few minutes. I ran outside and got a ladder. Several roofs were already off of other buildings. The wind returned, and the tempest resumed. I saw a second lieutenant walking by when a piece of tin roof flew like a Frisbee and hit him in the neck, decapitating him. He walked another step, fell, and spurted a big squirt of blood from where his head had been. After that, he just slowly drained and didn't squirt. It wasn't even realistic, although I knew it was; he was almost animated. Several troops were walking around in a daze, so I began barking orders and getting them to put auto parts on my roof. We put old wheels, bumpers, anything with weight to it, on the roof. One little guy was blown off the roof, but he was okay. The colonel later gave him the order of the rock (a heavy rock on a rope to hang from his neck for weight) at a formation.

When the wind couldn't pull the weight up anymore, I called everyone into the hooch for drinks. After a couple of drinks, the fear subsided for most of them, and we began talking about the moment again as the storm continued to wail. We were having a good time, and Captain D (my company commander) came through with a huge radio on his back and carrying a whip antenna, a bandoleer of ammo, an M-16, and C-rations for a week. He was beside himself with worry but had to show us he was the boss, and like Carrie Nation, he destroyed all our booze and went on to say that the camp was defenseless and we could be overrun with VC at any moment. I told him there was not one VC crazy enough to be out in this storm. He was wet and livid now, and we were dry and content.

The storm was now changing from heavy winds to heavy rains, and he sent us out with flak jackets, helmets, and weapons to guard the perimeter. We ended up on our feet for three days as repairs were affected on the barbwire and towers. My hooch was the only one that retained its roof through the typhoon. Staying awake the second night was nearly impossible. I obtained some hand flares and shot them into the garbage people had set up for ramshackle housing. They looked like card forts I'd built as a kid with boards leaning against whatever was around. No one was there during the typhoon, and I quickly had the place ablaze. It kept me awake, and we made it through the night. The day was exhausting, but I could stay awake, but on the third night, I started to go nuts.

I had to get REM sleep to empty my brain, or I got this overload. I began to hallucinate, and my thinking was really counterproductive. I did learn to sleep standing up. It wasn't a real deep sleep, but it was a desperate sleep to keep my wits. If we had been hit on the third night, I wouldn't have known if it were real or not. That captain was an idiot, and he could have gotten us all killed shooting each other. Captain D should have had us run four-hour rests. This would have sufficed to eliminate the visions, but he was misusing his power and should have been relieved from command. We survived, and no one died, but the potential for extreme error by the third day was large. When we finally got to rest, I couldn't even go to sleep. I just stared into space and thought about nothing, like a long daydream without the dreams.

The claymore was a landmine we used for protection in the wire around the camp. It was the size of a sheet of notebook paper folded once the long way and a little less than an inch thick. There were self-generating electrical plungers that looked like the controls for slot racers. The plastic explosive was like modeling clay inside and burned like sterno. In the cooler monsoon months, we would strip the mines of their charges and burn them for heat and light. I have to say that after we cleaned them out, the claymores were decoys only, so we put them out in plain sight instead of trying to conceal their presence.

One of our "friendly" pastimes was discharging CS (tear and nauseating gas) on an unsuspecting person. When someone was in his cot, another soldier would throw it under his bed. The unsuspecting victim would wake up drooling, and then tears would form if he opened his eyes. We decided on a truce amongst each other and felt we should share our passion with our beloved officer core. They had a club with four entrances, and we felt to show our appreciation and respect for their abilities, we should hit all four at once while they were imbibing liquid refreshment. We timed it for around nine o'clock at night, so everyone had some time to stock up on his favorite beverage. The club was centrally located, so we had hooches surrounding the club fixed up with ladders on their backsides. We opened the four doors at exactly nine o'clock and rolled in the delightful packages. We quickly ran around to the back of the hooches, climbed up on the roofs, and pulled the ladders up behind us. This would help ensure non- discovery if they fanned out to search for the perpetrators. From our concealed observation positions above the officers' normal sight line, we watched them stumble out of the club, heaving alcohol and cussing every imaginable profanity. I'm sure they would have loved to give us proper credit for their preparedness lesson, but we decided to be true heroes and not take the credit for the impromptu, on-the-job training session.

The military put in a new rehabilitation center for drug users on the other side of the base. Heroin was cheap in Vietnam, and a five-dollar-a-day user in- country would have to spend more than one hundred dollars for the same amount back in the States. Every GI had to have a urinalysis before returning to the United States. This was to check for drugs, and blood was drawn to check for social diseases. If you had caught something, you were missing in action until they could fix it, or you went to Thailand and were never seen again. We had in-company tests occasionally, and I was on CQ (Charge of Quarters, acting commander while everyone sleeps) one night when a couple of known heavy users were sitting in front of my desk discussing the urinalysis test in the morning. Now, I didn't have much use for heroin users most of the time, because they were such thieves to support their habits. These two were very concerned about getting caught and having to go to rehab and living out the hell of withdrawal. I jumped in to their conversation with a simple, "I know how to beat the test." They were all ears.

I told them I was chemistry major in college and to neutralize a base substance like heroin you needed a strong acid to cover all the trace elements and ions. (This was all total bullshit.) The exact quantity required would be a quart of vinegar each, ingested at least six hours prior to the test, to ensure a "clean" test. They bought it and went out and drank a quart each of vinegar. The next morning, I was just getting off CQ and went to take my test like everyone else, and the two of them were laughing it up and getting ready to take their test. Well, they did and flunked. The look on their faces was priceless as they told the sergeant that there was a mistake, and the test had to be wrong. After I took mine, I was curious where they were going, and I walked the mile over to the new center. To my surprise, one of my old fraternity brothers, Ron F, was there. (He was one of the guys cut by glass at the TKE house in college.) He was a small Howdy Doody looking guy and a backstabber from college. He was borderline gay but didn't have the guts to come out. He was always quite feminine but was a good dresser and had nice manners. I was surprised to see him, because he hated ROTC in college and always avoided sports and guns. Apparently, he was drafted after school and went for rehab to stay out of combat but ended up where they needed rehabilitation. I talked to him for a while, and he showed me the facility where the guys went to dry out. I asked him how many were in his program, and he said it was just up to sixty-eight. I found out a little later that all sixty-eight patients went back to heroin. I asked him if he went to town, and he said never, and he never left his area. He was scared to death about everything. We said our "tearful" good-byes and I never saw him again. What are the odds of that encounter?

Knowledge of the rehabilitation center sparked my next plan of action. Jesse B was one of the PX guys in my hooch. I first met him by catching him stealing a carton of cigarettes out of my locker. I pulled the bishop's candlesticks (short story from Les Misérables) routine on him from literature and offered him a second carton also. He was destroyed mentally with guilt, and we became friends. He had a heroin problem and smoked it (no needles) but was addicted nonetheless. He was getting near the end of his tour, and I knew he'd be caught in a drug test if he didn't get clean soon. He liked to drink, so I hit on a plan. We all took shifts and kept Jesse drunk. We kept him so drunk that when he started to pee one time, he passed out fell straight backward and, like a fountain, peed straight up in the air and back down on himself. The other PX guy in my hooch was a sergeant, and he covered for Jesse at the PX. We kept him drunk for more than two weeks straight. And then we spent three days slowly just getting him high and then sobered him up. He had lost fifteen pounds and looked a little gaunt. We dressed him up, shined his shoes, and got him over to the urinalysis test. He passed, and we were relieved. He looked at us sheepishly and was a happy camper to be going home. I don't know if he went back to heroin when he got to the States, but he had the opportunity to stay straight and get back to his family. (Of course, I might have created another alcoholic, but it was the lesser of two evils.)

At the base, toilet paper was critical. Usually, if you went to the bathroom, the Stars & Stripes (Army propaganda newspaper) was what you tore up to use if it was a good day. I got my jeep and a two-wheel pull trailer to get Jesse to Da Nang and home. We drove him to out processing with all his stuff got him set up and wished him well. He didn't need any drinks for a while. We (I don't remember who else came with us, but it was another buddy) decided to go and have a few drinks in Da Nang. While we were there, I noticed how well supplied the Air Force troops were, so I decided we'd pay them a visit over by Monkey Mountain. We hit all the latrines and cleaned out every roll of toilet paper we could find in officers' and enlisted barracks. My fatigues were full of TP in all the large cargo pockets. We then found a couple of grocery bags and filled them too. It was late at night when we headed back, and when I hit the checkpoint at Freedom Hill, I was feeling my booze and ready for fun.

Freedom Hill had a big PX theatre and all our area artillery. They were well guarded, and the lone road was a narrow two-lane (one each way) on the side of a cliff. I ran the checkpoint; the speed limit at night was then 10 miles per hour. Sammy Hagar, who sang "I Can't Drive Fifty-Five," didn't have anything on me. The MP jeep put on its flashing red light and took up the chase. I floored it with delight, and adrenaline kicked in with the thrill of the chase. When I reached the other end (maybe two miles) the MPs had an armored personnel carrier, ten snipers, two machine gun nests, and several officers waiting with a roadblock. We stopped and got out, and I'm sure they thought they had the biggest drug or contraband bust of their lives. As they searched us and found our pockets full, the toilet paper was revealed, and the military policemen were quite baffled.

The officers began to question me once they figured out there was no dope. I told them I was returning from a routine ETS (when you leave the country and military) delivery of an enlisted man. The officer then questioned the pursuing MPs and asked them how fast we were going. The corporal answered he didn't know, because he couldn't keep up with us in the dark to get a reading on the speedometer. He asked me who my CO was, and I lied and said Captain B at Camp Viking. He called Captain B (I had worked with him in S-3) and asked him if I was in his charge and related the running of the checkpoint. Captain B said, "Send that son of a bitch directly to me whatever time he gets back!"

They let me go, and as I returned to the base, I gave the guards at the front gate toilet paper and then went to Captain B's hooch. He wanted to know what was going on. I produced a roll of toilet paper, and you'd have thought he died and went to heaven. He was the only officer at the base who had toilet paper (unless someone got some from home). All my buddies were happy campers. It's amazing what you miss and what matters in life. I really was a hero to these guys, and the morale was never higher. Money almost meant nothing there. Anyone would lend you anything you wanted without any collateral. Toilet paper couldn't be had for love or money, and the few who had a partial roll coveted it like Silas Marner and his gold. To suddenly bring in a jeep load was like irrigation to the desert. I can't remember feeling better about giving to my fellow man than at that moment.

February is the rainy time when monsoons hit. It rains steadily all day, and everything is wet. Your clothes, bedding, and even your food are damp. I was cold and freezing all the time, even though it was fifty or sixty degrees out. (When you're used to temperatures that top out above one hundred degrees, weather at fifty-five degrees is cold.) I wore my T-shirt, fatigues, and a field jacket and was still grateful for a can of sterno or C4 explosives fire. I would take the liner out of my helmet, use the steel cover like a pan, put in the C4, and light it. It was like a small furnace, and if my hands and feet were warm, the rest would follow. We had no Plexiglas, so the hooches only had screens. The moisture permeated everything. I was glad to get to S-3, because we had Plexiglas, and the damp didn't get in. I volunteered for more door gunner jobs to get above the damp and see the sun, but half the time, the choppers were grounded or we couldn't get above the soup.

Some of the dopers had a spider monkey. They must have ill-treated him, and I know they taught him to smoke pot and whatever. I saw him running terrified through the camp one night, and I squatted down and didn't move. He came to me (animals and little kids have always been attracted to me for some reason), he looked up at me, and then I held my arm out to him. He ran up it and went under my blouse (fatigue shirt with cargo pockets) and peeked out the top with his body inside. Two of the dopers came over to me, telling me they owned the monkey and I'd better give it back. I didn't say anything, and one of them reached for the monkey. He tried to bite the guy's hand and made a menacing screech. I told him the monkey was obviously emancipated and had found a safe environment. They saw I was serious and left, and I never heard from them again. The monkey stayed inside my blouse for several hours and then came out when I got him some carrots from the mess hall. He was a permanent resident of the hooch now and followed me everywhere. He was like a little kid that got into everything, but he liked to go through my chest and head of hair looking for lice or whatever.

I was told that spider monkeys socialize by grooming each other, so I used an old toothbrush on him and cleaned him up. He followed me to S-3, and we had a Mormon captain who was very proper. The monkey saw him with his pipe, and when Captain A set it down, the monkey immediately stole it like a bad kid and jumped up on the back-file cabinets where we could see him but not touch. He then began to try to smoke it, and everyone roared except Captain A. I named him after the captain for obvious reasons. I got the captain his pipe back later, but he was still perturbed and not impressed that I named the monkey after him.

After a while, the monkey knew his name and would show his teeth in an exaggerated smile. He was very entertaining but still looked to me as a mother or alpha male. I renamed him Bozo to give the Captain peace. When riding on me, Bozo was very aggressive to anyone he didn't know who approached us. When he followed behind me (he was always close like a little shadow), he would just get out of the way when someone else approached. He was always playing with himself and had an erection a few hours every day. I always hoped he'd find a female monkey, but I never saw one. Bozo seemed to deal with incoming rockets or fire okay, but he wanted to be really close to me even when I was on guard duty or at the tower. I think he picked up on my vibes, and I was so used to fire by this time that I didn't even take notice unless it was hitting within fifty feet or I could see the location of the originator (like a gun flash). Bozo did not come in the chopper when I pulled door gunner duty. He hated the noise they made and stayed hidden until I returned. We'd get shot at a lot in the chopper from the jungle, and I rarely knew where to shoot back. Fortunately, the fuel tank was double sealed, and I was never hit even though I was half out the side (we had 28 hits on the chopper by end of tour). Sometimes I'd shoot sharks for the papasan (male, local, Vietnamese) in their sampans (small outrigger boat). They'd paddle over to the thrashing shark, net him, and paddle quickly to shore before another shark began to eat the one that had been hit.

My helmet had a confederate flag on the front and a pink panther in a top hat on the back. I think the papasan knew me and that I was responsible for their family's food on many occasions, but I'm not sure. When I got back, Bozo would race out of his hideout and get back in my blouse to re-bond for a while before coming out. He was a good watch monkey and would tell me if anyone were approaching, so after a while, even the officers didn't object. We had dogs too that would bark only at Vietnamese. (They were Vietnamese mongrels, but they probably sensed they were more like pigs than pets, for dog meat was one of the locals' delicacies.) Sappers (Vietcong with satchel charges to blow up whatever they could) never hit our wire, probably because we had so many animals. When I left Vietnam, I left Bozo to his own. I tried to get him back to the states, but the paperwork would have taken months, and the money (two months' pay plus quarantine charges) was prohibitive. It was better that he stayed in his climate. I released him over at Monkey Mountain because of the name. He cried out to me when I drove off but didn't follow. I think he understood or finally smelled a female.

Willie (the guy in my first firefight position when I didn't think we were being attacked) wasn't a speedy hustler but a nice, solid Tennessee boy. He'd play cards with us on ready reaction force and in our casino or at the club. He loved to gamble and always lost his paycheck. He was getting short (ready to go back to the States), and we were on ready reaction force duty. This is where you stay dressed and fully armed all night in a central part of the base. If we got hit, it was our job to run to the action and fight until everyone else could get to his post. We always played poker all night and it kept us awake. Willie started to win that last week he was in-country. It didn't matter who dealt; he would win. We started playing three- card guts where the loser matches the pot and anyone who drops has to keep putting another ante in the pot. If three guys try, two will match the pot, and the winner drags the current pot. It keeps going until one person goes for it, and no one challenges. If I had a pair of kings and Willie had a pair of aces, if I bluffed, Willie would beat me with an ace high. If I dropped, he was bluffing. It was his night. I lost my entire month's payroll, and so did the other two guys. Willie walked out with four months' payroll, which almost made up for the many months he lost. He was so happy, and we were happy for him. He was going home fairly rich, by our standards, and we didn't care because we could die anytime. Money was really meaningless and few held the reverence for it like people did back in the States. I don't know if Willie went to reenlist, but he was set for a while. I can still see the whites of his eyes on his dark brown face, wide open and happy that his ship finally came in and never at a better time.

Our unit was getting ready to stand down, so we had to clean up all our vehicles to turn them over to the ARVN forces. They would not accept any vehicles with grease on them anywhere. We had to steam clean the engines and body and remove all the gas and oil. Oddly, I don't remember removing any coolant. I drove a deuce-and-a-half truck with my jeep in the back to the ARVN reclamation area on a peninsula near Monkey Mountain. At the base, we unloaded my faithful jeep, and we got a call that a red alert (known enemy activity) was in progress, and all roads were shut down indefinitely. They could get choppers to a LZ (Landing Zone) a couple of miles from where they were to pick us up at the ocean end of the land. I told the sergeant with us to call them and that my jeep would work for me. He said that the gas and oil were vacuumed out already, and there was no way it could start. I pushed it down a hill and let out the clutch, and she fired up. We all jumped in and drove to the LZ. It made it just fine and was starting to heat up and smoke a little when I turned it off. We could see some explosions on the roadway that was blocked by the red alert as we took off for Camp Viking. I still remember seeing the jeep next to the LZ as we flew away and knowing it would always work for me. How could I know those things? We could have been blown up going the other way or lost it walking the two miles. It's good to have a sense in crisis, and it's always better to be lucky than good.

At the end of March 1972, I was five months away from my two years. President Richard Nixon had proclaimed that anyone leaving Vietnam with six or fewer months left in the service would get an early out returning to the States. I fit the profile perfectly. You needed eighteen months or more to get your honorable discharge with full benefits, and I had nineteen (although three months were bad time in the stockade, I had cleaned my records out on the plane to Vietnam). With the entire officer training, a summer camp, crack squad, Pershing rifles, and rifle team, I felt no guilt at all. I packed my refrigerator with my stuff to go home and took my duffel bag and clothes except for my khakis, a set of fatigues, my shaving kit, and socks. I went back to Da Nang to await my Freedom Flight, take the drug and blood tests, and process out of country. Fear increased at this time too because I was so close to getting out that I became really cautious. Short-timers are notoriously careful and superstitious.

I just wanted to forget about it, so I drank. I quickly got to know the local girls there. After all, I was a pimp from up north at Red Beach. I decided to become a customer not a pimp, but sometimes you can't help a viewpoint. There were two girls working the base but not very well, and their communication skills were lacking, so I decided to keep my mind off personal eradication or maiming to give these girls an opportunity. Most of the guys in my area had money and nothing to do but wait for their turn to leave. I was anywhere from a week to ten days away from getting down to Saigon for the Freedom Flight.

One of the girls was very slight of build and skinny. She was almost a child to me, but I'm sure to her she was old for her years, depending on what she'd seen. I decided she could work the cherry boys and nineteen- year-olds. The other one (her name was Goldie, and one of her incisors was solid gold) was a little chunky, probably very chunky to a Vietnamese, but had the biggest breasts I'd ever seen on a local. Most of the guys were scared of getting a VD and had the short- timer's problem thinking these girls were Commie spies with razor blades in their vaginas or rare social diseases designed to kill Americans. I got to the PX and procured the necessary protection for the guys and stupidly did not use any myself. I decided to put on an in-person porno to encourage participation. I assembled the multitudes in a hooch with blankets hung from the ceiling that were strategically cut to allow voyeur participation. I slowly undressed Goldie with her back to me, thus allowing the viewer's full-frontal perusal. I could see them leering and hear them whispering. I lay down on the bed on my back and put Goldie on top with her posterior toward the crowd, allowing them to see penetration. I held her up high enough for her breasts to swing free as I plowed her from underneath. The crowd got louder and was constantly shushing each other. Goldie, who had tried for a week to make some money hustling, started smiling ear to ear at me. They couldn't see her face and were more involved with my member management at the time. We hammed it for a while for everyone's delight, and I had her face the crowd after I got off so they could once again see the whole package. Well, it worked, and I had two lines going. I brought cold beer over for the waiting gentlemen to consume and passed out condoms for everyone. Since I had stupidly ridden bareback, the concern for razor blades and death diseases had left.

The troops in the area forgot about their fears and troubles and just thought about the moment. Morale was at an all-time high for a holding area. I was very fortunate not to contract a disease like clap, because that would have stopped my processing to go home. We made a lot of money during the next few days, and I recovered expenses and a few bucks for grins, but this time I gave the bulk of the money to the girls. When I left, they cried and gave me a private little party for just the three of us. They made me their local dishes and sang some songs and laughed one more time. They both wanted to do me, but I was going home and said no and thanked them both. Oddly, they didn't stay with their pimp gone and left the base. Maybe they had enough money and wanted a rest and some safe time; heaven knows they'd earned it.

The trip home was exciting. We left on March 31, 1972. We all knew we had made it, and everyone wanted to party. The plane was a Flying Tiger Airline, and the stewardesses stayed away from us as much as possible. It did have a movie, which was John Wayne in The Cowboys. We were given the option of dinner or the movie, and we unanimously picked the movie. After the movie, the plane foolishly landed in Guam, which was a free-trade island. We could pick up a gallon of liquor, so I bought five fifths of Canadian Club. Most of the other guys bought their last cheap booze also. When we were airborne, the stewardesses hid again and would not even bring us water or ice. We didn't care and began to open and pass the bottles around. We were a drunken rabble in no time.

When we landed in Hawaii, I could hardly see and didn't even get off the plane while we refueled. I awoke before we landed and began drinking straight Canadian again. When we got to the bus taking us to Fort Lewis, Washington, we were plastered again. We were throwing our empty fifths at cars on the freeway. Fortunately, our aim was terrible. Some cars may have picked up glass in their tires, but fortunately, no windshields caved in. When we got off the bus, there was a welcome home sign in front of a mess hall. We were led inside for a steak dinner. The guys were grilling and trying to be nice, but we were beasts. We grabbed the steaks off the grill and made animal sounds as we tore into the meat, cooked or not. The local Army brought MPs over and extra enlisted men but no officers. They kept explaining that we wouldn't go home if we hit any officers. Apparently, they'd had problems before.

As soon as I could, I kept my promise to sit on a real flush toilet again and loved it. It was so clean and fresh. I was processed out in a day and had March 31 twice, because I crossed the international dateline. It was April 1, and I was on my way to the Seattle airport to go to Chicago. I was still in khakis, and the stateside guys were mad that I didn't have my greens. I had all my ribbons and rank on, but they said it was a summer uniform, and I was out of season. When I at last saw Chicago from the air, I finally felt like I was at home. Knowing I had really made it home alive and safe was quite relaxing.

Military Draft commitment back then was six years. Two active Army, two ready Reserve and two inactive reserve. If you were in combat your ready Reserve was changed to four years with no weekend meetings or summer camp like in ready reserve. I was married nine days before leaving for Vietnam, and I had another five days back with my bride when I took R&R (rest and relaxation, like a vacation) stateside for my sister's wedding. We spent our first year of wedded bliss apart and consummated through letter writing only. I completed military service April 1, 1972 and figured April Fools' Day was an appropriate date for my swan song. I had to adjust to a new climate and being a unit (we) and not a person.

For going overseas, I received twelve dollars a month extra, and for combat pay, I received sixty dollars a month. For two dollars a day, I had risked my life. The average age was nineteen. I was an old man coming home at twenty-four. Many places it was twenty-one to drink, and it was twenty-one to vote. You could give your life to your country, but you couldn't vote for the people who would send you there, and you couldn't even legally buy a drink to forget about going. I was always sought by the troops who needed booze, and I never questioned anyone who wanted some. I can't imagine anyone over there who was twenty-one refusing to buy a drink for a fellow soldier who wasn't old enough.

When I got off the plane in Chicago, there were war protesters who wanted to know if I was a baby killer and had other inane and uninformed questions. I didn't respond and felt like I was in a strange, foreign place. I was now an observer not a participant, and I felt like Robert De Niro in The Deer Hunter when he got home and didn't go to his own party. He sat across the street and watched until everyone left, and then he went in. People avoided Vietnam questions, and there were no parades or cheering. It was like you were severely handicapped, and everyone just wanted to ignore you and not deal with your issues. My own dad, who was in World War II, said he was glad I was home and then never said another word. I know that when he went home, people celebrated and bought drinks for him and made him feel wanted. The Vietnam veteran was scorned and avoided by the populace. We were very unpopular, and the best we got was "Glad you made it."

It took a year to reacclimatize myself and shake off the observation and get back into being a "normal" person. Things went okay until President Gerald Ford freed the runaways by granting amnesty. That was the worst thing the country ever did to the veteran. We stayed and did our time, and they deserted their country and weren't even punished. The politically correct assholes said they'd suffered enough, and it was time to heal. Well, okay, but give them two years in the Peace Corps or two years in the Army doing something. These were drafted deserters allowed to return to the very country they disrespected. We all felt cheap and wondered why we had gone. It still doesn't make sense to this day. That is a terrible example to give to future generations.

We weren't allowed to win the war, only sustain it. We weren't serving our country. The population abhorred us, we were considered losers, and if we deserted, we would be forgiven with no penalties. We took the risk, and what was the incentive? I made the best of a bad situation and kept up morale for many who could have sustained years of mental damage.

President Ford was never elected, yet he trashed a generation of military veterans by pardoning the draft dodgers and betrayed the public's trust by pardoning a guilty president. I then saw the movie Alfie with Michael Caine and finally let it go. The movie's theme song *'What's it all about?'* was my food for thought. Whoever said life has to be fair? Maudlin only eats you up, and you have to retain your sense of humor. If you can't keep your own head happy, what good will you ever be to anyone else?

EPILOGUE

This concludes my first twenty-five years. The next book will include reentering "normal society," having three children, pursuing advanced degrees, dealing with Secret Service confrontation, living through divorce, searching for new love and family, battling a long and costly custody fight, enduring hospitalization for Vietnam Agent Orange poisoning, seeing the birth of my first granddaughter, and having a family reunion on my father's side of the family. Next, I went on a Wounded Woman tour with my son Bob; almost faced death and a serious infection at the South Pole; and did three combat contractor tours in Iraq, Afghanistan, and the Middle East for a total of six years (2003–09). I finally found true love on the Internet with an exceptional woman from Brazil.

It will contain a Christian marriage in Islamic Muscat, Oman (very difficult), new family ties, a honeymoon in Thailand, and a return to the USA in 2007 with my new bride. A return to Iraq with the Marines on border patrol ensues, and then it's back home in 2009. My bride and I do a US tour to stepdaughter Martha's graduation. I learn government paperwork for contractor wounds, direct my wife for US citizenship, have a visit to the Netherlands for a new grandson, travel to Brazil, and meet new family. We moved to Hendersonville, North Carolina to keep my parents out of assisted living (parental prison) in 2012. My younger sister Lauren tragically died in 2013, and my lovely wife enrolled in a doctorate program, so I finally had the time to write this all down in retirement.

Red Beach Camp Viking Vietnam 1971

Fort Dix Nov 1970